CW00369142

LAST AND
FIRST MEN

LAST AND FIRST MEN

OLAF STAPLEDON

Disclaimer

Throughout the text readers may find that some of the language used and sentiments expressed are unacceptable by today's standards. These reflect the attitudes and usage common at the time the book was written. In no way do they reflect the attitude of the publishers.

This edition published in 2024 by Arcturus Publishing Limited
26/27 Bickels Yard, 151–153 Bermondsey Street,
London SE1 3HA

Copyright © Arcturus Holdings Limited

All rights reserved. No part of this publication may be reproduced, stored in a retrieval system, or transmitted, in any form or by any means, electronic, mechanical, photocopying, recording or otherwise, without prior written permission in accordance with the provisions of the Copyright Act 1956 (as amended). Any person or persons who do any unauthorised act in relation to this publication may be liable to criminal prosecution and civil claims for damages.

Cover design: Peter Ridley
Cover illustration: Alessandro Valdrighi

AD010725UK

Printed in the UK

CONTENTS

THE CHRONICLE

TIME SCALES

INTRODUCTION

William Olaf Stapledon was born on 10 May 1886 to Clibbett Stapledon and Emmeline Miller. Stapledon spent the first six years of his life with his parents in Port Said, Egypt, presumably due to the location of his family's firm. He was later educated at Abbotsholme School and Balliol College, Oxford, where he obtained a Bachelor of Arts in Modern History. He held several positions prior to becoming an author, including a short stint as a teacher at Manchester Grammar School. He also worked at a shipping office in Liverpool and even returned, briefly, to Port Said where the family firm was based.

During World War I, Stapledon served as an ambulance driver with the Friends' Ambulance Unit, culminating in his being awarded the Croix de Guerre – the military decoration of France – for his contributions. Several months later he married a maternal cousin Agnes Zena Miller. Stapledon and Miller had two children, a daughter and son, before moving permanently to West Kirby.

In 1925, Stapledon completed his PhD in philosophy at the University of Liverpool. He would later utilise his doctoral thesis as the basis of his first prose book, *A Modern Theory of Ethics*. Published in 1929, *A Modern Theory of Ethics* is a philosophical work exploring moral behaviours in the modern world. While the book was not widely read, it received praise from academic scholars, and was cited in a number of journals. Later, Stapledon shifted his focus to writing fiction in an attempt to appeal to the general public. This resulted in the publication of perhaps his most famous title, *Last and First Men*.

Published a year after his first book, *Last and First Men* is a revolutionary science-fiction novel that details the history of humanity across a two-billion-year period. Critics praised the novel as the first of its kind, and it has since been lauded for its profound influence on many notable science-fiction writers, such as C. S. Lewis and H. G. Wells. He later went on to publish several other books, including *Last Men in London*, *Nebula Maker* and *Odd John*.

Stapledon's novels commonly deal with forms of intelligence across universes, and the conflict between our higher and lower impulses. He is also known for advancing modern transhumanism – a movement that supports the employment of sophisticated technologies to better the human condition. Commonly referred to as the 'Father of Modern Science Fiction', his contributions to the science-fiction landscape have drawn praise from authors across genres and literary spheres, such as Virginia Woolf, H. P. Lovecraft and Doris Lessing.

Stapledon died on 6 September 1950 due to a heart attack. His remains were scattered on cliffs overlooking the Dee Estuary, a commonly featured location in many of his works. In 2014, almost sixty-four years after his death, Stapledon was inducted into the Science Fiction and Fantasy Hall of Fame at the Museum of Pop Culture in Seattle, Washington.

PREFACE

This is a work of fiction. I have tried to invent a story which may seem a possible, or at least not wholly impossible, account of the future of man; and I have tried to make that story relevant to the change that is taking place today in man's outlook.

To romance of the future may seem to be indulgence in ungoverned speculation for the sake of the marvellous. Yet controlled imagination in this sphere can be a very valuable exercise for minds bewildered about the present and its potentialities. Today we should welcome, and even study, every serious attempt to envisage the future of our race; not merely in order to grasp the very diverse and often tragic possibilities that confront us, but also that we may familiarize ourselves with the certainty that many of our most cherished ideals would seem puerile to more developed minds. To romance of the far future, then, is to attempt to see the human race in its cosmic setting, and to mould our hearts to entertain new values.

But if such imaginative construction of possible futures is to be at all potent, our imagination must be strictly disciplined. We must endeavour not to go beyond the bounds of possibility set by the particular state of culture within which we live. The merely fantastic has only minor power. Not that we should seek actually to prophesy what will as a matter of fact occur; for in our present state such prophecy is certainly futile, save in the simplest matters. We are not to set up as historians attempting to look ahead instead of backwards. We can only select a certain thread out of the tangle of many equally valid possibilities. But we must select with a purpose. The activity that we are undertaking is not science, but art; and the effect that it should have on the reader is the effect that art should have.

Yet our aim is not merely to create aesthetically admirable fiction.

We must achieve neither mere history, nor mere fiction, but myth. A true myth is one which, within the universe of a certain culture (living or dead), expresses richly, and often perhaps tragically, the highest admirations possible within that culture. A false myth is one which either violently transgresses the limits of credibility set by its own cultural matrix, or expresses admirations less developed than those of its culture's best vision. This book can no more claim to be true myth than true prophecy. But it is an essay in myth creation.

The kind of future which is here imagined, should not, I think, seem wholly fantastic, or at any rate not so fantastic as to be without significance, to modern Western individuals who are familiar with the outlines of contemporary thought. Had I chosen matter in which there was nothing whatever of the fantastic, its very plausibility would have rendered it unplausible. For one thing at least is almost certain about the future, namely, that very much of it will be such as we should call incredible. In one important respect, indeed, I may perhaps seem to have strayed into barren extravagance. I have supposed an inhabitant of the remote future to be communicating with us of today. I have pretended that he has the power of partially controlling the operations of minds now living, and that this book is the product of such influence. Yet even this fiction is perhaps not wholly excluded by our thought. I might, of course, easily have omitted it without more than superficial alteration of the theme. But its introduction was more than a convenience. Only by some such radical and bewildering device could I embody the possibility that there may be more in time's nature than is revealed to us. Indeed, only by some such trick could I do justice to the conviction that our whole present mentality is but a confused and halting first experiment.

If ever this book should happen to be discovered by some future individual, for instance by a member of the next generation sorting out the rubbish of his predecessors, it will certainly raise a smile; for very much is bound to happen of which no hint is yet discoverable. And indeed even in our generation circumstances may well change so unexpectedly and so radically that this book may very soon look ridiculous. But no matter. We of today must conceive our relation to the rest of the universe as best we can; and even if our images must seem fantastic to future men, they may none the less serve their purpose today.

Some readers, taking my story to be an attempt at prophecy, may deem it unwarrantably pessimistic. But it is not prophecy; it is myth, or an essay in myth. We all desire the future to turn out more happily than I have figured it. In particular we desire our present civilization to advance steadily toward some kind of Utopia. The thought that it may decay and collapse, and that all its spiritual treasure may be lost irrevocably, is repugnant to us. Yet this must be faced as at least a possibility. And this kind of tragedy, the tragedy of a race, must, I think, be admitted in any adequate myth.

And so, while gladly recognizing that in our time there are strong seeds of hope as well as of despair, I have imagined for æsthetic purposes that our race will destroy itself. There is today a very earnest movement for peace and international unity; and surely with good fortune and intelligent management it may triumph. Most earnestly we must hope that it will. But I have figured things out in this book in such a manner that this great movement fails. I suppose it incapable of preventing a succession of national wars; and I permit it only to achieve the goal of unity and peace after the mentality of the race has been undermined. May this not happen! May the League of Nations, or some more strictly cosmopolitan authority, win through before it is too late! Yet let us find room in our minds and in our hearts for the thought that the whole enterprise of our race may be after all but a minor and unsuccessful episode in a vaster drama, which also perhaps may be tragic.

American readers, if ever there are any, may feel that their great nation is given a somewhat unattractive part in the story. I have imagined the triumph of the cruder sort of Americanism over all that is best and most promising in American culture. May this not occur in the real world! Americans themselves, however, admit the possibility of such an issue, and will, I hope, forgive me for emphasizing it, and using it as an early turning-point in the long drama of Man.

Any attempt to conceive such a drama must take into account

whatever contemporary science has to say about man's own nature and his physical environment. I have tried to supplement my own slight knowledge of natural science by pestering my scientific friends. In particular, I have been very greatly helped by conversation with Professors P. G. H. Boswell, J. Johnstone, and J. Rice, of Liverpool. But they must not be held responsible for the many deliberate extravagances which, though they serve a purpose in the design, may jar upon the scientific ear.

To Dr. L. A. Reid I am much indebted for general comments, and to Mr. E. V. Rieu for many very valuable suggestions. To Professor and Mrs. L. C. Martin, who read the whole book in manuscript, I cannot properly express my gratitude for constant encouragement and criticism. To my wife's devastating sanity I owe far more than she supposes.

Before closing this preface I would remind the reader that throughout the following pages the speaker, the first person singular, is supposed to be, not the actual writer, but an individual living in the extremely distant future.

O. S.

WEST KIRBY
July, 1930

INTRODUCTION

BY ONE OF THE LAST MEN

This book has two authors, one contemporary with its readers, the other an inhabitant of an age which they would call the distant future. The brain that conceives and writes these sentences lives in the time of Einstein. Yet I, the true inspirer of this book, I who have begotten it upon that brain, I who influence that primitive being's conception, inhabit an age which, for Einstein, lies in the very remote future.

The actual writer thinks he is merely contriving a work of fiction. Though he seeks to tell a plausible story, he neither believes it himself, nor expects others to believe it. Yet the story is true. A being whom you would call a future man has seized the docile but scarcely adequate brain of your contemporary, and is trying to direct its familiar processes for an alien purpose. Thus a future epoch makes contact with your age. Listen patiently; for we who are the Last Men earnestly desire to communicate with you, who are members of the First Human Species. We can help you, and we need your help.

You cannot believe it. Your acquaintance with time is very imperfect, and so your understanding of it is defeated. But no matter. Do not perplex yourselves about this truth, so difficult to you, so familiar to us of a later aeon. Do but entertain, merely as a fiction, the idea that the thought and will of individuals future to you may intrude, rarely and with difficulty, into the mental processes of some of your contemporaries. Pretend that you believe this, and that the following chronicle is an authentic message from the Last Men. Imagine the consequences of such a belief. Otherwise I cannot give life to the great history which it is my task to tell.

When your writers romance of the future, they too easily imagine a progress toward some kind of Utopia, in which beings like themselves

live in unmitigated bliss among circumstances perfectly suited to a
fixed human nature. I shall not describe any such paradise. Instead, I
shall record huge fluctuations of joy and woe, the results of changes
not only in man's environment but in his fluid nature. And I must
tell how, in my own age, having at last achieved spiritual maturity
and the philosophic mind, man is forced by an unexpected crisis to
embark on an enterprise both repugnant and desperate.

I invite you, then, to travel in imagination through the aeons that
lie between your age and mine. I ask you to watch such a history
of change, grief, hope, and unforeseen catastrophe, as has nowhere
else occurred, within the girdle of the Milky Way. But first, it is well
to contemplate for a few moments the mere magnitudes of cosmical
events. For, compressed as it must necessarily be, the narrative that
I have to tell may seem to present a sequence of adventures and
disasters crowded together, with no intervening peace. But in fact
man's career has been less like a mountain torrent hurtling from
rock to rock, than a great sluggish river, broken very seldom by
rapids. Ages of quiescence, often of actual stagnation, filled with the
monotonous problems and toils of countless almost identical lives,
have been punctuated by rare moments of racial adventure. Nay,
even these few seemingly rapid events themselves were in fact often
long-drawn-out and tedious. They acquire a mere illusion of speed
from the speed of the narrative.

The receding depths of time and space, though they can indeed be
haltingly conceived even by primitive minds, cannot be imaged save
by beings of a more ample nature. A panorama of mountains appears
to naive vision almost as a flat picture, and the starry void is a roof
pricked with light. Yet in reality, while the immediate terrain could be
spanned in an hour's walking, the sky-line of peaks holds within it
plain beyond plain. Similarly with time. While the near past and the
near future display within them depth beyond depth, time's remote
immensities are foreshortened into flatness. It is almost inconceivable
to simple minds that man's whole history should be but a moment in
the life of the stars, and that remote events should embrace within
themselves aeon upon aeon.

In your day you have learnt to calculate something of the magnitudes of time and space. But to grasp my theme in its true proportions, it is necessary to do more than calculate. It is necessary to brood upon these magnitudes, to draw out the mind toward them, to feel the littleness of your here and now, and of the moment of civilization which you call history. You cannot hope to image, as we do, such vast proportions as one in a thousand million, because your sense-organs, and therefore your perceptions, are too coarse-grained to discriminate so small a fraction of their total field. But you may at least, by mere contemplation, grasp more constantly and firmly the significance of your calculations.

Men of your day, when they look back into the history of their planet, remark not only the length of time but also the bewildering acceleration of life's progress. Almost stationary in the earliest period of the earth's career, in your moment it seems headlong. Mind in you, it is said, not merely stands higher than ever before in respect of percipience, knowledge, insight, delicacy of admiration, and sanity of will, but also it moves upward century by century ever more swiftly. What next? Surely, you think, there will come a time when there will be no further heights to conquer.

This view is mistaken. You underestimate even the foothills that stand in front of you, and never suspect that far above them, hidden by cloud, rise precipices and snow-fields. The mental and spiritual advances which, in your day, mind in the solar system has still to attempt, are overwhelmingly more complex, more precarious and dangerous, than those which have already been achieved. And though in certain humble respects you have attained full development, the loftier potencies of the spirit in you have not yet even begun to put forth buds.

Somehow, then, I must help you to feel not only the vastness of time and space, but also the vast diversity of mind's possible modes. But this I can only hint to you, since so much lies wholly beyond the range of your imagination.

Historians living in your day need grapple only with one moment of the flux of time. But I have to present in one book the essence not of centuries but of aeons. Clearly we cannot walk at leisure through such a tract, in which a million terrestrial years are but as a year is to your historians. We must fly. We must travel as you do in your aeroplanes, observing only the broad features of the continent. But since the flier sees nothing of the minute inhabitants below him, and since it is they who make history, we must also punctuate our flight with many descents, skimming as it were over the house-tops, and even alighting at critical points to speak face to face with individuals. And as the plane's journey must begin with a slow ascent from the intricate pedestrian view to wider horizons, so we must begin with a somewhat close inspection of that little period which includes the culmination and collapse of your own primitive civilization.

CHAPTER I

BALKAN EUROPE

1. THE EUROPEAN WAR AND AFTER

Observe now your own epoch of history as it appears to the Last Men.

Long before the human spirit awoke to clear cognizance of the world and itself, it sometimes stirred in its sleep, opened bewildered eyes, and slept again. One of these moments of precocious experience embraces the whole struggle of the First Men from savagery toward civilization. Within that moment, you stand almost in the very instant when the species attains its zenith. Scarcely at all beyond your own day is this early culture to be seen progressing, and already in your time the mentality of the race shows signs of decline.

The first, and some would say the greatest, achievement of your own 'Western' culture was the conceiving of two ideals of conduct, both essential to the spirit's well-being. Socrates, delighting in the truth for its own sake and not merely for practical ends, glorified unbiased thinking, honesty of mind and speech. Jesus, delighting in the actual human persons around him, and in that flavour of divinity which, for him, pervaded the world, stood for unselfish love of neighbours and of God. Socrates woke to the ideal of dispassionate intelligence, Jesus to the ideal of passionate yet self-oblivious worship. Socrates urged intellectual integrity, Jesus integrity of will. Each, of course, though starting with a different emphasis, involved the other.

Unfortunately both these ideals demanded of the human brain a degree of vitality and coherence of which the nervous system of the First Men was never really capable. For many centuries these twin stars enticed the more precociously human of human animals, in vain. And the failure to put these ideals in practice helped to engender in the race a cynical lassitude which was one cause of its decay.

There were other causes. The peoples from whom sprang Socrates and Jesus were also among the first to conceive admiration for Fate. In Greek tragic art and Hebrew worship of divine law, as also in the Indian resignation, man experienced, at first very obscurely, that vision of an alien and supernal beauty, which was to exalt and perplex him again and again throughout his whole career. The conflict between this worship and the intransigent loyalty to Life, embattled against Death, proved insoluble. And though few individuals were ever clearly conscious of the issue, the first human species was again and again unwittingly hampered in its spiritual development by this supreme perplexity.

While man was being whipped and enticed by these precocious experiences, the actual social constitution of his world kept changing so rapidly through increased mastery over physical energy, that his primitive nature could no longer cope with the complexity of his environment. Animals that were fashioned for hunting and fighting in the wild were suddenly called upon to be citizens, and moreover citizens of a world-community. At the same time they found themselves possessed of certain very dangerous powers which their petty minds were not fit to use. Man struggled; but, as you shall hear, he broke under the strain.

The European War, called at the time the War to End War, was the first and least destructive of those world conflicts which display so tragically the incompetence of the First Men to control their own nature. At the outset a tangle of motives, some honourable and some disreputable, ignited a conflict for which both antagonists were all too well prepared, though neither seriously intended it. A real difference of temperament between Latin France and Nordic Germany combined with a superficial rivalry between Germany and England, and a number of stupidly brutal gestures on the part of the German Government and military command, to divide the world into two camps; yet in such a manner that it is impossible to find any difference of principle between them. During the struggle each party was convinced that it alone stood for civilization. But in fact both succumbed now and again to impulses of sheer brutality, and both achieved acts not merely of heroism, but of generosity unusual among the First Men. For conduct which to clearer minds seems merely sane, was in those days to be performed only by rare vision and self-mastery.

As the months of agony advanced, there was bred in the warring peoples a genuine and even passionate will for peace and a united world. Out of the conflict of the tribes arose, at least for a while, a spirit loftier than tribalism. But this fervour lacked as yet clear guidance, lacked even the courage of conviction. The peace which followed the European War is one of the most significant moments of ancient history; for it epitomizes both the dawning vision and the incurable blindness, both the impulse toward a higher loyalty and the compulsive tribalism of a race which was, after all, but superficially human.

2. THE ANGLO-FRENCH WAR

One brief but tragic incident, which occurred within a century after the European War, may be said to have sealed the fate of the First Men. During this century the will for peace and sanity was already becoming a serious factor in history. Save for a number of most untoward accidents, to be recorded in due course, the party of peace might have dominated Europe during its most dangerous period; and, through Europe, the world. With either a little less bad luck or a fraction more of vision and self-control at this critical time, there might never have occurred that aeon of darkness, in which the First Men were presently to be submerged. For had victory been gained before the general level of mentality had seriously begun to decline, the attainment of the world state might have been regarded, not as an end, but as the first step toward true civilization. But this was not to be.

After the European War, the defeated nation, formerly no less militaristic than the others, now became the most pacific, and a stronghold of enlightenment. Almost everywhere, indeed, there had occurred a profound change of heart, but chiefly in Germany. The victors on the other hand, in spite of their real craving to be human and generous, and to found a new world, were led partly by their own timidity, partly by their governors' blind diplomacy, into all the vices against which they believed themselves to have been crusading. After a brief period in which they desperately affected amity for one another they began to indulge once more in physical conflicts. Of these conflicts, two must be observed.

The first outbreak, and the less disastrous for Europe, was a short and grotesque struggle between France and Italy. Since the fall of ancient Rome, the Italians had excelled more in art and literature than in martial achievement. But the heroic liberation of Italy in the nineteenth Christian century had made Italians peculiarly sensitive to national prestige; and since among Western peoples national vigour was measured in terms of military glory, the Italians were fired, by their success against a rickety foreign domination, to vindicate themselves more thoroughly against the charge of mediocrity in warfare. After the European War, however, Italy passed through a phase of social disorder and self-distrust. Subsequently a flamboyant but sincere national party gained control of the State, and afforded the Italians a new self-respect, based on reform of the social services, and on militaristic policy. Trains became punctual, streets clean, morals puritanical. Aviation records were won for Italy. The young, dressed up and taught to play at soldiers with real fire-arms, were persuaded to regard themselves as saviours of the nation, encouraged to shed blood, and used to enforce the will of the Government. The whole movement was engineered chiefly by a man whose genius in action combined with his rhetoric and crudity of thought to make him a very successful dictator. Almost miraculously he drilled the Italian nation into efficiency. At the same time, with great emotional effect and incredible lack of humour, he trumpeted Italy's self-importance, and her will to 'expand'. And since Italians were slow to learn the necessity of restricting their population, 'expansion' was a real need.

Thus it came about that Italy, hungry for French territory in Africa, jealous of French leadership of the Latin races, indignant at the protection afforded to Italian 'traitors' in France, became increasingly prone to quarrel with the most assertive of her late allies. It was a frontier incident, a fancied 'insult to the Italian flag', which at last caused an unauthorized raid upon French territory by a small party of Italian militia. The raiders were captured, but French blood was shed. The consequent demand for apology and reparation was calm, but subtly offensive to Italian dignity. Italian patriots worked themselves into short-sighted fury. The Dictator, far from daring to apologize, was forced to require the release of the captive militiamen, and finally to declare war. After a single sharp engagement the relentless armies of France pressed into North Italy. Resistance, at first heroic, soon became chaotic. In consternation the Italians woke from their dream of military glory. The populace turned against the Dictator whom they themselves had forced to declare war. In a theatrical but gallant attempt to dominate the Roman mob, he failed, and was killed. The new government made a hasty peace, ceding to France a frontier territory which she had already annexed for 'security'.

Thenceforth Italians were less concerned to outshine the glory of Garibaldi than to emulate the greater glory of Dante, Giotto and Galileo.

France had now complete mastery of the continent of Europe; but having much to lose, she behaved arrogantly and nervously. It was not long before peace was once more disturbed.

Scarcely had the last veterans of the European War ceased from wearying their juniors with reminiscence, when the long rivalry between France and England culminated in a dispute between their respective Governments over a case of sexual outrage said to have been committed by a French African soldier upon an Englishwoman. In this quarrel, the British Government happened to be definitely in the wrong, and was probably confused by its own sexual repressions. The outrage had never been committed. The facts which gave rise to the rumour were, that an idle and neurotic Englishwoman in the south of France, craving the embraces of a 'cave man', had seduced a Senegalese corporal in her own apartments. When, later, he had shown signs of boredom, she took revenge by declaring that he had attacked her indecently in the woods above the town. This rumour was such that the English were all too prone to savour and believe. At the same time, the magnates of the English Press could not resist this opportunity of trading upon the public's sexuality, tribalism and self-righteousness. There followed an epidemic of abuse, and occasional violence, against French subjects in England; and thus the party of fear and militarism in France was given the opportunity it had long sought. For the real cause of this war was connected with air power. France had persuaded the League of Nations (in one of its less intelligent moments) to restrict the size of military aeroplanes in such a manner that, while London lay within easy striking distance of the

French coast, Paris could only with difficulty be touched by England. This state of affairs obviously could not last long. Britain was agitating more and more insistently for the removal of the restriction. On the other hand, there was an increasing demand for complete aerial disarmament in Europe; and so strong was the party of sanity in France, that the scheme would almost certainly have been accepted by the French Government. On both counts, therefore, the militarists of France were eager to strike while yet there was opportunity.

In an instant, the whole fruit of this effort for disarmament was destroyed. That subtle difference of mentality which had ever made it impossible for these two nations to understand one another, was suddenly exaggerated by this provocative incident into an apparently insoluble discord. England reverted to her conviction that all Frenchmen were sensualists, while to France the English appeared, as often before, the most offensive of hypocrites. In vain did the saner minds in each country insist on the fundamental humanity of both. In vain, did the chastened Germans seek to mediate. In vain did the League, which by now had very great prestige and authority, threaten both parties with expulsion, even with chastisement. Rumour got about in Paris that England, breaking all her international pledges, was now feverishly building giant planes which would wreck France from Calais to Marseilles. And indeed the rumour was not wholly a slander, for when the struggle began, the British air force was found to have a range of intensive action far wider than was expected. Yet the actual outbreak of war took England by surprise. While the London papers were selling out upon the news that war was declared, enemy planes appeared over the city. In a couple of hours a third of London was in ruins, and half her population lay poisoned in the streets. One bomb, falling beside the British Museum, turned the whole of Bloomsbury into a crater, wherein fragments of mummies, statues, and manuscripts were mingled with the contents of shops, and morsels of salesmen and the intelligentsia. Thus in a moment was destroyed a large proportion of England's most precious relics and most fertile brains.

Then occurred one of those microscopic, yet supremely potent incidents which sometimes mould the course of events for centuries. During the bombardment a special meeting of the British Cabinet was held in a cellar in Downing Street. The party in power at the time was progressive, mildly pacifist, and timorously cosmopolitan. It had got itself involved in the French quarrel quite unintentionally. At this Cabinet meeting an idealistic member urged upon his colleagues the need for a supreme gesture of heroism and generosity on the part of Britain. Raising his voice with difficulty above the bark of English guns and the volcanic crash of French bombs, he suggested sending by radio the following message: 'From the people of England to the people of France. Catastrophe has fallen on us at your hands. In this hour of agony, all hate and anger have left us. Our eyes are opened. No longer can we think of ourselves as English merely, and you as merely French; all of us are, before all else, civilized beings. Do not imagine that we are defeated, and that this message is a cry for mercy. Our armament is intact, and our resources still very great. Yet, because of the revelation which has come to us today, we will not fight. No plane, no ship, no soldier of Britain shall commit any further act of hostility. Do what you will. It would be better even that a great people should be destroyed than that the whole race should be thrown into turmoil. But you will not strike again. As our own eyes have been opened by agony, yours now will be opened by our act of brotherhood. The spirit of France and the spirit of England differ. They differ deeply; but only as the eye differs from the hand. Without you, we should be barbarians. And without us, even the bright spirit of France would be but half expressed. For the spirit of France lives again in our culture and in our very speech; and the spirit of England is that which strikes from you your most distinctive brilliance.'

At no earlier stage of man's history could such a message have been considered seriously by any government. Had it been suggested during the previous war, its author would have been ridiculed, execrated, perhaps even murdered. But since those days, much had happened. Increased communication, increased cultural intercourse, and a prolonged vigorous campaign for cosmopolitanism, had changed the mentality of Europe. Even so, when, after a brief discussion, the Government ordered this unique message to be sent, its members were awed by their own act. As one of them expressed it, they were uncertain whether it was the devil or the deity that had possessed them, but possessed they certainly were.

That night the people of London (those who were left) experienced an exaltation of spirit. Disorganization of the city's life, overwhelming physical suffering and compassion, the consciousness of an unprecedented spiritual act in which each individual felt himself to have somehow participated – these influences combined to produce, even in the bustle and confusion of a wrecked metropolis, a certain restrained fervour, and a deep peace of mind, wholly unfamiliar to Londoners.

Meanwhile the undamaged North knew not whether to regard the Government's sudden pacificism as a piece of cowardice or as a superbly courageous gesture. Very soon, however, they began to make a virtue of necessity, and incline to the latter view. Paris itself was divided by the message into a vocal party of triumph and a silent party of bewilderment. But as the hours advanced, and the former urged a policy of aggression, the latter found voice for the cry, 'Viva l'Angleterre, viva l'humanité'. And so strong by now was the will for cosmopolitanism that the upshot would almost certainly have been a triumph of sanity, had there not occurred in England an accident which tilted the whole precarious course of events in the opposite direction.

The bombardment had occurred on a Friday night. On Saturday the repercussions of England's great message were echoing throughout the nations. That evening, as a wet and foggy day was achieving its pallid sunset, a French plane was seen over the western outskirts of London. It gradually descended, and was regarded by onlookers as a messenger of peace. Lower and lower it came. Something was seen to part from it and fall. In a few seconds an immense explosion occurred in the neighbourhood of a great school and a royal palace. There was hideous destruction in the school. The palace escaped. But, chief disaster for the cause of peace, a beautiful and extravagantly popular young princess was caught by the explosion. Her body, obscenely mutilated, but still recognizable to every student of the illustrated papers, was impaled upon some high park-railings beside the main thoroughfare toward the city. Immediately after the explosion the enemy plane crashed, burst into flame, and was destroyed with its occupants.

A moment's cool thinking would have convinced all onlookers that this disaster was an accident, that the plane was a belated straggler in distress, and no messenger of hate. But, confronted with the mangled bodies of schoolboys, and harrowed by cries of agony and terror, the populace was in no state for ratiocination. Moreover there was the princess, an overwhelmingly potent sexual symbol and emblem of tribalism, slaughtered and exposed before the eyes of her adorers.

The news was flashed over the country, and distorted of course in such a manner as to admit no doubt that this act was the crowning deviltry of sexual fiends beyond the Channel. In an hour the mood of London was changed, and the whole population of England succumbed to a paroxysm of primitive hate far more extravagant than any that had occurred even in the war against Germany. The British air force, all too well equipped and prepared, was ordered to Paris.

Meanwhile in France the militaristic government had fallen, and the party of peace was now in control. While the streets were still thronged by its vociferous supporters, the first bomb fell. By Monday morning Paris was obliterated. There followed a few days of strife between the opposing armaments, and of butchery committed upon the civilian populations. In spite of French gallantry, the superior organization, mechanical efficiency, and more cautious courage of the British air force soon made it impossible for a French plane to leave the ground. But if France was broken, England was too crippled to pursue her advantage. Every city of the two countries was completely disorganized. Famine, riot, looting, and above all the rapidly accelerating and quite uncontrollable spread of disease, disintegrated both States, and brought war to a standstill.

Indeed, not only did hostilities cease, but also both nations were too shattered even to continue hating one another. The energies of each were for a while wholly occupied in trying to prevent complete annihilation by famine and pestilence. In the work of reconstruction they had to depend very largely on help from outside. The management of each country was taken over, for the time, by the League of Nations.

It is significant to compare the mood of Europe at this time with that which followed the European War. Formerly, though there had been a real effort toward unity, hate and suspicion continued to find expression in national policies. There was much wrangling about indemnities, reparations, securities; and the division of the whole continent into two hostile camps persisted, though by then it was purely artificial and sentimental. But after the Anglo-French War, a very different mood prevailed. There was no mention of reparations, no possibility of seeking security by alliances. Patriotism simply faded out, for the time, under the influence of extreme disaster. The two enemy peoples co-operated with the League in the work of reconstructing not only each one itself, but each one the other. This change of heart was due partly to the temporary collapse of the whole national organization, partly to the speedy dominance of each nation by pacifist and anti-nationalist Labour, partly to the fact that the League was powerful enough to inquire into and publish the whole story of the origins of the war, and expose each combatant to itself and to the world in a sorry light.

We have now observed in some detail the incident which stands out in man's history as perhaps the most dramatic example of petty cause and mighty effect. For consider. Through some miscalculation, or a mere defect in his instruments, a French airman went astray, and came to grief in London after the sending of the peace message. Had this not happened, England and France would not have been wrecked. And, had the war been nipped at the outset, as it almost was, the party of sanity throughout the world would have been very greatly strengthened; the precarious will to unity would have gained the conviction which it lacked, would have dominated man not merely during the terrified revulsion after each spasm of national strife, but as a permanent policy based on mutual trust. Indeed so delicately balanced were man's primitive and developed impulses at this time, that but for this trivial accident, the movement which was started by England's peace message might have proceeded steadily and rapidly toward the unification of the race. It might, that is, have attained its goal, before, instead of after, the period of mental deterioration, which in fact resulted from a long epidemic of wars. And so the first Dark Age might never have occurred.

3. EUROPE AFTER THE ANGLO-FRENCH WAR

A subtle change now began to affect the whole mental climate of the planet. This is remarkable, since, viewed for instance from America or China, this war was, after all, but a petty disturbance, scarcely more than a brawl between quarrelsome statelets, an episode in the decline of a senile civilization. Expressed in dollars, the damage was not impressive to the wealthy West and the potentially wealthy East. The British Empire, indeed, that unique banyan tree of peoples, was henceforward less effective in world diplomacy; but since the bond that held it together was by now wholly a bond of sentiment, the Empire was not disintegrated by the misfortune of its parent trunk. Indeed, a common fear of American economic imperialism was already helping the colonies to remain loyal.

Yet this petty brawl was in fact an irreparable and far-reaching disaster. For in spite of those differences of temperament which had forced the English and French into conflict, they had co-operated, though often unwittingly, in tempering and clarifying the mentality of Europe. Though their faults played a great part in wrecking Western civilization, the virtues from which these vices sprang were needed for the salvation of a world prone to uncritical romance. In spite of the inveterate blindness and meanness of France in international policy, and the even more disastrous timidity of England, their influence on culture had been salutary, and was at this moment sorely needed. For, poles asunder in tastes and ideals, these two peoples were yet alike in being on the whole more sceptical, and in their finest individuals more capable of dispassionate yet creative intelligence, than any other Western people. This very character produced their distinctive faults, namely, in the English a caution that amounted often to moral cowardice, and in the French a certain myopic complacency and cunning, which masqueraded as realism. Within each nation there was, of course, great variety. English minds were of many types. But most were to some extent distinctively English; and hence the special character of England's influence in the world. Relatively detached, sceptical, cautious, practical, more tolerant than others, because more complacent and less prone to fervour, the typical Englishman was capable both of generosity and of spite, both of heroism and of timorous or cynical abandonment of ends proclaimed as vital to the race. French and English alike might sin against humanity, but in different manners. The French sinned blindly, through a strange inability to regard France dispassionately.

The English sinned through faint-heartedness, and with open eyes. Among all nations they excelled in the union of common sense and vision. But also among all nations they were most ready to betray their visions in the name of common sense. Hence their reputation for perfidy.

Differences of national character and patriotic sentiment were not the most fundamental distinctions between men at this time. Although in each nation a common tradition or cultural environment imposed a certain uniformity on all its members, yet in each nation every mental type was present, though in different proportions. The most significant of all cultural differences between men, namely, the difference between the tribalists and the cosmopolitans, traversed the national boundaries. For throughout the world something like a new, cosmopolitan 'nation' with a new all-embracing patriotism was beginning to appear. In every land there was by now a salting of awakened minds who, whatever their temperament and politics and formal faith, were at one in respect of their allegiance to humanity as a race or as an adventuring spirit. Unfortunately this new loyalty was still entangled with old prejudices. In some minds the defence of the human spirit was sincerely identified with the defence of a particular nation, conceived as the home of all enlightenment. In others, social injustice kindled a militant proletarian loyalty, which, though at heart cosmopolitan, infected alike its champions and its enemies with sectarian passions.

Another sentiment, less definite and conscious than cosmopolitanism, also played some part in the minds of men, namely loyalty toward the dispassionate intelligence, and perplexed admiration of the world which it was beginning to reveal, a world august, immense, subtle, in which, seemingly, man was doomed to play a part minute but tragic. In many races there had, no doubt, long existed some fidelity toward the dispassionate intelligence. But it was England and France that excelled in this respect. On the other hand, even in these two nations there was much that was opposed to this allegiance. These, like all peoples of the age, were liable to bouts of insane emotionalism. Indeed the French mind, in general so clear sighted, so realistic, so contemptuous of ambiguity and mist, so detached in all its final valuations, was yet so obsessed with the idea 'France' as to be wholly incapable of generosity in international affairs. But it was France, with England, that had chiefly inspired the intellectual integrity which was the rarest and brightest thread of Western culture, not only within the territories of these two nations, but throughout Europe and America. In the seventeenth and eighteenth Christian centuries, the French and English had conceived, more clearly than other peoples, an interest in the objective world for its own sake, had founded physical science, and had fashioned out of scepticism the most brilliantly constructive of mental instruments. At a later stage it was largely the French and English who, by means of this instrument, had revealed man and the physical universe in something like their true proportions; and it was chiefly the elect of these two peoples that had been able to exult in this bracing discovery.

With the eclipse of France and England this great tradition of dispassionate cognizance began to wane. Europe was now led by Germany. And the Germans, in spite of their practical genius, their scholarly contributions to history, their brilliant science and austere philosophy, were at heart romantic. This inclination was both their strength and their weakness. Thereby they had been inspired to their finest art and their most profound metaphysical speculation. But thereby they were also often rendered un-self-critical and pompous. More eager than Western minds to solve the mystery of existence, less sceptical of the power of human reason, and therefore more inclined to ignore or argue away recalcitrant facts, the Germans were courageous systematizers. In this direction they had achieved greatly. Without them, European thought would have been chaotic. But their passion for order and for a systematic reality behind the disorderly appearances, rendered their reasoning all too often biased. Upon shifty foundations they balanced ingenious ladders to reach the stars. Thus, without constant ribald criticism from across the Rhine and the North Sea, the Teutonic soul could not achieve full self-expression. A vague uneasiness about its own sentimentalism and lack of detachment did indeed persuade this great people to assert its virility now and again by ludicrous acts of brutality, and to compensate for its dream life by ceaseless hard-driven and brilliantly successful commerce; but what was needed was a far more radical self-criticism.

Beyond Germany, Russia. Here was a people whose genius needed, even more than that of the Germans, discipline under the critical intelligence. Since the Bolshevic revolution, there had risen in the scattered towns of this immense tract of corn and forest, and still more in the metropolis, an original mode of art and thought, in which were blended a passion of iconoclasm, a vivid sensuousness, and yet also a very remarkable and essentially mystical or intuitive power of detachment from all private cravings. America and Western Europe were interested first in the individual human life, and only secondarily in the social whole. For these peoples, loyalty involved a reluctant self-sacrifice, and the ideal was ever a person, excelling in prowess of various kinds. Society was but the necessary matrix of this jewel. But the Russians, whether by an innate gift, or through the influence of agelong political tyranny, religious devotion, and a truly social revolution, were prone to self-contemptuous interest in groups, prone, indeed, to a spontaneous worship of whatever was conceived as loftier than the individual man, whether society, or God, or the blind forces of nature. Western Europe could reach by way of the intellect a precise conception of man's littleness and irrelevance when regarded as an alien among the stars; could even glimpse from this standpoint the cosmic theme in which all human striving is but one contributory factor. But the Russian mind, whether orthodox or Tolstoyan or fanatically materialist, could attain much the same conviction intuitively, by direct perception, instead of after an arduous intellectual pilgrimage; and, reaching it, could rejoice in it. But because of this independence of intellect, the experience was confused, erratic, frequently misinterpreted; and its effect on conduct was rather explosive than directive. Great indeed was the need that the West and East of Europe should strengthen and temper one another.

After the Bolshevic revolution a new element appeared in Russian culture, and one which had not been known before in any modern state. The old regime was displaced by a real proletarian government, which, though an oligarchy, and sometimes bloody and fanatical, abolished the old tyranny of class, and encouraged the humblest citizen to be proud of his partnership in the great community. Still more important, the native Russian disposition not to take material possessions very seriously co-operated with the political revolution, and brought about such a freedom from the snobbery of wealth as was quite foreign to the West. Attention which elsewhere was absorbed in the massing or display of money was in Russia largely devoted either to spontaneous instinctive enjoyments or to cultural activity.

In fact it was among the Russian townsfolk, less cramped by tradition than other city-dwellers, that the spirit of the First Men was beginning to achieve a fresh and sincere readjustment to the facts of its changing world. And from the townsfolk something of the new way of life was spreading even to the peasants; while in the depths of Asia a hardy and ever-growing population looked increasingly to Russia, not only for machinery, but for ideas. There were times when it seemed that Russia might transform the almost universal autumn of the race into a new spring.

After the Bolshevic revolution the New Russia had been boycotted by the West, and had therefore passed through a stage of self-conscious extravagance. Communism and naïve materialism became the dogmas of a new crusading atheist church. All criticism was suppressed, even more rigorously than was the opposite criticism in other countries; and Russians were taught to think of themselves as saviours of mankind. Later, however, as economic isolation began to hamper the Bolshevic state, the new culture was mellowed and broadened. Bit by bit, economic intercourse with the West was restored, and with it cultural intercourse increased. The intuitive mystical detachment of Russia began to define itself, and so consolidate itself, in terms of the intellectual detachment of the best thought of the West. Iconoclasm was harnessed. The life of the senses and of impulse was tempered by a new critical movement. Fanatical materialism, whose fire had been derived from a misinterpreted, but intense, mystical intuition of dispassionate Reality, began to assimilate itself to the far more rational stoicism which was the rare flower of the West. At the same time, through intercourse with peasant culture and with the peoples of Asia, the new Russia began to grasp in one unifying act of apprehension both the grave disillusion of France and England and the ecstasy of the East.

The harmonizing of these two moods was now the chief spiritual need of mankind. Failure to integrate them into an all-dominant sentiment could not but lead to racial insanity. And so in due course it befell. Meanwhile this task of integration was coming to seem more and more urgent to the best minds in Russia, and might have been finally accomplished had they been longer illumined by the cold light of the West.

But this was not to be. The intellectual confidence of France and England, already shaken through progressive economic eclipse at the hands of America and Germany, was now undermined. For many decades England had watched these newcomers capture her markets. The loss had smothered her with a swarm of domestic problems, such as could never be solved save by drastic surgery; and this was a course which demanded more courage and energy than was possible to a people without hope. Then came the war with France, and harrowing disintegration. No delirium seized her, such as occurred in France; yet her whole mentality was changed, and her sobering influence in Europe was lessened.

As for France, her cultural life was now grievously reduced. It might, indeed, have recovered from the final blow, had it not already been slowly poisoned by gluttonous nationalism. For love of France was the undoing of the French. They prized the truly admirable spirit of France so extravagantly, that they regarded all other nations as barbarians.

Thus it befell that in Russia the doctrines of communism and materialism, products of German systematists, survived uncriticized. On the other hand, the practice of communism was gradually undermined. For the Russian state came increasingly under the influence of Western, and especially American, finance. The materialism of the official creed also became a farce, for it was foreign to the Russian mind. Thus between practice and theory there was, in both respects, a profound inconsistency. What was once a vital and promising culture became insincere.

4. THE RUSSO-GERMAN WAR

The discrepancy between communist theory and individualist practice in Russia was one cause of the next disaster which befell Europe. Between Russia and Germany there should have been close partnership, based on interchange of machinery and corn. But the theory of communism stood in the way, and in a strange manner. Russian industrial organization had proved impossible without American capital; and little by little this influence had transformed the communistic system. From the Baltic to the Himalayas and the Behring Straits, pasture, timber lands, machine-tilled corn-land, oil fields, and a spreading rash of industrial towns, were increasingly dependent on American finance and organization. Yet not America, but the far less individualistic Germany, had become in the Russian mind the symbol of capitalism. Self-righteous hate of Germany compensated Russia for her own betrayal of the communistic ideal. This perverse antagonism was encouraged by the Americans; who, strong in their own individualism and prosperity, and by now contemptuously tolerant of Russian doctrines, were concerned only to keep Russian finance to themselves. In truth, of course, it was America that had helped Russia's self-betrayal; and it was the spirit of America that was most alien to the Russian spirit. But American wealth was by now indispensable to Russia; so the hate due to America had to be borne vicariously by Germany.

The Germans, for their part, were aggrieved that the Americans had ousted them from a most profitable field of enterprise, and in particular from the exploitation of Russian Asiatic oil. The economic life of the human race had for some time been based on coal, but latterly oil had been found a far more convenient source of power; and as the oil store of the planet was much smaller than its coal store, and the expenditure of oil had of course been wholly uncontrolled and wasteful, a shortage was already being felt. Thus the national ownership of the remaining oil fields had become a main factor in politics and a fertile source of wars. America, having used up most of her own supplies, was now anxious to compete with the still prolific sources under Chinese control, by forestalling Germany in Russia. No wonder the Germans were aggrieved. But the fault was their own. In the days when Russian communism had been seeking to convert the world, Germany had taken over England's leadership of individualistic Europe. While greedy for trade with Russia, she had been at the same time frightened of contamination by Russian social doctrine, the more so because communism had at first made some headway among the German workers. Later, even when sane industrial reorganization in Germany had deprived communism of its appeal to the workers, and thus had rendered it impotent, the habit of anti-communist vituperation persisted.

Thus the peace of Europe was in constant danger from the bickerings of two peoples who differed rather in ideals than in practice. For the one, in theory communistic, had been forced to delegate many of the community's rights to enterprising individuals; while the other, in theory organized on a basis of private business, was becoming ever more socialized.

Neither party desired war. Neither was interested in military glory, for militarism as an end was no longer reputable. Neither was professedly nationalistic, for nationalism, though still potent, was no longer vaunted. Each claimed to stand for internationalism and peace, but accused the other of narrow patriotism. Thus Europe, though more pacific than ever before, was doomed to war.

Like most wars, the Anglo-French War had increased the desire for peace, yet made peace less secure. Distrust, not merely the old distrust of nation for nation, but a devastating distrust of human nature, gripped men like the dread of insanity. Individuals who thought of themselves as wholehearted Europeans, feared that at any moment they might succumb to some ridiculous epidemic of patriotism and participate in the further crippling of Europe.

This dread was one cause of the formation of a European Confederacy, in which all the nations of Europe, save Russia, surrendered their sovereignty to a common authority and actually pooled their armaments. Ostensibly the motive of this act was peace; but America interpreted it as directed against herself, and withdrew from the League of Nations. China, the 'natural enemy' of America, remained within the League, hoping to use it against her rival.

From without, indeed, the Confederacy at first appeared as a close-knit whole; but from within it was known to be insecure, and in every serious crisis it broke. There is no need to follow the many minor wars of this period, though their cumulative effect was serious, both economically and psychologically. Europe did at last, however, become something like a single nation in sentiment, though this unity was brought about less by a common loyalty than by a common fear of America.

Final consolidation was the fruit of the Russo-German War, the cause of which was partly economic and partly sentimental. All the peoples of Europe had long watched with horror the financial conquest of Russia by the United States, and they dreaded that they also must presently succumb to the same tyrant. To attack Russia, it was thought, would be to wound America in her only vulnerable spot. But the actual occasion of the war was sentimental. Half a century after the Anglo-French War, a second-rate German author published a typically German book of the baser sort. For as each nation had its characteristic virtues, so also each was prone to characteristic follies. This book was one of those brilliant but extravagant works in which the whole diversity of existence is interpreted under a single formula, with extreme detail and plausibility, yet with amazing naïveté. Highly astute within its own artificial universe, it was none the less in wider regard quite uncritical. In two large volumes the author claimed that the cosmos was a dualism in which a heroic and obviously Nordic spirit ruled by divine right over an un-self-disciplined, yet servile and obviously Slavonic spirit. The whole of history, and of evolution, was interpreted on this principle; and of the contemporary world it was said that the Slavonic element was poisoning Europe. One phrase in particular caused fury in Moscow, 'the anthropoid face of the Russian sub-man'.

Moscow demanded apology and suppression of the book. Berlin regretted the insult, but with its tongue in its cheek; and insisted on the freedom of the press. There followed a crescendo of radio hate, and war.

The details of this war do not matter to one intent upon the history of mind in the solar system, but its result was important. Moscow, Leningrad and Berlin were shattered from the air. The whole West of Russia was flooded with the latest and deadliest poison gas, so that, not only was all animal and vegetable life destroyed, but also the soil between the Black Sea and the Baltic was rendered infertile and uninhabitable for many years. Within a week the war was over, for the reason that the combatants were separated by an immense territory in which life could not exist. But the effects of the war were lasting. The Germans had set going a process which they could not stop. Whiffs of the poison continued to be blown by fickle winds into every country of Europe and Western Asia. It was spring-time; but save in the Atlantic coast-lands the spring flowers shrivelled in the bud, and every young leaf had a withered rim. Humanity also suffered; though, save in the regions near the seat of war, it was in general only the children and the old people who suffered greatly. The poison spread across the Continent in huge blown tresses, broad as principalities, swinging with each change of wind. And wherever it strayed, young eyes, throats, and lungs were blighted like the leaves.

America, after much debate, had at last decided to defend her interests in Russia by a punitive expedition against Europe. China began to mobilize her forces. But long before America was ready to strike, news of the widespread poisoning changed her policy. Instead of punishment, help was given. This was a fine gesture of goodwill. But also, as was observed in Europe, instead of being costly, it was profitable; for inevitably it brought more of Europe under American financial control.

The upshot of the Russo-German War, then, was that Europe was unified in sentiment by hatred of America, and that European mentality definitely deteriorated. This was due in part to the emotional influence of the War itself, partly to the socially damaging effects of the poison. A proportion of the rising generation had been rendered sickly for life. During the thirty years which intervened before the Euro-American war, Europe was burdened with an exceptional weight of invalids. First-class intelligence was on the whole rarer than before, and was more strictly concentrated on the practical work of reconstruction.

Even more disastrous for the human race was the fact that the recent Russian cultural enterprise of harmonizing Western intellectualism and Eastern mysticism was now wrecked.

CHAPTER II

EUROPE'S DOWNFALL

1. EUROPE AND AMERICA

Over the heads of the European tribes two mightier peoples regarded each other with increasing dislike. Well might they; for the one cherished the most ancient and refined of all surviving cultures, while the other, youngest and most self-confident of the great nations, proclaimed her novel spirit as the spirit of the future.

In the Far East, China, already half American, though largely Russian and wholly Eastern, patiently improved her rice lands, pushed forward her railways, organized her industries, and spoke fair to all the world. Long ago, during her attainment of unity and independence, China had learnt much from militant Bolshevism. And after the collapse of the Russian state it was in the East that Russian culture continued to live. Its mysticism influenced India. Its social ideal influenced China. Not indeed that China took over the theory, still less the practice, of communism; but she learnt to entrust herself increasingly to a vigorous, devoted and despotic party, and to feel in terms of the social whole rather than individualistically. Yet she was honeycombed with individualism, and in spite of her rulers she had precipitated a submerged and desperate class of wage slaves.

In the Far West, the United States of America openly claimed to be custodians of the whole planet. Universally feared and envied, universally respected for their enterprise, yet for their complacency very widely despised, the Americans were rapidly changing the whole character of man's existence. By this time every human being throughout the planet made use of American products, and there was no region where American capital did not support local labour. Moreover the American press, gramophone, radio, cinematograph and televisor ceaselessly drenched the planet with American thought. Year by year the ether reverberated with echoes of New York's pleasures and the religious fervours of the Middle West. What wonder, then, that America, even while she was despised, irresistibly moulded the whole human race. This, perhaps, would not have mattered, had America been able to give of her very rare best. But inevitably only her worst could be propagated. Only the most vulgar traits of that potentially great people could get through into the minds of foreigners by means of these crude instruments. And so, by the floods of poison issuing from this people's baser members, the whole world, and with it the nobler parts of America herself, were irrevocably corrupted.

For the best of America was too weak to withstand the worst. Americans had indeed contributed amply to human thought. They had helped to emancipate philosophy from ancient fetters. They had served science by lavish and rigorous research. In astronomy, favoured by their costly instruments and clear atmosphere, they had done much to reveal the dispositions of the stars and galaxies. In literature, though often they behaved as barbarians, they had also conceived new modes of expression, and moods of thought not easily appreciated in Europe. They had also created a new and brilliant architecture. And their genius for organization worked upon a scale that was scarcely conceivable, let alone practicable, to other peoples. In fact their best minds faced old problems of theory and of valuation with a fresh innocence and courage, so that fogs of superstition were cleared away wherever these choice Americans were present. But these best were after all a minority in a huge wilderness of opinionated self-deceivers, in whom, surprisingly, an outworn religious dogma was championed with the intolerant optimism of youth. For this was essentially a race of bright, but arrested, adolescents. Something lacked which should have enabled them to grow up. One who looks back across the aeons to this remote people can see their fate already woven of their circumstance and their disposition, and can appreciate the grim jest that these, who seemed to themselves gifted to rejuvenate the planet, should have plunged it, inevitably, through spiritual desolation into senility and age-long night.

Inevitably. Yet here was a people of unique promise, gifted innately beyond all other peoples. Here was a race brewed of all the races, and mentally more effervescent than any. Here were intermingled Anglo-Saxon stubbornness, Teutonic genius for detail and systematization, Italian gaiety, the intense fire of Spain, and the more mobile Celtic flame. Here also was the sensitive and stormy Slav, a youth-giving Negroid infusion, a faint but subtly stimulating trace of the Red Man, and in the West a sprinkling of the Mongol. Mutual intolerance no doubt isolated these diverse stocks to some degree; yet the whole was increasingly one people, proud of its individuality, of its success, of its idealistic mission in the world, proud also of its optimistic and anthropocentric view of the universe. What might not this energy have achieved, had it been more critically controlled, had it been forced to attend to life's more forbidding aspects! Direct tragic experience might perhaps have opened the hearts of this people. Intercourse with a more mature culture might have refined their intelligence. But the very success which had intoxicated them rendered them also too complacent to learn from less prosperous competitors.

Yet there was a moment when this insularity promised to wane. So long as England was a serious economic rival, America inevitably regarded her with suspicion. But when England was seen to be definitely in economic decline, yet culturally still at her zenith, America conceived a more generous interest in the last and severest phase of English thought. Eminent Americans themselves began to whisper that perhaps their unrivalled prosperity was not after all good evidence either of their own spiritual greatness or of the moral rectitude of the universe. A minute but persistent school of writers began to affirm that America lacked self-criticism, was incapable of seeing the joke against herself, was in fact wholly devoid of that detachment and resignation which was the finest, though of course the rarest, mood of latter-day England. This movement might well have infused throughout the American people that which was needed to temper their barbarian egotism, and open their ears once more to the silence beyond man's strident sphere. Once more, for only latterly had they been seriously deafened by the din of their own material success. And indeed, scattered over the continent throughout this whole period, many shrinking islands of true culture contrived to keep their heads above the rising tide of vulgarity and superstition. These it was that had looked to Europe for help, and were attempting a rally when England and France blundered into that orgy of emotionalism and murder which exterminated so many of their best minds and permanently weakened their cultural influence.

Subsequently it was Germany that spoke for Europe. And Germany was too serious an economic rival for America to be open to her influence. Moreover German criticism, though often emphatic, was too heavily pedantic, too little ironical, to pierce the hide of American complacency. Thus it was that America sank further and further into Americanism. Vast wealth and industry, and also brilliant invention, were concentrated upon puerile ends. In particular the whole of American life was organized around the cult of the powerful individual, that phantom ideal which Europe herself had only begun to outgrow in her last phase. Those Americans who wholly failed to realize this ideal, who remained at the bottom of the social ladder, either consoled themselves with hopes for the future, or stole symbolical satisfaction by identifying themselves with some popular star, or gloated upon their American citizenship, and applauded the arrogant foreign policy of their government. Those who achieved power were satisfied so long as they could merely retain it, and advertise it uncritically in the conventionally self-assertive manners.

It was almost inevitable that when Europe had recovered from the Russo-German disaster she should come to blows with America; for she had long chafed under the saddle of American finance, and the daily life of Europeans had become more and more cramped by the presence of a widespread and contemptuous foreign 'aristocracy' of American business men. Germany alone was comparatively free from this domination, for Germany was herself still a great economic power. But in Germany, no less than elsewhere, there was constant friction with the Americans.

Of course neither Europe nor America desired war. Each was well aware that war would mean the end of business prosperity, and for Europe very possibly the end of all things; for it was known that man's power of destruction had recently increased, and that if war were waged relentlessly, the stronger side might exterminate the other. But inevitably an 'incident' at last occurred which roused blind rage on each side of the Atlantic. A murder in South Italy, a few ill-considered remarks in the European Press, offensive retaliation in the American Press accompanied by the lynching of an Italian in the Middle West, an uncontrollable massacre of American citizens in Rome, the dispatch of an American air fleet to occupy Italy, interception by the European air fleet, and war was in existence before ever it had been declared. This aerial action resulted, perhaps unfortunately for Europe, in a momentary check to the American advance. The enemy was put on his mettle, and prepared a crushing blow.

2. THE ORIGINS OF A MYSTERY

While the Americans were mobilizing their whole armament, there occurred the really interesting event of the war. It so happened that an international society of scientific workers was meeting in England at Plymouth, and a young Chinese physicist had expressed his desire to make a report to a select committee. As he had been experimenting to find means for the utilization of subatomic energy by the annihilation of matter, it was with some excitement that, according to instruction, the forty international representatives travelled to the north coast of Devon and met upon the bare headland called Hartland Point.

It was a bright morning after rain. Eleven miles to the north-west, the cliffs of Lundy Island displayed their markings with unusual detail. Sea-birds wheeled about the heads of the party as they seated themselves on their raincoats in a cluster upon the rabbit-cropped turf.

They were a remarkable company, each one of them a unique person, yet characterized to some extent by his particular national type. And all were distinctively 'scientists' of the period. Formerly this would have implied a rather uncritical leaning toward materialism, and an affectation of cynicism; but by now it was fashionable to profess an equally uncritical belief that all natural phenomena were manifestations of the cosmic mind. In both periods, when a man passed beyond the sphere of his own serious scientific work he chose his beliefs irresponsibly, according to his taste, much as he chose his recreation or his food.

Of the individuals present we may single out one or two for notice. The German, an anthropologist, and a product of the long-established cult of physical and mental health, sought to display in his own athletic person the characters proper to Nordic man. The Frenchman, an old but still sparkling psychologist, whose queer hobby was the collecting of weapons, ancient and modern, regarded the proceedings with kindly cynicism. The Englishman, one of the few remaining intellectuals of his race, compensated for the severe study of physics by a scarcely less devoted research into the history of English expletives and slang, delighting to treat his colleagues to the fruits of his toil. The West African president of the Society was a biologist, famous for his interbreeding of man and ape.

When all were settled, the President explained the purpose of the meeting. The utilization of subatomic energy had indeed been achieved, and they were to be given a demonstration.

The young Mongol stood up, and produced from a case an instrument rather like the old-fashioned rifle. Displaying this object, he spoke as follows, with that quaintly stilted formality which had once been characteristic of all educated Chinese: 'Before describing the details of my rather delicate process, I will illustrate its importance by showing what can be done with the finished product. Not only can I initiate the annihilation of matter, but also I can do so at a distance and in a precise direction. Moreover, I can inhibit the process. As a means of destruction, my instrument is perfect. As a source of power for the constructive work of mankind, it has unlimited potentiality. Gentlemen, this is a great moment in the history of Man. I am about to render into the hands of organized intelligence the means to stop for ever man's internecine brawls. Henceforth this great Society, of which you are the élite, will beneficently rule the planet. With this little instrument you will stop the ridiculous war; and with another, which I shall soon perfect, you will dispense unlimited industrial power wherever you consider it needed. Gentlemen, with the aid of this handy instrument which I have the honour to demonstrate, you are able to become absolute masters of this planet.'

Here the representative of England muttered an archaism whose significance was known only to himself, 'Gawd 'elp us!' In the minds of some of those foreigners who were not physicists this quaint expression was taken to be a technical word having some connexion with the new source of energy.

The Mongol continued. Turning towards Lundy, he said, 'That island is no longer inhabited, and as it is something of a danger to shipping, I will remove it.' So saying he aimed his instrument at the distant cliff, but continued speaking. 'This trigger will stimulate the ultimate positive and negative charges which constitute the atoms at a certain point on the rock face to annihilate each other. These stimulated atoms will infect their neighbours, and so on indefinitely. This second trigger, however, will stop the actual annihilation. Were I to refrain from using it, the process would indeed continue indefinitely, perhaps until the whole of the planet had disintegrated.'

There was an anxious movement among the spectators, but the young man took careful aim, and pressed the two triggers in quick succession. No sound from the instrument. No visible effect upon the smiling face of the island. Laughter began to gurgle from the Englishman, but ceased. For a dazzling point of light appeared on the remote cliff. It increased in size and brilliance, till all eyes were blinded in the effort to continue watching. It lit up the under parts of the clouds and blotted out the sun-cast shadows of gorse bushes beside the spectators. The whole end of the island facing the mainland was now an intolerable scorching sun. Presently, however, its fury was veiled in clouds of steam from the boiling sea. Then suddenly the whole island, three miles of solid granite, leaped asunder; so that a covey of great rocks soared heavenward, and beneath them swelled more slowly a gigantic mushroom of steam and debris. Then the sound arrived. All hands were clapped to ears, while eyes still strained to watch the bay, pocked white with the hail of rocks. Meanwhile a great wall of sea advanced from the centre of turmoil. This was seen to engulf a coasting vessel, and pass on toward Bideford and Barnstaple.

The spectators leaped to their feet and clamoured, while the young author of this fury watched the spectacle with exultation, and some surprise at the magnitude of these mere after-effects of his process.

The meeting was now adjourned to a neighbouring chapel to hear the report of the research. As the representatives were filing through the door it was observed that the steam and smoke had cleared, and that open sea extended where had been Lundy. Within the chapel, the great Bible was decorously removed and the windows thrown open, to dispel somewhat the odour of sanctity. For though the early and spiritistic interpretations of relativity and the quantum theory had by now accustomed men of science to pay their respects to the religions, many of them were still liable to a certain asphyxia when they were actually within the precincts of sanctity. When the scientists had settled themselves upon the archaic and unyielding benches, the President explained that the chapel authorities had kindly permitted this meeting because they realized that, since men of science had gradually discovered the spiritual foundation of physics, science and religion must henceforth be close allies. Moreover the purpose of this meeting was to discuss one of those supreme mysteries which it was the glory of science to discover and religion to transfigure. The President then complimented the young dispenser of power upon his triumph, and called upon him to address the meeting.

At this point, however, the aged representative of France intervened, and was granted a hearing. Born almost a hundred and forty years earlier, and preserved more by native intensity of spirit than by the artifices of the regenerator, this ancient seemed to speak out of a remote and wiser epoch. For in a declining civilization it is often the old who see furthest and see with youngest eyes. He concluded a rather long, rhetorical, yet closely reasoned speech as follows: 'No doubt we are the intelligence of the planet; and because of our consecration to our calling, no doubt we are comparatively honest. But alas, even we are human. We make little mistakes now and then, and commit little indiscretions. The possession of such power as is offered us would not bring peace. On the contrary it would perpetuate our national hates. It would throw the world into confusion. It would undermine our own integrity, and turn us into tyrants. Moreover it would ruin science. And – well, when at last through some little error the world got blown up, the disaster would not be regrettable. I know that Europe is almost certainly about to be destroyed by those vigorous but rather spoilt children across the Atlantic. But distressing as this must be, the alternative is far worse. No, Sir! Your very wonderful toy would be a gift fit for developed minds; but for us, who are still barbarians – no, it must not be. And so, with deep regret I beg you to destroy your handiwork, and, if it were possible, your memory of your marvellous research. But above all breathe no word of your process to us, or to any man.'

The German then protested that to refuse would be cowardly. He briefly described his vision of a world organized under organized science, and inspired by a scientifically organized religious dogma. 'Surely,' he said, 'to refuse were to refuse the gift of God, of that God whose presence in the humblest quantum we have so recently and so surprisingly revealed.' Other speakers followed, for and against; but it soon grew clear that wisdom would prevail. Men of science were by now definitely cosmopolitan in sentiment. Indeed so far were they from nationalism, that on this occasion the representative of America had urged acceptance of the weapon, although it would be used against his own countrymen.

Finally, however, and actually by a unanimous vote, the meeting, while recording its deep respect for the Chinese scientist, requested, nay ordered, that the instrument and all account of it should be destroyed.

The young man rose, drew his handiwork from its case, and fingered it. So long did he remain thus standing in silence with eyes fixed on the instrument, that the meeting became restless. At last, however, he spoke. 'I shall abide by the decision of the meeting. Well, it is hard to destroy the fruit of ten years' work, and such fruit, too. I expected to have the gratitude of mankind; but instead I am an outcast.' Once more he paused. Gazing out of the window, he now drew from his pocket a field-glass, and studied the western sky. 'Yes, they are American. Gentlemen, the American air fleet approaches.'

The company leapt to its feet and crowded to the windows. High in the west a sparse line of dots stretched indefinitely into the north and the south. Said the Englishman, 'For God's sake use your damned tool once more, or England's done. They must have smashed our fellows over the Atlantic.'

The Chinese scientist turned his eyes on the President. There was a general cry of 'Stop them'. Only the Frenchman protested. The representative of the United States raised his voice and said, 'They are my people, I have friends up there in the sky. My own boy is probably there. But they're mad. They want to do something hideous.

They're in the lynching mood. Stop them.' The Mongol still gazed at the President, who nodded. The Frenchman broke down in senile tears. Then the young man, leaning upon the window sill, took careful aim at each black dot in turn. One by one, each became a blinding star, then vanished. In the chapel, a long silence. Then whispers; and glances at the Chinaman, expressive of anxiety and dislike.

There followed a hurried ceremony in a neighbouring field. A fire was lit. The instrument and the no less murderous manuscript were burnt. And then the grave young Mongol, having insisted on shaking hands all round, said, 'With my secret alive in me, I must not live. Some day a more worthy race will re-discover it, but today I am a danger to the planet. And so I, who have foolishly ignored that I live among savages, help myself now by the ancient wisdom to pass hence.' So saying, he fell dead.

3. EUROPE MURDERED

Rumour spread by voice and radio throughout the world. An island had been mysteriously exploded. The American fleet had been mysteriously annihilated in the air. And in the neighbourhood where these events had occurred, distinguished scientists were gathered in conference. The European Government sought out the unknown saviour of Europe, to thank him, and secure his process for their own use. The President of the scientific society gave an account of the meeting and the unanimous vote. He and his colleagues were promptly arrested, and 'pressure', first moral and then physical, was brought to bear on them to make them disclose the secret; for the world was convinced that they really knew it, and were holding it back for their own purposes.

Meanwhile it was learned that the American air commander, after he had defeated the European fleet, had been instructed merely to 'demonstrate' above England while peace was negotiated. For in America, big business had threatened the government with boycott if unnecessary violence were committed in Europe. Big business was by now very largely international in sentiment, and it was realized that the destruction of Europe would inevitably unhinge American finance. But the unprecedented disaster to the victorious fleet roused the Americans to blind hate, and the peace party was submerged.

Thus it turned out that the Chinaman's one hostile act had not saved England, but doomed her.

For some days Europeans lived in panic dread, knowing not what horror might at any moment descend on them. No wonder, then, that the Government resorted to torture in order to extract the secret from the scientists. No wonder that out of the forty individuals concerned, one, the Englishman, saved himself by deceit. He promised to do his best to 'remember' the intricate process. Under strict supervision, he used his own knowledge of physics to experiment in search of the Chinaman's trick. Fortunately, however, he was on the wrong scent. And indeed he knew it. For though his first motive was mere self-preservation, later he conceived the policy of indefinitely preventing the dangerous discovery by directing research along a blind alley. And so his treason, by seeming to give the authority of a most eminent physicist to a wholly barren line of research, saved this undisciplined and scarcely human race from destroying its planet.

The American people, sometimes tender even to excess, were now collectively insane with hate of the English and of all Europeans. With cold efficiency they flooded Europe with the latest and deadliest of gases, till all the peoples were poisoned in their cities like rats in their holes. The gas employed was such that its potency would cease within three days. It was therefore possible for an American sanitary force to take charge of each metropolis within a week after the attack. Of those who first descended into the great silence of the murdered cities, many were unhinged by the overwhelming presence of dead populations. The gas had operated first upon the ground level, but, rising like a tide, it had engulfed the top stories, the spires, the hills. Thus, while in the streets lay thousands who had been overcome by the first wave of poison, every roof and pinnacle bore the bodies of those who had struggled upwards in the vain hope of escaping beyond the highest reach of the tide. When the invaders arrived they beheld on every height prostrate and contorted figures.

Thus Europe died. All centres of intellectual life were blotted out, and of the agricultural regions only the uplands and mountains were untouched. The spirit of Europe lived henceforth only in a piece-meal and dislocated manner in the minds of Americans, Chinese, Indians, and the rest.

There were indeed the British Colonies, but they were by now far less European than American. The war had, of course, disintegrated the British Empire. Canada sided with the United States. South Africa and India declared their neutrality at the outbreak of war. Australia, not through cowardice, but through conflict of loyalties, was soon reduced to neutrality. The New Zealanders took to their mountains and maintained an insane but heroic resistance for a year. A simple and gallant folk, they had almost no conception of the European spirit, yet obscurely and in spite of their Americanization they were loyal to it, or at least to that symbol of one aspect of Europeanism, 'England'. Indeed so extravagantly loyal were they, or so innately dogged and opinionated, that when further resistance became impossible, many of them, both men and women, killed themselves rather than submit.

But the most lasting agony of this war was suffered, not by the defeated, but by the victors. For when their passion had cooled the Americans could not easily disguise from themselves that they had committed murder. They were not at heart a brutal folk, but rather a kindly. They liked to think of the world as a place of innocent pleasure-seeking, and of themselves as the main purveyors of delight. Yet they had been somehow drawn into this fantastic crime; and henceforth an all-pervading sense of collective guilt warped the American mind. They had ever been vainglorious and intolerant; but now these qualities in them became extravagant even to insanity. Both as individuals and collectively, they became increasingly frightened of criticism, increasingly prone to blame and hate, increasingly self-righteous, increasingly hostile to the critical intelligence, increasingly superstitious.

Thus was this once noble people singled out by the gods to be cursed, and the minister of curses.

CHAPTER III

AMERICA AND CHINA

1. THE RIVALS

After the eclipse of Europe, the allegiance of men gradually crystallized into two great national or racial sentiments, the American and the Chinese. Little by little all other patriotisms became mere local variants of one or other of these two major loyalties. At first, indeed, there were many internecine conflicts. A detailed history of this period would describe how North America, repeating the welding process of the ancient 'American Civil War', incorporated within itself the already Americanized Latins of South America; and how Japan, once the bully of young China, was so crippled by social revolutions that she fell a prey to American Imperialism; and how this bondage turned her violently Chinese in sentiment, so that finally she freed herself by an heroic war of independence, and joined the Asiatic Confederacy, under Chinese leadership.

A full history would also tell of the vicissitudes of the League of Nations. Although never a cosmopolitan government, but an association of national governments, each concerned mainly for its own sovereignty, this great organization had gradually gained a very real prestige and authority over all its members. And in spite of its many short-comings, most of which were involved in its fundamental constitution, it was invaluable as the great concrete focusing point of the growing loyalty toward humanity. At first its existence had been precarious; and indeed it had only preserved itself by an extreme caution, amounting almost to servility toward the 'great powers'. Little by little, however, it had gained moral authority to such an extent that no single power, even the mightiest, dared openly and in cold blood either to disobey the will of the League or reject the findings of the High Court. But, since human loyalty was still in the main national rather than cosmopolitan, situations were all too frequent in which a nation would lose its head, run amok, throw its pledges to the winds, and plunge into fear-inspired aggression. Such a situation had produced the Anglo-French War. At other times the nations would burst apart into two great camps, and the League would be temporarily forgotten in their disunion. This happened in the Russo-German War, which was possible only because America favoured Russia, and China favoured Germany. After the destruction of Europe, the world had for a while consisted of the League on one side and America on the other. But the League was dominated by China, and no longer stood for cosmopolitanism. This being so, those whose loyalty was genuinely human worked hard to bring America once more into the fold, and at last succeeded.

In spite of the League's failure to prevent the 'great' wars, it worked admirably in preventing all the minor conflicts which had once been a chronic disease of the race. Latterly, indeed, the world's peace was absolutely secure, save when the League itself was almost equally divided. Unfortunately, with the rise of America and China, this kind of situation became more and more common. During the war of North and South America an attempt was made to re-create the League as a Cosmopolitan Sovereignty, controlling the pooled armaments of all nations. But, though the cosmopolitan will was strong, tribalism was stronger. The upshot was that, over the Japanese question, the League definitely split into two Leagues, each claiming to inherit universal sovereignty from the old League, but each in reality dominated by a kind of supernational sentiment, the one American, the other Chinese.

This occurred within a century after the eclipse of Europe. The second century completed the process of crystallization into two systems, political and mental. On the one hand was the wealthy and close-knit American Continental Federation, with its poor relations, South Africa, Australia, New Zealand, the bedridden remains of Western Europe, and part of the soulless body that was Russia. On the other hand were Asia and Africa. In fact the ancient distinction between East and West had now become the basis of political sentiment and organization.

Within each system there were of course real differences of culture, of which the chief was the difference between the Chinese and Indian mentalities. The Chinese were interested in appearances, in the sensory, the urbane, the practical; while the Indians inclined to seek behind appearances for some ultimate reality, of which this life, they said, was but a passing aspect. Thus the average Indian never took to heart the practical social problem in all its seriousness. The ideal of perfecting this world was never an all-absorbing interest to him; since he had been taught to believe that this world was mere shadow. There was, indeed, a time when China had mentally less in common with India than with the West, but fear of America had drawn the two great Eastern peoples together. They agreed at least in earnest hate of that strange blend of the commercial traveller, the missionary, and the barbarian conqueror, which was the American abroad.

China, owing to her relative weakness and irritation caused by the tentacles of American industry within her, was at this time more nationalistic than her rival, America, indeed, professed to have outgrown nationalism, and to stand for political and cultural world unity. But she conceived this unity as a Unity under American organization; and by culture she meant Americanism. This kind of cosmopolitanism was regarded by Asia and Africa without sympathy. In China a concerted effort had been made to purge the foreign element from her culture. Its success, however, was only superficial. Pigtails and chopsticks had once more come into vogue among the leisured, and the study of Chinese classics was once more compulsory in all schools. Yet the manner of life of the average man remained American. Not only did he use American cutlery, shoes, gramophones, domestic labour-saving devices, but also his alphabet was European, his vocabulary was permeated by American slang, his newspapers and radio were American in manner, though anti-American in politics. He saw daily in his domestic television screen every phase of American private life and every American public event. Instead of opium and joss sticks, he affected cigarettes and chewing gum.

His thought also was largely a Mongolian variant of American thought. For instance, since his was a non-metaphysical mind, but since also some kind of metaphysics is unavoidable, he accepted the naïvely materialistic metaphysics which had been popularized by the earliest Behaviourists. In this view the only reality was physical energy, and the mind was but the system of the body's movements in response to stimulus. Behaviourism had formerly played a great part in purging the best Western minds of superstition; and indeed at one time it was the chief growing point of thought.

This early, pregnant, though extravagant, doctrine it was that had been absorbed by China. But in its native land Behaviourism had gradually been infected by the popular demand for comfortable ideas, and had finally changed into a curious kind of spiritism, according to which, though the ultimate reality was indeed physical energy, this energy was identified with the divine spirit. The most dramatic feature of American thought in this period was the merging of Behaviourism and Fundamentalism, a belated and degenerate mode of Christianity. Behaviourism itself, indeed, had been originally a kind of inverted Puritan faith, according to which intellectual salvation involved acceptance of a crude materialistic dogma, chiefly because it was repugnant to the self-righteous, and unintelligible to intellectuals of the earlier schools. The older Puritans trampled down all fleshy impulses; these newer Puritans trampled no less self-righteously upon the spiritual cravings. But in the increasingly spiritistic inclination of physics itself, Behaviourism and Fundamentalism had found a meeting place. Since the ultimate stuff of the physical universe was now said to be multitudinous and arbitrary 'quanta' of the activity of 'spirits', how easy was it for the materialistic and the spiritistic to agree! At heart, indeed, they were never far apart in mood, though opposed in doctrine. The real cleavage was between the truly spiritual view on the one hand, and the spiritistic and materialistic on the other. Thus the most materialistic of Christian sects and the most doctrinaire of scientific sects were not long in finding a formula to express their unity, their denial of all those finer capacities which had emerged to be the spirit of man.

These two faiths were at one in their respect for crude physical movement. And here lay the deepest difference between the American and the Chinese minds. For the former, activity, any sort of activity, was an end in itself; for the latter, activity was but a progress toward the true end, which was rest, and peace of mind. Action was to be undertaken only when equilibrium was disturbed.

And in this respect China was at one with India. Both preferred contemplation to action.

Thus in China and India the passion for wealth was less potent than in America. Wealth was the power to set things and people in motion; and in America, therefore, wealth came to be frankly regarded as the breath of God, the divine spirit immanent in man. God was the supreme Boss, the universal Employer. His wisdom was conceived as a stupendous efficiency, his love as munificence towards his employees. The parable of the talents was made the corner-stone of education; and to be wealthy, therefore, was to be respected as one of God's chief agents. The typical American man of big business was one who, in the midst of a show of luxury, was at heart ascetic. He valued his splendour only because it advertised to all men that he was of the elect. The typical Chinese wealthy man was one who savoured his luxury with a delicate and lingering palate, and was seldom tempted to sacrifice it to the barren lust of power.

On the other hand, since American culture was wholly concerned with the values of the individual life, it was more sensitive than the Chinese with regard to the well-being of humble individuals. Therefore industrial conditions were far better under American than under Chinese capitalism. And in China both kinds of capitalism existed side by side. There were American factories in which the Chinese operatives thrived on the American system, and there were Chinese factories in which the operatives were by comparison abject wage-slaves. The fact that many Chinese industrial workers could not afford to keep a motor-car, let alone an aeroplane, was a source of much self-righteous indignation amongst American employers. And the fact that this fact did not cause a revolution in China, and that Chinese employers were able to procure plenty of labour in spite of the better conditions in American factories, was a source of perplexity. But in truth what the average Chinese worker wanted was not symbolical self-assertion through the control of privately owned machines, but security of life, and irresponsible leisure. In the earlier phase of 'modern' China there had indeed been serious explosions of class hatred. Almost every one of the great Chinese industrial centres had, at some point in its career, massacred its employers, and declared itself an independent communist city-state. But communism was alien to China, and none of these experiments was permanently successful. Latterly, when the rule of the Nationalist Party had become secure, and the worst industrial evils had been abolished, class feeling had given place to a patriotic loathing of American interference and American hustle, and those who worked under American employers were often called traitors.

The Nationalist Party was not, indeed, the soul of China; but it was, so to speak, the central nervous system, within which the soul presided as a controlling principle. The Party was an intensely practical yet idealistic organization, half civil service, half religious order, though violently opposed to every kind of religion. Modelled originally on the Bolshevic Party of Russia, it had also drawn inspiration from the native and literary civil service of old China, and even from the tradition of administrative integrity which had been the best, the sole, contribution of British Imperialism to the East. Thus, by a route of its own, the Party had approached the ideal of the Platonic governors. In order to be admitted to the Party, it was necessary to do two things, to pass a very strict written examination on Western and Chinese social theory, and to come through a five years' apprenticeship in actual administrative work. Outside the Party, China was still extremely corrupt; for peculation and nepotism were not censured, so long as they were kept decently hidden. But the Party set a brilliant example of self-oblivious devotion; and this unheard-of honesty was one source of its power. It was universally recognized that the Party man was genuinely interested in social rather than private matters; and consequently he was trusted. The supreme object of his loyalty was not the Party, but China, not indeed the mass of Chinese individuals, whom he regarded with almost the same nonchalance as he regarded himself, but the corporate unity and culture of the race.

The whole executive power in China was now in the hands of members of the Party, and the final legislative authority was the Assembly of Party Delegates. Between these two institutions stood the President. Sometimes no more than chairman of the Executive Committee, this individual was now and then almost a dictator, combining in himself the attributes of Prime Minister, Emperor, and Pope. For the head of the Party was the head of the state; and like the ancient emperors, he became the symbolical object of ancestor worship.

The Party's policy was dominated by the Chinese respect for culture. Just as Western states had been all too often organized under the will for military prestige, so the new China was organized under the will for prestige of culture. For this end the American state was reviled as the supreme example of barbarian vulgarity; and so patriotism was drawn in to strengthen the cultural policy of the Party. It was boasted that, while indeed in America every man and woman might hope to fight a way to material wealth, in China every intelligent person could actually enjoy the cultural wealth of the race. The economic policy of the Party was based on the principle of affording to all workers security of livelihood and full educational opportunity. (In American eyes, however, the livelihood thus secured was scarcely fit for beasts, and the education provided was out of date and irreligious.) The Party took good care to gather into itself all the best of every social class, and also to encourage in the unintelligent masses a respect for learning, and the illusion that they themselves shared to some extent in the national culture.

But in truth this culture, which the common people so venerated in their superiors and mimicked in their own lives, was scarcely less superficial than the cult of power against which it was pitted. For it was almost wholly a cult of social rectitude and textual learning; not so much of the merely literary learning which had obsessed ancient China, as of the vast corpus of contemporary scientific dogma, and above all of pure mathematics. In old days the candidate for office had to show minute but uncritical knowledge of classical writers; now he had to give proof of a no less barren agility in describing the established formula of physics, biology, psychology, and more particularly of economics and social theory. And though never encouraged to puzzle over the philosophical basis of mathematics, he was expected to be familiar with the intricacy of at least one branch of that vast game of skill. So great was the mass of information forced upon the student, that he had no time to think of the mutual implications of the various branches of his knowledge.

Yet there was a soul in China. And in this elusive soul of China the one hope of the First Men now lay. Scattered throughout the Party was a minority of original minds, who were its source of inspiration and the growing point of the human spirit in this period. Well aware of man's littleness, these thinkers regarded him none the less as the crown of the universe. On the basis of a positivistic and rather perfunctory metaphysic, they built a social ideal and a theory of art. Indeed, in the practice and appreciation of art they saw man's highest achievement. Pessimistic about the remote future of the race, and contemptuous of American evangelism, they accepted as the end of living the creation of an intricately unified pattern of human lives set in a fair environment. Society, the supreme work of art (so they put it), is a delicate and perishable texture of human intercourse. They even entertained the possibility that in the last resort, not only the individual's life, but the whole career of the race, might be tragic, and to be valued according to the standards of tragic art. Contrasting their own spirit with that of the Americans, one of them had said, 'America, a backward youth in a playroom equipped with luxury and electric power, pretends that his mechanical toy moves the world. China, a gentleman walking in his garden in the evening, admires the fragrance and the order all the more because in the air is the first nip of winter, and in his ear rumour of the irresistible barbarian.'

In this attitude there was something admirable, and sorely needed at the time; but also there was a fatal deficiency. In its best exponents it rose to a detached yet fervent salutation of existence, but all too easily degenerated into a supine complacency, and a cult of social etiquette. In fact it was ever in danger of corruption through the inveterate Chinese habit of caring only for appearances. In some respects the spirit of America and the spirit of China were complementary, since the one was restless and the other bland, the one zealous and the other dispassionate, the one religious, the other artistic, the one superficially mystical or at least romantic, the other classical and rationalistic, though too easy-going for prolonged rigorous thought. Had they co-operated, these two mentalities might have achieved much. On the other hand, in both there was an identical and all-important lack. Neither of them was disturbed and enlightened by that insatiable lust for the truth, that passion for the free exercise of critical intelligence, the gruelling hunt for reality, which had been the glory of Europe and even of the earlier

America, but now was no longer anywhere among the First Men. And, consequent on this lack, another disability crippled them. Both were by now without that irreverent wit which individuals of an earlier generation had loved to exercise upon one another and on themselves, and even on their most sacred values.

In spite of this weakness, with good luck they might have triumphed. But, as I shall tell, the spirit of America undermined the integrity of China, and thereby destroyed its one chance of salvation. There befell, in fact, one of those disasters, half inevitable and half accidental, which periodically descended on the First Men, as though by the express will of some divinity who cared more for the excellence of his dramatic creation than for the sentient puppets which he had conceived for its enacting.

2. THE CONFLICT

After the Euro-American War there occurred first a century of minor national conflicts, and then a century of strained peace, during which America and China became more and more irksome to each other. At the close of this period the great mass of men were in theory far more cosmopolitan than nationalist, yet the inveterate tribal spirit lurked within each mind, and was ever ready to take possession. The planet was now a delicately organized economic unit, and big business in all lands was emphatically contemptuous of patriotism. Indeed the whole adult generation of the period was consciously and without reserve internationalist and pacifist. Yet this logically unassailable conviction was undermined by a biological craving for adventurous living. Prolonged peace and improved social conditions had greatly reduced the danger and hardship of life, and there was no socially harmless substitute to take the place of war in exercising the primitive courage and anger of animals fashioned for the wild. Consciously men desired peace, unconsciously they still needed some such gallantry as war afforded. And this repressed combative disposition ever and again expressed itself in explosions of irrational tribalism.

Inevitably a serious conflict at last occurred. As usual the cause was both economic and sentimental. The economic cause was the demand for fuel. A century earlier a very serious oil famine had so sobered the race that the League of Nations had been able to impose a system of cosmopolitan control upon the existing oil fields, and even the coal fields. It had also imposed strict regulations as to the use of these invaluable materials. Oil in particular was only to be used for enterprises in which no other source of power would serve. The cosmopolitan control of fuel was perhaps the supreme achievement of the League, and it remained a fixed policy of the race long after the League had been superseded. Yet, by a choice irony of fate, this quite unusually sane policy contributed largely to the downfall of civilization. By means of it, as will later transpire, the end of coal was postponed into the period when the intelligence of the race was so deteriorated that it could no longer cope with such a crisis. Instead of adjusting itself to the novel situation, it simply collapsed.

But at the time with which we are at present dealing, means had recently been found of profitably working the huge deposits of fuel in Antarctica. This vast supply unfortunately lay technically beyond the jurisdiction of the World Fuel Control Board. America was first in the field, and saw in Antarctic fuel a means for her advancement, and for her self-imposed duty of Americanizing the planet. China, fearful of Americanization, demanded that the new sources should be brought under the jurisdiction of the Board. For some years feeling had become increasingly violent on this point, and both peoples had by now relapsed into the crude old nationalistic mood. War began to seem almost inevitable.

The actual occasion of conflict, however, was, as usual, an accident. A scandal was brought to light about child labour in certain Indian factories. Boys and girls under twelve were being badly sweated, and in their abject state their only adventure was precocious sex. The American Government protested, and in terms which assumed that America was the guardian of the world's morals. India immediately held up the reform which she had begun to impose, and replied to America as to a busy-body. America threatened an expedition to set things right, 'backed by the approval of all the morally sensitive races of the earth'. China now intervened to keep the peace between her rival and her partner, and undertook to see that the evil should be abolished, if America would withdraw her extravagant slanders against the Eastern conscience. But it was too late. An American bank in China was raided, and its manager's severed head was kicked along the street. The tribes of men had once more smelled blood. War was declared by the West upon the East.

Of the combatants, Asia, with North Africa, formed geographically the more compact system, but America and her dependents were economically more organized. At the outbreak of war neither side had any appreciable armament, for war had long ago been 'outlawed'. This fact, however, made little difference; since the warfare of the period could be carried on with great effect simply by the vast swarms of civil aircraft, loaded with poison, high explosives, disease microbes, and the still more lethal 'hypobiological' organisms, which contemporary science sometimes regarded as the simplest living matter, sometimes as the most complex molecules.

The struggle began with violence, slackened, and dragged on for a quarter of a century. At the close of this period, Africa was mostly in the hands of America. But Egypt was an uninhabitable no-man's land, for the South Africans had very successfully poisoned the sources of the Nile. Europe was under Chinese military rule. This was enforced by armies of sturdy Central-Asiatics, who were already beginning to wonder why they did not make themselves masters of China also. The Chinese language, with European alphabet, was taught in all schools. In England, however, there were no schools, and no population; for early in the war, an American air-base had been established in Ireland, and England had been repeatedly devastated. Airmen passing over what had been London, could still make out the lines of Oxford Street and the Strand among the green and grey tangle of ruins. Wild nature, once so jealously preserved in national 'beauty spots' against the incursion of urban civilization, now rioted over the whole island. At the other side of the world, the Japanese islands had been similarly devastated in the vain American effort to establish there an air-base from which to reach the heart of the enemy. So far, however, neither China nor America had been very seriously damaged; but recently the American biologists had devised a new malignant germ, more infectious and irresistible than anything hitherto known. Its work was to disintegrate the highest levels of the nervous system, and therefore to render all who were even slightly affected incapable of intelligent action; while a severe attack caused paralysis and finally death. With this weapon the American military had already turned one Chinese city into a bedlam; and wandering bacilli had got into the brains of several high officials throughout the province, rendering their behaviour incoherent. It was becoming the fashion to attribute all one's blunders to a touch of the new microbe. Hitherto no effective means of resisting the spread of this plague had been discovered. And as in the early stages of the disease the patient became restlessly active, undertaking interminable and objectless journeys on the flimsiest pretexts, it seemed probable that the 'American madness' would spread throughout China.

On the whole, then, the military advantage lay definitely with the Americans; but economically they were perhaps the more damaged, for their higher standard of prosperity depended largely on foreign investment and foreign trade. Throughout the American continent there was now real poverty and serious symptoms of class war, not indeed between private workers and employers, but between workers and the autocratic military governing caste which inevitably war had created. Big business had at first succumbed to the patriotic fever, but had soon remembered that war is folly and ruinous to trade. Indeed upon both sides the fervour of nationalism had lasted only a couple of years, after which the lust of adventure had given place to mere dread of the enemy. For on each side the populace had been nursed into the belief that its foe was diabolic. When a quarter of a century had passed since there had been free intercourse between the two peoples, the real mental difference which had always existed between them appeared to many almost as a difference of biological species. Thus in America the Church preached that no Chinaman had a soul. Satan, it was said, had tampered with the evolution of the Chinese race when first it had emerged from the pre-human animal. He had contrived that it should be cunning, but wholly without tenderness. He had induced in it an insatiable sensuality, and wilful blindness toward the divine, toward that superbly masterful energy-for-energy's-sake which was the glory of America. Just as in a prehistoric era the young race of mammals had swept away the sluggish, brutish and demoded reptiles, so now, it was said, young soulful America was destined to rid the planet of the reptilian Mongol. In China, on the other hand, the official view was that the Americans were a typical case of biological retrogression. Like all parasitic organisms, they had thriven by specializing in one low-grade mode of behaviour at the expense of their higher nature; and now, 'tape-worms of the planet', they were starving out the higher capacities of the human race by their frantic acquisitiveness.

Such were the official doctrines. But the strain of war had latterly produced on each side a grave distrust of its own government, and an emphatic will for peace at any price. The governments hated the peace party even more than each other, since their existence now depended on war. They even went so far as to inform one another of the clandestine operations of the pacifists, discovered by their own secret service in enemy territory.

Thus when at last big business and the workers on each side of the Pacific had determined to stop the war by concerted action, it was very difficult for their representatives to meet.

3. ON AN ISLAND IN THE PACIFIC

Save for the governments, the whole human race now earnestly desired peace; but opinion in America was balanced between the will merely to effect an economic and political unification of the world, and a fanatical craving to impose American culture on the East. In China also there was a balance of the purely commercial readiness to sacrifice ideals for the sake of peace and prosperity, and the will to preserve Chinese culture. The two individuals who were to meet in secret for the negotiation of peace were typical of their respective races; in both of them the commercial and cultural motives were present, though the commercial was by now most often dominant.

It was in the twenty-sixth year of the war that two seaplanes converged by night from the East and West upon an island in the Pacific, and settled on a secluded inlet. The moon, destined in another age to smother this whole equatorial region with her shattered body, now merely besparkled the waves. From each plane a traveller emerged, and rowed himself ashore in a rubber coracle. The two men met upon the beach, and shook hands, the one with ceremony, the other with a slightly forced brotherliness. Already the sun peered over the wall of the sea, shouting his brilliance and his heat. The Chinese, taking off his air-helmet, uncoiled his pigtail with a certain emphasis, stripped off his heavy coverings, and revealed a sky-blue silk pyjama suit, embroidered with golden dragons. The other, glancing with scarcely veiled dislike at this finery, flung off his wraps and displayed the decent grey coat and breeches with which the American business men of this period unconsciously symbolized their reversion to Puritanism. Smoking the Chinese envoy's cigarettes, the two sat down to re-arrange the planet.

The conversation was amicable, and proceeded without hitch; for there was agreement about the practical measures to be adopted. The government in each country was to be overthrown at once. Both representatives were confident that this could be done if it could be attempted simultaneously on each side of the Pacific; for in both countries finance and the people could be trusted. In place of the national governments, a World Finance Directorate was to be created. This was to be composed of the leading commercial and industrial magnates of the world, along with representatives of the workers' organizations. The American representative should be the first president of the Directorate, and the Chinese the first vice-president. The Directorate was to manage the whole economic re-organization of the world. In particular, industrial conditions in the East were to be brought into line with those of America, while on the other hand the American monopoly of Antarctica was to be abolished. That rich and almost virgin land was to be subjected to the control of the Directorate.

Occasionally during the conversation reference was made to the great cultural difference between the East and West; but both the negotiants seemed anxious to believe that this was only a minor matter which need not be allowed to trouble a business discussion.

At this point occurred one of those incidents which, minute in themselves, have disproportionately great effects. The unstable nature of the First Men made them peculiarly liable to suffer from such accidents, and especially so in their decline.

The talk was interrupted by the appearance of a human figure swimming round a promontory into the little bay. In the shallows she arose, and walked out of the water towards the creators of the World State. A bronze young smiling woman, completely nude, with breasts heaving after her long swim, she stood before them, hesitating. The relation between the two men was instantly changed, though neither was at first aware of it.

'Delicious daughter of Ocean,' said the Chinese, in that somewhat archaic and deliberately un-American English which the Asiatics now affected in communication with foreigners, 'what is there that these two despicable land animals can do for you? For my friend, I cannot answer, but I at least am henceforth your slave.' His eyes roamed carelessly, yet as it were with perfect politeness, all over her body. And she, with that added grace which haloes women when they feel the kiss of an admiring gaze, pressed the sea from her hair and stood at the point of speech.

But the American protested, 'Whoever you are, please do not interrupt us. We are really very busy discussing a matter of great importance, and we have no time to spare. Please go. Your nudity is offensive to one accustomed to civilized manners. In a modern country you would not be allowed to bathe without a costume. We are growing very sensitive on this point.'

A distressful but enhancing blush spread under the wet bronze, and the intruder made as if to go. But the Chinese cried, 'Stay! We have almost finished our business talk. Refresh us with your presence. Bring the realities back into our discussion by permitting us to contemplate for a while the perfect vase line of your waist and thigh. Who are you? Of what race are you? My anthropological studies fail to place you. Your skin is fairer than is native here, though rich with sun. Your breasts are Grecian. Your lips are chiselled with a memory of Egypt. Your hair, night though it was, is drying with a most bewildering hint of gold. And your eyes, let me observe them. Long, subtle, as my countrywomen's, unfathomable as the mind of India, they yet reveal themselves to your new slave as not wholly black, but violet as the zenith before dawn. Indeed this exquisite unity of incompatibles conquers both my heart and my understanding.'

During this harangue her composure was restored, though she glanced now and then at the American, who kept ever removing his gaze from her.

She answered in much the same diction as the other; but, surprisingly, with an old-time English accent, 'I am certainly a mongrel. You might call me, not daughter of Ocean, but daughter of Man; for wanderers of every race have scattered their seed on this island. My body, I know, betrays its diverse ancestry in a rather queer blend of characters. My mind is perhaps unusual too, for I have never left this island. And though it is actually less than a quarter of a century since I was born, a past century has perhaps had more meaning for me than the obscure events of today. A hermit taught me. Two hundred years ago he lived actively in Europe; but towards the end of his long life he retreated to this island. As an old man he loved me. And day by day he gave me insight into the great spirit of the past; but of this age he gave me nothing. Now that he is dead, I struggle to familiarize myself with the present, but I continue to see everything from the angle of another age. And so,' (turning to the American) 'if I have offended against modern customs, it is because my insular mind has never been taught to regard nakedness as indecent. I am very ignorant, truly a savage. If only I could gain experience of your great world! If ever this war ends, I must travel.'

'Delectable,' said the Chinese, 'exquisitely proportioned, exquisitely civilized savage! Come with me for a holiday in modern China. There you can bathe without a costume, so long as you are beautiful.'

She ignored this invitation, and seemed to have fallen into a reverie. Then absently she continued, 'Perhaps I should not suffer from this restlessness, this craving to experience the world, if only I were to experience motherhood instead. Many of the islanders from time to time have enriched me with their embraces. But with none of them could I permit myself to conceive. They are dear; but not one of them is at heart more than a child.'

The American became restless. But again the Mongol intervened, with lowered and deepened voice. 'I,' he said, 'I, the Vice-President of the World Finance Directorate, shall be honoured to afford you the opportunity of motherhood.'

She regarded him gravely, then smiled as on a child who asks more than it is reasonable to give. But the American rose hastily. Addressing the silken Mongol, he said, 'You probably know that the American Government is in the act of sending a second poison fleet to turn your whole population insane, more insane than you are already. You cannot defend yourselves against this new weapon; and if I am to save you, I must not trifle any longer. Nor must you, for we must act simultaneously. We have settled all that matters for the moment. But before I leave, I must say that your behaviour toward this woman has very forcibly reminded me that there is something wrong with the Chinese way of thought and life. In my anxiety for peace, I overlooked my duty in this respect. I now give you notice that when the Directorate is established, we Americans must induce you to reform these abuses, for the world's sake and your own.'

The Chinese rose and answered, 'This matter must be settled locally. We do not expect you to accept our standards, so do not you expect us to accept yours.' He moved toward the woman, smiling. And the smile outraged the American.

We need not follow the wrangle which now ensued between the two representatives, each of whom, though in a manner cosmopolitan in sentiment, was heartily contemptuous of the other's values. Suffice it that the American became increasingly earnest and dictatorial, the other increasingly careless and ironical. Finally the American raised his voice and presented an ultimatum. 'Our treaty of world-union', he said, 'will remain unsigned unless you add a clause promising drastic reforms, which, as a matter of fact, my colleagues had already proposed as a condition of co-operation. I had decided to withhold them, in case they should wreck our treaty; but now I see they are essential. You must educate your people out of their lascivious and idle ways, and give them modern scientific religion. Teachers in your schools and universities must pledge themselves to the modern fundamentalized physics and behaviourism, and must enforce worship of the Divine Mover. The change will be difficult, but we will help you. You will need a strong order of Inquisitors, responsible to the Directorate. They will see also to the reform of your people's sexual frivolity in which you squander so much of the Divine Energy. Unless you agree to this, I cannot stop the war. The law of God must be kept, and those who know it must enforce it.'

The woman interrupted him. 'Tell me, what is this "God" of yours? The Europeans worshipped love, not energy. What do you mean by energy? Is it merely to make engines go fast, and to agitate the ether?'

He answered flatly, as if repeating a lesson, 'God is the all-pervading spirit of movement which seeks to actualize itself wherever it is latent. God has appointed the great American people to mechanize the universe.' He paused, contemplating the clean lines of his sea-plane. Then he continued with emphasis, 'But come! Time is precious. Either you work for God, or we trample you out of God's way.'

The woman approached him, saying, 'There is certainly something great in this enthusiasm. But somehow, though my heart says you are right, my head is doubting still. There must be a mistake somewhere.'

'Mistake!' he laughed, overhanging her with his mask of power. 'When a man's soul is action, how can he be mistaken that action is divine? I have served the great God, Energy, all my life, from garage boy to World President. Has not the whole American people proved its faith by its success?'

With rapture, but still in perplexity, she gazed at him. 'There's something terribly wrong-headed about you Americans,' she said, 'but certainly you are great.' She looked him in the eyes. Then suddenly she laid a hand on him, and said with conviction, 'Being what you are, you are probably right. Anyhow you are a man, a real man. Take me. Be the father of my boy. Take me to the dangerous cities of America to work with you.'

The President was surprised with sudden hunger for her body, and she saw it; but he turned to the Vice-President and said, 'She has seen where the truth lies. And you? War, or co-operation in God's work?'

'The death of our bodies, or the death of our minds,' said the Chinese, but with a bitterness that lacked conviction; for he was no fanatic. 'Well, since the soul is only the harmoniousness of the body's behaviour, and since, in spite of this little dispute, we are agreed that the co-ordination of activity is the chief need of the planet today, and since in respect of our differences of temperament this lady has judged in favour of America, and moreover since, if there is any virtue in our Asiatic way of life, it will not succumb to a little propaganda, but rather will be strengthened by opposition – since all these matters are so, I accept your terms. But it would be undignified in China to let this great change be imposed upon her externally. You must give me time to form in Asia a native and spontaneous party of Energists, who will themselves propagate your gospel, and perhaps give it an elegance which, if I may say so, it has not yet. Even this we will do to secure the cosmopolitan control of Antarctica.'

Thereupon the treaty was signed; but a new and secret codicil was drawn up and signed also, and both were witnessed by the Daughter of Man, in a clear, round, old-fashioned script.

Then, taking a hand of each, she said, 'And so at last the world is united. For how long, I wonder. I seem to hear my old master's voice scolding, as though I had been rather stupid. But he failed me, and I have chosen a new master, Master of the World.'

She released the hand of the Asiatic, and made as if to draw the American away with her. And he, though he was a strict monogamist with a better half waiting for him in New York, longed to crush her sun-clad body to his Puritan cloth. She drew him away among the palm trees.

The Vice-President of the World sat down once more, lit a cigarette, and meditated, smiling.

CHAPTER IV

AN AMERICANIZED PLANET

1. THE FOUNDATION OF THE FIRST WORLD STATE

We have now reached that point in the history of the First Men when, some three hundred and eighty terrestrial years after the European War, the goal of world unity was at last achieved – not, however, before the mind of the race had been seriously crippled.

There is no need to recount in detail the transition from rival national sovereignties to unitary control by the World Financial Directorate. Suffice it that by concerted action in America and China the military governments found themselves hamstrung by the passive resistance of cosmopolitan big business. In China this process was almost instantaneous and bloodless; in America there was serious disorder for a few weeks, while the bewildered government attempted to reduce its rebels by martial law. But the population was by now eager for peace; and, although a few business magnates were shot, and a crowd of workers here and there mown down, the opposition was irresistible. Very soon the governing clique collapsed.

The new order consisted of a vast system akin to guild socialism, yet at bottom individualistic. Each industry was in theory democratically governed by all its members, but in practice was controlled by its dominant individuals. Co-ordination of all industries was effected by a World Industrial Council, whereon the leaders of each industry discussed the affairs of the planet as a whole. The status of each industry on the Council was determined partly by its economic power in the world, partly by public esteem. For already the activities of men were beginning to be regarded as either 'noble' or 'ignoble'; and the noble were not necessarily the most powerful economically. Thus upon the Council appeared an inner ring of noble 'industries', which were, in approximate order of prestige, Finance, Flying, Engineering, Surface Locomotion, Chemical Industry, and Professional Athletics.

But the real seat of power was not the Council, not even the inner ring of the Council, but the Financial Directorate. This consisted of a dozen millionaires, with the American President and the Chinese Vice-President at their head.

Within this august committee internal dissensions were inevitable. Shortly after the system had been inaugurated the Vice-President sought to overthrow the President by publishing his connection with a Polynesian woman who now styled herself the Daughter of Man. This piece of scandal was expected to enrage the virtuous American public against their hero. But by a stroke of genius the President saved both himself and the unity of the world. Far from denying the charge, he gloried in it. In that moment of sexual triumph, he said, a great truth had been revealed to him. Without this daring sacrifice of his private purity, he would never have been really fit to be President of the World; he would have remained simply an American. In this lady's veins flowed the blood of all races, and in her mind all cultures mingled. His union with her, confirmed by many subsequent visits, had taught him to enter into the spirit of the East, and had given him a broad human sympathy such as his high office demanded. As a private individual, he insisted, he remained a monogamist with a wife in New York; and, as a private individual, he had sinned, and must suffer for ever the pangs of conscience. But as President of the World, it was incumbent upon him to espouse the World. And since nothing could be said to be real without a physical basis, this spiritual union had to be embodied and symbolized by his physical union with the Daughter of Man. In tones of grave emotion he described through the microphone how, in the presence of that mystical woman, he had suddenly triumphed over his private moral scruples; and how, in a sudden access of the divine energy, he had consummated his marriage with the World in the shade of a banana tree.

The lovely form of the Daughter of Man (decently clad) was transmitted by television to every receiver in the world. Her face, blended of Asia and the West, became a most potent symbol of human unity. Every man on the planet became in imagination her lover. Every woman identified herself with this supreme woman.

Undoubtedly there was some truth in the plea that the Daughter of Man had enlarged the President's mind, for his policy had been unexpectedly tactful toward the East. Often he had moderated the American demand for the immediate Americanization of China. Often he had persuaded the Chinese to welcome some policy which at first they had regarded with suspicion.

The President's explanation of his conduct enhanced his prestige both in America and Asia. America was hypnotized by the romantic religiosity of the story. Very soon it became fashionable to be a strict monogamist with one domestic wife, and one 'symbolical' wife in the East, or in another town, or a neighbouring street, or with several such in various localities. In China the cold tolerance with which the President was first treated was warmed by this incident into something like affection. And it was partly through his tact, or the influence of his symbolical wife, that the speeding up of China's Americanization was effected without disorder.

For some months after the foundation of the World State, China had been wholly occupied in coping with the plague of insanity, called 'the American madness', with which her former enemy had poisoned her. The coast region of North China had been completely disorganized. Industry, agriculture, transport, were at a standstill. Huge mobs, demented and starving, staggered about the country devouring every kind of vegetable matter and wrangling over the flesh of their own dead. It was long before the disease was brought under control; and indeed for years afterwards an occasional outbreak would occur, and cause panic throughout the land.

To some of the more old-fashioned Chinese it appeared as though the whole population had been mildly affected by the germ; for throughout China a new sect, apparently a spontaneous native growth, calling themselves Energists, began to preach a new interpretation of Buddhism in terms of the sanctity of action. And, strange to say, this gospel throve to such an extent that in a few years the whole educational system was captured by its adherents, though not without a struggle with the reactionary members of the older universities. Curiously enough, however, in spite of this general acceptance of the New Way, in spite of the fact that the young of China were now taught to admire movement in all its forms, in spite of a much increased wage-scale, which put all workers in possession of private mechanical locomotion, the masses of China continued at heart to regard action as a mere means toward rest. And when at last a native physicist pointed out that the supreme expression of energy was the tense balance of forces within the atom, the Chinese applied the doctrine to themselves, and claimed that in them quiescence was the perfect balance of mighty forces. Thus did the East contribute to the religion of this age. The worship of activity was made to include the worship of inactivity. And both were founded on the principles of natural science.

2. THE DOMINANCE OF SCIENCE

Science now held a position of unique honour among the First Men. This was not so much because it was in this field that the race long ago during its high noon had thought most rigorously, nor because it was through science that men had gained some insight into the nature of the physical world, but rather because the application of scientific principles had revolutionized their material circumstances. The once fluid doctrines of science had by now begun to crystallize into a fixed and intricate dogma; but inventive scientific intelligence still exercised itself brilliantly in improving the technique of industry, and thus completely dominated the imagination of a race in which the pure intellectual curiosity had waned. The scientist was regarded as an embodiment, not merely of knowledge, but of power; and no legends of the potency of science seemed too fantastic to be believed.

A century after the founding of the first World State a rumour began to be heard in China about the supreme secret of scientific religion, the awful mystery of Gordelpus, by means of which it should be possible to utilize the energy locked up in the opposition of proton and electron. Long ago discovered by a Chinese physicist and saint, this invaluable knowledge was now reputed to have been preserved ever since among the *élite* of science, and to be ready for publication as soon as the world seemed fit to possess it. The new sect of Energists claimed that the young Discoverer was himself an incarnation of Buddha, and that, since the world was still unfit for the supreme revelation, he had entrusted his secret to the Scientists. On the side of Christianity a very similar legend was concerned with the same individual. The Regenerate Christian Brotherhood, by now overwhelmingly the most powerful of the Western Churches,

regarded the Discoverer as the Son of God, who, in this his Second
Coming, had proposed to bring about the millennium by publishing
the secret of divine power; but, finding the peoples still unable to
put in practice even the more primitive gospel of love which was
announced at his First Coming, he had suffered martyrdom for
man's sake, and had entrusted his secret to the Scientists.

The scientific workers of the world had long ago organized
themselves as a close corporation. Entrance to the International
College of Science was to be obtained only by examination and the
payment of high fees. Membership conferred the title of 'Scientist',
and the right to perform experiments. It was also an essential
qualification for many lucrative posts. Moreover, there were said
to be certain technical secrets which members were pledged not to
reveal. Rumour had it that in at least one case of minor blabbing the
traitor had shortly afterwards mysteriously died.

Science itself, the actual corpus of natural knowledge, had by now
become so complex that only a tiny fraction of it could be mastered
by one brain. Thus students of one branch of science knew practically
nothing of the work of others in kindred branches. Especially was
this the case with the huge science called Subatomic Physics.
Within this were contained a dozen studies, any one of which was
as complex as the whole of the physics of the Nineteenth Christian
Century. This growing complexity had rendered students in one
field ever more reluctant to criticize, or even to try to understand,
the principles of other fields. Each petty department, jealous of
its own preserves, was meticulously respectful of the preserves of
others. In an earlier period the sciences had been co-ordinated and
criticized philosophically by their own leaders and by the technical
philosophers. But, philosophy, as a rigorous technical discipline, no
longer existed. There was, of course, a vague framework of ideas, or
assumptions, based on science, and common to all men, a popular
pseudo-science, constructed by the journalists from striking phrases
current among scientists. But actual scientific workers prided
themselves on the rejection of this ramshackle structure, even while
they themselves were unwittingly assuming it. And each insisted
that his own special subject must inevitably remain unintelligible
even to most of his brother scientists.

Under these circumstances, when rumour declared that the mystery of Gordelpus was known to the physicists, each department of subatomic physics was both reluctant to deny the charge explicitly in its own case, and ready to believe that some other department really did possess the secret. Consequently the conduct of the scientists as a body strengthened the general belief that they knew and would not tell.

About two centuries after the formation of the first World State, the President of the World declared that the time was ripe for a formal union of science and religion, and called a conference of the leaders of these two great disciplines. Upon that island in the Pacific which had become the Mecca of cosmopolitan sentiment, and was by now one vast many-storied, and cloud-capped Temple of Peace, the heads of Buddhism, Mohammedanism, Hinduism, the Regenerate Christian Brotherhood and the Modern Catholic Church in South America, agreed that their differences were but differences of expression. One and all were worshippers of the Divine Energy, whether expressed in activity, or in tense stillness. One and all recognized the saintly Discoverer as either the last and greatest of the prophets or an actual incarnation of divine Movement. And these two concepts were easily shown, in the light of modern science, to be identical.

In an earlier age it had been the custom to single out heresy and extirpate it with fire and sword. But now the craving for uniformity was fulfilled by explaining away differences, amid universal applause.

When the Conference had registered the unity of the religions, it went on to establish the unity of religion and science. All knew, said the President, that some of the scientists were in possession of the supreme secret, though, wisely, they would not definitely admit it. It was time, then, that the organizations of Science and Religion should be merged, for the better guidance of men. He, therefore, called upon the International College of Science to nominate from amongst themselves a select body, which should be sanctified by the Church, and called the Sacred Order of Scientists. These custodians of the supreme secret were to be kept at public expense. They were to devote themselves wholly to the service of science, and in particular to research into the most scientific manner of worshipping the Divine Gordelpus.

Of the scientists present, some few looked distinctly uncomfortable, but the majority scarcely concealed their delight under dignified and thoughtful hesitation. Amongst the priests also two expressions were visible; but on the whole it was felt that the Church must gain by thus gathering into herself the unique prestige of science. And so it was that the Order was founded which was destined to become the dominant force in human affairs until the downfall of the first world civilization.

3. MATERIAL ACHIEVEMENT

Save for occasional minor local conflicts, easily quelled by the World Police, the race was now a single social unit for some four thousand years. During the first of these millennia material progress at least was rapid, but subsequently there was little change until the final disintegration. The whole energy of man was concentrated on maintaining at a constant pitch the furious routine of his civilization, until, after another three thousand years of lavish expenditure, certain essential sources of power were suddenly exhausted. Nowhere was there the mental agility to cope with this novel crisis. The whole social order collapsed.

We may pass over the earlier stages of this fantastic civilization, and examine it as it stood just before the fatal change began to be felt.

The material circumstances of the race at this time would have amazed all its predecessors, even those who were in the true sense far more civilized beings. But to us, the Last Men, there is an extreme pathos and even comicality, not only in this most thorough confusion of material development with civilization, but also in the actual paucity of the vaunted material development itself, compared with that of our own society.

All the continents, indeed, were by now minutely artificialized. Save for the many wild reserves which were cherished as museums and playgrounds, not a square mile of territory was left in a natural state. Nor was there any longer a distinction between agricultural and industrial areas. All the continents were urbanized, not of course in the manner of the congested industrial cities of an earlier age, but none the less urbanized. Industry and agriculture interpenetrated everywhere. This was possible partly through the great development of aerial communication, partly through a no less remarkable improvement of architecture. Great advances in artificial materials had enabled the erection of buildings in the form of slender pylons which, rising often to a height of three miles, or even more, and founded a quarter of a mile beneath the ground, might yet occupy a ground plan of less than half a mile across. In section these structures were often cruciform; and on each floor, the centre of the long-armed cross consisted of an aerial landing, providing direct access from the air for the dwarf private aeroplanes which were by now essential to the life of every adult. These gigantic pillars of architecture, prophetic of the still mightier structures of an age to come, were scattered over every continent in varying density. Very rarely were they permitted to approach one another by a distance less than their height; on the other hand, save in the arctic, they were very seldom separated by more than twenty miles. The general appearance of every country was thus rather like an open forest of lopped tree-trunks, gigantic in stature. Clouds often encircled the middle heights of these artificial peaks, or blotted out all but the lower stories. Dwellers in the summits were familiar with the spectacle of a dazzling ocean of cloud, dotted on all sides with steep islands of architecture. Such was the altitude of the upper floors that it was sometimes necessary to maintain in them, not merely artificial heating, but artificial air pressure and oxygen supply.

Between these columns of habitation and industry, the land was everywhere green or brown with the seasonal variations of agriculture, park, and wild reserve. Broad grey thoroughfares for heavy freight traffic netted every continent; but lighter transport and the passenger services were wholly aerial. Over all the more populous districts the air was ever aswarm with planes up to a height of five miles, where the giant air-liners plied between the continents.

The enterprise of an already distant past had brought every land under civilization. The Sahara was a lake district, crowded with sun-proud holiday resorts. The arctic islands of Canada, ingeniously warmed by directed tropical currents, were the homes of vigorous northerners. The coasts of Antarctica, thawed in the same manner, were permanently inhabited by those engaged in exploiting the mineral wealth of the hinterland.

Much of the power needed to keep this civilization in being was drawn from the buried remains of prehistoric vegetation, in the form of coal. Although after the foundation of the World State the fuel of Antarctica had been very carefully husbanded, the new supply of oil had given out in less than three centuries, and men were forced to drive their aeroplanes by electricity generated from coal. It soon became evident, however, that even the unexpectedly rich coal-fields of Antarctica would not last for ever. The cessation of oil had taught men a much needed lesson, had made them feel the reality of the power problem. At the same time the cosmopolitan spirit, which was learning to regard the whole race as compatriots, was also beginning to take a broader view temporally, and to see things with the eyes of remote generations. During the first and sanest thousand years of the World State, there was a widespread determination not to incur the blame of the future by wasting power. Thus not only was there serious economy (the first large-scale cosmopolitan enterprise), but also efforts were made to utilize more permanent sources of power. Wind was used extensively. On every building swarms of windmills generated electricity, and every mountain range was similarly decorated, while every considerable fall of water forced its way through turbines. More important still was the utilization of power derived from volcanoes and from borings into the subterranean heat. This, it had been hoped, would solve the whole problem of power, once and for all. But even in the earlier and more intelligent period of the World State inventive genius was not what it had been, and no really satisfactory method was found. Consequently at no stage of this civilization did volcanic sources do more than supplement the amazingly rich coal seams of Antarctica. In this region coal was preserved at far greater depths than elsewhere, because, by some accident, the earth's central heat was not here fierce enough (as it was elsewhere) to turn the deeper beds into graphite. Another possible source of power was known to exist in the ocean tides; but the use of this was forbidden by the S.O.S. because, since tidal motion was so obviously astronomical in origin, it had come to be regarded as sacred.

Perhaps the greatest physical achievement of the First World State in its earlier and more vital phase had been in preventive medicine. Though the biological sciences had long ago become stereotyped in respect of fundamental theories, they continued to produce many practical benefits. No longer did men and women have to dread for themselves or those dear to them such afflictions as cancer, tuberculosis, angina pectoris, the rheumatic diseases, and the terrible disorders of the nervous system. No longer were there sudden microbic devastations. No longer was childbirth an ordeal, and womanhood itself a source of suffering. There were no more chronic invalids, no more life-long cripples. Only senility remained; and even this could be repeatedly alleviated by physiological rejuvenation. The removal of all these ancient sources of weakness and misery, which formerly had lamed the race and haunted so many individuals either with definite terrors or vague and scarcely conscious despond, brought about now a pervading buoyancy and optimism impossible to earlier peoples.

4. THE CULTURE OF THE FIRST WORLD STATE

Such was the physical achievement of this civilization. Nothing half so artificial and intricate and prosperous had ever before existed. An earlier age, indeed, had held before itself some such ideal as this; but its nationalistic mania prevented it from attaining the necessary economic unity. This latter-day civilization, however, had wholly outgrown nationalism, and had spent many centuries of peace in consolidating itself. But to what end? The terrors of destitution and ill-health having been abolished, man's spirit was freed from a crippling burden, and might have dared great adventures. But unfortunately his intelligence had by now seriously declined. And so this age, far more than the notorious 'nineteenth century', was the great age of barren complacency.

Every individual was a well-fed and physically healthy human animal. He was also economically independent. His working day was never more than six hours, often only four. He enjoyed a fair share of the products of industry; and in his long holidays he was free to wander in his own aeroplane all over the planet. With good luck he might find himself rich, even for those days, at forty; and if fortune had not favoured him, he might yet expect affluence before he was eighty, when he could still look forward to a century of active life.

But in spite of this material prosperity he was a slave. His work and his leisure consisted of feverish activity, punctuated by moments of listless idleness which he regarded as both sinful and unpleasant. Unless he was one of the furiously successful minority, he was apt to be haunted by moments of brooding, too formless to be called meditation, and of yearning, too blind to be called desire. For he and all his contemporaries were ruled by certain ideas which prevented them from living a fully human life.

Of these ideas one was the ideal of progress. For the individual, the goal imposed by his religious teaching was continuous advancement in aeronautical prowess, legal sexual freedom, and millionaireship. For the race also the ideal was progress, and progress of the same unintelligent type. Ever more brilliant and extensive aviation, ever more extensive legal sexual intercourse, ever more gigantic manufacture, and consumption, were to be co-ordinated in an ever more intricately organized social system. For the last three thousand years, indeed, progress even of this rude kind had been minute; but this was a source of pride rather than of regret. It implied that the goal was already almost attained, the perfection which should justify the release of the secret of divine power, and the inauguration of an era of incomparably mightier activity.

For the all-pervading idea which tyrannized over the race was the fanatical worship of movement. Gordelpus, the Prime Mover, demanded of his human embodiments swift and intricate activity, and the individual's prospect of eternal life depended on the fulfilment of this obligation. Curiously, though science had long ago destroyed the belief in personal immortality as an intrinsic attribute of man, a complementary belief had grown up to the effect that those who justified themselves in action were preserved eternally, by special miracle, in the swift spirit of Gordelpus. Thus from childhood to death the individual's conduct was determined by the obligation to produce as much motion as possible, whether by his own muscular activity or by the control of natural forces. In the hierarchy of industry three occupations were honoured almost as much as the Sacred Order of Scientists, namely, flying, dancing, and athletics. Every one practised all three of these crafts to some extent, for they were imposed by religion; but the professional fliers and aeronautical engineers, and the professional dancers and athletes, were a privileged class.

Several causes had raised flying to a position of unique honour. As a means of communication it was of extreme practical importance; and as the swiftest locomotion it constituted the supreme act of worship. The accident that the form of the aeroplane was reminiscent of the main symbol of the ancient Christian religion lent flying an additional mystical significance. For though the spirit of Christianity was lost, many of its symbols had been preserved in the new faith. A more important source of the dominance of flying was that, since warfare had long ceased to exist, aviation of a gratuitously dangerous kind was the main outlet for the innate adventurousness of the human animal. Young men and women risked their lives fervently for the glory of Gordelpus and their own salvation, while their seniors took vicarious satisfaction in this endless festival of youthful prowess. Indeed apart from the thrills of devotional aerial acrobats, it is unlikely that the race would so long have preserved its peace and its unity. On each of the frequent Days of Sacred Flight special rituals of communal and solo aviation were performed at every religious centre. On these occasions the whole sky would be intricately patterned with thousands of planes, wheeling, tumbling, soaring, plunging, in perfect order and at various altitudes, the dance at one level being subtly complementary to the dance at others. It was as though the spontaneous evolutions of many distinct flocks of redshank and dunlin were multiplied a thousand-fold in complexity, and subordinated to a single ever-developing terpsichorean theme. Then suddenly the whole would burst asunder to the horizon, leaving the sky open for the quartets, duets and solos of the most brilliant stars of flight. At night also, regiments of planes bearing coloured lights would inscribe on the zenith ever-changing and symbolical patterns of fire. Besides these aerial dances, there had existed for eight hundred years a custom of spelling out periodically in a dense flight of planes six thousand miles long the sacred rubrics of the gospel of Gordelpus, so that the living word might be visible to other planets.

In the life of every individual, flying played a great part. Immediately after birth he was taken up by a priestess of flight and dropped, clinging to a parachute, to be deftly caught upon the wings of his father's plane. This ritual served as a substitute for contraception (forbidden as an interference with the divine energy); for since in many infants the old simian grasping-instinct was atrophied, a large proportion of the new-born let go and were smashed upon the paternal wings. At adolescence the individual (male or female) took charge of a plane for the first time, and his life was subsequently punctuated by severe aeronautical tests. From middle age onwards, namely as a centenarian, when he could no longer hope to rise in the hierarchy of active flight, he continued to fly daily for practical purposes.

The two other forms of ritual activity, dancing and athletics, were scarcely less important. Nor were they confined wholly to the ground. For certain rites were celebrated by dances upon the wings of a plane in mid air.

Dancing was especially associated with the Negro race, which occupied a very peculiar position in the world at this time. As a matter of fact the great colour distinctions of mankind were now beginning to fade. Increased aerial communication had caused the black, brown, yellow and white stocks so to mingle that everywhere there was by now a large majority of the racially indistinguishable. Nowhere was there any great number of persons of marked racial character. But each of the ancient types was liable to crop up now and again in isolated individuals, especially in its ancient homeland. These 'throw-backs' were customarily treated in special and historically appropriate manners. Thus, for instance, it was to 'sports' of definite Negro character that the most sacred dancing was entrusted.

In the days of the nations, the descendants of emancipated African slaves in North America had greatly influenced the artistic and religious life of the white population, and had inspired a cult of Negroid dancing which survived till the end of the First Men. This was partly due to the sexual and primitive character of Negro dancing, sorely needed in a nation ridden by sexual taboos. But it had also a deeper source. The American nation had acquired its slaves by capture, and had long continued to spurn their descendants. Later it unconsciously compensated for its guilt by a cult of the Negro spirit. Thus when American culture dominated the planet, the pure Negroes became a sacred caste. Forbidden many of the rights of citizenship, they were regarded as the private servants of Gordelpus. They were both sacred and outcast. This dual role was epitomized in an extravagant ritual which took place once a year in each of the great national parks. A white woman and a Negro, both chosen for their prowess in dance, performed a long and symbolical ballet, which culminated in a ritual act of sexual violation, performed in full view of the maddened spectators. This over, the Negro knifed his victim, and fled through the forest pursued by an exultant mob. If he reached sanctuary, he became a peculiarly sacred object for the rest of his life. But if he was caught, he was torn to pieces or drenched with inflammable spirit and burned. Such was the superstition of the First Men at this time that the participants in this ceremony were seldom reluctant; for it was firmly believed that both were assured of eternal life in Gordelpus. In America this Sacred Lynching was the most popular of all festivals; for it was both sexual and bloody, and afforded a fierce joy to the masses whose sex-life was restricted and secret. In India and Africa the violator was always an 'Englishman', when such a rare creature could be found. In China the whole character of the ceremony was altered; for the violation became a kiss, and the murder a touch with a fan.

One other race, the Jews, were treated with a similar combination of honour and contempt, but for very different reasons. In ancient days their general intelligence, and in particular their financial talent, had co-operated with their homelessness to make them outcasts; and now, in the decline of the First Men, they retained the fiction, if not strictly the fact, of racial integrity. They were still outcasts, though indispensable and powerful. Almost the only kind of intelligent activity which the First Men could still respect was financial operation, whether private or cosmopolitan. The Jews had made themselves invaluable in the financial organization of the world state, having far outstripped the other races because they alone had preserved a furtive respect for pure intelligence. And so, long after intelligence had come to be regarded as disreputable in ordinary men and women, it was expected of the Jews. In them it was called satanic cunning, and they were held to be embodiments of the powers of evil, harnessed in the service of Gordelpus. Thus in time the Jews had made something like 'a corner' in intelligence. This precious commodity they used largely for their own purposes; for two thousand years of persecution had long ago rendered them permanently tribalistic, subconsciously if not consciously. Thus when they had gained control of the few remaining operations which demanded originality rather than routine, they used this advantage chiefly to strengthen their own position in the world. For, though relatively bright, they had suffered much of the general coarsening and limitation which had beset the whole world. Though capable to some extent of criticizing the practical means by which ends should be realized, they were by now wholly incapable of criticizing the major ends which had dominated their race for thousands of years. In them intelligence had become utterly subservient to tribalism. There was thus some excuse for the universal hate and even physical repulsion with which they were regarded; for they alone had failed to make the one great advance, from tribalism to a cosmopolitanism which in other races was no longer merely theoretical. There was good reason also for the respect which they received, since they retained and used somewhat ruthlessly a certain degree of the most distinctively human attribute, intelligence.

In primitive times the intelligence and sanity of the race had been preserved by the inability of its unwholesome members to survive. When humanitarianism came into vogue, and the unsound were tended at public expense, this natural selection ceased. And since these unfortunates were incapable alike of prudence and of social responsibility, they procreated without restraint, and threatened to infect the whole species with their rottenness. During the zenith of Western Civilization, therefore, the subnormal were sterilized. But the latter-day worshippers of Gordelpus regarded both sterilization and contraception as a wicked interference with the divine potency. Consequently the only restriction on population was the suspension of the new-born from aeroplanes, a process which, though it eliminated weaklings, favoured among healthy infants rather the primitive than the highly developed. Thus the intelligence of the race steadily declined. And no one regretted it.

The general revulsion from intelligence was a corollary of the adoration of instinct, and this in turn was an aspect of the worship of activity. Since the unconscious source of human vigour was the divine energy, spontaneous impulse must so far as possible never be thwarted. Reasoning was indeed permitted to the individual within the sphere of his official work, but never beyond. And not even specialists might indulge in reasoning and experiment without obtaining a licence for the particular research. The licence was expensive, and was only granted if the goal in view could be shown to be an increase of world activity. In old times certain persons of morbid curiosity had dared to criticize the time-honoured methods of doing things, and had suggested 'better' methods not convenient to the Sacred Order of Scientists. This had to be stopped. By the fourth millennium of the World State the operations of civilization had become so intricately stereotyped that novel situations of a major order never occurred.

One kind of intellectual pursuit in addition to finance was, indeed, honoured, namely mathematical calculation. All ritual movements, all the motions of industrial machinery, all observable natural phenomena, had to be minutely described in mathematical formulae. The records were filed in the sacred archives of the S.O.S. And there they remained. The vast enterprise of mathematical description was the main work of the scientists, and was said to be the only means by which the evanescent thing, movement, could be passed into the eternal being of Gordelpus.

The cult of instinct did not result simply in a life of ungoverned impulse. Far from it. For the fundamental instinct, it was said, was the instinct to worship Gordelpus in action, and this should rule all the other instincts. Of these, the most important and sacred was the sexual impulse, which the First Men had ever tended to regard as both divine and obscene. Sex, therefore, was now very strictly controlled. Reference to sexuality, save by circumlocution, was forbidden by law. Persons who remarked on the obvious sexual significance of the religious dances, were severely punished. No sexual activity and no sex knowledge were permitted to the individual until he had won his (or her) wings. Much information, of a distorted and perverted nature could, indeed, be gained meanwhile by observation of the religious writings and practices; but officially these sacred matters were all given a metaphysical, not a sexual interpretation. And though legal maturity, the Wing-Winning, might occur as early as the age of fifteen, sometimes it was not attained till forty. If at that age the individual still failed in the test, he or she was forbidden sexual intercourse and information for ever.

In China and India this extravagant sexual taboo was somewhat mitigated. Many easy-going persons had come to feel that the imparting of sex knowledge to the 'immature' was only wrong when the medium of communication was the sacred American language. They therefore made use of the local patois. Similarly, sexual activity of the 'immature' was permissible so long as it was performed solely in the wild reserves, and without American speech. These subterfuges, however, were condemned by the orthodox, even in Asia.

When a man had won his wings, he was formally initiated into the mystery of sex and all its 'biologico-religious' significance. He was also allowed to take a 'domestic wife', and after a much more severe aviation test, any number of 'symbolical' wives. Similarly with the woman. These two kinds of partnership differed greatly. The 'domestic' husband and wife appeared in public together, and their union was indissoluble. The 'symbolic' union, on the other hand, could be dissolved by either party. Also it was too sacred ever to be revealed, or even mentioned, in public.

A very large number of persons never passed the test which sanctioned sexuality. These either remained virgin, or indulged in sexual relations which were not only illegal but sacrilegious. The successful, on the other hand, were apt to consummate sexually every casual acquaintance.

Under these circumstances it was natural that there should exist among the sexually submerged part of the population certain secret cults which sought escape from harsh reality into worlds of fantasy. Of these illicit sects, two were most widespread. One was a perversion of the ancient Christian faith in a God of Love. All love, it was said, is sexual; therefore in worship, private or public, the individual must seek a direct sexual relation with God. Hence arose a grossly phallic cult, very contemptible to those more fortunate persons who had no need of it.

The other great heresy was derived partly from the energy of repressed intellective impulses, and was practised by persons of natural curiosity who, nevertheless, shared the universal paucity of intelligence. These pathetic devotees of intellect were inspired by Socrates. That great primitive had insisted that clear thought is impossible without clear definition of terms, and that without clear thinking man misses fullness of being. These his last disciples were scarcely less fervent admirers of truth than their master, yet they missed his spirit completely. Only by knowing the truth, they said, can the individual attain immortality; only by defining can he know the truth. Therefore, meeting together in secret, and in constant danger of arrest for illicit intellection, they disputed endlessly about the definition of things. But the things which they were concerned to define were not the basic concepts of human thought; for these, they affirmed, had been settled once for all by Socrates and his immediate followers. Therefore, accepting these as true, and grossly misunderstanding them, the ultimate Socratics undertook to define all the processes of the world state and the ritual of the established religion, all the emotions of men and women, all the shapes of noses, mouths, buildings, mountains, clouds, and in fact the whole superficies of their world. Thus they believe that they emancipated themselves from the philistinism of their age, and secured comradeship with Socrates in the hereafter.

5. DOWNFALL

The collapse of this first world-civilization was due to the sudden failure of the supplies of coal. All the original fields had been sapped centuries earlier, and it should have been obvious that those more recently discovered could not last for ever. For some thousands of years the main supply had come from Antarctica. So prolific was this continent that latterly a superstition had arisen in the clouded minds of the world-citizens that it was in some mysterious manner inexhaustible. Thus when at last, in spite of strict censorship, the news began to leak out that even the deepest possible borings had failed to reveal further vegetable deposits of any kind, the world was at first incredulous.

The sane policy would have been to abolish the huge expense of power on ritual flying, which used more of the community's resources than the whole of productive industry. But to believers in Gordelpus such a course was almost unthinkable. Moreover it would have undermined the flying aristocracy. This powerful class now declared that the time had come for the release of the secret of divine power, and called on the S.O.S. to inaugurate the new era. Vociferous agitation in all lands put the scientists in an awkward plight. They gained time by declaring that, though the moment of revelation was approaching, it had not yet arrived; for they had received a divine intimation that this failure of coal was imposed as a supreme test of man's faith. The service of Gordelpus in ritual flight must be rather increased than reduced. Spending a bare minimum of its power on secular matters, the race must concentrate upon religion. When Gordelpus had evidence of their devotion and trust, he would permit the scientists to save them.

Such was the prestige of science that at first this explanation was universally accepted. The ritual flights were maintained. All luxury trades were abolished, and even vital services were reduced to a minimum. Workers thus thrown out of employment were turned over to agricultural labour; for it was felt that the use of mechanical power in mere tillage must be as soon as possible abolished. These changes demanded far more organizing ability than was left in the race. Confusion was widespread, save here and there where serious organization was attempted by certain Jews.

The first result of this great movement of economy and self-denial was to cause something of a spiritual awakening among many who had formerly lived a life of bored ease. This was augmented by the widespread sense of crisis and impending marvels. Religion, which, in spite of its universal authority in this age, had become a matter of ritual rather than of inward experience, began to stir in many hearts – not indeed as a movement of true worship, but rather as a vague awe, not unmixed with self-importance.

But as the novelty of this enthusiasm dwindled, and life became increasingly uncomfortable, even the most zealous began to notice with horror that in moments of inactivity they were prone to doubts too shocking to confess. And as the situation worsened, even a life of ceaseless action could not suppress these wicked fantasies.

For the race was now entering upon an unprecedented psychological crisis, brought about by the impact of the economic disaster upon a permanently unwholesome mentality. Each individual, it must be remembered, had once been a questioning child, but had been taught to shun curiosity as the breath of Satan. Consequently the whole race was suffering from a kind of inverted repression, a repression of the intellective impulses. The sudden economic change, which affected all classes throughout the planet, thrust into the focus of attention a shocking curiosity, an obsessive scepticism, which had hitherto been buried in the deepest recesses of the mind.

It is not easy to conceive the strange mental disorder that now afflicted the whole race, symbolizing itself in some cases by fits of actual physical vertigo. After centuries of prosperity, of routine, of orthodoxy, men were suddenly possessed by a doubt which they regarded as diabolical. No one said a word of it; but in each man's own mind the fiend raised a whispering head, and each was haunted by the troubled eyes of his fellows. Indeed the whole changed circumstances of his life jibed at his credulity.

Earlier in the career of the race, this world crisis might have served to wake men into sanity. Under the first pressure of distress they might have abandoned the extravagances of their culture. But by now the ancient way of life was too deeply rooted. Consequently, we observe the fantastic spectacle of a world engaged, devotedly and even heroically, on squandering its resources in vast aeronautical displays, not through single-minded faith in their rightness and efficacy, but solely in a kind of desperate automatism. Like those little rodents whose migration became barred by an encroachment of the sea, so that annually they drowned themselves in thousands, the First Men helplessly continued in their ritualistic behaviour; but unlike the lemmings, they were human enough to be at the same time oppressed by unbelief, an unbelief which, moreover, they dared not recognize.

To gain a clearer view of this strange state of mind, let us watch the conduct of an individual. An important but typical incident occurred on the north coast of Baffin Island, now a great timber area dotted with residential pylons. The final preparations were being made for the great New Year Flight, in which the island intended to dazzle the rest of the archipelago. In every building the aerial landings thronged with planes and busy fliers. One of these planes was being given its finishing touches by a mother, while her boy watched, or lent a hand. Like many others, that afternoon she was in an overwrought state. Food had long been unwholesome and scanty. The central heating had been cruelly diminished, and the upper stories of the pylon were arctic. The lad had made matters worse by ragging her with innocently blasphemous suggestions, with which at heart she could not but sympathize. Why bother about the ceremony? Why not use their ration of power to go shopping in the South? Sure Gordelpus could not want his people to waste power in air shows when they were starving and freezing. She would never want him to starve, just to show he loved her. Gordelpus must be a beast if he liked that sort of thing. And anyhow it was dangerous to do flying-stunts when she was all empty and wobbly. In vain she had silenced him with the correct answers, for she herself was not convinced by them. Her hands blundered, her vision was obscured by tears. A spanner slipped, and she barked her knuckles.

The two drifted to the window and looked out across the dark carpet of forest, actually so hilly, yet so level in this lofty view. The western sky was colouring. Two distant buildings stood against it, giants of dark rectitude.

'The sun is setting,' she said, 'and we are not ready.' Silently the two worked on the place for a while, till a siren sounded wailing, threateningly. While they hurried into their flying clothes, the great air-doors slid open, and an arctic wind leapt at them. Both climbed into the machine and waited. The boy crunched a precious biscuit. Another scream of the siren, and they shot out into the glowing void. They became an insignificant unit in a swarm of planes that had issued from every floor of the building to climb the violet zenith. From the distant pylons arose a similar smoke of fliers.

At first the exhilaration of flight, and the hypnotic presence of a vast aerial multitude, banished all troubles. Almost every flier attained for a while that ecstasy of action which was both the glory and the undoing of the First Men. Hour after hour they looped and wheeled, climbed, poised and dived, weaving kaleidoscopic patterns on the darkness with their coloured lights. They were a tumultuous yet ordered galaxy, spread out from horizon to horizon.

Overhead, Sirius winded; Orion lounged unimpressed.

Now in the New Year ceremony the movement of the dance was arranged to accelerate steadily from midnight up to the climax of dawn. And the dancers expected to be strengthened with an increasing fervour which should blot out fatigue. But on this occasion many of the fliers were shocked to find themselves hampered by physical exhaustion and spiritual lassitude. Amongst these were the mother and her boy. In him, exhilaration had given place to brooding, to furtive critical introspection of the whole circumstance of his life. He thought of himself as a fledgling that a hawk had snatched up aloft, crushing its incompetent wings. The hawk was not his mother, but some invisible spirit of flight, in whose grip she was also powerless. Presently this reverie gave way to anxiety, for he noticed that the control of the plane was becoming erratic.

And now the supreme moment was at hand. Already the Eastern sky was warm. The whole aerial population raced toward it, and soared vertically, higher and higher, till they flashed into the sunlight, inscribing the holy name on the sky in letters of massed flight. Then they dropped backwards into the darkness. Again and again they leapt, flashed, dropped, until at last the sun touched the hill tops beneath them.

The mother's icy hands fumbled at their work. Her head reeled. All night she had fought alternately against two enemies, despair, and increasing tendency to fall asleep. Again and again she had plucked herself from the rising tide of somnolence; again and again she had wakened to the stark fact that her boy and herself were helpless in a doomed world. At last, in a vision born of exhaustion and misery, she seemed to herself to see beneath her the whole globe of the earth in all its detail, its squared forests and tillage, its long-shadowed towers, its arctic channels, where old men vainly sought for a way to the golden East, and naively gathered pyrites, its Greenland's icy mountains, its India, and Africa, and through its oddly transparent depths to irrigated Australia. How queer the people looked there, all upside-down! Lunatics! All the planet was seen to be peopled with lunatics; and over it spread the fiery and mindless desert of the sky. She put her hands over her eyes. The plane strayed for a few seconds unguided, then spun, and crashed among the pine trees.

Others also came to grief that night. There were casualties in every land. Some blundered in the wild acrobatics at dawn, and went headlong to death. Some, appalled by disillusion, deliberately wrecked themselves. Some few dared to break rank and fly off in sacrilegious independence – till they were shot down for treason against Gordelpus.

Meanwhile the scientists were earnestly and secretly delving in the ancient literature of their science, in hope of discovering the forgotten talisman. They undertook also clandestine experiments, but upon a false trail laid by the wily English contemporary of the Discoverer. The main results were, that several researchers were poisoned or electrocuted, and a great college was blown up. This event impressed the populace, who supposed the accident to be due to an overdaring exercise of the divine potency. The misunderstanding inspired the desperate scientists to rig further impressive 'miracles', and moreover to use them to dispel the increasing restlessness of hungry industrial workers. Thus when a deputation arrived outside the offices of Cosmopolitan Agriculture to demand more flour for industrialists, Gordelpus miraculously blew up the ground on which they stood, and flung their bodies among the onlookers. When the agriculturists of China struck to obtain a reasonable allowance of electric power for their tillage, Gordelpus affected them with an evil atmosphere, so that they choked and died in thousands. Stimulated in this manner by direct divine intervention, the doubting and disloyal elements of the world population recovered their faith and their docility. And so the world jogged on for a while, as nearly as possible as it had done for the last four thousand years, save for a general increase of hunger and ill-health.

But inevitably, as the conditions of life became more and more severe. docility gave place to desperation. Daring spirits began publicly to question the wisdom, and even the piety, of so vast an expenditure of power upon ritual flight, when prime necessities such as food and clothing were becoming so scarce. Did not this helpless devotion merely ridicule them in the divine eyes? God helps him who helps himself. Already the death-rate had risen alarmingly. Emaciated and ragged persons were beginning to beg in public places. In certain districts whole populations were starving, and the Directorate did nothing for them. Yet, elsewhere, harvests were being wasted for lack of power to reap them. In all lands an angry clamour arose for the inauguration of the new era.

The scientists were by now panic-stricken. Nothing had come of their researches, and it was evident that in future all wind and water-power must be devoted to the primary industries. Even so, there was starvation ahead for many. The President of the Physical Society suggested to the Directorate that ritual flying should at once be reduced by half as a compromise with Gordelpus. Immediately the hideous truth, which few hitherto had dared to admit even to themselves, was blurted out upon the ether by a prominent Jew: the whole hoary legend of the divine secret was a lie, else why were the physicists temporizing? Dismay and rage spread over the planet. Everywhere the people rose against the scientists, and against the governing authority which they controlled. Massacres and measures of retaliation soon developed into civil wars. China and India declared themselves free national states, but could not achieve internal unity. In America, ever a stronghold of science and religion, the Government maintained its authority for a while; but as its seat became less secure, its methods became more ruthless. Finally it made the mistake of using not merely poison gas, but microbes; and such was the decayed state of medical science that no one could invent a means of restraining their ravages. The whole American continent succumbed to a plague of pulmonary and nervous diseases. The ancient 'American Madness', which long ago had been used against China, now devastated America. The great stations of water-power and wind-power were wrecked by lunatic mobs who sought vengeance upon anything associated with authority. Whole populations vanished in an orgy of cannibalism.

In Asia and Africa, some semblance of order was maintained for a while. Presently, however, the American Madness spread to these continents also, and very soon all living traces of their civilization vanished.

Only in the most natural fertile areas of the world could the diseased remnant of a population now scrape a living from the soil. Elsewhere, utter desolation. With easy strides the jungle came back into its own.

CHAPTER V

THE FALL OF THE FIRST MEN

1. THE FIRST DARK AGE

We have reached a period in man's history rather less than five thousand years after the life of Newton. In this chapter we must cover about one hundred and fifteen thousand years, and in the next chapter another ten million years. That will bring us to a point as remotely future from the First World State as the earliest anthropoids were remotely past. During the first tenth of the first million years after the fall of the World State, during a hundred thousand years, man remained in complete eclipse. Not till the close of this span, which we will call the First Dark Age, did he struggle once more from savagery through barbarism into civilization and then his renaissance was relatively brief. From its earliest beginnings to its end, it covered only fifteen thousand years; and in its final agony the planet was so seriously damaged that mind lay henceforth in deep slumber for ten more millions of years. This was the Second Dark Age. Such is the field which we must observe in this and the following chapter.

It might have been expected that, after the downfall of the First World State, recovery would have occurred within a few generations. Historians have, indeed, often puzzled over the cause of this surprisingly complete and lasting degradation. Innate human nature was roughly the same immediately after as immediately before the crisis; yet minds that had easily maintained a world-civilization in being, proved quite incapable of building a new order on the ruins of the old. Far from recovering, man's estate rapidly deteriorated till it had sunk into abject savagery.

Many causes contributed to this result, some relatively superficial and temporary, some profound and lasting. It is as though Fate, directing events toward an allotted end, had availed herself of many diverse instruments, none of which would have sufficed alone, though all worked together irresistibly in the same sense. The immediate cause of the helplessness of the race during the actual crisis of the World State was of course the vast epidemic of insanity and still more widespread deterioration of intelligence, which resulted from the use of microbes. This momentary seizure made it impossible for man to check his downfall during its earliest and least unmanageable stage. Later, when the epidemic was spent, even though civilization was already in ruins, a concerted effort of devotion might yet have rebuilt it on a more modest plan. But among the First Men only a minority had ever been capable of wholehearted devotion. The great majority were by nature too much obsessed by private impulses. And in this black period, such was the depth of disillusion and fatigue, that even normal resolution was impossible. Not only man's social structure but the structure of the universe itself, it seemed, had failed. The only reaction was supine despair. Four thousand years of routine had deprived human nature of all its suppleness. To expect these things to refashion their whole behaviour, were scarcely less unreasonable than to expect ants, when their nest was flooded, to assume the habits of water beetles.

But a far more profound and lasting cause doomed the First Men to lie prone for a long while, once they had fallen. A subtle physiological change, which it is tempting to call 'general senescence of the species', was undermining the human body and mind. The chemical equilibrium of each individual was becoming more unstable, so that, little by little, man's unique gift of prolonged youth was being lost. Far more rapidly than of old, his tissues failed to compensate for the wear and tear of living. This disaster was by no means inevitable; but it was brought on by influences peculiar to the make-up of the species, and aggravated artificially. For during some thousands of years man had been living at too high a pressure in a biologically unnatural environment, and had found no means of compensating his nature for the strain thus put upon it.

Conceive, then, that after the fall of the First World State, the generations slid rapidly through dusk into night. To inhabit those centuries was to live in the conviction of universal decay, and under the legend of a mighty past. The population was derived almost wholly from the agriculturists of the old order, and since agriculture had been considered a sluggish and base occupation, fit only for sluggish natures, the planet was now peopled with yokels. Deprived of power, machinery, and chemical fertilizers, these bumpkins were hard put to it to keep themselves alive. And indeed only a tenth of their number survived the great disaster. The second generation knew civilization only as a legend. Their days were filled with ceaseless tillage, and in banding together to fight marauders. Women became once more sexual and domestic chattels. The family, or tribe of families, became the largest social whole. Endless brawls and feuds sprang up between valley and valley, and between the tillers and the brigand swarms. Small military tyrants rose and fell; but no permanent unity of control could be maintained over a wide region. There was no surplus wealth to spend on such luxuries as governments and trained armies.

Thus without appreciable change the millennia dragged on in squalid drudgery. For these latter-day barbarians were hampered by living in a used planet. Not only were coal and oil no more, but almost no mineral wealth of any kind remained within reach of their feeble instruments and wits. In particular the minor metals, needed for so many of the multifarious activities of developed material civilization, had long ago disappeared from the more accessible depths of the earth's crust. Tillage moreover was hampered by the fact that iron itself, which was no longer to be had without mechanical mining, was now inaccessible. Men had been forced to resort once more to stone implements, as their first human ancestors had done. But they lacked both the skill and the persistence of the ancients. Not for them the delicate flaking of the Paleoliths nor the smooth symmetry of the Neoliths. Their tools were but broken pebbles, chipped improvements upon natural stones. On almost every one they engraved the same pathetic symbol, the Swastika or cross, which had been used by the First Men as a sacred emblem throughout their existence, though with varying significance. In this instance it had originally been the figure of an aeroplane diving to destruction, and had been used by the rebels to symbolize the downfall of Gordelpus and the State. But subsequent generations reinterpreted the emblem as the sign manual of a divine ancestor, and as a memento of the golden age from which they were destined to decline for ever, or until the gods should intervene. Almost one might say that in its persistent use of this symbol the first human species unwittingly epitomized its own dual and self-thwarting nature.

The idea of irresistible decay obsessed the race at this time. The generation which brought about the downfall of the World State oppressed its juniors with stories of past amenities and marvels, and hugged to itself the knowledge that the young men had not the wit to rebuild such complexity. Generation by generation, as the circumstance of actual life became more squalid, the legend of past glory became more extravagant. The whole mass of scientific knowledge was rapidly lost, save for a few shreds which were of practical service even in savage life. Fragments of the old culture were indeed preserved in the tangle of folk-lore that meshed the globe, but they were distorted beyond recognition. Thus there was a widespread belief that the world had begun as fire, and that life had evolved out of the fire. After the apes had appeared, evolution ceased (so it was said), until divine spirits came down and possessed the female apes, thereby generating human beings. Thus had arisen the golden age of the divine ancestors. But unfortunately after a while the beast in man had triumphed over the god, so that progress had given place to age-long decay. And indeed decay was now unavoidable, until such time as the gods should see fit to come down to cohabit with women and fire the race once more. This faith in the second coming of the gods persisted here and there throughout the First Dark Age, and consoled men for their vague conviction of degeneracy.

Even at the close of the First Dark Age, the ruins of the ancient residential pylons still characterized every landscape, often with an effect of senile domination over the hovels of latter-day savages. For the living races dwelt beneath these relics like puny grandchildren playing around the feet of their fathers' once mightier fathers. So well had the past built, and with such durable material, that even after a hundred millennia the ruins were still recognizably artefacts. Though for the most part they were of course by now little more than pyramids of debris overgrown with grass and brushwood, most of them retained some stretch of standing wall, and here and there a favoured specimen still reared from its rubble-encumbered base a hundred foot or so of cliff, punctured with windows. Fantastic legends now clustered round these relics. In one myth the men of

old had made for themselves huge palaces which could fly. For a
thousand years (an aeon to these savages) men had dwelt in unity,
and in reverence of the gods; but at last they had become puffed up
with their own glory, and had undertaken to fly to the sun and moon
and the field of stars, to oust the gods from their bright home. But
the gods sowed discord among them, so that they fell a-fighting one
another in the upper air, and their swift palaces crashed down to the
earth in thousands, to be monuments of man's folly for ever after. In
yet another saga it was the men themselves who were winged. They
inhabited dovecotes of masonry, with summits overtopping the stars
and outraging the gods; who therefore destroyed them. Thus in one
form or another, this theme of the downfall of the mighty fliers of
old tyrannized over these abject peoples. Their crude tillage, their
hunting, their defence against the reviving carnivora, were hampered
at every turn by fear of offending the gods by any innovation.

2. THE RISE OF PATAGONIA

As the centuries piled up, the human species had inevitably
diverged once more into many races in the various geographical
areas. And each race consisted of a swarm of tribes, each ignorant
of all but its immediate neighbours. After many millennia this vast
diversification of stocks and cultures made it possible for fresh
biological transfusions and revivifications to occur. At last, after
many racial copulations, a people arose in whom the ancient dignity
of humanity was somewhat restored. Once more there was a real
distinction between the progressive and the backward regions,
between 'primitive' and relatively enlightened cultures.

This rebirth occurred in the Southern Hemisphere. Complex
climatic changes had rendered the southern part of South America
a fit nursery for civilization. Further, an immense warping of the
earth's crust to the east and south of Patagonia, had turned what was
once a relatively shallow region of the ocean into a vast new land
connecting America with Antarctica by way of the former Falkland
Islands and South Georgia, and stretching thence east and north-east
into the heart of the Atlantic.

It happened also that in South America the racial conditions were
more favourable than elsewhere. After the fall of the First World

State the European element in this region had dwindled, and the ancient 'Indian' and Peruvian stock had come into dominance. Many thousands of years earlier, this race had achieved a primitive civilization of its own. After its ruin at the hands of the Spaniards, it had seemed a broken and negligible thing; yet it had ever kept itself curiously aloof in spirit from its conquerors. Though the two stocks had mingled inextricably, there remained ever in the remoter parts of this continent a way of life which was foreign to the dominant Americanism. Superficially Americanized, it remained fundamentally 'Indian' and unintelligible to the rest of the world. Throughout the former civilization this spirit had lain dormant like a seed in winter; but with the return of barbarism it had sprouted, and quietly spread in all directions. From the interaction of this ancient primitive culture and the many other racial elements left over in the continent from the old cosmopolitan civilization, civil life was to begin once more. Thus in a manner the Incas were at last to triumph over their conquerors.

Various causes, then, combined in South America, and especially in the new and virgin plains of Patagonia, to bring the First Dark Age to an end. The great theme of mind began to repeat itself. But in a minor key. For a grave disability hampered the Patagonians. They began to grow old before their adolescence was completed. In the days of Einstein, an individual's youth lasted some twenty-five years, and under the World State it had been artificially doubled. After the downfall of civilization the increasing natural brevity of the individual life was no longer concealed by artifice, and at the end of the First Dark Age a boy of fifteen was already settling into middle age. Patagonian civilization at its height afforded considerable ease and security of life, and enabled man to live to seventy or even eighty; but the period of sensitive and supple youth remained at the very best little more than a decade and a half. Thus the truly young were never able to contribute to culture before they were already at heart middle-aged. At fifteen their bones were definitely becoming brittle, their hair grizzled, their faces lined. Their joints and muscles were stiffening, their brains were no longer quick to learn new adjustments, their fervour was evaporating.

It may seem strange that under these circumstances any kind of civilization could be achieved by the race, that any generation should ever have been able to do more than learn the tricks of its elders. Yet in fact, though progress was never swift, it was steady. For though these beings lacked much of the vigour of youth, they were compensated somewhat by escaping much of youth's fevers and distractions. The First Men, in fact, were now a race whose wild oats had been sown; and though their youthful escapades had somewhat crippled them, they had now the advantage of sobriety and singleness of purpose. Though doomed by lassitude, and a certain fear of extravagance, to fall short of the highest achievements of their predecessors, they avoided much of the wasteful incoherence and mental conflict which had tortured the earlier civilization at its height, though not in its decline. Moreover, because their animal nature was somewhat subdued, the Patagonians were more capable of dispassionate cognition, and more inclined toward intellectualism. They were a people in whom rational behaviour was less often subverted by passion, though more liable to fail through mere indolence or faint-heartedness. Though they found detachment relatively easy, theirs was the detachment of mere lassitude, not the leap from the prison of life's cravings into a more spacious world.

One source of the special character of the Patagonian mind was that in it the sexual impulse was relatively weak. Many obscure causes had helped to temper that lavish sexuality in respect of which the first human species differed from all other animals, even the continuously sexual apes. These causes were diverse, but they combined to produce in the last phase of the life of the species a general curtailment of excess energy. In the Dark Age the severity of the struggle for existence had thrust the sexual interest back almost into the subordinate place which it occupies in the animal mind. Coitus became a luxury only occasionally desired, while self-preservation had become once more an urgent and ever-present necessity. When at last life began to be easier, sexuality remained in partial eclipse, for the forces of racial 'senescence' were at work. Thus the Patagonian culture differed in mood from all the earlier cultures of the First Men. Hitherto it had been the clash of sexuality and social taboo that had generated half the fervour and half the delusions of the race. The excess energy of a victorious species, directed by circumstance into the great river of sex, and dammed by social convention, had been canalized for a thousand labours. And though often it would break loose and lay all waste before it, in the main it had been turned to good account. At all times indeed, it had been prone to escape in all directions and carve out channels for itself, as a lopped tree stump sends forth not one but a score of shoots. Hence the richness, diversity, incoherence, violent and uncomprehended cravings and enthusiasms, of the earlier peoples. In the Patagonians there was no such luxuriance. That they were not highly sexual was not in itself a weakness. What mattered was that the springs of energy which formerly happened to flood into the channel of sex were themselves impoverished.

Conceive, then, a small and curiously sober people established east of the ancient Bahia Blanca, and advancing century by century over the plains and up the valleys. In time it reached and encircled the heights which were once the island of South Georgia, while to the north and west it spread into the Brazilian highlands and over the Andes. Definitely of higher type than any of their neighbours, definitely more vigorous and acute, the Patagonians were without serious rivals. And since by temperament they were peaceable and conciliatory, their cultural progress was little delayed, either by military imperialism or internal strife. Like their predecessors in the northern hemisphere, they passed through phases of disruption and union, retrogression and regeneration; but their career was on the whole more steadily progressive, and less dramatic, than anything that had occurred before. Earlier peoples had leapt from barbarism to civil life and collapsed again within a thousand years. The slow march of the Patagonians took ten times as long to pass from a tribal to a civic organization.

Eventually they comprised a vast and highly organized community of autonomous provinces, whose political and cultural centre lay upon the new coast north-east of the ancient Falkland Islands, while its barbarian outskirts included much of Brazil and Peru. The absence of serious strife between the various parts of this 'empire' was due partly to an innately pacific disposition, partly to a genius for organization. These influences were strengthened by a curiously potent tradition of cosmopolitanism, or human unity, which had been born in the agony of disunion before the days of the World State, and was so burnt into men's hearts that it survived as an element of myth even through the Dark Age. So powerful was this tradition, that even when the sailing ships of Patagonia had founded colonies in remote Africa and Australia, these new communities remained at heart one with the mother country. Even when the almost Nordic culture of the new and temperate Antarctic coasts had outshone the ancient centre, the political harmony of the race was never in danger.

3. THE CULT OF YOUTH

The Patagonians passed through all the spiritual phases that earlier races had experienced, but in a distinctive manner. They had their primitive tribal religion, derived from the dark past, and based on the fear of natural forces. They had their monotheistic impersonation of Power as a vindictive Creator. Their most adored racial hero was a god-man who abolished the old religion of fear. They had their phases, also, of devout ritual and their phases of rationalism, and again their phases of empirical curiosity.

Most significant for the historian who would understand their special mentality is the theme of the god-man; so curiously did it resemble, yet differ from, similar themes in earlier cultures of the first human species. He was conceived as eternally adolescent, and as mystically the son of all men and women. Far from being the Elder Brother, he was the Favourite Child; and indeed he epitomizes that youthful energy and enthusiasm which the race now guessed was slipping away from it. Though the sexual interest of this people was weak, the parental interest was curiously strong. But the worship of the Favourite Son was not merely parental; it expressed also both the individual's craving for his own lost youth, and his obscure sense that the race itself was senescent.

It was believed that the prophet had actually lived a century as a fresh adolescent. He was designated the Boy who Refused to Grow Up. And this vigour of will was possible to him, it was said, because in him the feeble vitality of the race was concentrated many millionfold. For he was the fruit of all parental passion that ever was and would be; and as such he was divine. Primarily he was the Son of Man, but also he was God. For God, in this religion, was no prime Creator but the fruit of man's endeavour. The Creator was brute power, which had quite inadvertently begotten a being nobler than itself. God, the adorable, was the eternal outcome of man's labour in time, the eternally realized promise of what man himself should become. Yet though this cult was based on the will for a young-hearted future, it was also overhung by a dread, almost at times a certainty, that in fact such a future would never be, that the race was doomed to grow old and die, that spirit could never conquer the corruptible flesh, but must fade and vanish. Only by taking to heart the message of the Divine Boy, it was said, could man hope to escape this doom.

Such was the legend. It is instructive to examine the reality. The actual individual, in whom this myth of the Favourite Son was founded, was indeed remarkable. Born of shepherd parents among the Southern Andes, he had first become famous as the leader of a romantic 'youth movement'; and it was this early stage of his career that won him followers. He urged the young to set an example to the old, to live their own life undaunted by conventions, to enjoy, to work hard but briefly, to be loyal comrades. Above all, he preached the religious duty of remaining young in spirit. No one, he said, need grow old, if he willed earnestly not to do so, if he would but keep his soul from falling asleep, his heart open to all rejuvenating influences and shut to every breath of senility. The delight of soul in soul, he said, was the great rejuvenator; it re-created both lover and beloved. If Patagonians would only appreciate each other's beauty without jealousy, the race would grow young again. And the mission of his ever-increasing Band of Youth was nothing less than the rejuvenation of man.

The propagation of this attractive gospel was favoured by a seeming miracle. The prophet turned out to be biologically unique among Patagonians. When many of his coevals were showing signs of senescence, he remained physically young. Also he possessed a sexual vigour which to the Patagonians seemed miraculous. And since sexual taboo was unknown, he exercised himself so heartily in love-making, that he had paramours in every village, and presently his offspring were numbered in hundreds. In this respect his followers strove hard to live up to him, though with small success. But it was not only physically that the prophet remained young. He preserved also a striking youthful agility of mind. His sexual prodigality, though startling to his contemporaries, was in him a temperate overflow of surplus energy. Far from exhausting him, it refreshed him. Presently, however, this exuberance gave place to a more sober life of work and meditation. It was in this period that he began to differentiate himself mentally from his fellows. For at twenty-five, when most Patagonians were deeply settled into a mental groove, he was still battling with successive waves of ideas, and striking out into the unknown. Not till he was forty, and still physically in earlier prime, did he gather his strength and deliver himself of his mature gospel. This, his considered view of existence, turned out to be almost unintelligible to Patagonians. Though in a sense it was an expression of their own culture, it was an expression upon a plane of vitality to which very few of them could ever reach.

The climax came when, during a ceremony in the supreme temple of the capital city, while the worshippers were all prostrated before the hideous image of the Creator, the ageless prophet strode up to the altar, regarded first the congregation and then the god, burst into a hearty peal of laughter, slapped the image resoundingly, and cried, 'Ugly, I salute you! Not as almighty, but as the greatest of all jokers. To have such a face, and yet to be admired for it! To be so empty, and yet so feared!' Instantly there was a hubbub. But such was the young iconoclast's god-like radiance, confidence, unexpectedness, and such his reputation as the miraculous Boy, that when he turned upon the crowd, they fell silent, and listened to his scolding.

'Fools!' he cried. 'Senile infants! If God really likes your adulation, and all this hugger-mugger, it is because he enjoys the joke against you, and against himself, too. You are too serious, yet not serious enough; too solemn, and all for puerile ends. You are so eager for life, that you cannot live. You cherish your youth so much that it flies from you. When I was a boy, I said, "Let us keep young"; and you applauded, and went about hugging your toys and refusing to grow up. What I said was not bad for a boy, but it was not enough. Now I am a man; and I say, "For God's sake, grow up!" Of course we must keep young; but it is useless to keep young if we do not also grow up, and never stop growing up. To keep young, surely, is just to keep supple and keen; and to grow up is not at all a mere sinking into stiffness and into disillusion, but a rising into ever finer skill in all the actions of the game of living. There is something else, too, which is a part of growing up – to see that life is really, after all, a game; a terribly serious game, no doubt, but none the less a game. When we play a game, as it should be played, we strain every muscle to win; but all the while we care less for winning than for the game. And we play the better for it. When barbarians play against a Patagonian team, they forget that it is a game, and go mad for victory. And then how we despise them! If they find themselves losing, they turn savage; if winning, blatant. Either way, the game is murdered, and they cannot see that they are slaughtering a lovely thing. How they pester and curse the umpire, too! I have done that myself, of course, before now; not in games but in life. I have actually cursed the umpire of life. Better so, anyhow, than to insult him with presents, in the hope of being favoured; which is what you are doing here, with your salaams and your vows. I never did that. I merely hated him. Then later I learned to laugh at him, or rather at the thing you set up in his place. But now at last I see him clearly, and laugh with him, at myself, for having missed the spirit of the game. But as for you! Coming here to fawn and whine and cadge favours of the umpire!'

At this point the people rushed toward him to seize him. But he checked them with a young laugh that made them love while they hated. He spoke again.

'I want to tell you how I came to learn my lesson. I have a queer love for clambering about the high mountains; and once when I was up among the snow-fields and precipices of Aconcagua, I was caught in a blizzard. Perhaps some of you may know what storms can be like in the mountains. The air became a hurtling flood of snow. I was swallowed up and carried away. After many hours of floundering, I fell into a snow-drift. I tried to rise, but fell again and again, till my head was buried. The thought of death enraged me, for there was still so much that I wanted to do. I struggled frantically, vainly. Then suddenly – how can I put it? – I saw the game that I was losing, and it was good. Good, no less to lose than to win. For it was the game, now, not victory, that mattered. Hitherto I had been blindfold, and a slave to victory; suddenly I was free, and with sight. For now I saw myself, and all of us, through the eyes of the umpire. It was as though a play-actor were to see the whole play, with his own part in it, through the author's eyes, from the auditorium. Here was I, acting the part of a rather fine man who had come to grief through his own carelessness before his work was done. For me, a character in the play, the situation was hideous; yet for me, the spectator, it had become excellent, within a wider excellence. I saw that it was equally so with all of us, and with all the worlds. For I seemed to see a thousand worlds taking part with us in the great show. And I saw everything through the calm eyes, the exultant, almost derisive, yet not unkindly, eyes of the playwright.

'Well, it had seemed that my exit had come; but no, there was still a cue for me. Somehow I was so strengthened by this new view of things that I struggled out of the snow-drift. And here I am once more. But I am a new man. My spirit is free. While I was a boy, I said, "Grow more alive"; but in those days I never guessed that there was an aliveness far intenser than youth's flicker, a kind of still incandescence. Is there no one here who knows what I mean? No one who at least desires this keener living? The first step is to outgrow this adulation of life itself, and this cadging obsequiousness toward Power. Come! Put it away! Break the ridiculous image in your hearts, as I now smash this idol.'

So saying he picked up a great candlestick and shattered the image. Once more there was an uproar, and the temple authorities had him arrested. Not long afterwards he was tried for sacrilege and executed. For this final extravagance was but the climax of many indiscretions, and those in power were glad to have so obvious a pretext for extinguishing this brilliant but dangerous lunatic.

But the cult of the Divine Boy had already become very popular, for the earlier teaching of the prophet expressed the fundamental craving of the Patagonians. Even his last and perplexing message was accepted by his followers, though without real understanding. Emphasis was laid upon the act of iconoclasm, rather than upon the spirit of his exhortation.

Century by century, the new religion, for such it was, spread over the civilized world. And the race seemed to have been spiritually rejuvenated to some extent by widespread fervour. Physically also a certain rejuvenation took place; for before his death this unique biological 'sport', or throw-back to an earlier vitality, produced some thousands of sons and daughters; and they in turn propagated the good seed far and wide. Undoubtedly it was this new strain that brought about the golden age of Patagonia, greatly improving the material conditions of the race, carrying civilization into the northern continents and attacking problems of science and philosophy with renewed ardour.

But the revival was not permanent. The descendants of the prophet prided themselves too much on violent living. Physically, sexually, mentally, they over-reached themselves and became enfeebled. Moreover, little by little the potent strain was diluted and overwhelmed by intercourse with the greater volume of the innately 'senile'; so that, after a few centuries, the race returned to its middle-aged mood. At the same time the vision of the Divine Boy was gradually distorted. At first it had been youth's ideal of what youth should be, a pattern woven of fanatical loyalty, irresponsible gaiety, comradeship, physical gusto, and not a little pure devilry. But insensibly it became a pattern of that which was expected of youth by sad maturity. The violent young hero was sentimentalized into the senior's vision of childhood, naïve and docile. All that had been violent was forgotten; and what was left became a whimsical and appealing stimulus to the parental impulses. At the same time this phantom was credited with all the sobriety and caution which are so easily appreciated by the middle-aged.

Inevitably this distorted image of youth became an incubus upon the actual young men and women of the race. It was held up as the model social virtue; but it was a model to which they could never conform without doing violence to their best nature, since it was not any longer an expression of youth at all. Just as, in an earlier age, women had been idealized and at the same time hobbled, so now, youth.

Some few, indeed, throughout the history of Patagonia, attained a clearer vision of the prophet. Fewer still were able to enter into the spirit of his final message, in which his enduring youthfulness raised him to a maturity alien to Patagonia. For the tragedy of this people was not so much their 'senescence' as their arrested growth. Feeling themselves old, they yearned to be young again. But, through fixed immaturity of mind, they could never recognize that the true, though unlooked-for, fulfilment of youth's passionate craving is not the mere achievement of the ends of youth itself, but an advance into a more awake and far-seeing vitality.

4. THE CATASTROPHE

It was in these latter days that the Patagonians discovered the civilization that had preceded them. In rejecting the ancient religion of fear, they had abandoned also the legend of a remote magnificence, and had come to regard themselves as pioneers of the mind. In the new continent which was their homeland there were, of course, no relics of the ancient order; and the ruins that besprinkled the older regions had been explained as mere freaks of nature. But latterly, with the advance of natural knowledge, archaeologists had reconstructed something of the forgotten world. And the crisis came when, in the basement of a shattered pylon in China, they found a store of metal plates (constructed of an immensely durable artificial element), on which were embossed crowded lines of writing. These objects were, in fact, blocks from which books were printed a thousand centuries earlier. Other deposits were soon discovered, and bit by bit the dead language was deciphered. Within three centuries the outline of the ancient culture was laid bare; and presently the whole history of man's rise and ruin fell upon this latter-day civilization with crushing effect, as though an ancient pylon were to have fallen on a village of wigwams at its foot. The pioneers discovered that all the ground which they had so painfully won from the wild had been conquered long ago, and lost; that on the material side their glory was nothing beside the glory of the past; and that in the sphere of mind they had established only a few scattered settlements where formerly was an empire. The Patagonian system of natural knowledge had been scarcely further advanced than that of pre-Newtonian Europe. They had done little more than conceive the scientific spirit and unlearn a few superstitions. And now suddenly they came into a vast inheritance of thought.

This in itself was a gravely disturbing experience for a people of strong intellectual interest. But even more overwhelming was the discovery, borne in on them in the course of their research, that the past had been not only brilliant but crazy, and that in the long run the crazy element had completely triumphed. For the Patagonian mind was by now too sane and empirical to accept the ancient knowledge without testing it. The findings of the archaeologists were handed over to the physicists and other scientists, and the firm thought and valuation of Europe and America at their zenith were soon distinguished from the degenerate products of the World State.

The upshot of this impact with a more developed civilization was dramatic and tragic. It divided the Patagonians into loyalists and rebels, into those who clung to the view that the new learning was a satanic lie, and those who faced the facts. To the former party the facts were thoroughly depressing; the latter, though overawed, found in them a compelling majesty, and also a hope. That the earth was a mote among the star-clouds was the least subversive of the new doctrines, for the Patagonians had already abandoned the geocentric view. What was so distressing to the reactionaries was the theory that an earlier race had long ago possessed and spent the vitality that they themselves so craved. The party of progress, on the other hand, urged that this vast new knowledge must be used; and that, thus equipped, Patagonia might compensate for lack of youthfulness by superior sanity.

This divergence of will resulted in a physical conflict such as had never before occurred in the Patagonian world. Something like nationalism emerged. The more vigorous Antarctic coasts became modern, while Patagonia itself clung to the older culture. There were several wars, but as physics and chemistry advanced in Antarctica, the Southerners were able to devise engines of war which the Northerners could not resist. In a couple of centuries the new 'culture' had triumphed. The world was once more unified.

Hitherto Patagonian civilization had been of a medieval type. Under the influence of physics and chemistry it began to change. Wind- and water-power began to be used for the generation of electricity. Vast mining operations were undertaken in search of the metals and other minerals which no longer occurred at easy depths. Architecture began to make use of steel. Electrically driven aeroplanes were made, but without real success. And this failure was symptomatic; for the Patagonians were not sufficiently foolhardy to master aviation, even had their planes been more efficient. They themselves naturally attributed their failure wholly to lack of a convenient source of power, such as the ancient petrol. Indeed this lack of oil and coal hampered them at every turn. Volcanic power, of course, was available; but, never having been really mastered by the more resourceful ancients, it defeated the Patagonians completely.

As a matter of fact, in wind and water they had all that was needed. The resources of the whole planet were available, and the world population was less than a hundred million. With this source alone they could never, indeed, have competed in luxury with the earlier World State, but they might well have achieved something like Utopia.

But this was not to be. Industrialism, though accompanied by only a slow increase of population, produced in time most of the social discords which had almost ruined their predecessors. To them it appeared that all their troubles would be solved if only their material power were far ampler. This strong and scarcely rational conviction was a symptom of their ruling obsession, the craving for increased vitality.

Under these circumstances it was natural that one event and one strand of ancient history should fascinate them. The secret of limitless material power had once been known and lost. Why should not Patagonians rediscover it, and use it, with their superior sanity, to bring heaven on earth? The ancients, no doubt, did well to forgo this dangerous source of power; but the Patagonians, level-headed and single-minded, need have no fear. Some, indeed, considered it less important to seek power than to find a means of checking biological senescence; but, unfortunately, though physical science had advanced so rapidly, the more subtle biological sciences had remained backward, largely because among the ancients themselves little more had been done than to prepare their way. Thus it happened that the most brilliant minds of Patagonia, fascinated by the prize at stake, concentrated upon the problem of matter. The state encouraged this research by founding and endowing laboratories whose avowed end was this sole work.

The problem was difficult, and the Patagonian scientists, though intelligent, were somewhat lacking in grit. Only after some five hundred years of intermittent research was the secret discovered, or partially so. It was found possible, by means of a huge initial expenditure of energy, to annihilate the positive and negative electric charges in one not very common kind of atom. But this limitation mattered not at all; the human race now possessed an inexhaustible source of power which could be easily manipulated and easily controlled. But though controllable, the new gift was not foolproof; and there was no guarantee that those who used it might not use it foolishly, or inadvertently let it get out of hand.

Unfortunately, at the time when the new source of energy was discovered, the Patagonians were more divided than of old. Industrialism, combined with the innate docility of the race, had gradually brought about a class cleavage more extreme even than that of the ancient world, though a cleavage of a curiously different kind. The strongly parental disposition of the average Patagonian prevented the dominant class from such brutal exploitation as had formerly occurred. Save during the first century of industrialism, there was no serious physical suffering among the proletariat. A paternal government saw to it that all Patagonians were at least properly fed and clothed, that all had ample leisure and opportunities of amusement. At the same time they saw to it also that the populace became more and more regimented. As in the First World State, civil authority was once more in the hands of a small group of masters of industry, but with a difference. Formerly the dominant motive of big business had been an almost mystical passion for the creation of activity; now the ruling minority regarded themselves as standing towards the populace *in loco parentis*, and aimed at creating 'a young-hearted people, simple, gay, vigorous and loyal'. Their ideal of the state was something between a preparatory school under a sympathetic but strict adult staff, and a joint-stock company, in which the shareholders retained only one function, to delegate their powers thankfully to a set of brilliant directors.

That the system had worked so well and survived so long was due not only to innate Patagonian docility, but also to the principle by which the governing class recruited itself. One lesson at least had been learnt from the bad example of the earlier civilization, namely respect for intelligence. By a system of careful testing, the brightest children were selected from all classes and trained to be governors. Even the children of the governors themselves were subjected to the same examination, and only those who qualified were sent to the 'schools for young governors'. Some corruption no doubt existed, but in the main this system worked. The children thus selected were very carefully trained in theory and practice, as organizers, scientists, priests and logicians.

The less brilliant children of the race were educated very differently from the young governors. It was impressed on them that they were less able than the others. They were taught to respect the governors as superior beings, who were called upon to serve the community in specially skilled and arduous work, simply because of their ability. It would not be true to say that the less intelligent were educated merely to be slaves; rather they were expected to be the docile, diligent and happy sons and daughters of the fatherland. They were taught to be loyal and optimistic. They were given vocational training for their various occupations, and encouraged to use their intelligence as much as possible upon the plane suited to it; but the affairs of the state and the problems of religion and theoretical science were strictly forbidden. The official doctrine of the beauty of youth was fundamental in their education. They were taught all the conventional virtues of youth, and in particular modesty and simplicity. As a class they were extremely healthy, for physical training was a very important part of education in Patagonia. Moreover, the universal practice of sun-bathing, which was a religious rite, was especially encouraged among the proletariat, as it was believed to keep the body 'young' and the mind placid. The leisure of the governed class was devoted mostly to athletics and other sport, physical and mental. Music and other forms of art were also practised, for these were considered fit occupations for juveniles. The government exercised a censorship over artistic products, but it was seldom enforced; for the common folk of Patagonia were mostly too phlegmatic and too busy to conceive anything but the most obvious and respectable art. They were fully occupied with work and pleasure. They suffered no sexual restraints. Their impersonal interests were satisfied with the official religion of youth-worship and loyalty to the community.

This placid condition lasted for some four hundred years after the first century of industrialism. But as time passed the mental difference between the two classes increased. Superior intelligence became rarer and rarer among the proletariat; the governors were recruited more and more from their own offspring, until finally they became an hereditary caste. The gulf widened. The governors began to lose all mental contact with the governed. They made a mistake which could never have been committed had their psychology kept pace with their other sciences. Ever confronted with the workers' lack of intelligence, they came to treat them more and more as children, and forgot that, though simple, they were grown men and women who needed to feel themselves as free partners in a great human enterprise. Formerly this illusion of responsibility had been sedulously encouraged. But as the gulf widened the proletarians were treated rather as infants than as adolescents, rather as well-cared-for domestic animals than as human beings. Their lives became more and more minutely, though benevolently, systematized for them. At the same time less care was taken to educate them up to an understanding and appreciation of the common human enterprise. Under these circumstances the temper of the people changed. Though their material condition was better than had ever been known before, save under the First World State, they became listless, discontented, mischievous, ungrateful to their superiors.

Such was the state of affairs when the new source of energy was discovered. The world community consisted of two very different elements, first a small, highly intellectual caste, passionately devoted to the state and to the advancement of culture amongst themselves; and, second, a much more numerous population of rather obtuse, physically well-cared-for, and spiritually starved industrialists. A serious clash between the two classes had already occurred over the use of a certain drug, favoured by the people for the bliss it produced, forbidden by the governors for its evil after-effects. The drug was abolished; but the motive was misinterpreted by the proletariat. This incident brought to the surface a hate that had for long been gathering strength in the popular mind, though unwittingly.

When rumour got afoot that in future mechanical power would be unlimited, the people expected a millennium. Every one would have his own limitless source of energy. Work would cease. Pleasure would be increased to infinity. Unfortunately the first use made of the new power was extensive mining at unheard-of depths in search of metals and other minerals which had long ago ceased to be available near the surface. This involved difficult and dangerous work for the miners. There were casualties. Riots occurred. The new power was used upon the rioters with murderous effect, the governors declaring that, though their paternal hearts bled for their foolish children, this chastisement was necessary to prevent worse evils. The workers were urged to face their troubles with that detachment which the Divine Boy had preached in his final phase; but this advice was greeted with the derision which it deserved. Further strikes, riots, assassinations. The proletariat had scarcely more power against their masters than sheep against the shepherd, for they had not the brains for large-scale organization. But it was through one of these pathetically futile rebellions that Patagonia was at last destroyed.

A petty dispute had occurred in one of the new mines. The management refused to allow miners to teach their trade to their sons; for vocational education, it was said, should be carried on professionally. Indignation against this interference with parental authority caused a sudden flash of the old rage. A power unit was seized, and after a bout of insane monkeying with the machinery, the mischief-makers inadvertently got things into such a state that at last the awful djin of physical energy was able to wrench off his fetters and rage over the planet. The first explosion was enough to blow up the mountain range above the mine. In those mountains were huge tracts of the critical element, and these were detonated by rays from the initial explosion. This sufficed to set in action still more remote tracts of the elements. An incandescent hurricane spread over the whole of Patagonia, reinforcing itself with fresh atomic fury wherever it went. It raged along the line of the Andes and the Rockies, scorching both continents with its heat. It undermined and blew up the Behring Straits, spread like a brood of gigantic fiery serpents into Asia, Europe and Africa. Martians, already watching the earth as a cat a bird beyond its spring, noted that the brilliance of the neighbour planet was suddenly enhanced. Presently the oceans began to boil here and there with submarine commotion. Tidal waves mangled the coasts and floundered up the valleys. But in time the general sea level sank considerably through evaporation and the opening of chasms in the ocean floor. All volcanic regions became fantastically active. The polar caps began to melt, but prevented the arctic regions from being calcined like the rest of the planet. The atmosphere was a continuous dense cloud of moisture, fumes and dust, churned in ceaseless hurricanes. As the fury of the electromagnetic collapse proceeded, the surface temperature of the planet steadily increased, till only in the Arctic and a few favoured corners of the sub-Arctic could life persist.

Patagonia's death agony was brief. In Africa and Europe a few remote settlements escaped the actual track of the eruptions, but succumbed in a few weeks to the hurricanes of steam. Of the two hundred million members of the human race, all were burnt or roasted or suffocated within three months – all but thirty-five, who happened to be in the neighbourhood of the North Pole.

CHAPTER VI

TRANSITION

1. THE FIRST MEN AT BAY

By one of those rare tricks of fortune, which are as often favourable as hostile to humanity, an Arctic exploration ship had recently been embedded in the pack-ice for a long drift across the Polar sea. She was provisioned for four years, and when the catastrophe occurred she had already been at sea for six months. She was a sailing vessel; the expedition had been launched before it was practicable to make use of the new source of power. The crew consisted of twenty-eight men and seven women. Individuals of an earlier and more sexual race, proportioned thus, in such close proximity and isolation, would almost certainly have fallen foul of one another sooner or later. But to Patagonians the arrangement was not intolerable. Besides managing the whole domestic side of the expedition, the seven women were able to provide moderate sexual delight for all, for in this people the female sexuality was much less reduced than the male. There were, indeed, occasional jealousies and feuds in the little community, but these were subordinated to a strong *esprit de corps*. The whole company had, of course, been very carefully chosen for comradeship, loyalty, and health, as well as for technical skill. All claimed descent from the Divine Boy. All were of the governing class. One quaint expression of the strongly parental Patagonian temperament was that a pair of diminutive pet monkeys was taken with the expedition.

The crew's first intimation of the catastrophe was a furious hot wind that melted the surface of the ice. The sky turned black. The Arctic summer became a weird and sultry night, torn by fantastic thunderstorms. Rain crashed on the ship's deck in a continuous waterfall. Clouds of pungent smoke and dust irritated the eyes and nose. Submarine earthquakes buckled the pack-ice.

A year after the explosion, the ship was labouring in tempestuous and berg-strewn water near the Pole. The bewildered little company now began to feel its way south; but, as they proceeded, the air became more fiercely hot and pungent, the storms more savage. Another twelve months were spent in beating about the Polar sea, ever and again retreating north from the impossible southern weather. But at length conditions improved slightly, and with great difficulty these few survivors of the human race approached their original objective in Norway, to find that the lowlands were a scorched and lifeless desert, while on the heights the valley vegetation was already struggling to establish itself, in patches of sickly green. Their base town had been flattened by a hurricane, and the skeletons of its population still lay in the streets. They coasted further south. Everywhere the same desolation. Hoping that the disturbance might be merely local, they headed round the British Isles and doubled back on France. But France turned out to be an appalling chaos of volcanoes. With a change of wind, the sea around them was infuriated with falling debris, often red hot. Miraculously they got away and fled north again. After creeping along the Siberian coast they were at last able to find a tolerable resting-place at the mouth of one of the great rivers. The ship was brought to anchor, and the crew rested. They were a diminished company, for six men and two women had been lost on the voyage.

Conditions even here must recently have been far more severe, since much of the vegetation had been scorched, and dead animals were frequent. But evidently the first fury of the vast explosion was now abating.

By this time the voyagers were beginning to realize the truth. They remembered the half jocular prophecies that the new power would sooner or later wreck the planet, prophecies which had evidently been all too well founded. There had been a world-wide disaster; and they themselves had been saved only by their remoteness and the Arctic ice from a fate that had probably overwhelmed all their fellow men.

So desperate was the outlook for a handful of exhausted persons on a devastated planet, that some urged suicide. All dallied with the idea, save a woman, who had unexpectedly become pregnant. In her the strong parental disposition of her race was now awakened, and she implored the party to make a fight for the sake of her child. Reminded that the baby would only be born into a life of hardship, she reiterated with more persistence than reason, 'My baby must live.'

The men shrugged their shoulders. But as their tired bodies recovered after the recent struggle, they began to realize the solemnity of their position. It was one of the biologists who expressed a thought which was already present to all. There was at least a chance of survival, and if ever men and women had a sacred duty, surely these had, for they were now the sole trustees of the human spirit. At whatever cost of toil and misery they must people the earth again.

This common purpose now began to exalt them, and brought them all into a rare intimacy. 'We are ordinary folk,' said the biologist, 'but somehow we must become great.' And they were, indeed, in a manner made great by their unique position. In generous minds a common purpose and common suffering breed a deep passion of comradeship, expressed perhaps not in words but in acts of devotion. These, in their loneliness and their sense of obligation, experienced not only comradeship, but a vivid communion with one another as instruments of a sacred cause.

The party now began to build a settlement beside the river. Though the whole area had, of course, been devastated, vegetation had soon revived, from roots and seeds, buried or wind-borne. The countryside was now green with those plants that had been able to adjust themselves to the new climate. Animals had suffered far more seriously. Save for the Arctic fox, a few small rodents, and one herd of reindeer, none were left but the dwellers in the actual Arctic seas, the Polar bear, various cetaceans, and seals. Of fish there were plenty. Birds in great numbers had crowded out of the south, and had died off in thousands through lack of food, but certain species were already adjusting themselves to the new environment. Indeed, the whole remaining fauna and flora of the planet was passing through a phase of rapid and very painful readjustment. Many well-established species had wholly failed to get a footing in the new world, while certain hitherto insignificant types were able to forge ahead.

The party found it possible to grow maize and even rice from seed brought from a ruined store in Norway. But the great heat, frequent torrential rain, and lack of sunlight, made agriculture laborious and precarious. Moreover, the atmosphere had become seriously impure, and the human organism had not yet succeeded in adapting itself. Consequently the party were permanently tired and liable to disease.

The pregnant woman had died in child-birth, but her baby lived. It became the party's most sacred object, for it kindled in every mind the strong parental disposition so characteristic of Patagonians.

Little by little the numbers of the settlement were reduced by sickness, hurricanes and volcanic gases. But in time they achieved a kind of equilibrium with their environment, and even a certain strenuous amenity of life. As their prosperity increased, however, their unity diminished. Differences of temperament began to be dangerous. Among the men two leaders had emerged, or rather one leader and a critic. The original head of the expedition had proved quite incapable of dealing with the new situation, and had at last committed suicide. The company had then chosen the second navigating officer as their chief, and had chosen him unanimously. The other born leader of the party was a junior biologist, a man of very different type. The relations of these two did much to determine the future history of man, and are worthy of study in themselves; but here we can only glance at them. In all times of stress the navigator's authority was absolute, for everything depended on his initiative and heroic example. But in less arduous periods, murmurs arose against him for exacting discipline when discipline seemed unnecessary. Between him and the young biologist there grew up a strange blend of hostility and affection; for the latter, though critical, loved and admired the other, and declared that the survival of the party depended on this one man's practical genius.

Three years after their landing, the community, though reduced in numbers and in vitality, was well established in a routine of hunting, agriculture and building. Three fairly healthy infants rejoiced and exasperated their elders. With security, the navigator's genius for action found less scope, while the knowledge of the scientists became more valuable. Plant and poultry-breeding were beyond the range of the heroic leader, and in prospecting for minerals he was equally helpless. Inevitably as time passed he and the other navigators grew restless and irritable; and at last, when the leader decreed that the party should take to the ship and explore for better land, a serious dispute occurred. All the sea-farers applauded; but the scientists, partly through clearer understanding of the calamity that had befallen the planet, partly through repugnance at the hardship involved, refused to go.

Violent emotions were aroused; but both sides restrained themselves through well-tried mutual respect and loyalty to the community. Then suddenly sexual passion set a light to the tinder. The woman who, by general consent, had come to be queen of the settlement, and was regarded as sacred to the leader, asserted her independence by sleeping with one of the scientists. The leader surprised them, and in sudden rage killed the young man. The little community at once fell into two armed factions, and more blood was shed. Very soon, however, the folly and sacrilege of this brawl became evident to these few survivors of a civilized race, and after a parley a grave decision was made.

The company was to be divided. One party, consisting of five men and two women, under the young biologist, was to remain in the settlement. The leader himself, with the remaining nine men and two women, were to navigate the ship toward Europe, in search of a better land. They promised to send word, if possible, during the following year.

With this decision taken the two parties once more became amicable. All worked to equip the pioneers. When at last it was the time of departure, there was a solemn leave-taking. Every one was relieved at the cessation of a painful incompatibility; but more poignant than relief was the distressed affection of those who had so long been comrades in a sacred enterprise.

It was a parting even more momentous than was supposed. For from this act arose at length two distinct human species.

Those who stayed behind heard no more of the wanderers, and finally concluded that they had come to grief. But in fact they were driven west and south-west past Iceland, now a cluster of volcanoes, to Labrador. On this voyage through fantastic storms and oceanic convulsions they lost nearly half their number, and were at last unable to work the ship. When finally they were wrecked on a rocky coast, only the carpenter's mate, two women, and the pair of monkeys succeeded in clambering ashore.

These found themselves in a climate far more sultry than Siberia; but like Siberia, Labrador contained uplands of luxuriant vegetation. The man and his two women had at first great difficulty in finding food, but in time they adapted themselves to a diet of berries and roots. As the years passed, however, the climate undermined their mentality and their descendants sank into abject savagery, finally degenerating into a type that was human only in respect of its ancestry.

The little Siberian settlement was now hard-pressed but single-minded. Calculation had convinced the scientists that the planet would not return to its normal state for some millions of years; for though the first and superficial fury of the disaster had already ceased, the immense pent-up energy of the central explosions would take millions of years to leak out through volcanic vents. The leader of the party, by rare luck a man of genius, conceived their situation thus. For millions of years the planet would be uninhabitable save for a fringe of Siberian coast. The human race was doomed for ages to a very restricted and uncongenial environment. All that could be hoped for was the persistence of a mere remnant of civilized humanity, which should be able to lie dormant until a more favourable epoch. With this end in view the party must propagate itself, and make some possibility of cultured life for its offspring. Above all it must record in some permanent form as much as it could remember of Patagonian culture. 'We are the germ,' he said. 'We must play for safety, mark time, preserve man's inheritance. The chances against us are almost overwhelming, but just possibly we shall win through.'

And so in fact they did. Several times almost exterminated at the outset, these few harassed individuals preserved their spark of humanity. A close inspection of their lives would reveal an intense personal drama; for, in spite of the sacred purpose which united them, almost as muscles in one limb, they were individuals of different temperaments. The children, moreover, caused jealousy between their parentally hungry elders. There was ever a subdued, and sometimes an open, rivalry to gain the affection of these young things, these few and precious buds on the human stem. Also there was sharp disagreement about their education. For though all the elders adored them simply for their childishness, one at least, the visionary leader of the party, thought of them chiefly as potential vessels of the human spirit, to be moulded strictly for their great function. In this perpetual subdued antagonism of aims and temperaments the little society lived from day to day, much as a limb functions in the antagonism of its muscles.

The adults of the party devoted much of their leisure during the long winters to the heroic labour of recording the outline of man's whole knowledge. This task was very dear to the leader, but the others often grew weary of it. To each person a certain sphere of culture was assigned; and after he or she had thought out a section and scribbled it down on slate, it was submitted to the company for criticism, and finally engraved deeply on tablets of hard stone. Many thousands of such tablets were produced in the course of years, and were stored in a cave which was carefully prepared for them. Thus was recorded something of the history of the earth and of man, the outlines of physics, chemistry, biology, psychology, and geometry. Each scribe set down also in some detail a summary of his own special study, and added a personal manifesto of his own views about existence. Much ingenuity was spent in devising a vast pictorial dictionary and grammar, with which, it was hoped, the remote future might interpret the whole library.

Years passed while this immense registration of human thought was still in progress. The founders of the settlement grew feebler while the eldest of the next generation were still adolescent. Of the two women, one had died and the other was almost a cripple, both martyrs to the task of motherhood. A youth, an infant boy, and four girls of various ages – on these the future of man now depended. Unfortunately these precious beings had suffered from their very preciousness. Their education had been bungled. They had been both pampered and oppressed. Nothing was thought too good for them, but they were overwhelmed with cherishing and teaching. Thus they came to hold the elders at arm's length, and to weary of the ideals imposed on them. Brought into a ruined world without their own consent, they refused to accept the crushing obligation toward an improbable future. Hunting, and the daily struggle of a pioneering age, afforded their spirits full exercise in courage, mutual loyalty, and interest in one another's personality. They would live for the present only, and for the tangible reality, not for a culture which they knew only by hearsay. In particular, they loathed the hardship of engraving endless verbiage upon granitic slabs.

The crisis came when the eldest girl had crossed the threshold of physical maturity. The leader told her that it was her duty to begin bearing children at once, and ordered her to have intercourse with her half-brother, his own son. Having herself assisted at the last birth, which had destroyed her mother, she refused; and when pressed she dropped her graving tool and fled. This was the first serious act of rebellion. In a few years the older generation was deposed from authority. A new way of life, more active, more dangerous, zestful and careless, resulted in a lowering of the community's standard of comfort and organization, but also in greater health and vitality. Experiments in plant and stock-breeding were neglected, buildings went out of repair; but great feats of hunting and exploration were undertaken. Leisure was given over to games of hazard and calculation, to dancing, singing and romantic story-telling. Music and romance, indeed, were now the main expression of the finer nature of these beings, and became the vehicles of obscure religious experience. The intellectualism of the elders was ridiculed. What could their poor sciences tell of reality, of the many-faced, never-for-a-moment-the-same, superbly inconsequent, and ever-living Real? Man's intelligence was all right for hunting and tillage in the world of common sense; but if he rode it further afield, he would find himself in a desert, and his soul would starve. Let him live as nature prompted. Let him keep the young god in his heart alive. Let him give free play to the struggling, irrational, dark vitality that sought to realize itself in him not as logic but as beauty.

The tablets were now engraved only by the aged.

But one day, after the infant boy had reached the early Patagonian adolescence, his curiosity was roused by the tail-like hind limbs of a seal. The old people timidly encouraged him. He made other biological observations, and was led on to envisage the whole drama of life on the planet, and to conceive loyalty to the cause which they had served.

Meanwhile, sexual and parental nature had triumphed where schooling had failed. The young things inevitably fell in love with each other, and in time several infants appeared.

Thus, generation by generation, the little settlement maintained itself with varying success, varying zestfulness, and varying loyalty toward the future. With changing conditions the population fluctuated, sinking as low as two men and one woman, but increasing gradually up to a few thousand, the limit set by the food capacity of their strip of coast. In the long run, though circumstances did not prevent material survival, they made for mental decline. For the Siberian coast remained a tropical land bounded on the south by a forest of volcanoes; and consequently in the long run the generations declined in mental vigour and subtlety. This result was perhaps due in part to too intensive inbreeding; but this factor had also one good effect. Though mental vigour waned, certain desirable characteristics were consolidated. The founders of the group represented the best remaining stock of the first human species. They had been chosen for their hardihood and courage, their native loyalty, their strong cognitive interest. Consequently, in spite of phases of depression, the race not only survived but retained its curiosity and its group feeling. Even while the ability of men decreased, their will to understand, and their sense of racial unity, remained. Though their conception of man and the universe gradually sank into crude myth, they preserved a strong unreasoning loyalty towards the future, and toward the now sacred stone library which was rapidly becoming unintelligible to them. For thousands and even millions of years, after the species had materially changed its nature, there remained a vague admiration for mental prowess, a confused tradition of a noble past, and pathetic loyalty toward a still nobler future. Above all, internecine strife was so rare that it served only to strengthen the clear will to preserve the unity and harmony of the race.

2. THE SECOND DARK AGE

We must now pass rapidly over the Second Dark Age, observing merely those influences which were to affect the future of humanity.

Century by century the pent energy of the vast explosion dispersed itself; but not till many hundred thousand years had passed did the swarms of upstart volcanoes begin to die, and not till after millions of years did the bulk of the planet become once more a possible home for life.

During this period many changes took place. The atmosphere became clearer, purer and less turbulent. With the fall of temperature, frost and snow appeared occasionally in the Arctic regions, and in due course the Polar caps were formed again. Meanwhile, ordinary geological processes, augmented by the strains to which the planet was subjected by increased internal pressure, began to change the continents. South America mostly collapsed into the hollows blasted beneath it, but a new land rose to join Brazil with West Africa. The East Indies and Australia became a continuous continent. The huge mass of Thibet sank deeply into its disturbed foundations, lunged west, and buckled Afghanistan into a range of peaks nearly forty thousand feet above the sea. Europe sank under the Atlantic. Rivers writhed shiftingly hither and thither upon the continents, like tortured worms. New alluvial areas were formed. New strata were laid upon one another under new oceans. New animals and plants developed from the few surviving Arctic species, and spread south through Asia and America. In the new forests and grasslands appeared various specialized descendants of the reindeer, and swarms of rodents. Upon these preyed the large and small descendants of the Arctic fox, of which one species, a gigantic wolflike creature, rapidly became the 'King of Beasts' in the new order, and remained so, until it was ousted by the more slowly modified offspring of the polar bears. A certain genus of seals, reverting to the ancient terrestrial habit, had developed a slender snake-like body and an almost swift, and very serpentine, mode of locomotion among the coastal sand-dunes. There it was wont to stalk its rodent prey, and even follow them into their burrows. Everywhere there were birds. Many of the places left vacant by the destruction of the ancient fauna were now filled by birds which had discarded flight and developed pedestrian habits. Insects, almost exterminated by the great conflagration, had afterwards increased so rapidly, and had refashioned their types with such versatility, that they soon reached almost to their ancient profusion. Even more rapid was the establishment of the new micro-organisms. In general, among all the beasts and plants of the earth there was a great change of habit, and a consequent overlaying of old body-forms with new forms adapted to a new way of life.

The two human settlements had fared very differently. That of Labrador, oppressed by a more sweltering climate, and unsupported by the Siberian will to preserve human culture, sank into animality; but ultimately it peopled the whole West with swarming tribes. The human beings in Asia remained a mere handful throughout the ten million years of the Second Dark Age. An incursion of the sea cut them off from the south. The old Taimyr Peninsula, where their settlements clustered, became the northern promontory of an island whose coasts were the ancient valley-edges of the Yenessi, the Lower Tunguska and the Lena. As the climate became less oppressive, the families spread toward the southern coast of the island, but the sea checked them. Temperate conditions enabled them to regain a certain degree of culture. But they had no longer the capacity to profit much from the new clemency of nature, for the previous ages of tropical conditions had undermined them. Moreover, toward the end of the ten million years of the Second Dark Age, the Arctic climate spread south into their island. Their crops failed, the rodents that formed their chief cattle dwindled, their few herds of deer faded out through lack of food. Little by little this scanty human race degenerated into a mere remnant of Arctic savages. And so they remained for a million years. Psychologically they were so crippled that they had almost completely lost the power of innovation. When their sacred quarries in the hills were covered with ice, they had not the wit to use stone from the valleys, but were reduced to making implements of bone. Their language degenerated into a few grunts to signify important acts, and a more complex system of emotional expressions. For emotionally these creatures still preserved a certain refinement. Moreover, though they had almost wholly lost the power of intelligent innovation, their instinctive responses were often such as a more enlightened intelligence would justify. They were strongly social, deeply respectful of the individual human life, deeply parental, and often terribly earnest in their religion.

Not till long after the rest of the planet was once more covered with life, not till nearly ten million years after the Patagonian disaster, did a group of these savages, adrift on an iceberg, get blown southward across the sea to the mainland of Asia. Luckily, for Arctic conditions were increasing, and in time the islanders were extinguished.

The survivors settled in the new land and spread, century by century, into the heart of Asia. Their increase was very slow, for they were an infertile and inflexible race. But conditions were now extremely favourable. The climate was temperate; for Russia and Europe were now a shallow sea warmed by currents from the Atlantic. There were no dangerous animals save the small grey bears, an offshoot from the polar species, and the large wolf-like foxes. Various kinds of rodents and deer provided meat in plenty. There were birds of all sizes and habits. Timber, fruit, wild grains and other nourishing plants throve on the well-watered volcanic soil. The prolonged eruptions, moreover, had once more enriched the upper layers of the rocky crust with metals.

A few hundred thousand years in this new world sufficed for the human species to increase from a handful of individuals to a swarm of races. It was in the conflict and interfusion of these races, and also through the absorption of certain chemicals from the new volcanic soil, that humanity at last recovered its vitality.

CHAPTER VII

THE RISE OF THE SECOND MEN

1. THE APPEARANCE OF A NEW SPECIES

It was some ten million years after the Patagonian disaster that the first elements of a few human species appeared, in an epidemic of biological variations, many of which were extremely valuable. Upon this raw material the new and stimulating environment worked for some hundred thousand years until at last there appeared the Second Men.

Though of greater stature and more roomy cranium, these beings were not wholly unlike their predecessors in general proportions. Their heads, indeed, were large even for their bodies, and their necks massive. Their hands were huge, but finely moulded. Their almost titanic size entailed a seemingly excessive strength of support; their legs were stouter, even proportionately, than the legs of the earlier species. Their feet had lost the separate toes, and, by a strengthening and growing together of the internal bones, had become more efficient instruments of locomotion. During the Siberian exile the First Men had acquired a thick hairy covering, and most races of the Second Men retained something of this blonde hirsute appearance throughout their career. Their eyes were large, and often jade green, their features firm as carved granite, yet mobile and lucent. Of the second human species one might say that Nature had at last repeated and far excelled the noble but unfortunate type which she had achieved once, long ago, with the first species, in certain prehistoric cave-dwelling hunters and artists.

Inwardly the Second Men differed from the earlier species in that they had shed most of those primitive relics which had hampered the First Men more than was realized. Not only were they free of appendix, tonsils and other useless excrescences, but also their whole structure was more firmly knit into unity. Their chemical organization was such that their tissues were kept in better repair. Their teeth, though proportionately small and few, were almost completely immune from caries. Such was their glandular equipment that puberty did not begin till twenty; and not till they were fifty did they reach maturity. At about one hundred and ninety their powers began to fail, and after a few years of contemplative retirement they almost invariably died before true senility could begin. It was as though, when a man's work was finished, and he had meditated in peace upon his whole career, there were nothing further to hold his attention and prevent him from falling asleep. Mothers carried the foetus for three years, suckled the infant for five years, and were sterile during this period and for another seven years. Their climacteric was reached at about a hundred and sixty. Architecturally massive like their mates, they would have seemed to the First Men very formidable titanesses; but even those early half-human beings would have admired the women of the second species both for their superb vitality and for their brilliantly human expression.

In temperament the Second Men were curiously different from the earlier species. The same factors were present, but in different proportions, and in far greater subordination to the considered will of the individual. Sexual vigour had returned. But sexual interest was strangely altered. Around the ancient core of delight in physical and mental contact with the opposite sex there now appeared a kind of innately sublimated, and no less poignant, appreciation of the unique physical and mental forms of all kinds of live things. It is difficult for less ample natures to imagine this expansion of the innate sexual interest; for to them it is not apparent that the lusty admiration which at first directs itself solely on the opposite sex is the appropriate attitude to all the beauties of flesh and spirit in beast and bird and plant. Parental interest also was strong in the new species, but it too was universalized. It had become a strong innate interest in, and a devotion to, all beings that were conceived as in need of help. In the earlier species this passionate spontaneous altruism occurred only in exceptional persons. In the new species, however, all normal men and women experienced altruism as a passion. And yet at the same time primitive parenthood had become tempered to a less possessive and more objective love, which among the First

Men was less common than they themselves were pleased to believe. Assertiveness had also greatly changed. Formerly very much of a man's energy had been devoted to the assertion of himself as a private individual over against other individuals; and very much of his generosity had been at bottom selfish. But in the Second Men this competitive self-assertion, this championship of the most intimately known animal against all others, was greatly tempered. Formerly the major enterprises of society would never have been carried through had they not been able to annex to themselves the egoism of their champions. But in the Second Men the parts were reversed. Few individuals could ever trouble to exert themselves to the last ounce for merely private ends, save when those ends borrowed interest or import from some public enterprise. It was only his vision of a world-wide community of persons, and of his own function therein, that could rouse the fighting spirit in a man. Thus it was inwardly, rather than in outward physical characters, that the Second Men differed from the First. And in nothing did they differ more than in their native aptitude for cosmopolitanism. They had their tribes and nations. War was not quite unknown amongst them. But even in primitive times a man's most serious loyalty was directed toward the race as a whole; and wars were so hampered by impulses of kindliness toward the enemy that they were apt to degenerate into rather violent athletic contests, leading to an orgy of fraternization.

It would not be true to say that the strongest interest of these beings was social. They were never prone to exalt the abstraction called the state, or the nation, or even the world-commonwealth. For their most characteristic factor was not mere gregariousness but something novel, namely an innate interest in personality, both in the actual diversity of persons and in the ideal of personal development. They had a remarkable power of vividly intuiting their fellows as unique persons with special needs. Individuals of the earlier species had suffered from an almost insurmountable spiritual isolation from one another. Not even lovers, and scarcely even the geniuses with special insight into personality, ever had anything like accurate vision of one another. But the Second Men, more intensely and accurately self-conscious, were also more intensely and accurately conscious of one another. This they achieved by no unique faculty, but solely by a more ready interest in each other, a finer insight, and a more active imagination.

They had also a remarkable innate interest in the higher kinds of mental activity, or rather in the subtle objects of those activities. Even children were instinctively inclined toward a genuinely aesthetic interest in their world and their own behaviour, and also toward scientific inquiry and generalization. Small boys, for instance, would delight in collecting not merely such things as eggs or crystals, but mathematical formulae expressive of the different shapes of eggs and crystals, or of the innumerable rhythms of shells, fronds, leaflets, grass-nodes. And there was a wealth of traditional fairy-stories whose appeal was grounded in philosophical puzzles. Little children delighted to hear how the poor things called Illusions were banished from the Country of the Real, how one-dimensional Mr. Line woke up in a two-dimensional world, and how a brave young tune slew cacophonous beasts and won a melodious bride in that strange country where the landscape is all of sound and all living things are music. The First Men had attained to interest in science, mathematics, philosophy, only after arduous schooling, but in the Second Men there was a natural propensity for these activities, no less vigorous than the primitive instincts. Not, of course, that they were absolved from learning; but they had the same zest and facility in these matters as their predecessors had enjoyed only in humbler spheres.

In the earlier species, indeed, the nervous system had maintained only a very precarious unity, and was all too liable to derangement by the rebellion of one of its subordinate parts. But in the second species the highest centres maintained an almost absolute harmony among the lower. Thus the moral conflict between momentary impulse and considered will, and again between private and public interest, played a very subordinate part among the Second Men.

In actual cognitive powers, also, this favoured species far outstripped its predecessor. For instance, vision had greatly developed. The Second Men distinguished in the spectrum a new primary colour between green and blue; and beyond blue they saw, not a reddish blue, but again a new primary colour, which faded with increasing ruddiness far into the old ultraviolet. These two new primary colours were complementary to one another. At the other end of the spectrum they saw the infra-red as a peculiar purple. Further, owing to the very great size of their retina, and the multiplication of rods and cones, they discriminated much smaller fractions of their field of vision.

Improved discrimination combined with a wonderful fertility of mental imagery to produce a greatly increased power of insight into the character of novel situations. Whereas among the First Men, native intelligence had increased only up to the age of fourteen, among the Second Men it progressed up to forty. Thus an average adult was capable of immediate insight into problems which even the most brilliant of the First Men could only solve by prolonged reasoning. This superb clarity of mind enabled the second species to avoid most of those age-long confusions and superstitions which had crippled its predecessor. And along with great intelligence went a remarkable flexibility of will. In fact the Second Men were far more able than the First to break habits that were seen to be no longer justified.

To sum the matter, circumstance had thrown up a very noble species. Essentially it was of the same type as the earlier species, but it had undergone extensive improvements. Much that the First Men could only achieve by long schooling and self-discipline the Second Men performed with effortless fluency and delight. In particular, two capacities which for the First Men had been unattainable ideals were now realized in every normal individual, namely the power of wholly dispassionate cognition, and the power of loving one's neighbour as oneself, without reservation. Indeed, in this respect the Second Men might be called 'Natural Christians', so readily and constantly did they love one another in the manner of Jesus, and infuse their whole social policy with loving-kindness. Early in their career they conceived the religion of love, and they were possessed by it again and again, in diverse forms, until their end. On the other hand, their gift of dispassionate cognition helped them to pass speedily to the admiration of fate. And being by nature rigorous thinkers, they were peculiarly liable to be disturbed by the conflict between their religion of love and their loyalty to fate.

Well might it seem that the stage was now set for a triumphant and rapid progress of the human spirit. But though the second human species constituted a real improvement on the first, it lacked certain faculties without which the next great mental advance could not be made.

Moreover its very excellence involved one novel defect from which the First Men were almost wholly free. In the lives of humble individuals there are many occasions when nothing but an heroic effort can wrest their private fortunes from stagnation or decline, and set them pioneering in new spheres. Among the First Men this effort was often called forth by passionate regard for self. And it was upon the tidal wave of innumerable egoisms, blindly surging in one direction, that the first species was carried forward. But, to repeat, in the Second Men self-regard was never an over-mastering motive. Only at the call of social loyalty or personal love would a man spur himself to desperate efforts. Whenever the stake appeared to be mere private advancement, he was apt to prefer peace to enterprise, the delights of sport, companionship, art or intellect, to the slavery of self-regard. And so in the long run, though the Second Men were fortunate in their almost complete immunity from the lust of power and personal ostentation (which cursed the earlier species with industrialism and militarism), and though they enjoyed long ages of idyllic peace, often upon a high cultural plane, their progress toward full self-conscious mastery of the planet was curiously slow.

2. THE INTERCOURSE OF THREE SPECIES

In a few thousand years the new species filled the region from Afghanistan to the China Sea, overran India, and penetrated far into the new Australasian continent. Its advance was less military than cultural. The remaining tribes of the First Men, with whom the new species could not normally interbreed, were unable to live up to the higher culture that flooded round them and over them. They faded out.

For some further thousands of years the Second Men remained as noble savages, then passed rapidly through the pastoral into the agricultural stage. In this era they sent an expedition across the new and gigantic Hindu Kush to explore Africa. Here it was that they came upon the sub-human descendants of the ship's crew that had sailed from Siberia millions of years earlier. These animals had spread south through America and across the new Atlantic Isthmus into Africa.

Dwarfed almost to the knees of the superior species, bent so that as often as not they used their arms as aids to locomotion, flat-headed and curiously long-snouted, these creatures were by now more baboon-like than human. Yet in the wild state they maintained a very complicated organization into castes, based on the sense of smell. Their powers of scent, indeed, had developed at the expense of their intelligence. Certain odours, which had become sacred through their very repulsiveness, were given off only by individuals having certain diseases. Such individuals were treated with respect by their fellows; and though, in fact, they were debilitated by their disease, they were so feared that no healthy individual dared resist them. The characteristic odours were themselves graded in nobility, so that those individuals who bore only the less repulsive perfume, owed respect to those in whom a widespread rotting of the body occasioned the most nauseating stench. These plagues had the special effect of stimulating reproductive activity; and this fact was one cause both of the respect felt for them, and of the immense fertility of the species, such a fertility that, in spite of plagues and obtuseness, it had flooded two continents. For though the plagues were fatal, they were slow to develop. Further, though individuals far advanced in disease were often incapable of feeding themselves, they profited by the devotion of the healthy, who were well-pleased if they also became infected.

But the most startling fact about these creatures was that many of them had become enslaved to another species. When the Second Men had penetrated further into Africa they came to a forest region where companies of diminutive monkeys resisted their intrusion. It was soon evident that any interference with the imbecile and passive sub-humans in this district was resented by the monkeys. And as the latter made use of a primitive kind of bow and poisoned arrows, their opposition was seriously inconvenient to the invaders. The use of weapons and other tools, and a remarkable co-ordination in warfare, made it clear that in intelligence this simian species had far outstripped all creatures save man. Indeed, the Second Men were now face to face with the only terrestrial species which ever evolved so far as to compete with man in versatility and practical shrewdness.

As the invaders advanced, the monkeys were seen to round up

whole flocks of the sub-men and drive them out of reach. It was noticed also that these domesticated sub-men were wholly free from the diseases that infected their wild kinsfolk, who on this account greatly despised the healthy drudges. Later it transpired that the sub-men were trained as beasts of burden by the monkeys and that their flesh was a much relished article of diet. An arboreal city of woven branches was discovered, and was apparently in course of construction, for the sub-men were dragging timber and hauling it aloft, goaded by the bone-headed spears of the monkeys. It was evident also that the authority of the monkeys was maintained less by force than by intimidation. They anointed themselves with the juice of a rare aromatic plant, which struck terror into their poor cattle, and reduced them to abject docility.

Now the invaders were only a handful of pioneers. They had come over the mountains in search of metals, which had been brought to the earth's surface during the volcanic era. An amiable race, they felt no hostility toward the monkeys, but rather amusement at their habits and ingenuity. But the monkeys resented the mere presence of these mightier beings; and, presently collecting in the tree-tops in thousands, they annihilated the party with their poisoned arrows. One man alone escaped into Asia. In a couple of years he returned, with a host. Yet this was no punitive expedition, for the bland Second Men were strangely lacking in resentment. Establishing themselves on the outskirts of the forest region, they contrived to communicate and barter with the little people of the trees, so that after a while they were allowed to enter the territory unmolested, and begin their great metallurgical survey.

A close study of the relations of these very different intelligences would be enlightening, but we have no time for it. Within their own sphere the monkeys showed perhaps a quicker wit than the men; but only within very narrow limits did their intelligence work at all. They were deft at finding new means for the better satisfaction of their appetites. But they wholly lacked self-criticism. Upon a normal outfit of instinctive needs they had developed many acquired, traditional cravings, most of which were fantastic and harmful. The Second Men, on the other hand, though often momentarily outwitted by the monkeys, were in the long run incomparably more able and more sane.

The difference between the two species is seen clearly in their reaction to metals. The Second Men sought metal solely for the carrying on of an already well-advanced civilization. But the monkeys, when for the first time they saw the bright ingots, were fascinated. They had already begun to hate the invaders for their native superiority and their material wealth; and now this jealousy combined with primitive acquisitiveness to make the slabs of copper and tin become in their eyes symbols of power. In order to remain unmolested in their work, the invaders had paid a toll of the wares of their own country, of baskets, pottery and various specially designed miniature tools. But at the sight of the crude metal, the monkeys demanded a share of this noblest product of their own land. This was readily granted, since it did away with the need of bringing goods from Asia. But the monkeys had no real use for metal. They merely hoarded it, and became increasingly avaricious. No one had respect among them who did not laboriously carry a great ingot about with him wherever he went. And after a while it came to be considered actually indecent to be seen without a slab of metal. In conversation between the sexes this symbol of refinement was always held so as to conceal the genitals.

The more metal the monkeys acquired the more they craved. Blood was often shed in disputes over the possession of hoards. But this internecine strife gave place at length to a concerted movement to prevent the whole export of metal from their land. Some even suggested that the ingots in their possession should be used for making more effective weapons, with which to expel the invaders. This policy was rejected, not merely because there were none who could work up the crude metal, but because it was generally agreed that to put such a sacred material to any kind of service would be base.

The will to be rid of the invader was augmented by a dispute about the sub-men. These abject beings were treated very harshly by their masters. Not only were they overworked, but also they were tortured in cold blood, not precisely through lust in cruelty, but through a queer sense of humour, or delight in the incongruous. For instance, it afforded the monkeys a strangely innocent and extravagant pleasure to compel these cattle to carry on their work in an erect posture, which was by now quite unnatural to them, or to eat their own excrement or even their own young. If ever these tortures roused some exceptional sub-man to rebel, the monkeys flared into contemptuous rage at such a lack of humour, so incapable were they of realizing the subjective processes of others. To one another they could, indeed, be kindly and generous; but even among themselves the imp of humour would sometimes run riot. In any matter in which an individual was misunderstood by his fellows, he was sure to be gleefully baited, and often harried to death. But in the main it was only the slave-species that suffered.

The invaders were outraged by this cruel imbecility, and ventured to protest. To the monkeys the protest was unintelligible. What were cattle for, but to be used in the service of superior beings? Evidently, the monkeys thought, the invaders were after all lacking in the finer capacities of mind, since they failed to appreciate the beauty of the fantastic.

This and other causes of friction finally led the monkeys to conceive a means of freeing themselves for ever. The Second Men had proved to be terribly liable to the diseases of their wretched sub-human kinsfolk. Only by very rigorous quarantine had they stamped out the epidemic that had revealed this fact. Now partly for revenge, but partly also through malicious delight in the topsy-turvy, the monkeys determined to make use of this human weakness. There was a certain nut, very palatable to both taco and monkeys, which grew in a remote part of the country. The monkeys had already begun to barter this nut for extra metal; and the pioneering Second Men were arranging to send caravans laden with nuts into their own country. In this situation the monkeys found their opportunity. They carefully infected large quantities of nuts with the plagues rampant among those herds of sub-men which had not been domesticated. Very soon caravans of infected nuts were scattered over Asia. The effect upon a race wholly fresh to these microbes was disastrous. Not only were the pioneering settlements wiped out, but the bulk of the species also. The sub-men themselves had become adjusted to the microbes, and even reproduced more rapidly because of them. Not so the more delicately organized species. They died off like autumn leaves. Civilization fell to pieces. In a few generations Asia was peopled only by a handful of scattered savages, all diseased and mostly crippled.

But in spite of this disaster the species remained potentially the same. Within a few centuries it had thrown off the infection and had begun once more the ascent toward civilization. After another thousand years, pioneers again crossed the mountains and entered Africa. They met with no opposition. The precarious flicker of simian intelligence had long ago ceased. The monkeys had so burdened their bodies with metal and their minds with the obsession of metal, that at length the herds of sub-human cattle were able to rebel and devour their masters.

3. THE ZENITH OF THE SECOND MEN

For nearly a quarter of a million years the Second Men passed through successive phases of prosperity and decline. Their advance to developed culture was not nearly so steady and triumphal as might have been expected from a race of such brilliance. As with individuals, so with species, accidents are all too likely to defeat even the most cautious expectations. For instance, the Second Men were for a long time seriously hampered by a 'glacial epoch' which at its height imposed Arctic conditions even as far south as India. Little by little the encroaching ice crowded their tribes into the extremity of that peninsula, and reduced their culture to the level of the Esquimaux. In time, of course, they recovered, but only to suffer other scourges, of which the most devastating were epidemics of bacteria. The more recently developed and highly organized tissues of this species were peculiarly susceptible to disease, and not once but many times a promising barbarian culture or 'medieval' civilization was wiped out by plagues.

But of all the natural disasters which befell the Second Men, the worst was due to a spontaneous change in their own physical constitution. Just as the fangs of the ancient sabre-toothed tiger had finally grown so large that the beast could not eat, so the brain of the second human species threatened to outgrow the rest of its body. In a cranium that was originally roomy enough, this rare product of nature was now increasingly cramped; while a circulatory system, that was formerly quite adequate, was becoming more and more liable to fail in pumping blood through so cramped a structure. These two causes at last began to take serious effect. Congenital imbecility became increasingly common, along with all manner of acquired mental diseases. For some thousands of years the race remained in a most precarious condition, now almost dying out, now rapidly attaining an extravagant kind of culture in some region where physical nature happened to be peculiarly favourable. One of these precarious flashes of spirit occurred in the Yangtze valley as a sudden and brief effulgence of city states peopled by neurotics, geniuses and imbeciles. The lasting upshot of this civilization was a brilliant literature of despair, dominated by a sense of the difference between the actual and the potential in man and the universe. Later, when the race had attained its noontide glory, it was wont to brood upon this tragic voice from the past in order to remind itself of the underlying horror of existence.

Meanwhile, brains became more and more overgrown, and the race more and more disorganized. There is no doubt that it would have gone the way of the sabre-toothed tiger, simply through the fatal direction of its own physiological evolution, had not a more stable variety of this second human species at last appeared. It was in North America, into which, by way of Africa, the Second Men had long ago spread, that the roomier-skulled and stronger-hearted type first occurred. By great good fortune this new variety proved to be a dominant Mendelian character. And as it interbred freely with the older variety, a superbly healthy race soon peopled America. The species was saved.

But another hundred thousand years were to pass before the Second Men could reach their zenith. I must not dwell on this movement of the human symphony, though it is one of great richness. Inevitably many themes are now repeated from the career of the earlier species, but with special features, and transposed, so to speak, from the minor to the major key. Once more primitive cultures succeed one another, or pass into civilization, barbarian or 'medieval'; and in turn these fall or are transformed. Twice, indeed, the planet became the home of a single world-wide community which endured for many thousands of years, until misfortune wrecked it. The collapse is not altogether surprising, for unlike the earlier species, the Second Men had no coal and oil. In both these early world societies of the Second Men there was a complete lack of mechanical power. Consequently, though world-wide and intricate, they were in a manner 'medieval'. In every continent intensive and highly skilled agriculture crept from the valleys up the mountain sides and over the irrigated deserts. In the rambling garden-cities each citizen took his share of drudgery, practised also some fine handicraft, and yet had leisure for gaiety and contemplation. Intercourse within and between the five great continental communities had to be maintained by coaches, caravans and sailing ships. Sail, indeed, now came back into its own, and far surpassed its previous achievements. On every sea, fleets of great populous red-sailed clippers, wooden, with carved poops and prows, but with the sleek flanks of the dolphin carried the produce of every land, and the many travellers who delighted to spend a sabbatical year among foreigners.

So much, in the fullness of time, could be achieved, even without mechanical power, by a species gifted with high intelligence and immune from anti-social self-regard. But inevitably there came an end. A virus, whose subtle derangement of the glandular system was never suspected by a race still innocent of physiology, propagated throughout the world a mysterious fatigue. Century by century, agriculture withdrew from the hills and deserts, craftsmanship deteriorated, thought became stereotyped. And the vast lethargy produced a vast despond. At length the nations lost touch with one another, forgot one another, forgot their culture, crumbled into savage tribes. Once more Earth slept.

Many thousand years later, long after the disease was spent, several great peoples developed in isolation. When at last they made contact, they were so alien that in each there had to occur a difficult cultural revolution, not unaccompanied by bloodshed, before the world could once more feel as one. But this second world order endured only a few centuries, for profound subconscious differences now made it impossible for the races to keep wholeheartedly loyal to each other. Religion finally severed the unity which all willed but none could trust. An heroic nation of monotheists sought to impose its faith on a vaguely pantheist world. For the first and last time the Second Men stumbled into a world-wide civil war; and just because the war was religious it developed a brutality hitherto unknown. With crude artillery, but with fanaticism, the two groups of citizen armies harried one another. The fields were laid waste, the cities burned, the rivers, and finally the winds were poisoned. Long after that pitch of horror had been passed, at which an inferior species would have lost heart, these heroic madmen continued to organize destruction. And when at last the inevitable breakdown came, it was the more complete. In a sensitive species the devastating enlightenment which at last began to invade every mind, the overwhelming sense of treason against the human spirit, the tragic comicality of the whole struggle, sapped all energy. Not for thousands of years did the Second Men achieve once more a world-community. But they had learnt their lesson.

The third and most enduring civilization of the Second Men repeated the glorified medievalism of the first, and passed beyond it into a phase of brilliant natural science. Chemical fertilizers increased the crops, and therefore the world population. Wind and water-power was converted into electricity to supplement human and animal labour. At length, after many failures, it became possible to use volcanic and subterranean energy to drive dynamos. In a few years the whole physical character of civilization was transformed. Yet in this headlong passage into industrialism the Second Men escaped the errors of ancient Europe, America and Patagonia. This was due partly to their greater gift of sympathy, which, save during the one great aberration of the religious war, made them all in a very vivid manner members one of another. But partly also it was due to their combination of a practical common sense that was more than British, with a more than Russian immunity from the glamour of wealth, and a passion for the life of the mind that even Greece had never known. Mining and manufacture, even with plentiful electric power, were occupations scarcely less arduous than of old; but since each individual was implicated by vivid sympathy in the lives of all persons within his ken, there was little or no obsession with private economic power. The will to avoid industrial evils was effective, because sincere.

At its height, the culture of the Second Men was dominated by respect for the individual human personality. Yet contemporary individuals were regarded both as end and as means, as a stage toward far ampler individuals in the remote future. For, although they themselves were more long-lived than their predecessors, the

Second Men were oppressed by the brevity of human life, and the pettiness of the individual's achievement in comparison with the infinity round about him which awaited apprehension and admiration. Therefore they were determined to produce a race endowed with much greater natural longevity. Again, though they participated in one another far more than their predecessors, they themselves were dogged by despair at the distortion and error which spoiled every mind's apprehension of others. Like their predecessors, they had passed through all the more naïve phases of self-consciousness and other-consciousness, and through idealizations of various modes of personality. They had admired the barbarian hero, the romantical, the sensitive-subtle, the bluff and hearty, the decadent, the bland, the severe. And they had concluded that each person, while being himself an expression of some one mode of personality, should seek to be also sensitive to every other mode. They even conceived that the ideal community should be knit into one mind by each unique individual's direct telepathic apprehension of the experience of all his fellows. And the fact that this ideal seemed utterly unattainable wove through their whole culture a thread of darkness, a yearning for spiritual union, a horror of loneliness, which never seriously troubled their far more insulated predecessors.

This craving for union influenced the sexual life of the species. In the first place, so closely was the mental related to the physiological in their composition, that when there was no true union of minds, the sexual act failed to give conception. Casual sexual relations thus came to be regarded very differently from those which expressed a deeper intimacy. They were treated as a delightful embroidery on life, affording opportunity of much elegance, light-hearted tenderness, banter, and of course physical inebriation; but they were deemed to signify nothing more than the delight of friend in friend. Where there was a marriage of minds, but then only during the actual passion of communion, sexual intercourse almost always resulted in conception. Under these circumstances, intimate persons had often to practise contraception, but acquaintances never. And one of the most beneficial inventions of the psychologists was a technique of autosuggestion, which, at will, either facilitated conception, or prevented it, surely, harmlessly, and without inaesthetic accompaniments.

The sexual morality of the Second Men passed through all the phases known to the First Men; but by the time that they had established a single world-culture it had a form not known before. Not only were both men and women encouraged to have as much casual sexual intercourse as they needed for their enrichment, but also, on the higher plane of spiritual union, strict monogamy was deprecated. For in sexual union of this higher kind they saw a symbol of that communion of minds which they longed to make universal. Thus the most precious gift that a lover could bring to the beloved was not virginity but sexual experience. The union, it was felt, was the more pregnant the more each party could contribute from previous sexual and spiritual intimacy with others. Yet though as a principle monogamy was not applauded, the higher kind of union would in practice sometimes result in a life-long partnership. But since the average life was so much longer than among the First Men, such fortuitously perennial unions were often deliberately interrupted for a while, by a change of partners, and then restored with their vitality renewed. Sometimes, on the other hand, a group of persons of both sexes would maintain a composite and permanent marriage together. Sometimes such a group would exchange a member, or members, with another group, or disperse itself completely among other groups, to come together again years afterwards with enriched experience. In one form or another, this 'marriage of groups' was much prized, as an extension of the vivid sexual participation into an ampler sphere. Among the First Men the brevity of life made these novel forms of union impossible; for obviously no sexual, and no spiritual, relation can be developed with any richness in less than thirty years of close intimacy. It would be interesting to examine the social institutions of the Second Men at their zenith; but we have not time to spare for this subject, nor even for the brilliant intellectual achievements in which the species so far outstripped its predecessor. Obviously any account of the natural science and the philosophy of the Second Men would be unintelligible to readers of this book. Suffice it that they avoided the errors which had led the First Men into false abstraction, and into metaphysical theories which were at once sophisticated and naïve.

Not until after they had passed beyond the best work of the First Men in science and philosophy did the Second Men discover the remains of the great stone library in Siberia. A party of engineers happened upon it while they were preparing to sink a shaft for subterranean energy. The tablets were broken, disordered, weathered. Little by little, however, they were reconstructed and interpreted, with the aid of the pictorial dictionary. The finds were of extreme interest to the Second Men, but not in the manner which the Siberian party had intended, not as a store of scientific and philosophic truth, but as a vivid historical document. The view of the universe which the tablets recorded was both too naïve and too artificial; but the insight which they afforded into the mind of the earlier species was invaluable. So little of the old world had survived the volcanic epoch that the Second Men had failed hitherto to get a clear picture of their predecessors.

One item alone in this archaeological treasure had more than historical interest. The biologist leader of the little party in Siberia had recorded much of the sacred text of the Life of the Divine Boy. At the end of the record came the prophet's last words, which had so baffled Patagonia. This theme was full of meaning for the Second Men, as indeed it would have been even for the First Men in their prime. But whereas for the First Men the dispassionate ecstasy which the Boy had preached was rather an ideal than a fact of experience, the Second Men recognized in the prophet's words an intuition familiar to themselves. Long ago the tortured geniuses of the Yangtze cities had expressed this same intuition. Subsequently also it had often been experienced by the more healthy generations, but always with a certain shame. For it had become associated with morbid mentality. But now with growing conviction that it was wholesome, the Second Men had begun to grope for a wholesome expression of it. In the life and the last words of the remote apostle of youth they found an expression which was not wholly inadequate. The species was presently to be in sore need of this gospel.

The world community reached at length a certain relative perfection and equilibrium. There was a long summer of social harmony, prosperity, and cultural embellishment. Almost all that could be done by mind in the stage to which it had then reached seemed to have been done. Generations of long-lived, eager, and mutually delightful beings succeeded one another. There was a widespread feeling that the time had come for man to gather all his strength for a flight into some new sphere of mentality. The present type of human being, it was recognized, was but a rough and incoherent natural product. It was time for man to take control of himself and remake himself upon a nobler pattern. With this end in view, two great works were set afoot, research into the ideal of human nature, and research into practical means of remaking human nature. Individuals in all lands, living their private lives, delighting in each other, keeping the tissue of society alive and vigorous, were deeply moved by the thought that their world community was at last engaged upon this heroic task.

But elsewhere in the solar system life of a very different kind was seeking, in its own strange manner, ends incomprehensible to man, yet at bottom identical with his own ends. And presently the two were to come together, not in co-operation.

CHAPTER VIII

THE MARTIANS

1. THE FIRST MARTIAN INVASION

Upon the foothills of the new and titanic mountains that were once the Hindu Kush, were many holiday centres, whence the young men and women of Asia were wont to seek Alpine dangers and hardships for their souls' refreshment. It was in this district, and shortly after a summer dawn, that the Martians were first seen by men. Early walkers noticed that the sky had an unaccountably greenish tinge, and that the climbing sun, though free from cloud, was wan. Observers were presently surprised to see the green concentrate itself into a thousand tiny cloudlets, with clear blue between. Field-glasses revealed within each fleck of green some faint hint of a ruddy nucleus, and shifting strands of an infra-red colour, which would have been invisible to the earlier human race. These extraordinary specks of cloud were all of about the same size, the largest of them appearing smaller than the moon's disk; but in form they varied greatly, and were seen to be changing their shapes more rapidly than the natural cirrus which they slightly resembled. In fact, though there was much that was cloud-like in their form and motion, there was also something definite about them, both in their features and behaviour, which suggested life. Indeed they were strongly reminiscent of primitive amoeboid organisms seen through a microscope.

The whole sky was strewn with them, here and there in concentrations of unbroken green, elsewhere more sparsely. And they were observed to be moving. A general drift of the whole celestial population was setting toward one of the snowy peaks that dominated the landscape. Presently the foremost individuals reached the mountain's crest, and were seen to be creeping down the rock-face with a very slow amoeboid action.

Meanwhile a couple of aeroplanes, electrically driven, had climbed the sky to investigate the strange phenomenon at close quarters. They passed among the drifting cloudlets, and actually through many of them, without hindrance, and almost without being obscured from view.

On the mountain a vast swarm of the cloudlets was collecting, and creeping down the precipices and snow-fields into a high glacier valley. At a certain point, where the glacier dropped steeply to a lower level, the advance guard slowed down and stopped, while hosts of their fellows continued to pack in on them from behind. In half an hour the whole sky was once more clear, save for normal clouds; but upon the glacier lay what might almost have been an exceptionally dark solid-looking thunder-cloud, save for its green tinge and seething motion. For some minutes this strange object was seen to concentrate itself into a somewhat smaller bulk and become darker. Then it moved forward again, and passed over the cliffy end of the glacier into the pine-clad valley. An intervening ridge now hid it from its first observers.

Lower down the valley there was a village. Many of the inhabitants, when they saw the mysterious dense fume advancing upon them, took to their mechanical vehicles and fled; but some waited out of curiosity. They were swallowed up in a murky olive-brown fog, shot here and there with queer shimmering streaks of a ruddier tint. Presently there was complete darkness. Artificial lights were blotted out almost at arm's length. Breathing became difficult. Throats and lungs were irritated. Every one was seized with a violent attack of sneezing and coughing. The cloud streamed through the village, and seemed to exercise irregular pressures upon objects, not always in the general direction of movement but sometimes in the opposite direction, as though it were getting a purchase upon human bodies and walls, and actually elbowing its way along. Within a few minutes the fog lightened; and presently it left the village behind it, save for a few strands and whiffs of its smoke-like substance, which had become entangled in side-streets and isolated. Very soon, however, these seemed to get themselves clear and hurry to overtake the main body.

When the gasping villagers had somewhat recovered, they

sent a radio message to the little town lower down the valley, urging temporary evacuation. The message was not broadcast, but transmitted on a slender beam of rays. It so happened that the beam had to be directed through the noxious matter itself. While the message was being given, the cloud's progress ceased, and its outlines became vague and ragged. Fragments of it actually drifted away on the winds and dissipated themselves. Almost as soon as the message was completed, the cloud began to define itself again, and lay for a quarter of an hour at rest. A dozen bold young men from the town now approached the dark mass out of curiosity. No sooner did they come face to face with it, round a bend in the valley, than the cloud rapidly contracted, till it was no bigger than a house. Looking now something between a dense, opaque fume and an actual jelly, it lay still until the party had ventured within a few yards. Evidently their courage failed, for they were seen to turn. But before they had retreated three paces, a long proboscis shot out of the main mass with the speed of a chameleon's tongue, and enveloped them. Slowly it withdrew; but the young men had been gathered in with it. The cloud, or jelly, churned itself violently for some seconds, then ejected the bodies in a single chewed lump.

The murderous thing now elbowed itself along the road toward the town, leaned against the first house, crushed it, and proceeded to wander hither and thither, pushing everything down before it, as though it were a lava-stream. The inhabitants took to their heels, but several were licked up and slaughtered.

Powerful beam radiation was now poured into the cloud from all the neighbouring installations. Its destructive activity slackened, and once more it began to disintegrate and expand. Presently it streamed upwards as a huge column of smoke; and, at a great altitude, it dissipated itself again into a swarm of the original green cloudlets, noticeably reduced in numbers. These again faded into a uniform greenish tinge, which gradually vanished.

Thus ended the first invasion of the Earth from Mars.

2. LIFE ON MARS

Our concern is with humanity, and with the Martians only in relation to men. But in order to understand the tragic intercourse of the two planets, it is necessary to glance at conditions on Mars, and conceive something of those fantastically different yet fundamentally similar beings, who were now seeking to possess man's home.

To describe the biology, psychology and history of a whole world in a few pages is as difficult as it would be to give the Martians themselves in the same compass a true idea of man. Encyclopaedias, libraries, would be needed in either case. Yet, somehow, I must contrive to suggest the alien sufferings and delights, and the many aeons of struggle, which went to the making of these strange non-human intelligences, in some ways so inferior yet in others definitely superior to the human species which they encountered.

Mars was a world whose mass was about one-tenth that of the earth. Gravity therefore had played a less tyrannical part in Martian than in terrestrial history. The weakness of Martian gravity combined with the paucity of the planet's air envelope to make the general atmospheric pressure far lighter than on earth. Oxygen was far less plentiful. Water also was comparatively rare. There were no oceans or seas, but only shallow lakes and marshes, many of which dried up in summer. The climate of the planet was in general very dry, and yet very cold. Being without cloud, it was perennially bright with the feeble rays of a distant sun.

Earlier in the history of Mars, when there were more air, more water, and a higher temperature from internal heat, life had appeared in the coastal waters of the seas, and evolution had proceeded in much the same manner as on earth. Primitive life was differentiated into the fundamental animal and vegetable types. Multicellular structures appeared, and specialized themselves in diverse manners to suit diverse environments. A great variety of plant forms clothed the lands, often with forests of gigantic and slender-stemmed plumes. Mollusc-like and insect-like animals crept or swam, or shot themselves hither and thither in fantastic jumps. Huge spidery creatures of a type not wholly unlike crustaceans, or gigantic grasshoppers, bounded after their prey, and developed a versatility and cunning which enabled them to dominate the planet almost as, at a much later date, early man was to dominate the terrestrial wild.

But meanwhile a rapid loss of atmosphere, and especially of water vapour, was changing Martian conditions beyond the limits of adaptability of this early fauna and flora. At the same time a very different kind of vital organization was beginning to profit by the change. On Mars, as on the Earth, life had arisen from one of many 'subvital' forms. The new type of life on Mars evolved from another of these subvital kinds of molecular organization, one which had hitherto failed to evolve at all, and had played an insignificant part, save occasionally as a rare virus in the respiratory organs of animals. These fundamental subvital units of organization were ultra-microscopic, and indeed far smaller than the terrestrial bacteria, or even the terrestrial viruses. They originally occurred in the marshy ponds, which dried up every spring, and became depressions of baked mud and dust. Certain of their species, borne into the air upon dust particles, developed an extremely dry habit of life. They maintained themselves by absorbing chemicals from the wind-borne dust, and a very slight amount of moisture from the air. Also they absorbed sunlight by a photosynthesis almost identical with that of the Plants.

To this extent they were similar to the other living things, but they had also certain capacities which the other stock had lost at the very outset of its evolutionary career. Terrestrial organisms, and Martian organisms of the terrestrial type, maintained themselves as vital unities by means of nervous systems, or other forms of material contact between parts. In the most developed forms, an immensely complicated neural 'telephone' system connected every part of the body with a vast central exchange, the brain. Thus on the earth a single organism was without exception a continuous system of matter, which maintained a certain constancy of form. But from the distinctively Martian subvital unit there evolved at length a very different kind of complex organism, in which material contact of parts was not necessary either to co-ordination of behaviour or unity of consciousness. These ends were achieved upon a very different physical basis. The ultra-microscopic subvital members were sensitive to all kinds of etherial vibrations, directly sensitive, in a manner impossible to terrestrial life; and they could also initiate vibrations. Upon this basis Martian life developed at length the capacity of maintaining vital organization as a single conscious individual without continuity of living matter. Thus the typical

Martian organism was a cloudlet, a group of free-moving members dominated by a 'group-mind'. But in one species individuality came to inhere, for certain purposes, not in distinct cloudlets only, but in a great fluid system of cloudlets. Such was the single-minded Martian host which invaded the Earth.

The Martian organism depended, so to speak, not on 'telephone' wires, but on an immense crowd of mobile 'wireless stations', transmitting and receiving different wave-lengths according to their function. The radiation of a single unit was of course very feeble; but a great system of units could maintain contact with its wandering parts over a considerable distance.

One other important characteristic distinguished the dominant form of life on Mars. Just as a cell, in the terrestrial form of life, has often the power of altering its shape (whence the whole mechanism of muscular activity), so in the Martian form the free-floating ultra-microscopic unit might be specialized for generating around itself a magnetic field, and so either repelling or attracting its neighbours. Thus a system of materially disconnected units had a certain cohesion. Its consistency was something between a smoke-cloud and a very tenuous jelly. It had a definite, though ever-changing contour and resistant surface. By massed mutual repulsions of its constituent units it could exercise pressure on surrounding objects; and in its most concentrated form the Martian cloud-jelly could bring to bear immense forces which could also be controlled for very delicate manipulation. Magnetic forces were also responsible for the mollusc-like motion of the cloud as a whole over the ground, and again for the transport of lifeless material and living units from region to region within the cloud.

The magnetic field of repulsion and attraction generated by a subvital unit was much more restricted than its field of 'wireless' communication. Similarly with organized systems of units. Thus each of the cloudlets which the Second Men saw in their sky was an independent motor unit; but also it was in a kind of 'telepathic' communication with all its fellows. Indeed in every public enterprise, such as the terrestrial campaigns, almost perfect unity of consciousness was maintained within the limits of a huge field of radiation. Yet only when the whole population concentrated

itself into a small and relatively dense cloud-jelly, did it become
a single magnetic motor unit. The Martians, it should be noted,
had three possible forms, or formations, namely: first, an 'open
order' of independent and very tenuous cloudlets in 'telepathic'
communication, and often in strict unity as a group mind; second, a
more concentrated and less vulnerable corporate cloud; and third, an
extremely concentrated and formidable cloud-jelly.

Save for these very remarkable characteristics, there was no
really fundamental difference between the distinctively Martian
and the distinctively terrestrial forms of life. The chemical basis of
the former was somewhat more complicated than that of the latter;
and selenium played a part in it, to which nothing corresponded
in terrestrial life. The Martian organism, moreover, was unique
in that it fulfilled within itself the functions of both animal and
vegetable. But, save for these peculiarities, the two types of life
were biochemically much the same. Both needed material from the
ground, both needed sunlight. Each lived in the chemical changes
occurring in its own 'flesh'. Each, of course, tended to maintain
itself as an organic unity. There was a certain difference, indeed, in
respect of reproduction; for the Martian subvital units retained the
power of growth and sub-division. Thus the birth of a Martian cloud
arose from the sub-division of myriads of units within the parent
cloud, followed by their ejection as a new individual. And, as the
units were highly specialized for different functions, representatives
of many types had to pass into the new cloud.

In the earliest stages of evolution on Mars the units had become
independent of each other as soon as they parted in reproduction.
But later the hitherto useless and rudimentary power of emitting
radiation was specialized, so that, after reproduction, free
individuals came to maintain radiant contact with one another,
and to behave with ever-increasing co-ordination. Still later,
these organized groups themselves maintained radiant contact
with groups of their offspring, thus constituting larger individuals
with specialized members. With each advance in complexity the
sphere of radiant influence increased; until, at the zenith of Martian
evolution, the whole planet (save for the remaining animal and
vegetable representatives of the other and unsuccessful kind of

life) constituted sometimes a single biological and psychological individual. But this occurred as a rule only in respect of matters which concerned the species as a whole. At most times the Martian individual was a cloudlet, such as those which first astonished the Second Men. But in great public crises each cloudlet would suddenly wake up to find himself the mind of the whole race, sensing through many individuals, and interpreting his sensations in the light of the experience of the whole race.

The life which dominated Mars was thus something between an extremely well-disciplined army of specialized units, and a body possessed by one mind. Like an army, it could take any form without destroying its organic unity. Like an army it was sometimes a crowd of free-wandering units, yet at other times also it disposed itself in very special orders to fulfil special functions. Like an army it was composed of free, experiencing individuals who voluntarily submitted themselves to discipline. On the other hand, unlike an army, it woke occasionally into unified consciousness.

The same fluctuation between individuality and multiplicity which characterized the race as a whole, characterized also each of the cloudlets themselves. Each was sometimes an individual, sometimes a swarm of more primitive individuals. But while the race rather seldom rose to full individuality, the cloudlets declined from it only in very special circumstances. Each cloudlet was an organization of specialized groups formed of minor specialized groups, which in turn were composed of the fundamental specialized varieties of subvital units. Each free-roving group of free-roving units constituted a special organ, fulfilling some particular function in the whole. Thus some were specialized for attraction and repulsion, some for chemical operations, some for storing the sun's energy, some for emitting radiation, some for absorbing and storing water, some for special sensitivities, such as awareness of mechanical pressure and vibration, or temperature changes, or light rays. Others again were specialized to fulfil the function of the brain of man; but in a peculiar manner. The whole volume of the cloudlet vibrated with innumerable 'wireless' messages in very many wavelengths from the different 'organs'. It was the function of the 'brain' units to receive, and correlate, and interpret these messages in the light of past experience, and to initiate responses in the wave-lengths appropriate to the organs concerned.

All these subvital units, save a few types that were too highly specialized, were capable of independent life as air-borne bacteria or viruses. And whenever they lost touch with the radiation of the whole system, they continued to live their own simple lives until they were once more controlled. All were free-floating units, but normally they were under the influence of the cloudlet's system of electro-magnetic fields, and were directed hither and thither for their special functions. And under this influence some of them might be held rigidly in position in relation to one another. Such was the case of the organs of sight. In early stages of evolution, some of the units had specialized for carrying minute globules of water. Later, much larger droplets were carried, millions of units holding between them a still microscopic globule of life's most precious fluid. Ultimately this function was turned to good account in vision. Aqueous lenses as large as the eye of an ox, were supported by a scaffolding of units; while, at focal length from the lens, a rigid retina of units was held in position. Thus the Martian could produce eyes of every variety whenever he wanted them, and telescopes and microscopes too. This production and manipulation of visual organs was of course largely subconscious, like the focussing mechanism in man. But latterly the Martians had greatly increased their conscious control of physiological processes; and it was this achievement which facilitated their remarkable optical triumphs.

One other physiological function we must note before considering the Martian psychology. The fully evolved, but as yet uncivilized, Martian had long ago ceased to depend for his chemicals on wind -borne volcanic dust. Instead, he rested at night on the ground, like a knee-high mist on terrestrial meadows, and projected specialized tubular groups of units into the soil, like rootlets. Part of the day also had to be occupied in this manner. Somewhat later this process was supplemented by devouring the declining plant-life of the planet. But the final civilized Martians had greatly improved their methods of exploiting the ground and the sunlight, both by mechanical means and by artificial specialization of their own organs. Even so, however, as their activities increased, these vegetable functions became an ever more serious problem for them. They practised agriculture; but only a very small area of the arid planet could be induced to bear. It was terrestrial water and terrestrial vegetation that finally determined them to make the great voyage.

3. THE MARTIAN MIND

The Martian mind was of a very different type from the terrestrial – different, yet at bottom identical. In so strange a body, the mind was inevitably equipped with alien cravings, and alien manners of apprehending its environment. And with so different a history, it was confused by prejudices very unlike those of man. Yet it was none the less mind, concerned in the last resort with the maintenance and advancement of life, and the exercise of vital capacities. Fundamentally the Martian was like all other living beings, in that he delighted in the free working of his body and his mind. Yet superficially, he was as unlike man in mind as in body.

The most distinctive feature of the Martian, compared with man, was that his individuality was both far more liable to disruption, and at the same time immeasurably more capable of direct participation in the minds of other individuals. The human mind in its solid body maintained its unity and its dominance over its members in all normal circumstances. Only in disease was man liable to mental or physical dissociation. On the other hand, he was incapable of direct contact with other individuals, and the emergence of a 'super-mind' in a group of individuals was quite impossible. The Martian cloudlet, however, though he fell to pieces physically, and also mentally, far more readily than a man, might also at any moment wake up to be the intelligent mind of his race, might begin to perceive with the sense-organs of all other individuals, and experience thoughts and desires which were, so to speak, the resultant of all individual thoughts and desires upon some matter of general interest. But unfortunately, as I shall tell, the common mind of the Martians never woke into any order of mentality higher than that of the individual.

These differences between the Martian and the human psyche entailed characteristic advantages and disadvantages. The Martian, immune from man's inveterate selfishness and spiritual isolation from his fellows, lacked the mental coherence, the concentrated

attention and far-reaching analysis and synthesis, and again the
vivid self-consciousness and relentless self-criticism, which even
the First Men, at their best, had attained in some degree, and
which in the Second Men were still more developed. The Martians,
moreover, were hampered by being almost identical in character.
They possessed perfect harmony; but only through being almost
wholly in temperamental unison. They were all hobbled by their
sameness to one another. They were without that rich diversity of
personal character, which enabled the human spirit to cover so wide
a field of mentality. This infinite variety of human nature entailed,
indeed, endless wasteful and cruel personal conflicts in the first,
and even to some extent in the second, species of man; but also
it enabled every individual of developed sympathy to enrich his
spirit by intercourse with individuals whose temperament, thought
and ideals differed from his own. And while the Martians were little
troubled by internecine strife and the passion of hate, they were also
almost wholly devoid of the passion of love. The Martian individual
could admire, and be utterly faithful to, the object of his loyalty; but
his admiration was given, not to concrete and uniquely charactered
persons of the same order as himself, but at best to the vaguely
conceived 'spirit of the race'. Individuals like himself he regarded
merely as instruments or organs of the 'supermind'.

This would not have been amiss, had the mind of the race, into
which he so frequently awoke under the influence of the general
radiation, been indeed a mind of higher rank than his own. But it was
not. It was but a pooling of the percipience and thought and will of
the cloudlets. Thus it was that the superb loyalty of the Martians was
squandered upon something which was not greater than themselves
in mental calibre, but only in mere bulk.

The Martian cloudlet, like the human animal, had a complex
instinctive nature. By night and day, respectively, he was impelled
to perform the vegetative functions of absorbing chemicals from the
ground and energy from the sunlight. Air and water he also craved,
though he dealt with them, of course, in his own manner. He had
also his own characteristic instinctive impulses to move his 'body',
both for locomotion and manipulation. Martian civilization provided
an outlet for these cravings, both in the practice of agriculture and

in intricate and wonderfully beautiful cloud-dances and gymnastics. For these perfectly supple beings rejoiced in executing aerial evolutions, flinging out wild rhythmical streamers, intertwining with one another in spirals, concentrating into opaque spheres, cubes, cones, and all sorts of fantastical volumes. Many of these movements and shapes had intense emotional significance for them in relation to the operations of their life, and were executed with a religious fervour and solemnity.

The Martian had also his impulses of fear and pugnacity. In the remote past these had often been directed against hostile members of his own species; but since the race had become unified, they found exercise only upon other types of life and upon inanimate nature. Instinctive gregariousness was, of course, extremely developed in the Martian at the expense of instinctive self-assertion. Sexuality the Martian had not; there were no partners in reproduction. But his impulse to merge physically and mentally with other individuals, and wake up as the super-mind, had in it much that was characteristic of sex in man. Parental impulses, of a kind, he knew; but they were scarcely worthy of the name. He cared only to eject excessive living matter from his system, and to keep *en rapport* with the new individual thus formed, as he would with any other individual. He knew no more of the human devotion to children as budding personalities than of the subtle intercourse of male and female temperaments. By the time of the first invasion, however, reproduction had been greatly restricted; for the planet was fully populated, and each individual cloudlet was potentially immortal. Among the Martians there was no 'natural death', no spontaneous death through mere senility. Normally the cloudlet's members kept themselves in repair indefinitely by the reproduction of their constituent units. Diseases, indeed, were often fatal. And chief among them was a plague, corresponding to terrestrial cancer, in which the subvital units lost their sensitivity to radiation, so that they proceeded to live as primitive organisms and reproduced without restraint. As they also became parasitic on the unaffected units, the cloudlet inevitably died.

Like the higher kinds of terrestrial mammal, the Martians had strong impulses of curiosity. Having also many practical needs to fulfil as a result of their civilization, and being extremely well equipped by nature for physical experiment and microscopy, they had gone far in the natural sciences. In physics, astronomy, chemistry and even in the chemistry of life, man had nothing to teach them.

The vast corpus of Martian knowledge had taken many thousands of years to grow. All its stages, and its current achievements were recorded on immense scrolls of paper made from vegetable pulp, and stored in libraries of stone. For the Martians, curiously enough, had become great masons, and had covered much of their planet with buildings of feathery and toppling design, such as would have been quite impossible on earth. They had no need of buildings for habitation, save in the arctic regions; but as workshops, granaries, and store rooms of all sorts, buildings had become very necessary to the Martians. Moreover these extremely tenuous creatures took a peculiar joy in manipulating solids. Even their most utilitarian architecture blossomed with a sort of gothic or arabesque ornateness and fantasy, wherein the ethereal seemed to torture the substance of solid rocks into its own likeness.

At the time of the invasion, the Martians were still advancing intellectually; and, indeed, it was through an achievement in theoretical physics that they were able to leave their planet. They had long known that minute particles at the upper limit of the atmosphere might be borne into space by the pressure of the sun's rays at dawn and sunset. And at length they discovered how to use this pressure as the wind is used in sailing. Dissipating themselves into their ultra-microscopic units, they contrived to get a purchase on the gravitational fields of the solar system, as a boat's keel and rudder get a purchase on the water. Thus they were able to tack across to the earth as an armada of ultra-microscopic vessels. Arrived in the terrestrial sky, they re-formed themselves as cloudlets, swam through the dense air to the alpine summit, and climbed downwards, as a swimmer may climb down a ladder under water.

This achievement involved very intricate calculations and chemical inventions, especially for the preservation of life in transit and on an alien planet. It could never have been done save by beings with far-reaching and accurate knowledge of the physical world. But though in respect of 'natural knowledge' the Martians were so well advanced, they were extremely backward in all those spheres which may be called 'spiritual knowledge'. They had little understanding of their own mentality, and less of the place of mind in the cosmos. Though in a sense a highly intelligent species, they were at the same time wholly lacking in philosophical interest. They scarcely conceived, still less tackled, the problems which even the First Men had faced so often, though so vainly. For the Martians there was no mystery in the distinction between reality and appearance or in the relation of the one and the many, or in the status of good and evil. Nor were they ever critical of their own ideals. They aimed whole-heartedly at the advancement of the Martian super-individual. But what should constitute individuality, and its advancement, they never seriously considered. And the idea that they were under obligation also toward beings not included in the Martian system of radiation, proved wholly beyond them. For, though so clever, they were the most naïve of self-deceivers, and had no insight to see what it is that is truly desirable.

4. DELUSIONS OF THE MARTIANS

To understand how the Martians tricked themselves, and how they were finally undone by their own insane will, we must glance at their history.

The civilized Martians constituted the sole remaining variety of a species. That species itself, in the remote past, had competed with, and exterminated, many other species of the same general type. Aided by the changing climate, it had also exterminated almost all the species of the more terrestrial kind of fauna, and had thereby much reduced the vegetation which it was subsequently to need and foster so carefully. This victory of the species had been due partly to its versatility and intelligence, partly to a remarkable zest in ferocity, partly to its unique powers of radiation and sensitivity to radiation, which enabled it to act with a co-ordination impossible even to the most gregarious of animals. But, as with other species in biological history, the capacity by which it triumphed became at length a source of weakness. When the species reached a stage corresponding to primitive human culture, one of its races, achieving a still higher degree of radiant intercourse and physical unity, was able to behave as a single vital unit; and so it succeeded in exterminating all its rivals. Racial conflict had persisted for many thousands of years, but as soon as the favoured race had developed this almost absolute solidarity of will, its victory was sweeping, and was clinched by joyous massacre of the enemy.

But ever afterwards the Martians suffered from the psychological effects of their victory at the close of the epoch of racial wars. The extreme brutality with which the other races had been exterminated conflicted with the generous impulses which civilization had begun to foster, and left a scar upon the conscience of the victors. In self-defence they persuaded themselves that since they were so much more admirable than the rest, the extermination was actually a sacred duty. And their unique value, they said, consisted in their unique radiational development. Hence arose a gravely insincere tradition and culture, which finally ruined the species. They had long believed that the physical basis of consciousness must necessarily be a system of units directly sensitive to ethereal vibrations, and that organisms dependent on the physical contact of their parts were too gross to have any experience whatever. After the age of the racial massacres they sought to persuade themselves that the excellence, or ethical worth, of any organism depended upon the degree of complexity and unity of its radiation. Century by century they strengthened their faith in this vulgar doctrine, and developed also a system of quite irrational delusions and obsessions based upon an obsessive and passionate lust in radiation.

It would take too long to tell of all these subsidiary fantasies, and of the ingenious ways in which they were reconciled with the main body of sane knowledge. But one at least must be mentioned, because of the part it played in the struggle with man. The Martians knew, of course, that 'solid matter' was solid by virtue of the interlocking of the minute electromagnetic systems called atoms. Now rigidity had for them somewhat the same significance and prestige that air, breath, spirit, had for early man. It was in the quasi-solid form that Martians were physically most potent; and the maintenance of this form was exhausting and difficult. These facts combined in the Martian consciousness with the knowledge that rigidity was after all the outcome of interlocked electro-magnetic systems. Rigidity was thus endowed with a peculiar sanctity. The superstition was gradually consolidated, by a series of psychological accidents, into a fanatical admiration of all very rigid materials, but especially of hard crystals, and above all of diamonds. For diamonds were extravagantly resistant; and at the same time, as the Martians themselves put it, diamonds were superb jugglers with the ethereal radiation called light. Every diamond was therefore a supreme embodiment of the tense energy and eternal equilibrium of the cosmos, and must be treated with reverence. In Mars, all known diamonds were exposed to sunlight on the pinnacles of sacred buildings; and the thought that on the neighbour planet might be diamonds which were not properly treated, was one motive of the invasion.

Thus did the Martian mind, unwittingly side-tracked from its true development, fall sick, and strive ever more fanatically toward mere phantoms of its goal. In the early stages of the disorder, radiation was merely regarded as an infallible sign of mentality, and radiative complexity was taken as an infallible measure, merely, of spiritual worth. But little by little, radiation and mentality failed to be distinguished, and radiative organization was actually mistaken for spiritual worth.

In this obsession the Martians resembled somewhat the First Men during their degenerate phase of servitude to the idea of movement; but with a difference. For the Martian intelligence was still active, though its products were severely censored in the name of the 'spirit of the race'. Every Martian was a case of dual personality. Not merely was he sometimes a private consciousness, sometimes the consciousness of the race, but further, even as a private individual he was in a manner divided against himself. Though his practical allegiance to the super-individual was absolute, so that he condemned or ignored all thoughts and impulses that could not be assimilated to the public consciousness, he did in fact have such thoughts and impulses, as it were in the deepest recesses of his being. He very seldom noticed that he was having them, and whenever he did notice it, he was shocked and terrified; yet he did have them. They constituted an intermittent, sometimes almost a continuous, critical commentary on all his more reputable experience.

This was the great tragedy of the spirit on Mars. The Martians were in many ways extremely well equipped for mental progress and for true spiritual adventure, but through a trick of fortune which had persuaded them to prize above all else unity and uniformity, they were driven to thwart their own struggling spirits at every turn.

Far from being superior to the private mind, the public mind which obsessed every Martian was in many ways actually inferior. It had come into dominance in a crisis which demanded severe military co-ordination; and though, since that remote age, it had made great intellectual progress, it remained at heart a military mind. Its disposition was something between that of a field-marshal and the God of the ancient Hebrews. A certain English philosopher once described and praised the fictitious corporate personality of the state, and named it 'Leviathan'. The Martian superindividual was Leviathan endowed with consciousness. In this consciousness there was nothing hut what was easily assimilated and in accord with tradition. Thus the public mind was always intellectually and culturally behind the times. Only in respect of practical social organization did it keep abreast of its own individuals. Intellectual progress had always been initiated by private individuals, and had only penetrated the public mind when the mass of individuals had been privately infected by intercourse with the pioneers. The public consciousness itself initiated progress only in the sphere of social, military, and economic organization.

The novel circumstances which were encountered on the earth put the mentality of the Martians to a supreme test. For the unique enterprise of tackling a new world demanded the extremes of both public and private activity, and so led to agonizing conflicts within each private mind. For, while the undertaking was essentially social and even military, and necessitated very strict co-ordination and unity of action, the extreme novelty of the new environment demanded all the resources of the untrammelled private consciousness. Moreover the Martians encountered much on the earth which made nonsense of their fundamental assumptions. And in their brightest moments of private consciousness they sometimes recognized this fact.

CHAPTER IX

EARTH AND MARS

1. THE SECOND MEN AT BAY

Such were the beings that invaded the earth when the Second Men were gathering their strength for a great venture in artificial evolution. The motives of the invasion were both economic and religious. The Martians sought water and vegetable matter; but they came also in a crusading spirit, to 'liberate' the terrestrial diamonds.

Conditions on the earth were very unfavourable to the invaders. Excessive gravitation troubled them less than might have been expected. Only in their most concentrated form did they find it oppressive. More harmful was the density of the terrestrial atmosphere, which constricted the tenuous animate cloudlets very painfully, hindering their vital processes, and deadening all their movements. In their native atmosphere they swam hither and thither with ease and considerable speed; but the treacly air of the earth hampered them as a bird's wings are hampered under water. Moreover, owing to their extreme buoyancy as individual cloudlets, they were scarcely able to dive down so far as the mountain-tops. Excessive oxygen was also a source of distress; it tended to put them into a violent fever, which they had only been able to guard against very imperfectly. Even more damaging was the excessive moisture of the atmosphere, both through its solvent effect upon certain factors in the subvital units, and because heavy rain interfered with the physiological processes of the cloudlets and washed many of their materials to the ground.

The invaders had also to cope with the tissue of 'radio' messages that constantly enveloped the planet, and tended to interfere with their own organic systems of radiation. They were prepared for this to some extent; but 'beam wireless' at close range surprised, bewildered, tortured, and finally routed them; so that they fled back to

Mars, leaving many of their number disintegrated in the terrestrial air.

But the pioneering army (or individual, for throughout the adventure it maintained unity of consciousness) had much to report at home. As was expected, there was rich vegetation, and water was even too abundant. There were solid animals, of the type of the prehistoric Martian fauna, but mostly two-legged and erect. Experiment had shown that these creatures died when they were pulled to pieces, and that though the sun's rays affected them by setting up chemical action in their visual organs, they had no really direct sensitivity to radiation. Obviously, therefore, they must be unconscious. On the other hand, the terrestrial atmosphere was permanently alive with radiation of a violent and incoherent type. It was still uncertain whether these crude ethereal agitations were natural phenomena, mere careless offshoots of the cosmic mind, or whether they were emitted by a terrestrial organism. There was reason to suppose this last to be the case, and that the solid organisms were used by some hidden terrestrial intelligence as instruments; for there were buildings, and many of the bipeds were found within the buildings. Moreover, the sudden violent concentration of beam radiation upon the Martian cloud suggested purposeful and hostile behaviour. Punitive action had therefore been taken, and many buildings and bipeds had been destroyed. The physical basis of such a terrestrial intelligence was still to be discovered. It was certainly not in the terrestrial clouds, for these had turned out to be insensitive to radiation. Anyhow, it was obviously an intelligence of very low order, for its radiation was scarcely at all systematic, and was indeed excessively crude. One or two unfortunate diamonds had been found in a building. There was no sign that they were properly venerated.

The Terrestrials, on their side, were left in complete bewilderment by the extraordinary events of that day. Some had jokingly suggested that since the strange substance had behaved in a manner obviously vindictive, it must have been alive and conscious; but no one took the suggestion seriously. Clearly, however, the thing had been dissipated by beam radiation. That at least was an important piece of practical knowledge. But theoretical knowledge about the real nature of the clouds, and their place in the order of the universe, was for the present wholly lacking. To a race of strong cognitive interest and splendid scientific achievement, this ignorance was violently disturbing. It seemed to shake the foundations of the great structure of knowledge. Many frankly hoped, in spite of the loss of life in the first invasion, that there would soon be another opportunity for studying these amazing objects, which were not quite gaseous and not quite solid, not (apparently) organic, yet capable of behaving in a manner suggestive of life. An opportunity was soon afforded.

Some years after the first invasion the Martians appeared again, and in far greater force. This time, moreover, they were almost immune from man's offensive radiation. Operating simultaneously from all the alpine regions of the earth, they began to dry up the great rivers at their sources; and, venturing further afield, they spread over jungle and agricultural land, and stripped off every leaf. Valley after valley was devastated as though by endless swarms of locusts, so that in whole countries there was not a green blade left. The booty was carried off to Mars. Myriads of the subvital units, specialized for transport of water and food materials, were loaded each with a few molecules of the treasure, and dispatched to the home planet. The traffic continued indefinitely. Meanwhile the main body of the Martians proceeded to explore and loot. They were irresistible. For the absorption of water and leafage, they spread over the countryside as an impalpable mist which man had no means to dispel. For the destruction of civilization, they became armies of gigantic cloud-jellies, far bigger than the brute which had formed itself during the earlier invasion. Cities were knocked down and flattened, human beings masticated into pulp. Man tried weapon after weapon in vain.

Presently the Martians discovered the sources of terrestrial radiation in the innumerable wireless transmitting stations. Here at last was the physical basis of the terrestrial intelligence! But what a lowly creature! What a caricature of life! Obviously in respect of complexity and delicacy of organization these wretched immobile systems of glass, metal and vegetable compounds were not to be compared with the Martian cloud. Their only feat seemed to be that they had managed to get control of the unconscious bipeds who tended them.

In the course of their explorations the Martians also discovered a few more diamonds. The second human species had outgrown the barbaric lust for jewellery; but they recognized the beauty of gems and precious metals, and used them as badges of office. Unfortunately, the Martians, in sacking a town, came upon a woman who was wearing a large diamond between her breasts; for she was mayor of the town, and in charge of the evacuation. That the sacred stone should be used thus, apparently for the mere identification of cattle, shocked the invaders even more than the discovery of fragments of diamonds in certain cutting-instruments. The war now began to be waged with all the heroism and brutality of a crusade. Long after a rich booty of water and vegetable matter had been secured, long after the Terrestrials had developed an effective means of attack, and were slaughtering the Martian clouds with high-tension electricity in the form of artificial lightning flashes, the misguided fanatics stayed on to rescue the diamonds and carry them away to the mountain tops, where, years afterwards, climbers discovered them, arranged along the rock-edges in glittering files, like seabird's eggs. Thither the dying remnant of the Martian host had transported them with its last strength, scorning to save itself before the diamonds were borne into the pure mountain air, to be lodged with dignity. When the Second Men learned of this great hoard of diamonds, they began to be seriously persuaded that they had been dealing, not with a freak of physical nature, nor yet (as some said) with swarms of bacteria, but with organisms of a higher order. For how could the jewels have been singled out, freed from their metallic settings, and so carefully regimented on the rocks, save by conscious purpose? The murderous clouds must have had at least the pilfering mentality of jackdaws, since evidently they had been fascinated by the treasure. But the very action which revealed their consciousness suggested also that they were no more intelligent than the merely instinctive animals. There was no opportunity of correcting this error, since all the clouds had been destroyed.

The struggle had lasted only a few months. Its material effects on Man were serious but not insurmountable. Its immediate psychological effect was invigorating. The Second Men had long been accustomed to a security and prosperity that were almost utopian. Suddenly they were overwhelmed by a calamity which was quite unintelligible in terms of their own systematic knowledge.

Their predecessors, in such a situation, would have behaved with their own characteristic vacillation between the human and the sub-human. They would have contracted a fever of romantic loyalty, and have performed many random acts of secretly self-regarding self-sacrifice. They would have sought profit out of the public disaster, and howled at all who were more fortunate than themselves. They would have cursed their gods, and looked for more useful ones. But also, in an incoherent manner, they would sometimes have behaved reasonably, and would even have risen now and again to the standards of the Second Men. Wholly unused to large-scale human bloodshed, these more developed beings suffered an agony of pity for their mangled fellows. But they said nothing about their pity, and scarcely noticed their own generous grief; for they were busy with the work of rescue. Suddenly confronted with the need of extreme loyalty and courage, they exulted in complying, and experienced that added keenness of spirit which comes when danger is well faced. But it did not occur to them that they were bearing themselves heroically; for they thought they were merely behaving reasonably, showing common sense. And if any one failed in a tight place, they did not call him coward, but gave him a drug to clear his head; or, if that failed, they put him under a doctor. No doubt, among the First Men such a policy would not have been justified, for those bewildered beings had not the clear and commanding vision which kept all sane members of the second species constant in loyalty.

The immediate psychological effect of the disaster was that it afforded this very noble race healthful exercise for its great reserves of loyalty and heroism. Quite apart from this immediate invigoration, however, the first agony, and those many others which were to follow, influenced the Second Men for good and ill in a train of effects which may be called spiritual. They had long known very well that the universe was one in which there could be not only private but also great public tragedies; and their philosophy did not seek to conceal this fact. Private tragedy they were able to face with a bland fortitude, and even an ecstasy of acceptance, such as the earlier species had but rarely attained. Public tragedy, even world-tragedy, they declared should be faced in the same spirit. But to know world-tragedy in the abstract, is very different from the direct acquaintance with it. And now the Second Men, even while they held their attention earnestly fixed upon the practical work of defence, were determined to absorb this tragedy into the very depths of their being, to scrutinize it fearlessly, savour it, digest it, so that its fierce potency should henceforth be added to them. Therefore they did not curse their gods, nor supplicate them. They said to themselves, 'Thus, and thus, and thus, is the world. Seeing the depth we shall see also the height; and we shall praise both.'

But their schooling was yet scarcely begun. The Martian invaders were all dead, but their subvital units were dispersed over the planet as a virulent ultra-microscopic dust. For, though as members of the living cloud they could enter the human body without doing permanent harm, now that they were freed from their functions within the higher organic system, they became a predatory virus. Breathed into man's lungs, they soon adapted themselves to the new environment, and threw his tissues into disorder. Each cell that they entered overthrew its own constitution, like a state which the enemy has successfully infected with lethal propaganda through a mere handful of agents. Thus, though man was temporarily victor over the Martian super-individual, his own vital units were poisoned and destroyed by the subvital remains of his dead enemy. A race whose physique had been as utopian as its body politic, was reduced to timid invalidity. And it was left in possession of a devastated planet. The loss of water proved negligible; but the destruction of vegetation in all the war areas produced for a while a world famine such as the Second Men had never known. And the material fabric of civilization had been so broken that many decades would have to be spent in rebuilding it.

But the physical damage proved far less serious than the physiological. Earnest research discovered, indeed, a means of checking the infection; and, after a few years of rigorous purging, the atmosphere and man's flesh were clean once more. But the generations that had been stricken never recovered; their tissues had been too seriously corroded. Little by little, of course, there arose a fresh population of undamaged men and women. But it was a small population; for the fertility of the stricken had been much reduced. Thus the earth was now occupied by a small number of healthy persons below middle age and a very large number of ageing invalids. For many years these cripples had contrived to carry on the work of the world in spite of their frailty, but gradually they began to fail both in endurance and competence. For they were rapidly losing their grip on life, and sinking into a long-drawn-out senility, from which the Second Men had never before suffered; and at the same time the young, forced to take up work for which they were not yet equipped, committed all manner of blunders and crudities of which their elders would never have been guilty. But such was the general standard of mentality in the second human species, that what might have been an occasion for recrimination produced an unparalleled example of human loyalty at its best. The stricken generations decided almost unanimously that whenever an individual was declared by his generation to have outlived his competence, he should commit suicide. The younger generations, partly through affection, partly through dread of their own incompetence, were at first earnestly opposed to this policy. 'Our elders', one young man said, 'may have declined in vigour, but they are still beloved, and still wise. We dare not carry on without them.' But the elders maintained their point. Many members of the rising generation were no longer juveniles. And, if the body politic was to survive the economic crisis, it must now ruthlessly cut out all its damaged tissues. Accordingly the decision was carried out. One by one, as occasion demanded, the stricken 'chose the peace of annihilation', leaving a scanty, inexperienced, but vigorous, population to rebuild what had been destroyed.

Four centuries passed, and then again the Martian clouds appeared in the sky. Once more devastation and slaughter. Once more a complete failure of the two mentalities to conceive one another. Once more the Martians were destroyed. Once more the pulmonary plague, the slow purging, a crippled population, and generous suicide.

Again, and again they appeared, at irregular intervals for fifty thousand years. On each occasion the Martians came irresistibly fortified against whatever weapon humanity had last used against them. And so, by degrees, men began to recognize that the enemy was no merely instinctive brute, but intelligent. They therefore made attempts to get in touch with these alien minds, and make overtures for a peaceful settlement. But since obviously the negotiations had to be performed by human beings, and since the Martians always regarded human beings as the mere cattle of the terrestrial intelligence, the envoys were always either ignored or destroyed.

During each invasion the Martians contrived to dispatch a considerable bulk of water to Mars. And every time, not satisfied with this material gain, they stayed too long crusading, until man had found a weapon to circumvent their new defences; and then they were routed. After each invasion man's recovery was slower and less complete, while Mars, in spite of the loss of a large proportion of its population, was in the long run invigorated with the extra water.

2. THE RUIN OF TWO WORLDS

Rather more than fifty thousand years after their first appearance, the Martians secured a permanent footing on the Antarctic table-land and over-ran Australasia and South Africa. For many centuries they remained in possession of a large part of the earth's surface, practising a kind of agriculture, studying terrestrial conditions, and spending much energy on the 'liberation' of diamonds.

During the considerable period before their settlement their mentality had scarcely changed; but actual habitation of the earth now began to undermine their self-complacency and their unity. It was borne in upon certain exploring Martians that the terrestrial bipeds, though insensitive to radiation, were actually the intelligences of the planet. At first this fact was studiously shunned, but little by little it gripped the attention of all terrestrial Martians. At the same time they began to realize that the whole work of research into terrestrial conditions, and even the social construction of their colony, depended, not on the public mind, but on private individuals, acting in their private capacity. The colonial super-individual inspired only the diamond crusade, and the attempt to extirpate the terrestrial intelligence, or radiation. These various novel acts of insight woke the Martian colonists from an age-long dream. They saw that their revered super-individual was scarcely more than the least common measure of themselves, a bundle of atavistic fantasies and cravings, knit into one mind and gifted with a certain practical cunning. A rapid and bewildering spiritual renascence now came over the whole Martian colony. The central doctrine of it was that what was valuable in the Martian species was not radiation but mentality. These two utterly different things had been confused, and even identified, since the dawn of Martian civilization. At last they were clearly distinguished. A fumbling but sincere study of mind now began; and distinction was even made between the humbler and loftier mental activities.

There is no telling whither this renascence might have led, had it run its course. Possibly in time the Martians might have recognized worth even in minds other than Martian minds. But such a leap was at first far beyond them. Though they now understood that human animals were conscious and intelligent, they regarded them with no sympathy, rather indeed, with increased hostility. They still rendered allegiance to the Martian race, or brotherhood, just because it was in a sense one flesh, and, indeed, one mind. For they were concerned not to abolish but to re-create the public mind of the colony, and even that of Mars itself.

But the colonial public mind still largely dominated them in their more somnolent periods, and actually sent some of those who, in their private phases, were revolutionaries across to Mars for help against the revolutionary movement. The home planet was quite untouched by the new ideas. Its citizens co-operated whole-heartedly in an attempt to bring the colonists to their senses. But in vain. The colonial public mind itself changed its character as the centuries passed, until it became seriously alienated from Martian orthodoxy. Presently, indeed, it began to undergo a very strange and thorough metamorphosis, from which, conceivably, it might have emerged as the noblest inhabitant of the solar system. Little by little it fell into a kind of hypnotic trance. That is to say, it ceased to possess the attention of its private members, yet remained as a unity of their subconscious, or un-noticed mentality. Radiational unity of the colony was maintained, but only in this subconscious manner; and it was at that depth that the great metamorphosis began to take place under the fertilizing influence of the new ideas; which, so to speak, were generated in the tempest of the fully conscious mental revolution, and kept on spreading down into the oceanic depth of the subconsciousness. Such a condition was likely to produce in time the emergence of a qualitatively new and finer mentality, and to waken at last into a fully conscious super-individual of higher order than its own members. But meanwhile this trance of the public consciousness incapacitated the colony for that prompt and co-ordinated action which had been the most successful faculty of Martian life. The public mind of the home planet easily destroyed its disorderly offspring, and set about re-colonizing the earth.

Several times during the next three hundred thousand years this process repeated itself. The changeless and terribly efficient super-individual of Mars extirpated its own offspring on the earth, before it could emerge from the chrysalis. And the tragedy might have been repeated indefinitely, but for certain changes that took place in humanity.

The first few centuries after the foundation of the Martian colony had been spent in ceaseless war. But at last, with terribly reduced resources, the Second Men had reconciled themselves to the fact that they must live in the same world with their mysterious enemy. Moreover, constant observation of the Martians began to restore somewhat man's shattered self-confidence. For during the fifty thousand years before the Martian colony was founded his opinion of himself had been undermined. He had formerly been used to regarding himself as the sun's ablest child. Then suddenly a stupendous new phenomenon had defeated his intelligence. Slowly he had learned that he was at grips with a determined and versatile rival, and that this rival hailed from a despised planet. Slowly he had been forced to suspect that he himself was outclassed, outshone, by a race whose very physique was incomprehensible to man. But after the Martians had established a permanent colony, human scientists began to discover the real physiological nature of the Martian organism, and were comforted to find that it did not make nonsense of human science. Man also learned that the Martians, though very able in certain spheres, were not really of a high mental type. These discoveries restored human self-confidence. Man settled down to make the best of the situation. Impassable barriers of high-power electric current were devised to keep the Martians out of human territory, and men began patiently to rebuild their ruined home as best they could. At first there was little respite from the crusading zeal of the Martians, but in the second millennium this began to abate, and the two races left one another alone, save for occasional revivals of Martian fervour. Human civilization was at last reconstructed and consolidated, though upon a modest scale. Once more, though interrupted now and again by decades of agony, human beings lived in peace and relative prosperity. Life was somewhat harder than formerly, and the physique of the race was definitely less reliable than of old; but men and women still enjoyed conditions which most nations of the earlier species would have envied. The age of ceaseless personal sacrifice in service of the stricken community had ended at last. Once more a wonderful diversity of untrammelled personalities was put forth. Once more the minds of men and women were devoted without hindrance to the joy of skilled work, and all the subtleties of personal intercourse. Once more the passionate interest in one's fellows, which had for so long been hushed under the all-dominating public calamity, refreshed and enlarged the mind. Once more there was music, sweet and backward-hearkening towards a golden past. Once more a wealth of literature, and of the visual arts. Once more intellectual exploration into the nature of the physical world and the potentiality of mind. And once more the religious experience, which had for so long been coarsened and obscured by all the violent distractions and inevitable self-deceptions of war, seemed to be refining itself under the influence of reawakened culture.

In such circumstances the earlier and less sensitive human species might well have prospered indefinitely. Not so the Second Men. For their very refinement of sensibility made them incapable of shunning an ever-present conviction that in spite of all their prosperity they were undermined. Though superficially they seemed to be making a slow but heroic recovery they were at the same time suffering from a still slower and far more profound spiritual decline. Generation succeeded generation. Society became almost perfected, within its limited territory and its limitations of material wealth. The capacities of personality were developed with extreme subtlety and richness. At last the race proposed to itself once more its ancient project of re-making human nature upon a loftier plane. But somehow it had no longer the courage and self-respect for such work. And so, though there was much talk, nothing was done. Epoch succeeded epoch, and everything human remained apparently the same. Like a twig that has been broken but not broken off, man settled down to retain his life and culture, but could make no progress.

It is almost impossible to describe in a few words the subtle malady of the spirit that was undermining the Second Men. To say that they were suffering from an inferiority complex, would not be wholly false, but it would be a misleading vulgarization of the truth. To say that they had lost faith, both in themselves and in the universe, would be almost as inadequate. Crudely stated, their trouble was that, as a species, they had attempted a certain spiritual feat beyond the scope of their still-primitive nature. Spiritually they had over-reached themselves, broken every muscle (so to speak) and incapacitated themselves for any further effort. For they had determined to see their own racial tragedy as a thing of beauty, and they had failed. It was the obscure sense of this defeat that had poisoned them, for, being in many respects a very noble species, they could not simply turn their backs upon their failure and pursue the old way of life with the accustomed zest and thoroughness.

During the earliest Martian raids, the spiritual leaders of humanity had preached that the disaster must be an occasion for a supreme religious experience. While striving mightily to save their civilization, men must yet (so it was said) learn not merely to endure, but to admire, even the sternest issue. 'Thus and thus is the world. Seeing the depth, we shall see also the height, and praise both.' The whole population had accepted this advice. At first they had seemed to succeed. Many noble literary expressions were given forth, which seemed to define and elaborate, and even actually to create in men's hearts, this supreme experience. But as the centuries passed and the disasters were repeated, men began to fear that their forefathers had deceived themselves. Those remote generations had earnestly longed to feel the racial tragedy as a factor in the cosmic beauty; and at last they had persuaded themselves that this experience had actually befallen them. But their descendants were slowly coming to suspect that no such experience had ever occurred, that it would never occur to any man, and that there was in fact no such cosmic beauty to be experienced. The First Men would probably, in such a situation, have swung violently either into spiritual nihilism, or else into some comforting religious myth. At any rate, they were of too coarse-grained a nature to be ruined by a trouble so impalpable. Not so the Second Men. For they realized all too clearly that they were faced with the supreme crux of existence. And so, age after age the generations clung desperately to the hope that, if only they could endure a little longer, the light would break in on them. Even after the Martian colony had been three times established and destroyed by the orthodox race in Mars, the supreme preoccupation of the human species was with this religious crux. But afterwards, and very gradually, they lost heart. For it was borne in on them that either they themselves were by nature too obtuse to perceive this ultimate excellence of things (an excellence which they had strong reason to believe in intellectually, although they could not actually experience it), or the human race had utterly deceived itself, and the course of cosmic events after all was not significant, but a meaningless rigmarole.

It was this dilemma that poisoned them. Had they been still physically in their prime, they might have found fortitude to accept it, and proceed to the patient exfoliation of such very real excellencies as they were still capable of creating. But they had lost the vitality which alone could perform such acts of spiritual abnegation. All the wealth of personality, all the intricacies of personal relationship, all the complex enterprise of a very great community, all art, all intellectual research, had lost their savour. It is remarkable that a purely religious disaster should have warped even the delight of lovers in one another's bodies, actually taken the flavour out of food, and drawn a veil between the sun-bather and the sun. But individuals of this species, unlike their predecessors, were so closely integrated, that none of their functions could remain healthy while the highest was disordered. Moreover, the general slight failure of physique, which was the legacy of age-long war, had resulted in a recurrence of those shattering brain disorders which had dogged the earliest races of their species. The very horror of the prospect of racial insanity increased their aberration from reasonableness. Little by little, shocking perversions of desire began to terrify them. Masochistic and sadistic orgies alternated with phases of extravagant and ghastly revelry. Acts of treason against the community, hitherto almost unknown, at last necessitated a strict police system. Local groups organized predatory raids against one another. Nations appeared, and all the phobias that make up nationalism.

The Martian colonists, when they observed man's disorganization, prepared, at the instigation of the home planet, a very great offensive. It so happened that at this time the colony was going through its phase of enlightenment, which had always hitherto been followed sooner or later by chastisement from Mars. Many individuals were at the moment actually toying with the idea of seeking harmony with man, rather than war. But the public mind of Mars, outraged by this treason, sought to overwhelm it by instituting a new crusade. Man's disunion offered a great opportunity.

The first attack produced a remarkable change in the human race. Their madness seemed suddenly to leave them. Within a few weeks the national governments had surrendered their sovereignty to a central authority. Disorders, debauchery, perversions, wholly ceased. The treachery and self-seeking and corruption, which had by now been customary for many centuries, suddenly gave place to universal and perfect devotion to the social cause. The species was apparently once more in its right mind. Everywhere, in spite of the war's horrors, there was gay brotherliness, combined with a heroism, which clothed itself in an odd extravagance of jocularity.

The war went ill for man. The general mood changed to cold resolution. And still victory was with the Martians. Under the influence of the huge fanatical armies which were poured in from the home planet, the colonists had shed their tentative pacifism, and sought to vindicate their loyalty by ruthlessness. In reply the human race deserted its sanity, and succumbed to an uncontrollable lust for destruction. It was at this stage that a human bacteriologist announced that he had bred a virus of peculiar deadliness and transmissibility, with which it would be possible to infect the enemy, but at the cost of annihilating also the human race. It is significant of the insane condition of the human population at this time that, when these facts were announced and broadcast, there was no discussion of the desirability of using this weapon. It was immediately put in action, the whole human race applauding.

Within a few months the Martian colony had vanished, their home planet itself had received the infection, and its population was already aware that nothing could save it. Man's constitution was tougher than that of the animate clouds, and he appeared to be doomed to a somewhat more lingering death. He made no effort to save himself, either from the disease which he himself had propagated, or from the pulmonary plague which was caused by the disintegrated substance of the dead Martian colony. All the public processes of civilization began to fall to pieces; for the community was paralysed by disillusion, and by the expectation of death. Like a bee-hive that has no queen, the whole population of the earth sank into apathy. Men and women stayed in their homes, idling, eating whatever food they could procure, sleeping far into the mornings, and, when at last they rose, listlessly avoiding one another. Only the children could still be gay, and even they were oppressed by their elders' gloom. Meanwhile the disease was spreading. Household after household was stricken, and was left unaided by its neighbours. But the pain in each individual's flesh was strangely numbed by his more poignant distress in the spiritual defeat of the race. For such was the high development of this species, that even physical agony could not distract it from the racial failure. No one wanted to save himself; and each knew that his neighbours desired not his aid. Only the children, when the disease crippled them, were plunged into agony and terror. Tenderly, yet listlessly, their elders would then give them the last sleep. Meanwhile the unburied dead spread corruption among the dying. Cities fell still and silent. The corn was not harvested.

3. THE THIRD DARK AGE

So contagious and so lethal was the new bacterium, that its authors expected the human race to be wiped out as completely as the Martian colony. Each dying remnant of humanity, isolated from its fellows by the breakdown of communications, imagined its own last moments to be the last of man. But by accident, almost one might say by miracle, a spark of human life was once more preserved, to hand on the sacred fire. A certain stock or strain of the race, promiscuously scattered throughout the continents, proved less susceptible than the majority. And, as the bacterium was less vigorous in a hot climate, a few of these favoured individuals, who happened to be in the tropical jungle, recovered from the infection. And of these few a minority recovered also from the pulmonary plague which, as usual, was propagated from the dead Martians.

It might have been expected that from this human germ a new civilized community would have soon arisen. With such brilliant beings as the Second Men, surely a few generations, or at the most a few thousand years, should have sufficed to make up the lost ground.

But no. Once more it was in a manner the very excellence of the species that prevented its recovery, and flung the spirit of Earth into a trance which lasted longer than the whole previous career of mammals. Again and again, some thirty million times, the seasons were repeated; and throughout this period man remained as fixed in bodily and mental character as, formerly, the platypus. Members of the earlier human species must find it difficult to understand this prolonged impotence of a race far more developed than themselves. For here apparently were both the requisites of progressive culture, namely a world rich and unpossessed, and a race exceptionally able. Yet nothing was done.

When the plagues, and all the immense consequent putrefactions, had worked themselves off, the few isolated groups of human survivors settled down to an increasingly indolent tropical life. The fruits of past learning were not imparted to the young, who therefore grew up in extreme ignorance of almost everything beyond their immediate experience. At the same time the elder generation cowed their juniors with vague suggestions of racial defeat and universal futility. This would not have mattered, had the young themselves been normal; they would have reacted with fervent optimism. But they themselves were now by nature incapable of any enthusiasm. For, in a species in which the lower functions were so strictly disciplined under the higher, the long-drawn-out spiritual disaster had actually begun to take effect upon the germ-plasm; so that individuals were doomed before birth to lassitude, and to mentality in a minor key. The First Men, long ago, had fallen into a kind of racial senility through a combination of vulgar errors and indulgences. But the second species, like a boy whose mind has been too soon burdened with grave experience, lived henceforth in a sleep-walk.

As the generations passed, all the lore of civilization was shed, save the routine of tropical agriculture and hunting. Not that intelligence itself had waned. Not that the race had sunk into mere savagery. Lassitude did not prevent it from readjusting itself to suit its new circumstances. These sleep-walkers soon invented convenient ways of making, in the home and by hand, much that had hitherto been made in factories and by mechanical power. Almost without mental effort they designed and fashioned tolerable instruments out of wood and flint and bone. But though still intelligent, they had become by disposition, supine, indifferent. They would exert themselves only under the pressure of urgent primitive need. No man seemed capable of putting forth the full energy of a man. Even suffering had lost its poignancy. And no ends seemed worth pursuing that could not be realized speedily. The sting had gone out of experience. The soul was calloused against every goad. Men and women worked and played, loved and suffered; but always in a kind of rapt absent-mindedness. It was as though they were ever trying to remember something important which escaped them. The affairs of daily life seemed too trivial to be taken seriously. Yet that other, and supremely important thing, which alone deserved consideration, was so obscure that no one had any idea what it was. Nor indeed was anyone aware of this hypnotic subjection, any more than a sleeper is aware of being asleep.

The minimum of necessary work was performed, and there was even a dreamy zest in the performance, but nothing which would entail extra toil ever seemed worth while. And so, when adjustment to the new circumstances of the world had been achieved, complete stagnation set in. Practical intelligence was easily able to cope with a slowly changing environment, and even with sudden natural upheavals such as floods, earthquakes and disease epidemics. Man remained in a sense master of his world, but he had no idea what to do with his mastery. It was everywhere assumed that the sane end of living was to spend as many days as possible in indolence, lying in the shade. Unfortunately human beings had, of course, many needs which were irksome if not appeased, and so a good deal of hard work had to be done. Hunger and thirst had to be satisfied. Other individuals besides oneself had to be cared for, since man was cursed with sympathy and with a sentiment for the welfare of his group. The only fully rational behaviour, it was thought, would be general suicide, but irrational impulses made this impossible. Beatific drugs offered a temporary heaven. But, far as the Second Men had fallen, they were still too clear-sighted to forget that such beatitude is outweighed by subsequent misery.

Century by century, epoch by epoch, man glided on in this seemingly precarious, yet actually unshakable equilibrium. Nothing that happened to him could disturb his easy dominance over the beasts and over physical nature; nothing could shock him out of his racial sleep. Long-drawn-out climatic changes made desert, jungle and grassland fluctuate like the clouds. As the years advanced by millions, ordinary geological processes, greatly accentuated by the immense strains set up by the Patagonian upheaval, remodelled the surface of the planet. Continents were submerged, or lifted out of the sea, till presently there was little of the old configuration. And along with these geological changes went changes in the fauna and flora. The bacterium which had almost exterminated man had also wrought havoc amongst other mammals. Once more the planet had to be re-stocked, this time from the few surviving tropical species. Once more there was a great remaking of old types, only less revolutionary than that which had followed the Patagonian disaster. And since the human race remained minute, through the effects of its spiritual fatigue, other species were favoured. Especially the ruminants and the large carnivora increased and diversified themselves into many habits and forms.

But the most remarkable of all the biological trains of events in this period was the history of the Martian subvital units that had been disseminated by the slaughter of the Martian colony, and had then tormented men and animals with pulmonary diseases. As the ages passed, certain species of mammals so readjusted themselves that the Martian virus became not only harmless but necessary to their well-being. A relationship which was originally that of parasite and host became in time a true symbiosis, a co-operative partnership, in which the terrestrial animals gained something of the unique attributes of the vanished Martian organisms. The time was to come when Man himself should look with envy on these creatures, and finally make use of the Martian 'virus' for his own enrichment.

But meanwhile, and for many million years, almost all kinds of life were on the move, save Man. Like a ship-wrecked sailor, he lay exhausted and asleep on his raft, long after the storm had abated.

But his stagnation was not absolute. Imperceptibly, he was drifting on the oceanic currents of life, and in a direction far out of his original course. Little by little, his habit was becoming simpler, less artificial, more animal. Agriculture faded out, since it was no longer necessary in the luxuriant garden where man lived. Weapons of defence and of the chase became more precisely adapted to their restricted purposes, but at the same time less diversified and more stereotyped. Speech almost vanished; for there was no novelty left in experience. Familiar facts and familiar emotions were conveyed increasingly by gestures which were mostly unwitting. Physically, the species had changed little. Though the natural period of life was greatly reduced, this was due less to physiological change than to a strange and fatal increase of absent-mindedness in middle age. The individual gradually ceased to react to his environment; so that even if he escaped a violent death, he died of starvation.

Yet in spite of this great change, the species remained essentially human. There was no bestialization, such as had formerly produced a race of sub-men. These tranced remnants of the second human species were not beasts but innocents, simples, children of nature, perfectly adjusted to their simple life. In many ways their state was idyllic and enviable. But such was their dimmed mentality that they were never clearly aware even of the blessings they had, still less, of course, of the loftier experiences which had kindled and tortured their ancestors.

CHAPTER X

THE THIRD MEN IN THE WILDERNESS

1. THE THIRD HUMAN SPECIES

We have now followed man's career during some forty million years. The whole period to be covered by this chronicle is about two thousand million. In this chapter, and the next, therefore, we must accomplish a swift flight at great altitude over a tract of time more than three times as long as that which we have hitherto observed. This great expanse is no desert, but a continent teeming with variegated life, and many successive and very diverse civilizations. The myriads of human beings who inhabit it far outnumber the First and Second Men combined. And the content of each one of these lives is a universe, rich and poignant as that of any reader of this book.

In spite of the great diversity of this span of man's history, it is a single movement within the whole symphony, just as the careers of the First and of the Second Men are each a single movement. Not only is it a period dominated by a single natural human species and the artificial human species into which the natural species at length transformed itself; but, also, in spite of innumerable digressions, a single theme, a single mood of the human will, informs the whole duration. For now at last man's main energy is devoted to remaking his own physical and mental nature. Throughout the rise and fall of many successive cultures this purpose is progressively clarifying itself, and expressing itself in many tragic and even devastating experiments; until, toward the close of this immense period, it seems almost to achieve its end.

When the Second Men had remained in their strange racial trance for about thirty million years, the obscure forces that make for advancement began to stir in them once more. This reawakening was favoured by geological accident. An incursion of the sea gradually isolated some of their number in an island continent, which was once part of the North Atlantic ocean-bed. The climate of this island gradually cooled from sub-tropical to temperate and sub-arctic. The vast change of conditions caused in the imprisoned race a subtle chemical re-arrangement of the germ-plasm, such that there ensued an epidemic of biological variation. Many new types appeared, but in the long run one, more vigorous and better adapted than the rest, crowded out all competitors and slowly consolidated itself as a new species, the Third Men.

Scarcely more than half the stature of their predecessors, these beings were proportionally slight and lithe. Their skin was of a sunny brown, covered with a luminous halo of red-gold hairs, which on the head became a russet mop. Their golden eyes, reminiscent of the snake, were more enigmatic than profound. Their faces were compact as a cat's muzzle, their lips full, but subtle at the corners. Their ears, objects of personal pride and of sexual admiration, were extremely variable both in individuals and races. These surprising organs, which would have seemed merely ludicrous to the First Men, were expressive both of temperament and passing mood. They were immense, delicately involuted, of a silken texture, and very mobile. They gave an almost bat-like character to the otherwise somewhat feline heads. But the most distinctive feature of the Third Men was their great lean hands, on which were six versatile fingers, six antennae of living steel.

Unlike their predecessors, the Third Men were short-lived. They had a brief childhood and a brief maturity, followed (in the natural course) by a decade of senility, and death at about sixty. But such was their abhorrence of decrepitude, that they seldom allowed themselves to grow old. They preferred to kill themselves when their mental and physical agility began to decline. Thus, save in exceptional epochs of their history, very few lived to be fifty.

But though in some respects the third human species fell short of the high standard of its predecessor, especially in certain of the finer mental capacities, it was by no means simply degenerate. The admirable sensory equipment of the second species was retained, and even improved. Vision was no less ample and precise and colourful.

Touch was far more discriminate, especially in the delicately pointed sixth fingertip. Hearing was so developed that a man could run through wooded country blindfold without colliding with the trees. Moreover the great range of sounds and rhythms had acquired an extremely subtle gamut of emotional significance. Music was therefore one of the main preoccupations of the civilizations of this species.

Mentally the Third Men were indeed very unlike their predecessors. Their intelligence was in some ways no less agile; but it was more cunning than intellectual, more practical than theoretical. They were interested more in the world of sense-experience than in the world of abstract reason, and again far more in living things than in the lifeless. They excelled in certain kinds of art, and indeed also in some fields of science. But they were led into science more through practical, aesthetic or religious needs than through intellectual curiosity. In mathematics, for instance (helped greatly by the duodecimal system, which resulted from their having twelve fingers), they became wonderful calculators; yet they never had the curiosity to inquire into the essential nature of number. Nor, in physics, were they ever led to discover the more obscure properties of space. They were, indeed, strangely devoid of curiosity. Hence, though sometimes capable of a penetrating mystical intuition, they never seriously disciplined themselves under philosophy, nor tried to relate their mystical intuitions with the rest of their experience.

In their primitive phases the Third Men were keen hunters; but also, owing to their strong parental impulses, they were much addicted to making pets of captured animals. Throughout their career they displayed what earlier races would have called an uncanny sympathy with, and understanding of, all kinds of animals and plants. This intuitive insight into the nature of living things, and this untiring interest in the diversity of vital behaviour, constituted the dominating impulse throughout the whole career of the third human species. At the outset they excelled not only as hunters but as herdsmen and domesticators. By nature they were very apt in every kind of manipulation, but especially in the manipulation of living things. As a species they were also greatly addicted to play of all kinds, but especially to manipulative play, and above all to the playful manipulation of organisms. From the first they performed great feats of riding on the moose-like deer which they had domesticated. They tamed also a certain gregarious coursing beast. The pedigree of this great leonine wolf led, through the tropical survivors of the Martian plague, back to those descendants of the arctic fox which had over-run the world after the Patagonian disaster. This animal the Third Men trained not only to help them in shepherding and in the chase, but also to play intricate hunting games. Between this hound and its master or mistress there frequently arose a very special relation, a kind of psychical symbiosis, a dumb intuitive mutual insight, a genuine love, based on economic co-operation, but strongly toned also, in a manner peculiar to the third human species, with religious symbolism and frankly sexual intimacy.

As herdsmen and shepherds the Third Men very early practised selective breeding; and increasingly they became absorbed in the perfecting and enriching of all types of animals and plants. It was the boast of every local chieftain not only that the men of his tribe were more manly and the women more beautiful than all others, but also that the bears in his territory were the noblest and most bear-like of all bears, that the birds built more perfect nests and were more skilful fliers and singers than birds elsewhere. And so on, through all the animal and vegetable races.

This biological control was achieved at first by simple breeding experiments, but later and increasingly by crude physiological manipulation of the young animal, the foetus and (later still) the germ-plasm. Hence arose a perennial conflict, which often caused wars of a truly religious bitterness, between the tender-hearted, who shrank from the infliction of pain, and the passionately manipulative, who willed to create at whatever cost. This conflict, indeed, was waged not only between individuals but within each mind; for all were innately hunters and manipulators, but also all had intuitive sympathy even with the quarry which they tormented. The trouble was increased by a strain of sheer cruelty which occurred even in the most tender-hearted. This sadism was at bottom an expression of an almost mystical reverence for sensory experience. Physical pain, being the most intense of all sensed qualities, was apt to be thought the most excellent. It might be expected that this would lead rather to self-torture than to cruelty. Sometimes it did. But in general those who could not appreciate pain in their own flesh were yet able to persuade themselves that in inflicting pain on lower animals they were creating vivid psychic reality, and therefore high excellence. It was just the intense reality of pain, they said, that made it intolerable to men and animals. Seen with the detachment of the divine mind, it appeared in its true beauty. And even man, they declared, could appreciate its excellence when it occurred not in men but in animals.

Though the Third Men lacked interest in systematic thought, their minds were often concerned with matters outside the fields of private and social economy. They experienced not only aesthetic but mystical cravings. And though they were without any appreciation of those finer beauties of human personality, which their predecessors had admired as the highest attainment of life on the planet, the Third Men themselves, in their own way, sought to make the best of human nature, and indeed of animal nature. Man they regarded in two aspects. In the first place he was the noblest of all animals, gifted with unique aptitudes. He was, as was sometimes said, God's chief work of art. But secondly, since his special virtues were his insight into the nature of all living things and his manipulative capacity, he was himself God's eye and God's hand. These convictions were expressed over and over again in the religions of the Third Men, by the image of the deity as a composite animal, with wings of the albatross, jaws of the great wolf-dog, feet of the deer, and so on. For the human element was represented in this deity by the hands, the eyes, and the sexual organs of man. And between the divine hands lay the world, with all its diverse population. Often the world was represented as being the fruit of God's primitive potency, but also as in process of being drastically altered and tortured into perfection by the hands.

Most of the cultures of the Third Men were dominated by this obscure worship of Life as an all-pervading spirit, expressing itself in myriad diverse individuals. And at the same time the intuitive loyalty to living things and to a vaguely conceived life-force was often complicated by sadism. For in the first place it was recognized, of course, that what is valued by higher beings may be intolerable to lower; and, as has been said, pain itself was thought to be a superior excellence of this kind. And again in a second manner sadism expressed itself. The worship of Life, as agent or subject, was complemented by worship of environment, as object to life's subjectivity, as that which remains ever foreign to life, thwarting its enterprises, torturing it, yet making it possible, and, by its very resistance, goading it into nobler expressions. Pain, it was said, was the most vivid apprehension of the sacred and universal Object.

The thought of the third human species was never systematic. But in some such manner as the foregoing it strove to rationalize its obscure intuition of the beauty which includes at once Life's victory and defeat.

2. DIGRESSIONS OF THE THIRD MEN

Such, in brief, was the physical and mental nature of the third human species. In spite of innumerable distractions, the spirit of the Third Men kept on returning to follow up the thread of biological interest through a thousand variegated cultures. Again and again folk after folk would clamber out of savagery and barbarism into relative enlightenment; and mostly, though not always, the main theme of this enlightenment was some special mood either of biological creativeness or of sadism, or of both. To a man born into such a society, no dominant characteristic would be apparent. He would be impressed rather by the many-sidedness of human activities in his time. He would note a wealth of personal intercourse, of social organization and industrial invention, of art and speculation, all set in that universal matrix, the private struggle to preserve or express the self. Yet the historian may often see in a society, over and above this multifarious proliferation, some one controlling theme.

Again and again, then, at intervals of a few thousand or a few hundred thousand years, man's whim was imposed upon the fauna and flora of the earth, and at length directed to the task of remaking man himself. Again and again, through a diversity of causes, the effort collapsed, and the species sank once more into chaos. Sometimes indeed there was an interlude of culture in some quite different key. Once, early in the history of the species, and before its nature had become fixed, there occurred a non-industrial civilization of a genuinely intellectual kind, almost like that of Greece. Sometimes, but not often, the third human species fooled itself into an extravagantly industrial world civilization, in the manner of the Americanized

First Men. In general its interest was too much concerned with other matters to become entangled with mechanical devices. But on three occasions at least it succumbed. Of these civilizations one derived its main power from wind and falling water, one from the tides, one from the earth's internal heat. The first, saved from the worst evils of industrialism by the limitations of its power, lasted some hundred thousand years in barren equilibrium, until it was destroyed by an obscure bacterium. The second was fortunately brief; but its fifty thousand years of unbridled waste of tidal energy was enough to interfere appreciably with the orbit of the moon. This world-order collapsed at length in a series of industrial wars. The third endured a quarter of a million years as a brilliantly sane and efficient world organization. Throughout most of its existence there was almost complete social harmony with scarcely as much internal strife as occurs in a bee-hive. But once more civilization came at length to grief, this time through the misguided effort to breed special human types for specialized industrial pursuits.

Industrialism, however, was never more than a digression, a lengthy and disastrous irrelevance in the life of this species. There were other digressions. There were for instance cultures, enduring sometimes for several thousand years, which were predominantly musical. This could never have occurred among the First Men; but, as was said, the third species was peculiarly developed in hearing, and in emotional sensitivity to sound and rhythm. Consequently, just as the First Men at their height were led into the wilderness by an irrational obsession with mechanical contrivances, just as the Third Men themselves were many times undone by their own interest in biological control, so, now and again, it was their musical gift that hypnotized them.

Of these predominantly musical cultures the most remarkable was one in which music and religion combined to form a tyranny no less rigid than that of religion and science in the remote past. It is worth while to dwell on one of these episodes for a few moments.

The Third Men were very subject to a craving for personal immortality. Their lives were brief, their love of life intense. It seemed to them a tragic flaw in the nature of existence that the melody of the individual life must either fade into a dreary senility or be cut short, never to be repeated. Now music had a special significance for this race. So intense was their experience of it, that they were ready to regard it as in some manner the underlying reality of all things. In leisure hours, snatched from a toilful and often tragic life, groups of peasants would seek to conjure about them by song or pipe or viol a universe more beautiful, more real, than that of daily labour. Concentrating their sensitive hearing upon the inexhaustible diversity of tone and rhythm, they would seem to themselves to be possessed by the living presence of music, and to be transported thereby into a lovelier world. No wonder they believed that every melody was a spirit, leading a life of its own within the universe of music. No wonder they imagined that a symphony or chorus was itself a single spirit inhering in all its members. No wonder it seemed to them that when men and women listened to great music, the barriers of their individuality were broken down, so that they became one soul through communion with the music.

The prophet was born in a highland village where the native faith in music was intense, though quite unformulated. In time he learnt to raise his peasant audiences to the most extravagant joy and the most delicious sorrow. Then at last he began to think, and to expound his thoughts with the authority of a great bard. Easily he persuaded men that music was the reality, and all else illusion, that the living spirit of the universe was pure music, and that each individual animal and man, though he had a body that must die and vanish for ever, had also a soul that was music and eternal. A melody, he said, is the most fleeting of things. It happens and ceases. The great silence devours it, and seemingly annihilates it. Passage is essential to its being. Yet though for a melody, to halt is to die a violent death, all music, the prophet affirmed, has also eternal life. After silence it may occur again, with all its freshness and aliveness. Time cannot age it; for its home is in a country outside time. And that country, thus the young musician earnestly preached, is also the homeland of every man and woman, nay of every living thing that has any gift of music. Those who seek immortality, must strive to waken their tranced souls into melody and harmony. And according to their degree of musical originality and proficiency will be their standing in the eternal life.

The doctrine, and the impassioned melodies of the prophet, spread like fire. Instrumental and vocal music sounded from every pasture and corn plot. The government tried to suppress it, partly because it was thought to interfere with agricultural productivity, largely because its passionate significance reverberated even in the hearts of courtly ladies, and threatened to undo the refinement of centuries. Nay, the social order itself began to crumble. For many began openly to declare that what mattered was not aristocratic birth, nor even proficiency in the time-honoured musical forms (so much prized by the leisured), but the gift of spontaneous emotional expression in rhythm and harmony. Persecution strengthened the new faith with a glorious company of martyrs who, it was affirmed, sang triumphantly even in the flames.

One day the sacred monarch himself, hitherto a prisoner within the conventions, declared half sincerely, half by policy, that he was converted to his people's faith. Bureaucracy gave place to an enlightened dictatorship, the monarch assumed the title of Supreme Melody, and the whole social order was re-fashioned, more to the taste of the peasants. The subtle prince, backed by the crusading zeal of his people, and favoured by the rapid spontaneous spread of the faith in all lands, conquered the whole world, and founded the Universal Church of Harmony. The prophet himself, meanwhile, dismayed by his own too facile success, had retired into the mountains to perfect his art under the influence of their great quiet, or the music of wind, thunder and waterfall. Presently, however, the silence of the fells was shattered by the blare of military bands and ecclesiastical choirs, which the emperor had sent to salute him and conduct him to the metropolis. He was secured, though not without a scrimmage, and lodged in the High Temple of Music. There he was kept a prisoner, dubbed God's Big Noise, and used by the world-government as an oracle needing interpretation. In a few years the official music of the temple, and of deputations from all over the world, drove him into raving madness; in which state he was the more useful to the authorities.

Thus was founded the Holy Empire of Music, which gave order and purpose to the species for a thousand years. The sayings of the prophet, interpreted by a series of able rulers, became the foundation of a great system of law which gradually supplanted all local codes by virtue of its divine authority. Its root was madness; but its final expression was intricate common sense, decorated with harmless and precious flowers of folly. Throughout, the individual was wisely, but tacitly, regarded as a biological organism having definite needs or rights and definite social obligations; but the language in which this principle was expressed and elaborated was a jargon based on the fiction that every human being was a melody, demanding completion within a greater musical theme of society.

Toward the close of this millennium of order a schism occurred among the devout. A new and fervent sect declared that the true spirit of the musical religion had been stifled by ecclesiasticism. The founder of the religion had preached salvation by individual musical experience, by an intensely emotional communion with the Divine Music. But little by little, so it was said, the church had lost sight of this central truth, and had substituted a barren interest in the objective forms and principles of melody and counterpoint. Salvation, in the official view, was not to be had by subjective experience, but by keeping the rules of an obscure musical technique. And what was this technique? Instead of making the social order a practical expression of the divine law of music, churchmen and statesmen had misinterpreted these divine laws to suit mere social convenience, until the true spirit of music had been lost. Meanwhile on the other side a counter-revival took place. The self-centred and soul-saving mood of the rebels was ridiculed. Men were urged to care rather for the divine and exquisitely ordered forms of music itself than for their own emotion.

It was amongst the rebel peoples that the biological interest of the race, hitherto subordinate, came into its own. Mating, at least among the more devout sort of women, began to be influenced by the desire to have children who should be of outstanding musical brilliance and sensitivity. Biological sciences were rudimentary, but the general principle of selective breeding was known. Within a century this policy of breeding for music, or breeding 'soul', developed from a private idiosyncrasy into a racial obsession. It was so far successful that after a while a new type became common, and thrived upon the approbation and devotion of ordinary persons. These new beings were indeed extravagantly sensitive to music, so much so that the song of a sky-lark caused them serious torture by its banality, and in response to any human music of the kind which they approved, they invariably fell into a trance. Under the stimulus of music which was not to their taste they were apt to run amok and murder the performers.

We need not pause to trace the stages by which an infatuated race gradually submitted itself to the whims of these creatures of human folly, until for a brief period they became the tyrannical ruling caste of a musical theocracy. Nor need we observe how they reduced society to chaos; and how at length an age of confusion and murder brought mankind once more to its senses, but also into so bitter a disillusionment that the effort to re-orientate the whole direction of its endeavour lacked determination. Civilization fell to pieces and was not rebuilt till after the race had lain fallow for some thousands of years.

So ended perhaps the most pathetic of racial delusions. Born of a genuine and potent aesthetic experience, it retained a certain crazy nobility even to the end.

Many scores of other cultures occurred, separated often by long ages of barbarism, but they must be ignored in this brief chronicle. The great majority of them were mainly biological in spirit. Thus one was dominated by an obsessive interest in flight, and therefore in birds, another by the concept of metabolism, several by sexual creativity, and very many by some general but mostly unenlightened policy of eugenics. All these we must pass over, so that we may descend to watch the greatest of all the races of the third species torture itself into a new form.

3. THE VITAL ART

It was after an unusually long period of eclipse that the spirit of the third human species attained its greatest brilliance. We need not watch the stages by which this enlightenment was reached. Suffice it that the upshot was a very remarkable civilization, if such a word can be applied to an order in which agglomerations of architecture were unknown, clothing was used only when needed for warmth, and such industrial development as occurred was wholly subordinated to other activities.

Early in the history of this culture the requirements of hunting and agriculture, and the spontaneous impulse to manipulate live things, gave rise to a primitive but serviceable system of biological knowledge. Not until the culture had unified the whole planet, did biology itself give rise to chemistry and physics. At the same time a well-controlled industrialism, based first on wind and water, and later on subterranean heat, afforded the race all the material luxuries it desired, and much leisure from the business of keeping itself in existence. Had there not already existed a more powerful and all-dominating interest, industrialism itself would probably have hypnotized the race, as it had so many others. But in this race the interest in live things, which characterized the whole species, was dominant before industrialism began. Egotism among the Third Men could not be satisfied by the exercise of economic power, nor by the mere ostentation of wealth. Not that the race was immune from egotism. On the contrary, it had lost almost all that spontaneous altruism which had distinguished the Second Men. But in most periods the only kind of personal ostentation which appealed to the Third Men was directly connected with the primitive interest in 'pecunia'. To own many and noble beasts, whether they were economically productive or not, was ever the mark of respectability. The vulgar, indeed, were content with mere numbers, or at most with the conventional virtues of the recognized breeds. But the more refined pursued, and flaunted, certain very exact principles of aesthetic excellence in their control of living forms.

In fact, as the race gained biological insight, it developed a very remarkable new art, which we may call 'plastic vital art'. This was to become the chief vehicle of expression of the new culture. It was practised universally, and with religious fervour; for it was very closely connected with the belief in a life-god. The canons of this art, and the precepts of this religion, fluctuated from age to age, but in general certain basic principles were accepted. Or rather, though there was almost always universal agreement that the practice of vital art was the supreme goal, and should not be treated in a utilitarian spirit, there were two conflicting sets of principles which were favoured by opposed sets. One mode of vital art sought to evoke the full potentiality of each natural type as a harmonious and perfected nature, or to produce new types equally harmonious. The other prided itself on producing monsters. Sometimes a single capacity was developed at the expense of the harmony and welfare of the organism as a whole. Thus a bird was produced which could fly faster than any other bird; but it could neither reproduce nor even feed, and therefore had to be maintained artificially. Sometimes, on the other hand, certain characters incompatible in nature were forced upon a single organism, and maintained in precarious and torturing equilibrium. To give examples, one much-talked-of feat was the production of a carnivorous mammal in which the fore-limbs had assumed the structure of a bird's wings, complete with feathers. This creature could not fly, since its body was wrongly proportioned. Its only mode of locomotion was a staggering run with outstretched wings. Other examples of monstrosity were an eagle with twin heads, and a deer in which, with incredible ingenuity, the artists had induced the tail to develop as a head, with brain, sense organs, and jaws. In this monstrous art, interest in living things was infected with sadism through the preoccupation with fate, especially internal fate, as the divinity that shapes our ends. In its more vulgar forms, of course, it was a crude expression of egotistical lust in power.

This *motif* of the monstrous and the self-discrepant was less prominent than the other, the *motif* of harmonious perfection; but at all times it was apt to exercise at least a subconscious influence. The supreme aim of the dominant, perfection-seeking movement was to embellish the planet with a very diverse fauna and flora, with the human race as at once the crown and the instrument of terrestrial life. Each species, and each variety, was to have its place and fulfil its part in the great cycle of living types. Each was to be internally perfected to its function. It must have no harmful relics of a past manner of life; and its capacities must be in true accord with one another. But, to repeat, the supreme aim was not concerned merely with individual types, but with the whole vital economy of the planet. Thus, though there were to be types of every order from the most humble bacterium up to man, it was contrary to the canon of orthodox sacred art that any type should thrive by the destruction of a type higher than itself. In the sadistic mode of the art, however, a peculiarly exquisite tragic beauty was said to inhere in situations in which a lowly type exterminated a higher. There were occasions in the history of the race when the two sects indulged in bloody conflict because the sadists kept devising parasites to undermine the noble products of the orthodox.

Of those who practised vital art, and all did so to some extent, a few, though they deliberately rejected the orthodox principles, gained notoriety and even fame by their grotesques; while others, less fortunate, were ready to accept ostracism and even martyrdom, declaring that what they had produced was a significant symbol of the universal tragedy of vital nature. The great majority, however, accepted the sacred canon. They had therefore to choose one or other of certain recognized modes of expression. For instance, they might seek to enhance some extant type of organism, both by perfecting its capacities and by eliminating from it all that was harmful or useless. Or else, a more original and precarious work, they might set about creating a new type to fill a niche in the world, which had not yet been occupied. For this end they would select a suitable organism, and seek to remake it upon a new plan, striving to produce a creature of perfectly harmonious nature precisely adapted to the new way of life. In this kind of work sundry strict aesthetic principles must be observed. Thus it was considered bad art to reduce a higher type to a lower, or in any manner to waste the capacities of a type. And further, since the true end of art was not the production of individual types, but the production of a world-wide and perfectly systematic fauna and flora, it was inadmissible to harm even accidentally any type higher than that which it was intended to produce. For the practice of orthodox vital art was regarded as a co-operative enterprise. The ultimate artist, under God, was mankind as a whole; the ultimate work of art must be an ever more subtle garment of living forms for the adornment of the planet, and the delight of the supreme Artist, in relation to whom man was both creature and instrument.

Little was achieved, of course, until the applied biological sciences had advanced far beyond the high-water mark attained long ago during the career of the Second Men. Much more was needed than the rule-of-thumb principles of earlier breeders. It took this brightest of all the races of the third species many thousands of years of research to discover the more delicate principles of heredity, and to devise a technique by which the actual hereditary factors in the germ could be manipulated. It was this increasing penetration of biology itself that opened up the deeper regions of chemistry and physics. And owing to this historical sequence the latter sciences were conceived in a biological manner, with the electron as the basic organism, and the cosmos as an organic whole.

Imagine, then, a planet organized almost as a vast system of botanical and zoological gardens, or wild parks, interspersed with agriculture and industry. In every great centre of communications occurred annual and monthly shows. The latest creations were put through their paces, judged by the high priests of vital art, awarded distinctions, and consecrated with religious ceremony. At these shows some of the exhibits would be utilitarian, others purely aesthetic. There might be improved grains, vegetables, cattle, some exceptionally intelligent or sturdy variety of herdsman's dog, or a new micro-organism with some special function in agriculture or in human digestion. But also there would be the latest achievements in pure vital art. Great sleek-limbed, hornless, racing deer, birds or mammals adapted to some hitherto unfulfilled role, bears intended to outclass all existing varieties in the struggle for existence, ants with specialized organs and instincts, improvements in the relations of parasite and host, so as to make a true symbiosis in which the host profited by the parasite. And so on. And everywhere there would be the little unclad ruddy faun-like beings who had created these marvels. Shy forest-dwelling folk of Gurkha physique would stand beside their antelopes, vultures, or new great cat-like prowlers. A grave young woman might cause a stir by entering the grounds followed by several gigantic bears. Crowds would perhaps press round to examine the creatures' teeth or limbs, and she might scold the meddlers away from her patient flock. For the normal relation between man and beast at this time was one of perfect amity, rising, sometimes, in the case of domesticated animals, to an exquisite, almost painful, mutual adoration. Even the wild beasts never troubled to avoid man, still less to attack him, save in the special circumstances of the hunt and the sacred gladiatorial show.

These last need special notice. The powers of combat in beasts were admired no less than other powers. Men and women alike experienced a savage joy, almost an ecstasy, in the spectacle of mortal combat. Consequently there were formal occasions when different kinds of beasts were enraged against one another and allowed to fight to the death. Not only so, but also there were sacred contests between beast and man, between man and man, between woman and woman, and, most surprising to the readers of this book, between woman and man. For in this species, woman in her prime was not physically weaker than her partner.

4. CONFLICTING POLICIES

Almost from the first, vital art had been applied to some extent to man himself, though with hesitation. Certain great improvements had been effected, but only improvements about which there could be no two opinions. The many diseases and abnormalities left over from past civilizations were patiently abolished, and various more fundamental defects were remedied. For instance, teeth, digestion, glandular equipment and the circulatory system were greatly improved. Extreme good health and considerable physical beauty became universal. Child-bearing was made a painless and health-giving process. Senility was postponed. The standard of practical intelligence was appreciably raised. These reforms were made possible by a vast concerted effort of research and experiment supported by the world community. But private enterprise was also effective, for the relation between the sexes was much more consciously dominated by the thought of offspring than among the First Men. Every individual knew the characteristics of his or her hereditary composition, and knew what kinds of offspring were to be expected from intercourse of different hereditary types. Thus in courtship the young man was not content to persuade his beloved that his mind was destined by nature to afford her mind joyful completion; he sought also to persuade her that with his help she might bear children of a peculiar excellence. Consequently there was at all times going on a process of selective breeding towards the conventionally ideal type. In certain respects the ideal remained constant for many thousands of years. It included health, cat-like agility, manipulative dexterity, musical sensitivity, refined perception of rightness and wrongness in the sphere of vital art, and an intuitive practical judgment in all the affairs of life. Longevity, and the abolition of senility, were also sought, and partially attained. Waves of fashion sometimes directed sexual selection toward prowess in combat, or some special type of facial expression or vocal powers. But these fleeting whims were negligible. Only the permanently desired characters were actually intensified by private selective breeding.

But at length there came a time when more ambitious aims were entertained. The world-community was now a highly organized theocratic hierarchy, strictly but on the whole benevolently ruled by a supreme council of vital priests and biologists. Each individual, down to the humblest agricultural worker, had his special niche in society, allotted him by the supreme council or its delegates, according to his known heredity and the needs of society. This system, of course, sometimes led to abuse, but mostly it worked without serious friction. Such was the precision of biological knowledge that each person's mental calibre and special aptitudes were known beyond dispute, and rebellion against his lot in society would have been rebellion against his own heredity. This fact was universally known, and accepted without regret. A man had enough scope for emulation and triumph among his peers, without indulging in vague attempts to transcend his own nature, by rising into a superior hierarchical order. This state of affairs would have been impossible had there not been universal faith in the religion of life and the truth of biological science. Also it would have been impossible had not all normal persons been active practitioners of the sacred vital art, upon a plane suited to their capacity. Every individual adult of the rather scanty world-population regarded himself or herself as a creative artist, in however humble a sphere. And in general he, or she, was so fascinated by the work, that he was well content to leave social organization and control to those who were fitted for it. Moreover, at the back of every mind was the conception of society itself as an organism of specialized members. The strong sentiment for organized humanity tended, in this race, to master even its strong egotistical impulses, though not without a struggle.

It was such a society, almost unbelievable to the First Men, that now set about remaking human nature. Unfortunately there

were conflicting views about the goal. The orthodox desired only
to continue the work that had for long been on foot; though they
proposed greater enterprise and co-ordination. They would perfect
man's body, but upon its present plan; they would perfect his mind,
but without seeking to introduce anything new in essence. His
physique, percipience, memory, intelligence and emotional nature,
should be improved almost beyond recognition; but they must, it
was said, remain essentially what they always had been.

A second party, however, finally persuaded orthodox opinion to
amplify itself in one important respect. As has already been said, the
Third Men were prone to phases of preoccupation with the ancient
craving for personal immortality. This craving had often been strong
among the First Men; and even the Second Men, in spite of their
great gift of detachment, had sometimes allowed their admiration
for human personality to persuade them that souls must live for ever.
The short-lived and untheoretical Third Men, with their passion for
living things of all kinds, and all the diversity of vital behaviour,
conceived immortality in a variety of manners. In their final culture
they imagined that at death all living things whom the Life God
approved passed into another world, much like the familiar world,
but happier. There they were said to live in the presence of the deity,
serving him in untrammelled vital creativeness of sundry kinds.

Now it was believed that communication might occur between
the two worlds, and that the highest type of terrestrial life was that
which communicated most effectively, and further that the time had
now arrived for much fuller revelation of the life to come. It was
therefore proposed to breed highly specialized communicants whose
office should be to guide this world by means of advice from the
other. As among the First Men, this communication with the unseen
world was believed to take place in the mediumistic trance. The new
enterprise, then, was to breed extremely sensitive mediums, and to
increase the mediumistic powers of the average individual.

There was yet another party, whose aim was very different.
Man, they said, is a very noble organism. We have dealt with other
organisms so as to enhance in each its noblest attributes. It is time to
do the same with man. What is most distinctive in man is intelligent
manipulation, brain and hand. Now hand is really outclassed by

modern mechanisms, but brain will never be outclassed. Therefore we must breed strictly for brain, for intelligent co-ordination of behaviour. All the organic functions which can be performed by machinery, must be relegated to machinery, so that the whole vitality of the organism may be devoted to brain-building and brain-working. We must produce an organism which shall be no mere bundle of relics left over from its primitive ancestors and precariously ruled by a glimmer of intelligence. We must produce a man who is nothing but man. When we have done this we can, if we like, ask him to find out the truth about immortality. And also, we can safely surrender to him the control of all human affairs.

The governing caste were strongly opposed to this policy. They declared that, if it succeeded, it would only produce a most inharmonious being whose nature would violate all the principles of vital aesthetics. Man, they said, was essentially an animal, though uniquely gifted. His whole nature must be developed, not one faculty at the expense of others. In arguing thus, they were probably influenced partly by the fear of losing their authority; but their arguments were cogent, and the majority of the community agreed with them. Nevertheless a small group of the governors themselves were determined to carry through the enterprise in secret.

There was no need of secrecy in breeding communicants. The world state encouraged this policy and even set up institutions for its pursuit.

CHAPTER XI

MAN REMAKES HIMSELF

1. THE FIRST OF THE GREAT BRAINS

Those who sought to produce a super-brain embarked upon a great enterprise of research and experiment in a remote corner of the planet. It is unnecessary to tell in detail how they fared. Working first in secret, they later strove to persuade the world to approve of their scheme, but only succeeded in dividing mankind into two parties. The body politic was torn asunder. There were religious wars. But after a few centuries of intermittent bloodshed the two sects, those who sought to produce communicants and those who sought the super-brain, settled down in different regions to pursue their respective aims unmolested. In time each developed into a kind of nation, united by a religious faith and crusading spirit. There was little cultural intercourse between the two.

Those who desired to produce the super-brain employed four methods, namely selective breeding, manipulation of the hereditary factors in germ cells (cultivated in the laboratory), manipulation of the fertilized ovum (cultivated also in the laboratory), and manipulation of the growing body. At first they produced innumerable tragic abortions. These we need not observe. But at length, several thousand years after the earliest experiments, something was produced which seemed to promise success. A human ovum had been carefully selected, fertilized in the laboratory, and largely reorganized by artificial means. By inhibiting the growth of the embryo's body, and the lower organs of the brain itself, and at the same time greatly stimulating the growth of the cerebral hemispheres, the dauntless experimenters succeeded at last in creating an organism which consisted of a brain twelve feet across, and a body most of which was reduced to a mere vestige upon the under-surface of the brain. The only parts of the body which were allowed to attain the natural size were the arms and hands. These sinewy organs of manipulation were induced to key themselves at the shoulders into the solid masonry which formed the creature's house. Thus they were able to get a purchase for their work. The hands were the normal six-fingered hands of the Third Men, very greatly enlarged and improved. The fantastic organism was generated and matured in a building designed to house both it and the complicated machinery which was necessary to keep it alive. A self-regulating pump, electrically driven, served it as a heart. A chemical factory poured the necessary materials into its blood and removed waste products, thus taking the place of digestive organs and the normal battery of glands. Its lungs consisted of a great room full of oxidizing tubes, through which a constant wind was driven by an electric fan. The same fan forced air through the artificial organs of speech. These organs were so constructed that the natural nerve-fibres, issuing from the speech centres of the brain, could stimulate appropriate electrical controls so as to produce sounds identical with those which they would have produced from a living throat and mouth. The sensory equipment of this trunkless brain was a blend of the natural and the artificial. The optic nerves were induced to grow out along two flexible probosces, five feet long, each of which bore a huge eye at the end. But by a very ingenious alteration of the structure of the eye, the natural lens could be moved aside at will, so that the retina could be applied to any of a great diversity of optical instruments. The ears also could be projected upon stalks, and were so arranged that the actual nerve endings could be brought into contact with artificial resonators of various kinds, or could listen directly to the microscopic rhythms of the most minute organisms. Scent and taste were developed as a chemical sense, which could distinguish almost all compounds and elements by their flavour. Pressure, warmth and cold were detected only by the fingers, but there with great subtlety. Sensory pain was to have been eliminated from the organism altogether; but this end was not achieved.

The creature was successfully launched upon life, and was actually kept alive for four years. But though at first all went well, in his second year the unfortunate child, if such he may be called, began to suffer severe pain, and to show symptoms of mental derangement. In spite of all that his devoted foster-parents could do, he gradually sank into insanity and died. He had succumbed to his own brain weight and to certain failures in the chemical regulation of his blood.

We may overlook the next four hundred years, during which sundry vain attempts were made to repeat the great experiment more successfully. Let us pass on to the first true individual of the fourth human species. He was produced in the same artificial manner as his forerunners, and was designed upon the same general plan. His mechanical and chemical machinery, however, was far more efficient; and his makers expected that, owing to careful adjustments of the mechanisms of growth and decay, he would prove to be immortal. His general plan, also, was changed in one important respect. His makers built a large circular 'brain-turret' which they divided with many partitions, radiating from a central space, and covered everywhere with pigeon-holes. By a technique which took centuries to develop, they induced the cells of the growing embryonic brain to spread outwards, not as normal hemispheres of convolutions, but into the pigeon-holes which had been prepared for them. Thus the artificial 'cranium' had to be a roomy turret of ferro-concrete some forty feet in diameter. A door and a passage led from the outer world into the centre of the turret, and thence other passages radiated between tiers of little cupboards. Innumerable tubes of glass, metal and a kind of vulcanite conveyed blood and chemicals over the whole system. Electric radiators preserved an even warmth in every cupboard, and throughout the innumerable carefully protected channels of the nerve-fibres. Thermometers, dials, pressure gauges, indicators of all sorts, informed the attendants of every physical change in this strange half-natural, half-artificial system, this preposterous factory of mind.

Eight years after its inception the organism had filled its brain room, and attained the mentality of a new-born infant. His advance to maturity seemed to his foster-parents dishearteningly slow. Not till almost at the end of his fifth decade could he be said to have reached the mental standard of a bright adolescent. But there was no real reason for disappointment. Within another decade this pioneer of the Fourth Men had learned all that the Third Men could teach him, and had also seen that a great part of their wisdom was folly. In manual dexterity he could already vie with the best; but though manipulation afforded him intense delight, he used his hands almost wholly in service of his tireless curiosity. In fact, it was evident that curiosity was his main characteristic. He was a huge bump of curiosity equipped with most cunning hands. A department of state had been created to look after his nurture and education. An army of learned persons was kept in readiness to answer his impatient questions and assist him in his own scientific experiments. Now that he had attained maturity these unfortunate pundits found themselves hopelessly outclassed, and reduced to mere clerks, bottle-washers and errand-boys. Hundreds of his servants were for ever scurrying into every corner of the planet to seek information and specimens; and the significance of their errands was by now often quite beyond the range of their own intelligence. They were careful, however, not to let their ignorance appear to the public. On the contrary, they succeeded in gaining much prestige from the mere mysteriousness of their errands.

The great brain was wholly lacking in all normal instinctive responses, save curiosity and constructiveness. Instinctive fear he knew not, though of course he was capable of cold caution in any circumstances which threatened to damage him and hinder his passionate research. Anger he knew not, but only an adamantine firmness in the face of opposition. Normal hunger and thirst he knew not, but only an experience of faintness when his blood was not properly supplied with nutriment. Sex was wholly absent from his mentality. Instinctive tenderness and instinctive group-feeling were not possible to him, for he was without the bowels of mercy. The heroic devotion of his most intimate servants called forth no gratitude, but only cold approval.

At first he interested himself not at all in the affairs of the society which maintained him, served his every whim, and adored him. But in time he began to take pleasure in suggesting brilliant solutions of all the current problems of social organization. His advice was increasingly sought and accepted. He became autocrat of the state. His own intelligence and complete detachment combined with the people's superstitious reverence to establish him far more securely than any ordinary tyrant. He cared nothing for the petty troubles of his people, but he was determined to be served by a harmonious, healthy and potent race. And as relaxation from the more serious excitement of research in physics and astronomy, the study of human nature was not without attractions. It may seem strange that one so completely devoid of human sympathy could have the tact to govern a race of the emotional Third Men. But he had built up for himself a very accurate behaviouristic psychology; and like the skilful master of animals, he knew unerringly how much could be expected of his people, even though their emotions were almost wholly foreign to him. Thus, for instance, while he thoroughly despised their admiration of animals and plants, and their religion of life, he soon learned not to seem hostile to these obsessions, but rather to use them for his own ends. He himself was interested in animals only as material for experiments. In this respect his people readily helped him, partly because he assured them that his goal was the further improvement of all types, partly because they were fascinated by his complete disregard, in his experimentation, of the common technique for preventing pain. The orgy of vicarious suffering awakened in his people the long-suppressed lust in cruelty which, in spite of their intuitive insight into animal nature, was so strong a factor in the third human species.

Little by little the great brain probed the material universe and the universe of mentality. He mastered the principles of biological evolution, and constructed for his own delight a detailed history of life on earth. He learned, by marvellous archaeological technique, the story of all the earlier human peoples, and of the Martian episode, matters which had remained hidden from the Third Men. He discovered the principles of relativity and the quantum theory, the nature of the atom as a complex system of wave trains. He measured the cosmos; and with his delicate instruments he counted the planetary systems in many of the remote universes. He casually solved, to his own satisfaction at least, the ancient problems of good and evil, of mind and its object, of the one and the many, and of truth and error. He created many new departments of state for the purpose of recording his discoveries in an artificial language which he devised for the purpose. Each department consisted of many colleges of carefully bred and educated specialists who could understand the subject of their own department to some extent. But the co-ordination of all, and true insight into each, lay with the great brain alone.

2. THE TRAGEDY OF THE FOURTH MEN

When some three thousand years had passed since his beginning, the unique individual determined to create others of his kind. Not that he suffered from loneliness. Not that he yearned for love, or even for intellectual companionship. But solely for the undertaking of more profound research, he needed the co-operation of beings of his own mental stature. He therefore designed, and had built in various regions of the planet, turrets and factories like his own, though greatly improved. Into each he sent, by his servants, a cell of his own vestigial body, and directed how it should be cultivated so as to produce a new individual. At the same time he caused far-reaching operations to be performed upon himself, so that he should be remade upon a more ample plan. Of the new capacities which he inculcated in himself and his progeny the most important was direct sensitivity to radiation. This was achieved by incorporating in each brain tissue a specially bred strain of Martian parasites. These henceforth were to live in the great brain as integral members of each one of its cells. Each brain was also equipped with a powerful wireless transmitting apparatus. Thus should the widely scattered sessile population maintain direct 'telepathic' contact with one another.

The undertaking was successfully accomplished. Some ten thousand of these new individuals, each specialized for his particular locality and office, now constituted the Fourth Men. On the highest mountains were super-astronomers with vast observatories, whose instruments were partly artificial, partly natural excrescences of their own brains. In the very entrails of the planet others, specially adapted to heat, studied the subterranean forces, and were kept in 'telepathic' union with the astronomers. In the tropics, in the Arctic, in the forests, the deserts, and on the ocean floor, the Fourth Men indulged their immense curiosity; and in the homeland, around the father of the race, a group of great buildings housed a hundred individuals. In the service of this world-wide population, those races of Third Men which had originally co-operated to produce the new human species, tilled the land, tended the cattle, manufactured the immense material requisites of the new civilization, and satisfied their spirits with an ever more stereotyped ritual of their ancient vital art. This degradation of the whole race to a menial position had occurred slowly, imperceptibly.

But the result was none the less irksome. Occasionally there were sparks of rebellion, but they always failed to kindle serious trouble; for the prestige and persuasiveness of the Fourth Men were irresistible.

At length, however, a crisis occurred. For some three thousand years the Fourth Men had pursued their research with constant success, but latterly progress had been slow. It was becoming increasingly difficult to devise new lines of research. True, there was still much detail to be filled in, even in their knowledge of their own planet, and very much in their knowledge of the stars. But there was no prospect of opening up entirely new fields which might throw some light on the essential nature of things. Indeed, it began to dawn on them that they had scarcely plumbed a surface ripple of the ocean of mystery. Their knowledge seemed to them perfectly systematic, yet wholly enigmatic. They had a growing sense that though in a manner they knew almost everything, they really knew nothing.

The normal mind, when it experiences intellectual frustration, can seek recreation in companionship, or physical exercise, or art. But for the Fourth Men there was no such escape. These activities were impossible and meaningless to them. The Great Brains were wholeheartedly interested in the objective world, but solely as a vast stimulus to intellection, never for its own sake. They admired only the intellective process itself and the interpretative formulae and principles which it devised. They cared no more for men and women than for material in a test-tube, no more for one another than for mechanical calculators. Nay, of each one of them it might almost be said that he cared even for himself solely as an instrument of knowing. Many of the species had actually sacrificed their sanity, even in some cases their lives, to the obsessive lust of intellection.

As the sense of frustration became more and more oppressive, the Fourth Men suffered more and more from the one-sidedness of their nature. Though so completely dispassionate while their intellectual life proceeded smoothly, now that it was thwarted they began to be confused by foolish whims and cravings which they disguised from themselves under a cloak of excuses. Sessile and incapable of affection, they continually witnessed the free movement, the group life, the love-making of their menials. Such activities became an offence to them, and filled them with a cold jealousy, which it was altogether beneath their dignity to notice. The affairs of the serf-population began to be conducted by their masters with less than the accustomed justice. Serious grievances arose.

The climax occurred in connexion with a great revival of research, which, it was said, would break down the impalpable barriers and set knowledge in progress again. The Great Brains were to be multiplied a thousandfold, and the resources of the whole planet were to be devoted far more strictly than before to the crusade of intellection. The menial Third Men would therefore have to put up with more work and less pleasure. Formerly they would willingly have accepted this fate for the glory of serving the super-human brains. But the days of their blind devotion was past. It was murmured among them that the great experiment of their forefathers had proved a great disaster, and that the Fourth Men, the Great Brains, in spite of their devilish cunning, were mere abortions.

Matters came to a head when the tyrants announced that all useless animals must be slaughtered, since their upkeep was too great an economic burden upon the world-community. The vital art, moreover, was to be practised in future only by the Great Brains themselves. This announcement threw the Third Men into violent excitement, and divided them into two parties. Many of those whose lives were spent in direct service of the Great Brains favoured implicit obedience, though even these were deeply distressed. The majority, on the other hand, absolutely refused to permit the impious slaughter, or even to surrender their privileges as vital artists. For, they said, to kill off the fauna of the planet would be to violate the fair form of the universe by blotting out many of its most beautiful features. It would be an outrage to the Life-God, and he would surely avenge it. They therefore urged that the time was come for all true human beings to stand together and depose the tyrants. And this, they pointed out, could easily be done. It was only necessary to cut a few electric cables, connecting the Great Brains with the subterranean generating stations. The electric pumps would then cease to supply the brain-turrets with aerated blood. Or, in the few cases in which the Great Brains were so located that they could control their own source of power in wind or water, it was necessary merely to refrain from transporting food to their digestion-laboratories.

The personal attendants of the Great Brains shrank from such action; for their whole lives had been devoted, proudly and even in a manner lovingly, to service of the revered beings. But the agriculturists determined to withhold supplies. The Great Brains, therefore, armed their servitors with a diversity of ingenious weapons. Immense destruction was done; but since the rebels were decimated, there were not enough hands to work the fields. Some of the Great Brains, and many of their servants, actually died of starvation. And as hardship increased, the servants themselves began to drift over to the rebels. It now seemed certain to the Third Men that the Great Brains would very soon be impotent, and the planet once more under the control of natural beings. But the tyrants were not to be so easily defeated. Already for some centuries they had been secretly experimenting with a means of gaining a far more thorough dominion over the natural species. At the eleventh hour they succeeded.

In this undertaking they had been favoured by the results which a section of the natural species itself had produced long ago in the effort to breed specialized communicants to keep in touch with the unseen world. That sect, or theocratic nation, which had striven for many centuries toward this goal, had finally attained what they regarded as success. There came into existence an hereditary caste of communicants. Now, though these beings were subject to mediumistic trances in which they apparently conversed with denizens of the other world and received instructions about the ordering of matters terrestrial, they were in fact merely abnormally suggestible. Trained from childhood in the lore of the unseen world, their minds, during the trance, were amazingly fertile in developing fantasies based on that lore. Left to themselves, they were merely folk who were abnormally lacking in initiative and intelligence. Indeed, so naïve were they, and so sluggish, that they were mentally more like cattle than human beings. Yet under the influence of suggestion they became both intelligent and vigorous. Their intelligence, however, operating strictly in service of the suggestion, was wholly incapable of criticizing the suggestion itself.

There is no need to revert to the downfall of this theocratic society, beyond saying that, since both private and public affairs were regulated by reference to the sayings of the communicants, inevitably the state fell into chaos. The other community of the Third Men, that which was engaged upon breeding the Great Brains, gradually dominated the whole planet. The mediumistic stock, however, remained in existence, and was treated with a half-contemptuous reverence. The mediums were still generally regarded as in some manner specially gifted with the divine spirit, but they were now thought to be too holy for their sayings to have any relation to mundane affairs.

It was by means of this mediumistic stock that the Great Brains had intended to consolidate their position. Their earlier efforts may be passed over. But in the end they produced a race of living and even intelligent machines whose will they could control absolutely, even at a great distance. For the new variety of Third Men was 'telepathically' united with its masters. Martian units had been incorporated in its nervous system.

At the last moment the Great Brains were able to put into the field an army of these perfect slaves, which they equipped with the most efficient lethal weapons. The remnant of original servants discovered too late that they had been helping to produce their supplanters. They joined the rebels, only to share in the general destruction. In a few months all the Third Men, save the new docile variety, were destroyed; except for a few specimens which were preserved in cages for experimental purposes. And in a few years every type of animal that was not known to be directly or indirectly necessary to human life had been exterminated. None were preserved even as specimens, for the Great Brains had already studied them through and through.

But though the Great Brains were now absolute possessors of the Earth, they were after all no nearer their goal than before. The actual struggle with the natural species had provided them with an aim; but now that the struggle was over, they began to be obsessed once more with their intellectual failure. With painful clarity they realized that, in spite of their vast weight of neural tissue, in spite of their immense knowledge and cunning, they were practically no nearer the ultimate truth than their predecessors had been. Both were infinitely far from it.

For the Fourth Men, the Great Brains, there was no possible life but the life of intellect; and the life of intellect had become barren. Evidently something more than mere bulk of brain was needed for the solving of the deeper intellectual problems. They must, therefore, somehow create a new brain-quality, or organic formation of brain, capable of a mode of vision or insight impossible in their present state. They must learn somehow to remake their own brain-tissues upon a new plan. With this aim, and partly through unwitting jealousy of the natural and more balanced species which had created them, they began to use their captive specimens of that species for a great new enterprise of research into the nature of human brain-tissue. It was hoped thus to find some hint of the direction in which the new evolutionary leap should take place. The unfortunate specimens were therefore submitted to a thousand ingenious physiological and psychological tortures. Some were kept alive with their brains spread out permanently on a laboratory table, for microscopic observation during their diverse psychological reactions. Others were put into fantastic states of mental abnormality. Others were maintained in perfect health of body and mind, only to be felled at last by some ingeniously contrived tragic experience. New types were produced which, it was hoped, might show evidence of emergence into a qualitatively higher mode of mentality; but in fact they succeeded only in ranging through the whole gamut of insanity.

The research continued for some thousands of years, but gradually slackened, so utterly barren did it prove to be. As this frustration became more and more evident, a change began to come over the minds of the Fourth Men.

They knew, of course, that the natural species valued many things and activities which they themselves did not appreciate at all. Hitherto this had seemed a symptom merely of the low mental development of the natural species. But the behaviour of the unfortunate specimens upon whom they had been experimenting had gradually given the Fourth Men a greater insight into the likings and admirations of the natural species, so that they had learned to distinguish between those desires which were fundamental and those merely accidental cravings which clear thinking would have dismissed. In fact, they came to see that certain activities and certain objects were appreciated by these beings with the same clear-sighted conviction as they themselves appreciated knowledge. For instance, the natural human beings valued one another, and were sometimes capable of sacrificing themselves for the sake of others. They also valued love itself. And again they valued very seriously their artistic activities; and the activities of their bodies and of animal bodies appeared to them to have intrinsic excellence.

Little by little the Fourth Men began to realize that what was wrong with themselves was not merely their intellectual limitation, but, far more seriously, the limitation of their insight into values. And this weakness, they saw, was the result, not of paucity of intellective brain, but of paucity of body and lower brain tissues. This defect they could not remedy. It was obviously impossible to remake themselves so radically that they should become of a more normal type. Should they concentrate their efforts upon the production of new individuals more harmonious than themselves? Such a work, it might be supposed, would have seemed unattractive to them. But no. They argued thus: 'It is our nature to care most for knowing. Full knowledge is to be attained only by minds both more penetrating and more broadly based than ours. Let us, therefore, waste no more time in seeking to achieve the goal in ourselves. Let us seek rather to produce a kind of being, free from our limitations, in whom we may attain the goal of perfect knowledge vicariously. The producing of such a being will exercise all our powers, and will afford the highest kind of fulfilment possible to us. To refrain from this work would be irrational.'

Thus it came about that the artificial Fourth Men began to work in a new spirit upon the surviving specimens of the Third Men to produce their own supplanters.

3. THE FIFTH MEN

The plan of the proposed new human being was worked out in great detail before any attempt was made to produce an actual individual. Essentially he was to be a normal human organism, with all the bodily functions of the natural type; but he was to be perfected through and through. Care must be taken to give him the greatest possible bulk of brain compatible with such a general plan, but no more. Very carefully his creators calculated the dimensions and internal proportions which their creature must have. His brain could not be nearly as large as their own, since he would have to carry it about with him, and maintain it with his own physiological machinery. On the other hand, if it was to be at all larger than the natural brain, the rest of the organism must be proportionately sturdy. Like the Second Men, the new species must be titanic. Indeed, it must be such as to dwarf even those natural giants. The body, however, must not be so huge as to be seriously hampered by its own weight, and by the necessity of having bones so massive as to be unmanageable.

In working out the general proportions of the new man, his makers took into account the possibility of devising more efficient bone and muscle. After some centuries of patient experiment they did actually invent a means of inducing in germ cells a tendency toward far stronger bone-tissues and far more powerful muscle. At the same time they devised nerve-tissues more highly specialized for their particular functions. And in the new brain, so minute compared with their own, smallness was to be compensated for by efficiency of design, both in the individual cells and in their organization.

Further, it was found possible to economize somewhat in bulk and vital energy by improvements in the digestive system. Certain new models of micro-organisms were produced, which, living symbiotically in the human gut, should render the whole process of digestion easier, more rapid, and less erratic.

Special attention was given to the system of self-repair in all tissues, especially in those which had hitherto been the earliest to wear out. And at the same time the mechanism regulating growth and general senescence was so designed that the new man should reach maturity at the age of two hundred years, and should remain in full vigour, for at least three thousand years, when, with the first serious symptom of decay, his heart should suddenly cease functioning. There had been some dispute whether the new being should be endowed with perennial life, like his makers. But in the end it had been decided that, since he was intended only as a transitional type, it would be safer to allow him only a finite, though a prolonged, lifetime. There must be no possibility that he should be tempted to regard himself as life's final expression.

In sensory equipment, the new man was to have all the advantages of the Second and Third Men, and, in addition a still wider range and finer discrimination in every sense organ. More important was the incorporation of Martian units in the new model of germ cell. As the organism developed, these should propagate themselves and congregate in the cells of the brain, so that every brain area might be sensitive to ethereal vibrations, and the whole might emit a strong system of radiation. But care was taken that this 'telepathic' faculty of the new species should remain subordinate. There must be no danger that the individual should become a mere resonator of the herd.

Long-drawn-out chemical research enabled the Fourth Men to design also far-reaching improvements in the secretions of the new man, so that he should maintain both a perfect physiological equilibrium and a well-balanced temperament. For they were determined that though he should experience all the range of emotional life, his passions should not run into disastrous excess; nor should he be prone to some one emotion in season and out of season. It was necessary also to revise in great detail the whole system of natural reflexes, abolishing some, modifying others, and again strengthening others. All the more complex, 'instinctive' responses, which had persisted in man since the days of Pithecanthropus Erectus, had also to be meticulously revised, both in respect of the form of activity and the objects upon which they should be instinctively directed. Anger, fear, curiosity, humour, tenderness, egoism, sexual passion, and sociality must all be possible, but never uncontrollable. In fact, as with the Second Men, but more emphatically, the new type was to have an innate aptitude for, and inclination toward, all those higher activities and objects which, in the First Men, were only achieved after laborious discipline. Thus, while the design included self-regard, it also involved a disposition to prize the self chiefly as a social and intellectual being, rather than as a primeval savage. And while it included strong sociality, the group upon which instinctive interest was to be primarily directed was to be nothing less than the organized community of all minds. And again, while it included vigorous primitive sexuality and parenthood, it provided also those innate 'sublimations' which had occurred in the second species; for instance, the native aptitude for altruistic love of individual spirits of every kind, and for art and religion. Only by a miracle of pure intellectual skill could the cold-natured Great Brains, who were themselves doomed never to have actual experience of such activities, contrive, merely by study of the Third Men, to see their importance, and to design an organism splendidly capable of them. It was much as though a blind race, after studying physics, should invent organs of sight.

It was recognized, of course, that in a race in which the average life span should be counted in thousands of years, procreation must be very rare. Yet it was also recognized that, for full development of mind, not only sexual intercourse but parenthood was necessary in both sexes. This difficulty was overcome partly by designing a very prolonged infancy and childhood; which, necessary in themselves for the proper mental and physical growth of these complicated organisms, provided also a longer exercise of parenthood for the mature. At the same time the actual process of childbirth was designed to be as easy as among the Third Men. And it was expected that with its greatly improved physiological organization the infant would not need that anxious and absorbing care which had so seriously hobbled most mothers among the earlier races.

The mere sketching out of these preliminary specifications of an improved human being involved many centuries of research and calculation which taxed even the ingenuity of the Great Brains. Then followed a lengthy period of tentative experiment in the actual production of such a type. For some thousands of years little was done but to show that many promising lines of attack were after all barren. And several times during this period the whole work was held up by disagreements among the Great Brains themselves as to the policy to be adopted. Once, indeed, they took to violence, one party attacking the other with chemicals, microbes, and armies of human automata.

In short it was only after many failures, and after many barren epochs during which, for a variety of reasons, the enterprise was neglected, that the Fourth Men did at length fashion two individuals almost precisely of the type they had originally designed. These were produced from a single fertilized ovum, in laboratory conditions. Identical twins, but of opposite sexes, they became the Adam and Eve of a new and glorious human species, the Fifth Men.

It may fittingly be said of the Fifth Men that they were the first to attain true human proportions of body and mind. On average they were more than twice as tall as the First Men, and much taller than the Second Men. Their lower limbs had therefore to be extremely massive compared with the torso which they had to support. Thus, upon the ample pedestal of their feet, they stood like columns of masonry. Yet though their proportions were in a manner elephantine, there was a remarkable precision and even delicacy in the volumes that composed them. Their great arms and shoulders, dwarfed somewhat by their still mightier legs, were instruments not only of power but also of fine adjustment. Their hands also were fashioned both for power and for minute control; for, while the thumb and forefinger constituted a formidable vice, the delicate sixth finger had been induced to divide its tip into two Lilliputian fingers and a corresponding thumb. The contours of the limbs were sharply visible, for the body bore no hair, save for a close, thick skull-cap which, in the original stock, was of ruddy brown. The well-marked eyebrows, when drawn down, shaded the sensitive eyes from the sun. Elsewhere there was no need of hair, for the brown skin had been so ingeniously contrived that it maintained an even temperature alike in tropical and sub-Arctic climates, with no aid either from hair or clothes. Compared with the great body, the head was not large, though the brain capacity was twice that of the Second Men. In the original pair of individuals the immense eyes were of a deep violet, the features strongly moulded and mobile. These facial characters had not been specially designed, for they seemed unimportant to the Fourth Men; but the play of biological forces resulted in a face not unlike that of the Second Men, though with an added and indescribable expression which no human face had hitherto attained.

How from this pair of individuals the new population gradually arose; how at first it was earnestly fostered by its creators; how it subsequently asserted its independence and took control of its own destiny; how the Great Brains failed piteously to understand and sympathize with the mentality of their creatures, and tried to tyrannize over them; how for a while the planet was divided into two mutually intolerant communities, and was at last drenched with man's blood, until the human automata were exterminated, the Great

Brains starved or blown to pieces, and the Fifth Men themselves decimated; how, as a result of these events, a dense fog of barbarism settled once more upon the planet, so that the Fifth Men, like so many other races, had after all to start rebuilding civilization and culture from its very foundations; how all these things befell we must not in detail observe.

4. THE CULTURE OF THE FIFTH MEN

It is not possible to recount the stages by which the Fifth Men advanced toward their greatest civilization and culture; for it is that fully developed culture itself which concerns us. And even of their highest achievement, which persisted for so many millions of years, I can say but little, not merely because I must hasten to the end of my story, but also because so much of that achievement lies wholly beyond the comprehension of those for whom this book is intended. For I have at last reached that period in the history of man when he first began to reorganize his whole mentality to cope with matters whose very existence had been hitherto almost completely hidden from him. The old aims persist, and are progressively realized as never before; but also they become increasingly subordinate to the requirements of new aims which are more and more insistently forced upon him by his deepening experience. Just as the interests and ideals of the First Men lie beyond the grasp of their ape contemporaries, so the interests and ideals of the Fifth Men in their full development lie beyond the grasp of the First Men. On the other hand, just as, in the life of primitive man, there is much which would be meaningful even to the ape, so in the life of the Fifth Men much remains which is meaningful even to the First Men.

Conceive a world-society developed materially far beyond the wildest dreams of America. Unlimited power, derived partly from the artificial disintegration of atoms, partly from the actual annihilation of matter through the union of electrons and protons to form radiation, completely abolished the whole grotesque burden of drudgery which hitherto had seemed the inescapable price of civilization, nay of life itself. The vast economic routine of the world-community was carried on by the mere touching of appropriate buttons. Transport, mining, manufacture, and even agriculture were performed in this manner. And indeed in most cases the systematic co-ordination of these activities was itself the work of self-regulating machinery. Thus, not only was there no longer need for any human beings to spend their lives in unskilled monotonous labour, but further, much that earlier races would have regarded as highly skilled though stereotyped work, was now carried on by machinery. Only the pioneering of industry, the endless exhilarating research, invention, design and reorganization, which is incurred by an ever-changing society, still engaged the minds of men and women. And though this work was of course immense, it could not occupy the whole attention of a great world-community. Thus very much of the energy of the race was free to occupy itself with other no less difficult and exacting matters, or to seek recreation in its many admirable sports and arts. Materially every individual was a multi-millionaire, in that he had at his beck and call a great diversity of powerful mechanisms; but also he was a penniless friar, for he had no vestige of economic control over any other human being. He could fly through the upper air to the ends of the earth in an hour, or hang idle among the clouds all day long. His flying machine was no cumbersome aeroplane, but either a wingless aerial boat, or a mere suit of overalls in which he could disport himself with the freedom of a bird. Not only in the air, but in the sea also, he was free. He could stroll about the ocean bed, or gambol with the deep-sea fishes. And for habitation he could make his home, as he willed, either in a shack in the wilderness or in one of the great pylons which dwarfed the architecture even of the American age. He could possess this huge palace in loneliness and fill it with his possessions, to be automatically cared for without human service; or he could join with others and create a hive of social life. All these amenities he took for granted as the savage takes for granted the air which he breathes. And because they were as universally available as air, no one craved them in excess, and no one grudged another the use of them.

Yet the population of the earth was now very numerous. Some ten thousand million persons had their homes in the snow-capped pylons which covered the continents with an open forest of architecture. Between these great obelisks lay corn-land, park, and wilderness.

For there were very many areas of hill-country and forest which were preserved as playgrounds. And indeed one whole continent, stretching from the Tropics to the Arctic, was kept as nearly as possible in its natural state. This region was chosen mainly for its mountains; for since most of the Alpine tracts had by now been worn into insignificance by water and frost, mountains were much prized. Into this Wild Continent individuals of all ages repaired to spend many years at a time in living the life of primitive man without any aid whatever from civilization. For it was recognized that a highly sophisticated race, devoted almost wholly to art and science, must take special measures to preserve its contact with the primitive. Thus in the Wild Continent was to be found at any time a sparse population of 'savages', armed with flint and bone, or more rarely with iron, which they or their friends had wrested from the earth. These voluntary primitives were intent chiefly upon hunting and simple agriculture. Their scanty leisure was devoted to art, and meditation, and to savouring fully all the primeval human values. Indeed it was a hard life and a dangerous one that these intellectuals periodically imposed on themselves. And though of course they had zest in it, they often dreaded its hardship and the uncertainty that they would ever return from it. For the danger was very real. The Fifth Men had compensated for the Fourth Men's foolish destruction of the animals by creating a whole system of new types, which they set at large in the Wild Continent; and some of these creatures were extremely formidable carnivora, which man himself, armed only with primitive weapons, had very good reason to fear. In the Wild Continent there was inevitably a high death-rate. Many promising lives were tragically cut short. But it was recognized that from the point of view of the race this sacrifice was worth while, for the spiritual effects of the institution of periodic savagery were very real. Beings whose natural span was three thousand years, given over almost wholly to civilized pursuits, were greatly invigorated and enlightened by an occasional decade in the wild.

The culture of the Fifth Men was influenced in many respects by their 'telepathic' communication with one another. The obvious advantages of this capacity were now secured without its dangers. Each individual could isolate himself at will from the radiation of his fellows, either wholly or in respect of particular elements of his mental process; and thus he was in no danger of losing his individuality. But, on the other hand, he was immeasurably more able to participate in the experience of others than were beings for whom the only possible communication was symbolic. The result was that, though conflict of wills was still possible, it was far more easily resolved by mutual understanding than had ever been the case in earlier species. Thus there were no lasting and no radical conflicts, either of thought or desire. It was universally recognized that every discrepancy of opinion and of aim could be abolished by telepathic discussion. Sometimes the process would be easy and rapid; sometimes it could not be achieved without a patient and detailed 'laying of mind to mind', so as to bring to light the point where the difference originated.

One result of the general 'telepathic' facility of the species was that speech was no longer necessary. It was still preserved and prized, but only as a medium of art, not as a means of communication. Thinking, of course, was still carried on largely by means of words; but in communication there was no more need actually to speak the words than in thinking in private. Written language remained essential for the recording and storing of thought. Both language and the written expression of it had become far more complex and accurate than they had ever been, more faithful instruments for the expression and creation of thought and emotion.

'Telepathy' combined with longevity and the extremely subtle brain-structure of the species to afford each individual an immense number of intimate friendships, and some slight acquaintance actually with the whole race. This, I fear, must seem incredible to my readers, unless they can be persuaded to regard it as a symptom of the high mental development of the species. However that may be, it is a fact that each person was aware of every other, at least as a face, or a name, or the holder of a certain office. It is impossible to exaggerate the effects of this facility of personal intercourse. It meant that the species constituted at any moment, if not strictly a community of friends, at least a vast club or college. Further, since each individual saw his own mind reflected, as it were, in very many other minds, and since there was great variety of psychological types, the upshot in each individual was a very accurate self-consciousness.

In the Martians, 'telepathic' intercourse had resulted in a true group mind, a single psychical process embodied in the electro-magnetic radiation of the whole race; but this group-mind was inferior in calibre to the individual minds. All that was distinctive of an individual at his best failed to contribute to the group-mind. But in the fifth human species 'telepathy' was only a means of intercourse between individuals; there was no true group-mind. On the other hand, 'telepathic' intercourse occurred even on the highest planes of experience. It was by 'telepathic' intercourse in respect of art, science, philosophy, and the appreciation of personalities, that the public mind, or rather the public culture, of the Fifth Men had being. With the Martians, 'telepathic' union took place chiefly by elimination of the differences between individuals; with the Fifth Men 'telepathic' communication was, as it were, a kind of spiritual multiplication of mental diversity, by which each mind was enriched with the wealth of ten thousand million. Consequently each individual was, in a very real sense, the cultured mind of the species; but there were as many such minds as there were individuals. There was no additional racial mind over and above the minds of the individuals. Each individual himself was a conscious centre which participated in, and contributed to, the experience of all other centres.

This state of affairs would not have been possible had not the world community been able to direct so much of its interest and energy into the higher mental activities. The whole structure of society was fashioned in relation to its best culture. It is almost impossible to give even an inkling of the nature and aims of this culture, and to make it believable that a huge population should have spent scores of millions of years not wholly, not even chiefly, on industrial advancement, but almost entirely on art, science and philosophy, without ever repeating itself or falling into ennui. I can only point out that, the higher a mind's development, the more it discovers in the universe to occupy it.

Needless to say, the Fifth Men had early mastered all those paradoxes of physical science which had so perplexed the First Men. Needless to say, they had a very complete knowledge of the geography of the cosmos and of the atom. But again and again the very foundations of their science were shattered by some new discovery, so that they had patiently to reconstruct the whole upon an entirely new plan. At length, however, with the clear formulation of the principles of psycho-physics, in which the older psychology and the older physics were held, so to speak, in chemical combination, they seemed to have built upon the rock. In this science, the fundamental concepts of psychology were given a physical meaning, and the fundamental concepts of physics were stated in a psychological manner. Further, the most fundamental relations of the physical universe were found to be of the same nature as the fundamental principles of art. But, and herein lay mystery and horror even for the Fifth Men, there was no shred of evidence that this aesthetically admirable cosmos was the work of a conscious artist, nor yet that any mind would ever develop so greatly as to be able to appreciate the Whole in all its detail and unity.

Since art seemed to the Fifth Men to be in some sense basic to the cosmos, they were naturally very much preoccupied with artistic creation. Consequently, all those who were not social or economic organizers, or scientific researchers, or pure philosophers, were by profession creative artists or handicraftsmen. That is to say, they were engaged on the production of material objects of various kinds, whose form should be aesthetically significant to the perceiver. In some cases the material object was a pattern of spoken words, in others pure music, in others moving coloured shapes, in others a complex of steel cubes and bars, in others some translation of the human figure into a particular medium, and so on. But also the aesthetic impulse expressed itself in the production, by hand, of innumerable common utensils, indulging sometimes in lavish decoration, trusting at other times to the beauty of function. Every medium of art that had ever beers employed was employed by the Fifth Men, and innumerable new vehicles were also used. They prized on the whole more highly those kinds of art which were not static; but involved time as well as space; for as a race they were peculiarly fascinated by time.

These innumerable artists held that they were doing something of great importance. The cosmos was to be regarded as an aesthetic unity in four directions, and of inconceivable complexity. Human works of pure art were thought of as instruments through which man might behold and admire some aspect of the cosmic beauty. They were said to focus together features of the cosmos too vast and elusive for man otherwise to apprehend their form. The work of art was sometimes likened to a compendious mathematical formula expressive of some immense and apparently chaotic field of facts. But in the case of art, it was said, the unity which the artistic object elicited was one in which factors of vital nature and of mind itself were essential members.

The race thus deemed itself to be engaged upon a great enterprise both of discovery and creation in which each individual was both an originator of some unique contribution, and an appraiser of all.

Now, as the years advanced in millions and in decades of millions, it began to be noticed that the movement of world culture was in a manner spiral. There would be an age during which the interest of the race was directed almost wholly upon certain tracts or aspects of existence; and then, after perhaps a hundred thousand years, these would seem to have been fully cultivated, and would be left fallow. During the next epoch attention would be in the main directed to other spheres, and then afterwards to yet others, and again others. But at length a return would be made to the fields that had been deserted, and it would be discovered that they could now miraculously bear a million-fold the former crop. Thus, in both science and art man kept recurring again and again to the ancient themes, to work over them once more in meticulous detail and strike from them new truth and new beauty, such as, in the earlier epoch, he could never have conceived. Thus it was that, though science gathered to itself unfalteringly an ever wider and more detailed view of existence, it periodically discovered some revolutionary general principle in terms of which its whole content had to be given a new significance. And in art there would appear in one age works superficially almost identical with works of another age, yet to the discerning eye incomparably more significant. Similarly, in respect of human personality itself, those men and women who lived at the close of the aeon of the Fifth Men could often discover in the remote beginning of their own race beings curiously like themselves, yet, as it were, expressed in fewer dimensions than their own many-dimensional natures. As a map is like the mountainous land, or the picture like the landscape, or indeed as the point and the circle are like the sphere, so, and only so, the earlier Fifth Men resembled the flower of the species.

Such statements would be in a manner true of any period of steady cultural progress. But in the present instance they have a peculiar significance which I must now somehow contrive to suggest.

CHAPTER XII

THE LAST TERRESTRIALS

1. THE CULT OF EVANESCENCE

The Fifth Men had not been endowed with that potential immortality which their makers themselves possessed. And from the fact that they were mortal and yet long-lived, their culture drew its chief brilliance and poignancy. Beings for whom the natural span was three thousand years, and ultimately as much as fifty thousand, were peculiarly troubled by the prospect of death, and by the loss of those dear to them. The mere ephemeral kind of spirit, that comes into being and then almost immediately ceases, before it has entered at all deeply into consciousness of itself, can face its end with a courage that is half unwitting. Even its smart in the loss of other beings with whom it has been intimate is but a vague and dreamlike suffering. For the ephemeral spirit has no time to grow fully awake, or fully intimate with another, before it must lose its beloved, and itself once more fade into unconsciousness. But with the long-lived yet not immortal Fifth Men the case was different. Gathering to themselves experience of the cosmos, acquiring an ever more precise and vivid insight and appreciation, they knew that very soon all this wealth of the soul must cease to be. And in love, though they might be fully intimate not merely with one but with very many persons, the death of one of these dear spirits seemed an irrevocable tragedy, an utter annihilation of the most resplendent kind of glory, an impoverishment of the cosmos for evermore.

In their brief primitive phase, the Fifth Men, like so many other races, sought to console themselves by unreasoning faith in a life after death. They conceived, for instance, that at death terrestrial beings embarked upon a career continuous with earthly life, but far more ample, either in some remote planetary system, or in some wholly distinct orb of space-time. But though such theories were never disproved in the primitive era, they gradually began to seem not merely improbable but ignoble. For it came to be recognized that the resplendent glories of personality, even in that degree of beauty which now for the first time was attained, were not after all the extreme of glory. It was seen with pain, but also with exultation, that even love's demand that the beloved should have immortal life is a betrayal of man's paramount allegiance. And little by little it became evident that those who used great gifts, and even genius, to establish the truth of the after life, or to seek contact with their beloved dead, suffered from a strange blindness, and obtuseness of the spirit. Though the love which had misled them was itself a very lovely thing, yet they were misled. Like children, searching for lost toys, they wandered. Like adolescents seeking to recapture delight in the things of childhood, they shunned those more difficult admirations which are proper to the grown mind.

And so it became a constant aim of the Fifth Men to school themselves to admire chiefly even in the very crisis of bereavement, not persons, but that great music of innumerable personal lives, which is the life of the race. And quite early in their career they discovered an unexpected beauty in the very fact that the individual must die. So that, when they had actually come into possession of the means to make themselves immortal, they refrained, choosing rather merely to increase the life-span of succeeding generations to fifty thousand years. Such a period seemed to be demanded for the full exercise of human capacity; but immortality, they held, would lead to spiritual disaster.

Now as their science advanced they saw that there had been a time, before the stars were formed, when there was no possible footing for minds in the cosmos; and that there would come a time when mentality would be driven out of existence. Earlier human species had not needed to trouble about mind's ultimate fate; but for the long-lived Fifth Men the end, though remote, did not seem infinitely distant. The prospect distressed them. They had schooled themselves to live not for the individual but for the race; and now the life of the race itself was seen to be a mere instant between the endless void of the past and the endless void of the future. Nothing within their ken was more worthy of admiration than the organized progressive mentality of mankind; and the conviction that this most admired thing must soon cease, filled many of their less ample minds with horror and indignation. But in time the Fifth Men, like the Second Men long before them, came to suspect that even in this tragic brevity of mind's course there was a quality of beauty, more difficult than the familiar beauty, but also more exquisite. Even thus imprisoned in an instant, the spirit of man might yet plumb the whole extent of space, and also the whole past and the whole future; and so, from behind his prison bars, he might render the universe that intelligent worship which, they felt, it demanded of him. Better so, they said, than that he should fret himself with puny efforts to escape. He is dignified by his very weakness, and the cosmos by its very indifference to him.

For aeons they remained in this faith. And they schooled their hearts to acquiesce in it, saying, if it is so, it is best, and somehow we must learn to see that it is best. But what they meant by 'best' was not what their predecessors would have meant. They did not, for instance, deceive themselves by pretending that after all they themselves actually preferred life to be evanescent. On the contrary, they continued to long that it might be otherwise. But having discovered, both behind the physical order and behind the desires of minds, a fundamental principle whose essence was aesthetic, they were faithful to the conviction that whatever was fact must somehow in the universal view be fitting, right, beautiful, integral to the form of the cosmos. And so they accepted as right a state of affairs which in their own hearts they still felt grievously wrong. This conviction of the irrevocability of the past and of the evanescence of mind induced in them a great tenderness for all beings that had lived and ceased. Deeming themselves to be near the crest of life's achievement, blessed also with longevity and philosophic detachment, they were often smitten with pity for those humbler, briefer and less free spirits whose lot had fallen in the past. Moreover, themselves extremely complex, subtle, conscious, they conceived a generous admiration for all simple minds, for the early men, and for the beasts. Very strongly they condemned the action of their predecessors in destroying so many joyous and delectable creatures. Earnestly they sought to reconstruct in imagination all those beings that blind intellectualism had murdered. Earnestly they delved in the near and the remote past so as to recover as much as possible of the history of life on the planet. With meticulous love they would figure out the life stories of extinct types, such as the brontosaurus, the hippopotamus, the chimpanzee, the Englishman, the American, as also of the still extant amoeba. And while they could not but relish the comicality of these remote beings, their amusement was the outgrowth of affectionate insight into simple natures, and was but the obverse of their recognition that the primitive is essentially tragic, because blind. And so, while they saw that the main work of man must have regard to the future, they felt that he owed also a duty toward the past. He must preserve it in his own mind, if not actually in life at least in being. In the future lay glory, joy, brilliance of the spirit. The future needed service, not pity, not piety; but in the past lay darkness, confusion, waste, and all the cramped primitive minds, bewildered, torturing one another in their stupidity, yet one and all in some unique manner, beautiful.

The reconstruction of the past, not merely as abstract history but with the intimacy of the novel, thus became one of the main preoccupations of the Fifth Men. Many devoted themselves to this work, each individual specializing very minutely in some particular episode of human or animal history, and transmitting his work into the culture of the race. Thus increasingly the individual felt himself to be a single flicker between the teeming gulf of the never-more and the boundless void of the not-yet. Himself a member of a very noble and fortunate race, his zest in existence was tempered, deepened, by a sense of the presence, the ghostly presence, of the myriad less fortunate beings in the past. Sometimes, and especially in epochs when the contemporary world seemed most satisfactory and promising, this piety toward the primitive and the past became the dominant activity of the race, giving rise to alternating phases of rebellion against the tyrannical nature of the cosmos, and faith that in the universal view, after all, this horror must be right. In this latter mood it was held that the very irrevocability of the past dignified all past existents, and dignified the cosmos, as a work of tragic art is dignified by the irrevocability of disaster. It was this mood of acquiescence and faith which in the end became the characteristic attitude of the Fifth Men for many millions of years.

But a bewildering discovery was in store for the Fifth Men, a discovery which was to change their whole attitude toward existence. Certain obscure biological facts began to make them suspect, on purely empirical grounds, that past events were not after all simply non-existent, that though no longer existent in the temporal manner, they had eternal existence in some other manner. The effect of this increasing suspicion about the past was that a once harmonious race was divided for a while into two parties, those who insisted that the formal beauty of the universe demanded the tragic evanescence of all things, and those who determined to show that living minds could actually reach back into past events in all their pastness.

The readers of this book are not in a position to realize the poignancy of the conflict which now threatened to wreck humanity. They cannot approach it from the point of view of a race whose culture had consisted of an age-long schooling in admiration of an ever-vanishing cosmos. To the orthodox it seemed that the new view was iconoclastic, impertinent, vulgar. Their opponents, on the other hand, insisted that the matter must be decided dispassionately, according to the evidence. They were also able to point out that this devotion to evanescence was after all but the outcome of the conviction that the cosmos must be supremely noble. No one, it was said, really had direct vision of evanescence as in itself an excellence. So heartfelt was the dispute that the orthodox party actually broke off all 'telepathic' communication with the rebels, and even went so far as to plan their destruction. There can be no doubt that if violence had actually been used the human race would have succumbed; for in a species of such high mental development internecine war would have been a gross violation of its nature. It would never have been able to live down so shameful a spiritual disaster. Fortunately, however, at the eleventh hour, common sense prevailed. The iconoclasts were permitted to carry on their research, and the whole race awaited the result.

2. EXPLORATION OF TIME

This first attack upon the nature of time involved an immense co-operative work, both theoretical and practical. It was from biology that the first hint had come that the past persisted. And it would be necessary to restate the whole of biology and the physical sciences in terms of the new idea. On the practical side it was necessary to undertake a great campaign of experiment, physiological and psychological. We cannot stay to watch this work. Millions of years passed by. Sometimes, for thousands of years at a spell, temporal research was the main preoccupation of the race: sometimes it was thrust into the background, or completely ignored, during epochs which were dominated by other interests. Age after age passed, and always the effort of man in this sphere remained barren. Then at last there was a real success.

A child had been selected from among those produced by an age-long breeding enterprise, directed towards the mastery of time. From infancy this child's brain had been very carefully controlled physiologically. Psychologically also he had been subjected to a severe treatment, that he might be properly schooled for his strange task. In the presence of several scientists and historians he was put into a kind of trance, and brought out of it again, half an hour later. He was then asked to give an account 'telepathically' of his experiences during the trance. Unfortunately he was now so shattered that his evidence was almost unintelligible. After some months of rest he was questioned again, and was able to describe a curious episode which turned out to be a terrifying incident in the girlhood of his dead mother. He seemed to have seen the incident through her eyes, and to have been aware of all her thoughts. This alone proved nothing, for he might have received the information from some living mind. Once more, therefore, and in spite of his entreaties, he was put into the peculiar trance. On waking he told a rambling story of 'little red people living in a squat white tower'. It was clear that he was referring to the Great Brains and their attendants. But once more, this proved nothing; and before the account was finished the child died.

Another child was chosen, but was not put to the test until late in adolescence. After an hour of the trance, he woke and became terribly agitated, but forced himself to describe an episode which the historians assigned to the age of the Martian invasions. The importance of this incident lay in his account of a certain house with a carved granite portico, situated at the head of a waterfall in a mountain valley. He said he had found himself to be an old woman, and that he, or she, was being hurriedly helped out of the house by the other inmates. They watched a formless monster creep down the valley, destroy their house, and mangle two persons who failed to get away in time. Now this house was not at all typical of the Second Men, but must have expressed the whim of some freakish individual. From evidence derived from the boy himself, it proved possible to locate the valley with reference to a former mountain, known to history. No valley survived in that spot; but deep excavations revealed the ancient slopes, the fault that had occasioned the waterfall, and the broken pillars.

This and many similar incidents confirmed the Fifth Men in their new view of time. There followed an age in which the technique of direct inspection of the past was gradually improved, but not without tragedy. In the early stages it was found impossible to keep the 'medium' alive for more than a few weeks after his venture into the past. The experience seemed to set up a progressive mental disintegration which produced first insanity, then paralysis, and, within a few months, death. This difficulty was at last overcome. By one means and another a type of brain was produced capable of undergoing the strain of supra-temporal experience without fatal results. An increasingly large proportion of the rising generation had now direct access to the past, and were engaged upon a great restatement of history in relation to their first-hand experience; but their excursions into the past were uncontrollable. They could not go where they wanted to go, but only where fate flung them. Nor could they go of their own will, but only through a very complicated technique, and with the cooperation of experts. After a time the process was made much easier, in fact, too easy. The unfortunate medium might slip so easily into the trance that his days were eaten up by the past. He might suddenly fall to the ground, and lie rapt, inert, dependent on artificial feeding, for weeks, months, even for years. Or a dozen times in the same day he might be flung into a dozen different epochs of history. Or, still more distressing, his experience of past events might not keep pace with the actual rhythm of those events themselves. Thus he might behold the events of a month, or even a lifetime, fantastically accelerated so as to occupy a trance of no more than a day's duration. Or, worse, he might find himself sliding backwards down the vista of the hours and experiencing events in an order the reverse of the natural order. Even the magnificent brains of the Fifth Men could not stand this. The result was maniacal behaviour, followed by death. Another trouble also beset these first experimenters. Supra-temporal experience proved to be like a dangerous and habit-forming drug. Those who ventured into the past might become so intoxicated that they would try to spend every moment of their natural lives in roaming among past events. Thus gradually they would lose touch with the present, live in absent-minded brooding, fail to react normally to their environment, turn socially worthless, and often come actually to physical disaster through inability to look after themselves.

Many more thousands of years passed before these difficulties and dangers were overcome. At length, however, the technique of supra-temporal experience was so perfected that every individual could at will practise it with safety, and could, within limits, project his vision into any locality of space-time which he desired to inspect. It was only possible, however, to see past events through the mind of some past organism, no longer living. And in practice only human minds, and to some extent the minds of the higher mammals, could be entered. The explorer retained throughout his adventure his own personality and system of memory. While experiencing the past individual's perceptions, memories, thoughts, desires, and in fact the whole process and content of the past mind, the explorer continued to be himself, and to react in terms of his own character, now condemning, now sympathizing, now critically enjoying the spectacle.

The task of explaining the mechanism of this new faculty occupied the scientists and philosophers of the species for a very long period. The final account, of course, cannot be presented save by parable; for it was found necessary to recast many fundamental concepts in order to interpret the facts coherently. The only hint that I can give of the explanation is in saying, metaphorically of course, that the living brain had access to the past, not by way of some mysterious kind of racial memory, nor by some equally impossible journey up the stream of time, but by a partial awakening, as it were, into eternity, and into inspection of a minute tract of space-time through some temporal mind in the past, as though through an optical instrument.

In the early experiments the fantastic speeding, slowing and reversal of the temporal process resulted from disorderly inspection. As a reader may either skim the pages of a book, or read at a comfortable pace, or dwell upon one word, or spell the sentence backwards, so, unintentionally, the novice in eternity might read or misread the mind that was presented to him.

This new mode of experience, it should be noted, was the activity of living brains, though brains of a novel kind. Hence what was to be discovered 'through the medium of eternity' was limited by the particular exploring brain's capacity of understanding what was presented to it. And, further, though the actual supra-temporal contact with past events occupied no time in the brain's natural life, the assimilating of that moment of vision, the reduction of it to normal temporal memory in the normal brain structures, took time, and had to be done during the period of the trance. To expect the neural structure to record the experience instantaneously would be to expect a complicated machine to effect a complicated readjustment without a process of readjusting.

The access to the past had, of course, far-reaching effects upon the culture of the Fifth Men. Not only did it give them an incomparably more accurate knowledge of past events, and insight into the motives of historical personages, and into large-scale cultural movements, but also it effected a subtle change in their estimate of the importance of things. Though intellectually they had, of course, realized both the vastness and the richness of the past, now they realized it with an overwhelming vividness. Matters that had been known hitherto only historically, schematically, were now available to be lived through by intimate acquaintance. The only limit to such acquaintance was set by the limitations of the explorer's own brain-capacity. Consequently the remote past came to enter into a man and shape his mind in a manner in which only the recent past, through memory, had shaped him hitherto. Even before the new kind of experience was first acquired, the race had been, as was said, peculiarly under the spell of the past; but now it was infinitely more so. Hitherto the Fifth Men had been like stay-at-home folk who had read minutely of foreign parts, but had never travelled; now they had become travellers experienced in all the continents of human time. The presences that had hitherto been ghostly were now presences of flesh and blood seen in broad daylight. And so the moving instant called the present appeared no longer as the only, and infinitesimal, real, but as the growing surface of an everlasting tree of existence. It was now the past that seemed most real, while the future still seemed void, and the present merely the impalpable becomingness of the indestructible past.

The discovery that past events were after all persistent, and accessible, was of course for the Fifth Men a source of deep joy; but also it caused them a new distress. While the past was thought of as a mere gulf of non-existence, the inconceivably great pain, misery, baseness, that had fallen into that gulf, could be dismissed as done with; and the will could be concentrated wholly on preventing such horrors from occurring in the future. But now, along with past joy, past distress was found to be everlasting. And those who, in the course of their voyaging in the past, encountered regions of eternal agony, came back distraught. It was easy to remind these harrowed explorers that if pain was eternal, so also was joy. Those who had endured travel in the tragic past were apt to dismiss such assurances with contempt, affirming that all the delights of the whole population of time could not compensate for the agony of one tortured individual. And anyhow, they declared, it was obvious that there had been no preponderance of joy over pain. Indeed, save in the modern age, pain had been overwhelmingly in excess.

So seriously did these convictions prey upon the minds of the Fifth Men, that in spite of their own almost perfect social order, in which suffering had actually to be sought out as a tonic, they fell into despair. At all times, in all pursuits, the presence of the tragic past haunted them, poisoning their lives, sapping their strength. Lovers were ashamed of their delight in one another. As in the far-off days of sexual taboo, guilt crept between them, and held their spirits apart even while their bodies were united.

3. VOYAGING IN SPACE

It was while they were struggling in the grip of this vast social melancholy, and anxiously erasing some new vision by which to reinterpret or transcend the agony of the past, that the Fifth Men were confronted with a most unexpected physical crisis. It was discovered that something queer was happening to the moon; in fact, that the orbit of the satellite was narrowing in upon the earth in a manner contrary to all the calculations of the scientists.

The Fifth Men had long ago fashioned for themselves an all-embracing and minutely coherent system of natural sciences, every factor in which had been put to the test a thousand times and had never been shaken. Imagine, then, their bewilderment at this extraordinary discovery. In ages when science was still fragmentary, a subversive discovery entailed merely a reorganization of some one department of science; but by now, such was the coherence of knowledge, that any minute discrepancy of fact and theory must throw man into a state of complete intellectual vertigo.

The evolution of the lunar orbit had, of course, been studied from time immemorial. Even the First Men had learned that the moon must first withdraw from and subsequently once more approach the earth, till it should reach a critical proximity and begin to break up into a swarm of fragments likes the rings of Saturn. This view had been very thoroughly confirmed by the Fifth Men themselves. The satellite should have continued to withdraw for yet many hundreds of millions of years; but in fact it was now observed that not only had the withdrawal ceased, but a comparatively rapid approach had begun.

Observations and calculations were repeated, and ingenious theoretical explanations were suggested; but the truth remained completely hidden. It was left to a future and more brilliant species to discover the connexion between a planet's gravitation and its cultural development. Meanwhile, the Fifth Men knew only that the distance between the earth and the moon was becoming smaller with ever-increasing rapidity.

This discovery was a tonic to a melancholy race. Men turned from the tragic past to the bewildering present and the uncertain future.

For it was evident that, if the present acceleration of approach were to be maintained, the moon would enter the critical zone and disintegrate in less than ten million years; and, further, that the fragments would not maintain themselves as a ring, but would soon crash upon the earth. Heat generated by their impact would make the surface of the earth impossible as the home of life. A short-lived and short-sighted species might well have considered ten million years as equivalent to eternity. Not so the Fifth Men. Thinking primarily in terms of the race, they recognized at once that their whole social policy must now be dominated by this future catastrophe. Some there were indeed who at first refused to take the matter seriously, saying that there was no reason to believe that the moon's odd behaviour would continue indefinitely. But as the years advanced, this view became increasingly improbable. Some of those who had spent much of their lives in exploration of the past now sought to explore the future also, hoping to prove that human civilization would always be discoverable on the earth in no matter how remote a future. But the attempt to unveil the future by direct inspection failed completely. It was surmised, erroneously, that future events, unlike past events, must be strictly non-existent until their creation by the advancing present.

Clearly humanity must leave its native planet. Research was therefore concentrated on the possibility of flight through empty space, and the suitability of neighbouring worlds. The only alternatives were Mars and Venus. The former was by now without water and without atmosphere. The latter had a dense, moist atmosphere; but one which lacked oxygen. The surface of Venus, moreover, was known to be almost completely covered with a shallow ocean. Further the planet was so hot by day that, even at the poles, man in his present state would scarcely survive.

It did not take the Fifth Men many centuries to devise a tolerable means of voyaging in interplanetary space. Immense rockets were constructed, the motive power of which was derived from the annihilation of matter. The vehicle was propelled simply by the terrific pressure of radiation thus produced. 'Fuel' for a voyage of many months, or even years, could, of course, easily be carried, since the annihilation of a minute amount of matter produced a vast wealth of energy. Moreover, when once the vessel had emerged from the earth's atmosphere, and had attained full speed, she would, of course, maintain it without the use of power from the rocket apparatus. The task of rendering the 'ether ship' properly manageable and decently habitable proved difficult, but not insurmountable. The first vessel to take the ether was a cigar-shaped hull some three thousand feet long, and built of metals whose artificial atoms were incomparably more rigid than anything hitherto known. Batteries of 'rocket' apparatus at various points on the hull enabled the ship not only to travel forward, but to reverse, turn in any direction, or side-step. Windows of an artificial transparent element, scarcely less strong than the metal of the hull, enabled the voyagers to look around them. Within there was ample accommodation for a hundred persons and their provisions for three years. Air for the same period was manufactured in transit from protons and electrons stored under pressure comparable to that in the interior of a star. Heat was, of course, provided by the annihilation of matter. Powerful refrigeration would permit the vessel to approach the sun almost to the orbit of Mercury. An 'artificial gravity' system, based on the properties of the electro-magnetic field, could be turned on and regulated at will, so as to maintain a more or less normal environment for the human organism.

This pioneer ship was manned with a navigating crew and a company of scientists, and was successfully dispatched upon a trial trip. The intention was to approach close to the surface of the moon, possibly to circumnavigate it at an altitude of ten thousand feet, and to return without landing. For many days those on earth received radio messages from the vessel's powerful installation, reporting that all was going well. But suddenly the messages ceased, and no more was ever heard of the vessel. Almost at the moment of the last message, telescopes had revealed a sudden flash of light at a point on the vessel's course. It was therefore surmised that she had collided with a meteor and fused with the heat of the impact.

Other vessels were built and dispatched on trial voyages. Many failed to return. Some got out of control, and reported that they were heading for outer space or plunging toward the sun, their hopeless messages continuing until the last of the crew succumbed to suffocation. Other vessels returned successfully, but with crews haggard and distraught from long confinement in bad atmosphere. One, venturing to land on the moon, broke her back, so that the air rushed out of her, and her people died. After her last message was received, she was detected from the earth, as an added speck on the stippled surface of a lunar 'sea'.

As time passed, however, accidents became rarer; indeed, so rare that trips in the void began to be a popular form of amusement. Literature of the period reverberates with the novelty of such experiences, with the sense that man had at last learned true flight, and acquired the freedom of the solar system. Writers dwelt upon the shock of seeing, as the vessel soared and accelerated, the landscape dwindle to a mere illuminated disk or crescent, surrounded by constellations. They remarked also the awful remoteness and mystery which travellers experienced on these early voyages, with dazzling sunlight on one side of the vessel and dazzling bespangled night on the other. They described how the intense sun spread his corona against a black and star-crowded sky. They expatiated also on the overwhelming interest of approaching another planet; of inspecting from the sky the still visible remains of Martian civilization; of groping through the cloud banks of Venus to discover islands in her almost coastless ocean; of daring an approach to Mercury, till the heat became insupportable in spite of the best refrigerating mechanism; of feeling a way across the belt of the asteroids and onwards toward Jupiter, till shortage of air and provisions forced a return.

But though the mere navigation of space was thus easily accomplished, the major task was still untouched. It was necessary either to remake man's nature to suit another planet, or to modify conditions upon another planet to suit man's nature. The former alternative was repugnant to the Fifth Men. Obviously it would entail an almost complete refashioning of the human organism. No existing individual could possibly be so altered as to live in the present conditions of Mars or Venus. And it would probably prove impossible to create a new being, adapted to these conditions, without sacrificing the brilliant and harmonious constitution of the extant species.

On the other hand, Mars could not be made habitable without first being stocked with air and water; and such an undertaking seemed impossible. There was nothing for it, then, but to attack Venus. The polar surfaces of that planet, shielded by impenetrable depths of cloud, proved after all not unendurably hot. Subsequent generations might perhaps be modified so as to withstand even the sub-arctic and 'temperate' climates. Oxygen was plentiful, but it was all tied up in chemical combination. Inevitably so, since oxygen combines very readily, and on Venus there was no vegetable life to exhale the free gas and replenish the ever-vanishing supply. It was necessary, then, to equip Venus with an appropriate vegetation, which in the course of ages should render the planet's atmosphere hospitable to man. The chemical and physical conditions on Venus had therefore to be studied in great detail, so that it might be possible to design a kind of life which would have a chance of flourishing. This research had to be carried out from within the ether ships, or with gas helmets, since no human being could live in the natural atmosphere of the planet.

We must not dwell upon the age of heroic research and adventure which now began. Observations of the lunar orbit were showing that ten millions years was too long an estimate of the future habitability of the earth; and it was soon realized that Venus could not be made ready soon enough unless some more rapid change was set on foot. It was therefore decided to split up some of the ocean of the planet into hydrogen and oxygen by a vast process of electrolysis. This would have been a more difficult task, had not the ocean been relatively free from salt, owing to the fact that there was so little dry land to be denuded of salts by rain and river. The oxygen thus formed by electrolysis would be allowed to mix with the atmosphere. The hydrogen had to be got rid of somehow, and an ingenious method was devised by which it should be ejected beyond the limits of the atmosphere at so great a speed that it would never return. Once sufficient free oxygen had been produced, the new vegetation would replenish the loss due to oxidation. This work was duly set on foot. Great automatic electrolyzing stations were founded on several of the islands; and biological research produced at length a whole flora of specialized vegetable types to cover the land surface of the planet. It was hoped that in less than a million years Venus would be fit to receive the human race, and the race fit to live on Venus.

Meanwhile a careful survey of the planet had been undertaken. Its land surface, scarcely more than a thousandth that of the earth, consisted of an unevenly distributed archipelago of mountainous islands. The planet had evidently not long ago been through a mountain-forming era, for soundings proved its whole surface to be extravagantly corrugated. The ocean was subject to terrific storms and currents; for since the planet took several weeks to rotate, there was a great difference of temperature and atmospheric pressure between the almost arctic hemisphere of night and the sweltering hemisphere of day. So great was the evaporation, that open sky was almost never visible from any part of the planet's surface; and indeed the average day-time weather was a succession of thick fogs and fantastic thunderstorms. Rain in the evening was a continuous torrent. Yet before night was over the waves clattered with fragments of ice.

Man looked upon his future home with loathing, and on his birthplace with an affection which became passionate. With its blue sky, its incomparable starry nights, its temperate and varied continents, its ample spaces of agriculture, wilderness and park, its well-known beasts and plants, and all the material fabric of the most enduring of terrestrial civilizations, it seemed to the men and women who were planning flight almost a living thing imploring them not to desert it. They looked often with hate at the quiet moon, now visibly larger than the moon of history. They revised again and again their astronomical and physical theories, hoping for some flaw which should render the moon's observed behaviour less mysterious, less terrifying. But they found nothing. It was as though a fiend out of some ancient myth had come to life in the modern world, to interfere with the laws of nature for man's undoing.

4. PREPARING A NEW WORLD

Another trouble now occurred. Several electrolysis stations on Venus were wrecked, apparently by submarine eruption. Also, a number of etherships, engaged in surveying the ocean, mysteriously exploded. The explanation was found when one of these vessels, though damaged, was able to return to the earth. The commander reported that, when the sounding line was drawn up, a large spherical object was seen to be attached to it. Closer inspection showed that this object was fastened to the sounding apparatus by a hook, and was indeed unmistakably artificial, a structure of small metal plates riveted together. While preparations were being made to bring the object within the ship, it happened to bump against the hull, and then it exploded.

Evidently there must be intelligent life somewhere in the ocean of Venus. Evidently the marine Venerians resented the steady depletion of their aqueous world, and were determined to stop it. The terrestrials had assumed that water in which no free oxygen was dissolved could not support life. But observation soon revealed that in this world-wide ocean there were many living species, some sessile, others free-swimming, some microscopic, others as large as whales. The basis of life in these creatures lay not in photosynthesis and chemical combination, but in the controlled disintegration of radio-active atoms. Venus was particularly rich in these atoms, and still contained certain elements which had long ago ceased to exist on the earth. The oceanic fauna subsisted in the destruction of minute quantities of radio-active atoms throughout its tissues.

Several of the Venerian species had attained considerable mastery over their physical environment, and were able to destroy one another very competently with various mechanical contrivances. Many types were indeed definitely intelligent and versatile within certain limits. And of these intelligent types, one had come to dominate all the others by virtue of its superior intelligence, and had constructed a genuine civilization on the basis of radio-active power. These most developed of all the Venerian creatures were beings of about the size and shape of a swordfish. They had three manipulative organs, normally sheathed within the long 'sword', but capable of extension beyond its point, as three branched muscular tentacles. They swam with a curious screw-like motion of their bodies and triple tails. Three fins enabled them to steer. They had also organs of phosphorescence, vision, touch, and something analogous to hearing. They appeared to reproduce asexually, laying eggs in the ooze of the ocean bed. They had no need of nutrition in the ordinary sense; but in infancy they seemed to gather enough radio-active matter to keep them alive for many years. Each individual, when his stock was running out and he began to be feeble, was either destroyed by his juniors or buried in a radio-active mine, to rise from this living death in a few months completely rejuvenated.

At the bottom of the Venerian ocean these creatures thronged in cities of proliferated coral-like buildings, equipped with many complex articles, which must have constituted the necessities and luxuries of their civilization. So much was ascertained by the Terrestrials in the course of their submarine exploration. But the mental life of Venerians remained hidden. It was clear, indeed, that like all living things, they were concerned with self-maintenance and the exercise of their capacities; but of the nature of these capacities little was discoverable. Clearly they used some kind of symbolic language, based on mechanical vibrations set up in the water by the snapping claws of their tentacles. But their more complex activities were quite unintelligible. All that could be recorded with certainty was that they were much addicted to warfare, even to warfare between groups of one species; and that even in the stress of military disaster they maintained a feverish production of material articles of all sorts, which they proceeded to destroy and neglect.

One activity was observed which was peculiarly mysterious. At certain seasons three individuals, suddenly developing unusual luminosity, would approach one another with rhythmic swayings and tremors, and would then rise on their tails and press their bodies together. Sometimes at this stage an excited crowd would collect, whirling around the three like driven snow. The chief performers would now furiously tear one another to pieces with their crab-like pincers, till nothing was left but tangled shreds of flesh, the great swords, and the still twitching claws. The Terrestrials, observing these matters with difficulty, at first suspected some kind of sexual intercourse; but no reproduction was ever traced to this source. Possibly the behaviour had once served a biological end, and had now become a useless ritual. Possibly it was a kind of voluntary religious sacrifice. More probably it was of a quite different nature, unintelligible to the human mind.

As man's activities on Venus became more extensive, the Venerians became more energetic in seeking to destroy him. They could not come out of the ocean to grapple with him, for they were deep-sea organisms. Deprived of oceanic pressure, they would have burst. But they contrived to hurl high explosives into the centres of the islands, or to undermine them from tunnels. The work of electrolysis was thus very seriously hampered. And as all efforts to parley with the Venerians failed completely, it was impossible to effect a compromise. The Fifth Men were thus faced with a grave moral problem. What right had man to interfere in a world already possessed by beings who were obviously intelligent, even though their mental life was incomprehensible to man? Long ago man himself had suffered at the hands of Martian invaders, who doubtless regarded themselves as more noble than the human race. And now man was committing a similar crime. On the other hand, either the migration to Venus must go forward, or humanity must be destroyed; for it seemed quite certain by now that the moon would fall, and at no very distant date. And though man's understanding of the Venerians was so incomplete, what he did know of them strongly suggested that they were definitely inferior to himself in mental range. The judgment might, of course, be mistaken; the Venerians might after all be so superior to man that man could not get an inkling of their superiority. But this argument would apply equally to jelly-fish and micro-organisms. Judgment had to be passed according to the evidence available. So far as man could judge at all in the matter, he was definitely the higher type.

There was another fact to be taken into account. The life of the Venerian organism depended on the existence of radio-active atoms. Since those atoms are subject to disintegration, they must become rarer. Venus was far better supplied than the earth in this respect, but there must inevitably come a time when there would be no more radio-active matter in Venus. Now submarine research showed that the Venerian fauna had once been much more extensive, and that the increasing difficulty of procuring radio-active matter was already the great limiting factor of civilization. Thus the Venerians were doomed, and man would merely hasten their destruction.

It was hoped, of course, that in colonizing Venus mankind would be able to accommodate itself without seriously interfering with the native population. But this proved impossible for two reasons. In the first place, the natives seemed determined to destroy the invader even if they should destroy themselves in the process. Titanic explosions were engineered, which caused the invaders serious damage, but also strewed the ocean surface with thousands of dead Venerians. Secondly, it was found that, as electrolysis poured more and more free oxygen into the atmosphere, the ocean absorbed some of the potent element back into itself by solution; and this dissolved oxygen had a disastrous effect upon the oceanic organisms. Their tissues began to oxidize. They were burnt up, internally and externally, by a slow fire. Man dared not stop the process of electrolysis until the atmosphere had become as rich in oxygen as his native air. Long before this state was reached, it was already clear that the Venerians were beginning to feel the effects of the poison, and that in a few thousand years, at most, they would be exterminated. It was therefore determined to put them out of their misery as quickly as possible. Men could by now walk abroad on the islands of Venus, and indeed the first settlements were already being founded. They were thus able to build a fleet of powerful submarine vessels to scour the ocean and destroy the whole native fauna.

This vast slaughter influenced the mind of the fifth human species in two opposite directions, now flinging it into despair, now rousing it to grave elation. For on the one hand the horror of the slaughter produced a haunting guiltiness in all men's minds, an unreasoning disgust with humanity for having been driven to murder in order to save itself. And this guiltiness combined with the purely intellectual loss of self-confidence which had been produced by the failure of science to account for the moon's approach. It re-awakened, also, that other quite irrational sense of guilt which had been bred of sympathy with the everlasting distress of the past. Together, these three influences tended toward racial neurosis.

On the other hand a very different mood sometimes sprang from the same three sources. After all, the failure of science was a challenge to be gladly accepted; it opened up a wealth of possibilities hitherto unimagined. Even the unalterable distress of the past constituted a challenge; for in some strange manner the present and future, it was said, must transfigure the past. As for the murder of Venerian life, it was, indeed, terrible, but right. It had been committed without hate; indeed, rather in love. For as the navy proceeded with its relentless work, it had gathered much insight into the life of the natives, and had learned to admire, even in a sense to love, while it killed. This mood, of inexorable yet not ruthless will, intensified the spiritual sensibility of the species, refined, so to speak, its spiritual hearing, and revealed to it tones and themes in the universal music which were hitherto obscure.

Which of these two moods, despair or courage, would triumph? All depended on the skill of the species to maintain a high degree of vitality in untoward circumstances.

Man now busied himself in preparing his new home. Many kinds of plant life, derived from the terrestrial stock, but bred for the Venerian environment, now began to swarm on the islands and in the sea. For so restricted was the land surface, that great areas of ocean had to be given over to specially designed marine plants, which now formed immense floating continents of vegetable matter. On the least torrid islands appeared habitable pylons, forming an architectural forest, with vegetation on every acre of free ground. Even so, it would be impossible for Venus ever to support the huge population of the earth. Steps had therefore been taken to ensure that the birth-rate should fall far short of the death-rate; so that, when the time should come, the race might emigrate without leaving any living members behind. No more than a hundred million, it was reckoned, could live tolerably on Venus. The population had therefore to be reduced to a hundredth of its former size. And since, in the terrestrial community, with its vast social and cultural activity, every individual had fulfilled some definite function in society, it was obvious that the new community must be not merely small but mentally impoverished. Hitherto, each individual had been enriched by intercourse with a far more intricate and diverse social environment than would be possible on Venus.

Such was the prospect when at length it was judged advisable to leave the earth to its fate. The moon was now so huge that it periodically turned day into night, and night into a ghastly day. Prodigious tides and distressful weather conditions had already spoilt the amenities of the earth, and done great damage to the fabric of civilization. And so at length humanity reluctantly took flight. Some centuries passed before the migration was completed, before Venus had received, not only the whole remaining human population, but also representatives of many other species of organisms, and all the most precious treasures of man's culture.

CHAPTER XIII

HUMANITY ON VENUS

1. TAKING ROOT AGAIN

Man's sojourn on Venus lasted somewhat longer than his whole career on the Earth. From the days of Pithecanthropus to the final evacuation of his native planet he passed, as we have seen, through a bewildering diversity of form and circumstance, On Venus, though the human type was somewhat more constant biologically, it was scarcely less variegated in culture.

To give an account of this period, even on the minute scale that has been adopted hitherto, would entail another volume. I can only sketch its bare outline. The sapling, humanity, transplanted into foreign soil, withers at first almost to the root, slowly readjusts itself, grows into strength and a certain permanence of form, burgeons, season by season, with leaf and flower of many successive civilizations and cultures, sleeps winter by winter, through many ages of reduced vitality, but at length (to force the metaphor), avoids this recurrent defeat by attaining an evergreen constitution and a continuous efflorescence. Then once more, through the whim of Fate, it is plucked up by the roots and cast upon another world.

The first human settlers on Venus knew well that life would be a sorry business. They had done their best to alter the planet to suit human nature, but they could not make Venus into another Earth. The land surface was minute. The climate was almost unendurable. The extreme difference of temperature between the protracted day and night produced incredible storms, rain like a thousand contiguous waterfalls, terrifying electrical disturbances, and fogs in which a man could not see his own feet. To make matters worse, the oxygen supply was as yet barely enough to render the air breathable. Worse still, the liberated hydrogen was not always successfully ejected from the atmosphere. It would sometimes mingle with the air to form an explosive mixture, and sooner or later there would occur a vast atmospheric flash. Recurrent disasters of this sort destroyed the architecture and the human inhabitants of many islands, and further reduced the oxygen supply. In time, however, the increasing vegetation made it possible to put an end to the dangerous process of electrolysis.

Meanwhile, these atmospheric explosions crippled the race so seriously that it was unable to cope with a more mysterious trouble which beset it some time after the migration. A new and inexplicable decay of the digestive organs, which first occurred as a rare disease, threatened within a few centuries to destroy mankind. The physical effects of this plague were scarcely more disastrous than the psychological effects of the complete failure to master it; for, what with the mystery of the moon's vagaries and the deep-seated, unreasoning, sense of guilt produced by the extermination of the Venerians, man's self-confidence was already seriously shaken, and his highly organized mentality began to show symptoms of derangement. The new plague was, indeed, finally traced to something in the Venerian water, and was supposed to be due to certain molecular groupings, formerly rare, but subsequently fostered by the presence of terrestrial organic matter in the ocean. No cure was discovered.

And now another plague seized upon the enfeebled race. Human tissues had never perfectly assimilated the Martian units which were the means of 'telepathic' communication. The universal ill-health now favoured a kind of 'cancer' of the nervous system, which was due to the ungoverned proliferation of these units. The harrowing results of this disease may be left unmentioned. Century by century it increased; and even those who did not actually contract the sickness lived in constant terror of madness.

These troubles were aggravated by the devastating heat. The hope that, as the generations passed, human nature would adapt itself even to the more sultry regions, seemed to be unfounded. Far otherwise, within a thousand years the once-populous arctic and antarctic islands were almost deserted. Out of each hundred of the great pylons, scarcely more than two were inhabited, and these only by a few plague-stricken and broken-spirited human relics. These alone were left to turn their telescopes upon the earth and watch the unexpectedly delayed bombardment of their native world by the fragments of the moon.

Population decreased still further. Each brief generation was slightly less well developed than its parents. Intelligence declined. Education became superficial and restricted. Contact with the past was no longer possible. Art lost its significance, and philosophy its dominion over the minds of men. Even applied science began to be too difficult. Unskilled control of the sub-atomic sources of power led to a number of disasters, which finally gave rise to a superstition that all 'tampering with nature' was wicked, and all the ancient wisdom a snare of Man's Enemy. Books, instruments, all the treasures of human culture, were therefore burnt. Only the perdurable buildings resisted destruction. Of the incomparable world-order of the Fifth Men nothing was left but a few island tribes cut off from one another by the ocean, and from the rest of space-time by the depths of their own ignorance.

After many thousands of years human nature did begin to adapt itself to the climate and to the poisoned water without which life was impossible. At the same time a new variety of the fifth species now began to appear, in which the Martian units were not included. Thus at last the race regained a certain mental stability, at the expense of its faculty of 'telepathy', which man was not to regain until almost the last phase of his career. Meanwhile, though he had recovered somewhat from the effects of an alien world, the glory that had been was no more. Let us therefore hurry through the ages that passed before noteworthy events again occurred.

In early days on Venus men had gathered their foodstuff from the great floating islands of vegetable matter which had been artificially produced before the migration. But as the oceans became populous with modifications of the terrestrial fauna, the human tribes turned more and more to fishing. Under the influence of its marine environment, one branch of the species assumed such an aquatic habit that in time it actually began to develop biological adaptations for marine life. It is perhaps surprising that man was still capable of spontaneous variation; but the fifth human species was artificial, and had always been prone to epidemics of mutation. After some millions of years of variation and selection there appeared a very successful species of seal-like sub-men. The whole body was moulded to stream-lines. The lung capacity was greatly developed. The spine had elongated, and increased in flexibility. The legs were shrunken, grown together, and flattened into a horizontal rudder. The arms also were diminutive and fin-like, though they still retained the manipulative forefinger and thumb. The head had shrunk into the body and looked forward in the direction of swimming. Strong carnivorous teeth, emphatic gregariousness, and a new, almost human, cunning in the chase, combined to make these seal-men lords of the ocean. And so they remained for many million years, until a more human race, annoyed at their piscatorial success, harpooned them out of existence.

For another branch of the degenerated fifth species had retained a more terrestrial habit and the ancient human form. Sadly reduced in stature and in brain, these abject beings were so unlike the original invaders that they are rightly considered a new species, and may therefore be called the Sixth Men. Age after age they gained a precarious livelihood by grubbing roots upon the forest-clad islands, trapping the innumerable birds, and catching fish in the tidal inlets with ground bait. Not infrequently they devoured, or were devoured by, their seal-like relatives. So restricted and constant was the environment of these human remnants, that they remained biologically and culturally stagnant for some millions of years.

At length, however, geological events afforded man's nature once more the opportunity of change. A mighty warping of the planet's crust produced an island almost as large as Australia. In time this was peopled, and from the clash of tribes a new and versatile race emerged. Once more there was methodical tillage, craftsmanship, complex social organization, and adventure in the realm of thought.

During the next two hundred million years all the main phases of man's life on earth were many times repeated on Venus with characteristic differences. Theocratic empires; free and intellectualistic island cities; insecure overlordship of feudal archipelagos; rivalries of high priest and emperor; religious feuds over the interpretation of sacred scriptures; recurrent fluctuations of thought from naïve animism, through polytheism, conflicting monotheisms, and all the desperate 'isms' by which mind seeks to blur the severe outline of truth; recurrent fashions of comfort-seeking fantasy and cold intelligence; social disorders through the misuse of volcanic or wind power in industry; business empires and pseudo-communistic empires – all these forms flitted over the changing substance of mankind again and again, as in an enduring hearth fire there appear and vanish the infinitely diverse forms of flame and smoke. But all the while the brief spirits, in whose massed configurations these forms inhered, were intent chiefly on the primitive needs of food, shelter, companionship, crowd-lust, love-making, the two-edged relationship of parent and child, the exercise of muscle and intelligence in facile sport. Very seldom, only in rare moments of clarity, only after ages of misapprehension, did a few of them, here and there, now and again, begin to have the deeper insight into the world's nature and man's. And no sooner had this precious insight begun to propagate itself, than it would be blotted out by some small or great disaster, by epidemic disease, by the spontaneous disruption of society, by an access of racial imbecility, by a prolonged bombardment of meteorites, or by the mere cowardice and vertigo that dared not look down the precipice of fact.

2. THE FLYING MEN

We need not dwell upon these multitudinous reiterations of culture, but must glance for a moment at the last phase of this sixth human species, so that we may pass on to the artificial species which it produced.

Throughout their career the Sixth Men had often been fascinated by the idea of flight. The bird was again and again their most sacred symbol. Their monotheism was apt to be worship not of a god-man, but of a god-bird, conceived now as the divine sea-eagle, winged with power, now as the giant swift, winged with mercy, now as a disembodied spirit of air, and once as the bird-god that became man to endow the human race with flight, physical and spiritual.

It was inevitable that flight should obsess man on Venus, for the planet afforded but a cramping home for groundlings; and the riotous efflorescence of avian species shamed man's pedestrian habit. When in due course the Sixth Men attained knowledge and power comparable to that of the First Men at their height, they invented flying-machines of various types. Many times, indeed, mechanical flight was rediscovered and lost again with the downfall of civilization. But at its best it was regarded only as a makeshift. And when at length, with the advance of the biological sciences, the Sixth Men were in a position to influence the human organism itself, they determined to produce a true flying man. Many civilizations strove vainly for this result, sometimes half-heartedly, sometimes with religious earnestness. Finally the most enduring and brilliant of all the civilizations of the Sixth Men actually attained the goal.

The Seventh Men were pigmies, scarcely heavier than the largest of terrestrial flying birds. Through and through they were organized for flight. A leathery membrane spread from the foot to the tip of the immensely elongated and strengthened 'middle' finger. The three 'outer' fingers, equally elongated, served as ribs to the membrane; while the index and thumb remained free for manipulation. The body assumed the stream-lines of a bird, and was covered with a deep quilt of feathery wool. This, and the silken down of the flight-membranes, varied greatly from individual to individual in colouring and texture. On the ground the Seventh Men walked much as other human beings, for the flight-membranes were folded close to the legs and body, and hung from the arms like exaggerated sleeves. In flight the legs were held extended as a flattened tail, with the feet locked together by the big toes. The breastbone was greatly developed as a keel, and as a base for the muscles of flight. The other bones were hollow, for lightness, and their internal surfaces were utilized as supplementary lungs. For, like the birds, these flying men had to maintain a high rate of oxidation. A state which others would regard as fever was normal to them.

Their brains were given ample tracts for the organization of prowess in flight. In fact, it was found possible to equip the species with a system of reflexes for aerial balance, and a true, though artificial, instinctive aptitude for flight, and interest in flight. Compared with their makers their brain volume was of necessity small, but their whole neural system was very carefully organized. Also it matured rapidly, and was extremely facile in the acquirement of new modes of activity. This was very desirable; for the individual's natural life period was but fifty years, and in most cases it was deliberately cut short by some impossible feat at about forty, or whenever the symptoms of old age began to be felt.

Of all human species these bat-like Flying Men, the Seventh Men, were probably the most care-free. Gifted with harmonious physique and gay temperament, they came into a social heritage well adapted to their nature. There was no occasion for them, as there had often been for some others, to regard the world as fundamentally hostile to life, or themselves as essentially deformed. Of quick intelligence in respect of daily personal affairs and social organization, they were untroubled by the insatiable lust of understanding. Not that they were an unintellectual race, for they soon formulated a beautifully systematic account of experience. They clearly perceived, however, that the perfect sphere of their thought was but a bubble adrift in chaos. Yet it was an elegant bubble. And the system was true, in its own gay and frankly insincere manner, true as significant metaphor, not literally true. What more, it was asked, could be expected of human intellect? Adolescents were encouraged to study the ancient problems of philosophy, for no reason but to convince themselves of the futility of probing beyond the limits of the orthodox system. 'Prick the bubble of thought at any point', it was said, 'and you shatter the whole of it. And since thought is one of the necessities of human life, it must be preserved.'

Natural science was taken over from the earlier species with half-contemptuous gratitude, as a necessary means of sane adjustment to the environment. Its practical applications were valued as the ground of the social order; but as the millennia advanced, and society approached that remarkable perfection and stability which was to endure for many million years, scientific inventiveness became less and less needful, and science itself was relegated to the infant schools. History also was given in outline during childhood, and subsequently ignored.

This curiously sincere intellectual insincerity was due to the fact that the Seventh Men were chiefly concerned with matters other than abstract thought. It is difficult to give to members of the first human species an inkling of the great preoccupation of these Flying

Men. To say that it was flight would be true, yet far less than the truth. To say that they sought to live dangerously and vividly, to crowd as much experience as possible into each moment, would again be a caricature of the truth. On the physical plane indeed 'the universe of flight' with all the variety of peril and skill afforded by a tempestuous atmosphere, was every individual's chief medium of self-expression. Yet it was not flight itself, but the spiritual aspect of flight, which obsessed the species.

In the air and on the ground the Seventh Men were different beings. Whenever they exercised themselves in flight they suffered a remarkable change of spirit. Much of their time had to be spent on the ground, since most of the work upon which civilization rested was impossible in the air. Moreover, life in the air was life at high pressure, and necessitated spells of recuperation on the ground. In their pedestrian phase the Seventh Men were sober folk, mildly bored, yet in the main cheerful, humorously impatient of the drabness and irk of pedestrian affairs, but ever supported by memory and anticipation of the vivid life of the air. Often they were tired, after the strain of that other life, but seldom were they despondent or lazy. Indeed, in the routine of agriculture and industry they were industrious as the wingless ants. Yet they worked in a strange mood of attentive absent-mindedness; for their hearts were ever in the air. So long as they could have frequent periods of aviation, they remained bland even on the ground. But if for any reason such as illness they were confined to the ground for a long period, they pined, developed acute melancholia, and died. Their makers had so contrived them that with the onset of any very great pain or misery their hearts should stop. Thus they were to avoid all serious distress. But, in fact, this merciful device worked only on the ground. In the air they assumed a very different and more heroic nature, which their makers had not foreseen, though indeed it was a natural consequence of their design.

In the air the flying man's heart beat more powerfully. His temperature rose. His sensation became more vivid and more discriminate, his intelligence more agile and penetrating. He experienced a more intense pleasure or pain in all that happened to him. It would not be true to say that he became more emotional;

rather the reverse, if by emotionality is meant enslavement to the emotions. For the most remarkable features of the aerial phase was that this enhanced power of appreciation was dispassionate. So long as the individual was in the air, whether in lonely struggle with the storm, or in the ceremonial ballet with sky-darkening hosts of his fellows; whether in the ecstatic love dance with a sexual partner, or in solitary and meditative circlings far above the world; whether his enterprise was fortunate, or he found himself dismembered by the hurricane, and crashing to death; always the gay and the tragic fortunes of his own person were regarded equally with detached aesthetic delight. Even when his dearest companion was mutilated or destroyed by some aerial disaster, he exulted; though also he would give his own life in the hope of effecting a rescue. But very soon after he had returned to the ground he would be overwhelmed with grief, would strive vainly to recapture the lost vision, and would perhaps die of heart failure.

Even when, as happened occasionally in the wild climate of Venus, a whole aerial population was destroyed by some world-wide atmospheric tumult, the few broken survivors, so long as they could remain in the air, exulted. And actually while at length they sank exhausted toward the ground, toward certain disillusionment and death, they laughed inwardly. Yet an hour after they had alighted, their constitution would be changed, their vision lost. They would remember only the horror of the disaster, and the memory would kill them.

No wonder the Seventh Men grudged every moment that was passed on the ground. While they were in the air, of course, the prospect of a pedestrian interlude, or indeed of endless pedestrianism, though in a manner repugnant, would be accepted with unswerving gaiety; but while they were on the ground, they grudged bitterly to be there. Early in the career of the species the proportion of aerial to terrestrial hours was increased by a biological invention. A minute food plant was produced which spent the winter rooted in the ground, and the summer adrift in the sunlit upper air, engaged solely in photosynthesis. Henceforth the populations of the Flying Men were able to browse upon the bright pastures of the sky, like swallows. As the ages passed, material civilization became more and more simplified. Needs which could not be satisfied without terrestrial labour tended to be outgrown. Manufactured articles became increasingly rare. Books were no longer written or read. In the main, indeed, they were no longer necessary; but to some extent their place was taken by verbal tradition and discussion, in the upper air. Of the arts, music, spoken lyric and epic verse, and the supreme art of winged dance, were constantly practised. The rest vanished. Many of the sciences inevitably faded into tradition; yet the true scientific spirit was preserved in a very exact meteorology, a sufficient biology, and a human psychology surpassed only by the second and fifth species at their height. None of these sciences, however, was taken very seriously, save in its practical applications. For instance, psychology explained the ecstasy of flight very neatly as a febrile and 'irrational' beatitude. But no one was disconcerted by this theory; for every one, while on the wing, felt it to be merely an amusing half-truth.

The social order of the Seventh Men was in essence neither utilitarian, nor humanistic, nor religious, but aesthetic. Every act and every institution were to be justified as contributing to the perfect form of the community. Even social prosperity was conceived as merely the medium in which beauty should be embodied, the beauty, namely, of vivid individual lives harmoniously related. Yet not only for the individual, but even for the race itself (so the wise insisted), death on the wing was more excellent than prolonged life on the ground. Better, far better, would be racial suicide than a future of pedestrianism. Yet though both the individual and the race were conceived as instrumental to objective beauty, there was nothing religious, in any ordinary sense, in this conviction. The Seventh Men were completely without interest in the universal and the unseen. The beauty which they sought to create was ephemeral and very largely sensuous. And they were well content that it should he so. Personal immortality, said a dying sage, would be as tedious as an endless song. Equally so with the race. The lovely flame, of which we all are members, must die, he said, must die; for without death she would fall short of beauty.

For close on a hundred million terrestrial years this aerial society endured with little change. On many of the islands throughout this period stood even yet a number of the ancient pylons, though repaired almost beyond recognition. In these nests the men and women of the seventh species slept through the long Venerian nights, crowded like roosting swallows. By day the same great towers were sparsely peopled with those who were serving their turn in industry, while in the fields and on the sea others laboured. But most were in the air. Many would be skimming the ocean, to plunge, gannet-like, for fish. Many, circling over land or sea, would now and again swoop like hawks upon the wild-fowl which formed the chief meat of the species. Others, forty or fifty thousand feet above the waves, where even the plentiful atmosphere of Venus was scarcely capable of supporting them, would be soaring, circling, sweeping, for pure joy of flight. Others, in the calm and sunshine of high altitudes, would be hanging effortless upon some steady up-current of air for meditation and the rapture of mere percipience. Not a few love-intoxicated pairs would be entwining their courses in aerial patterns, in spires, cascades, and true love-knots of flight, presently to embrace and drop ten thousand feet in bodily union. Some would be driving hither and thither through the green mists of vegetable particles, gathering the manna in their open mouths. Companies, circling together, would be discussing matters social or aesthetic; others would be singing together, or listening to recitative epic verse. Thousands, gathering in the sky like migratory birds, would perform massed convolutions, reminiscent of the vast mechanical aerial choreography of the First World State, but more vital and expressive, as a bird's flight is more vital than the flight of any machine. And all the while there would be some, solitary or in companies, who, either in the pursuit of fish and wildfowl, or out of pure devilment, pitted their strength and skill against the hurricane, often tragically, but never without zest, and laughter of the spirit.

It may seem to some incredible that the culture of the Seventh Men should have lasted so long. Surely it must either have decayed through mere monotony and stagnation or have advanced into richer experience. But no. Generation succeeded generation, and each was too short-lived to outlast its young delight and discover boredom. Moreover, so perfect was the adjustment of these beings to their world, that even if they had lived for centuries they would have felt no need of change. Flight provided them with intense physical exhilaration, and with the physical basis of a genuine and ecstatic, though limited, spiritual experience. In this their supreme attainment they rejoiced not only in the diversity of flight itself, but also in the perceived beauties of their variegated world, and most of all, perhaps, in the thousand lyric and epic ventures of human intercourse in an aerial community.

The end of this seemingly everlasting elysium was nevertheless involved in the very nature of the species. In the first place, as the ages lengthened into aeons, the generations preserved less and less of the ancient scientific lore. For it became insignificant to them. The aerial community had no need of it. This loss of mere information did not matter so long as their condition remained unaltered; but in due course biological changes began to undermine them. The species had always been prone to a certain biological instability. A proportion of infants, varying with circumstances, had always been misshapen; and the deformity had generally been such as to make flight impossible. The normal infant was able to fly early in its second year. If some accident prevented it from doing so, it invariably fell into a decline and died before its third year was passed. But many of the deformed types, being the result of a partial reversion to the pedestrian nature, were able to live on indefinitely without flight. According to a merciful custom these cripples had always to be destroyed. But at length, owing to the gradual exhaustion of a certain marine salt essential to the high-strung nature of the Seventh Men, infants were more often deformed than true to type. The world population declined so seriously that the organized aerial life of the community could no longer be carried on according to the time-honoured aesthetic principles. No one knew how to check this racial decay, but many felt that with greater biological knowledge it might be avoided. A disastrous policy was now adopted. It was decided to spare a carefully selected proportion of the deformed infants, those namely which, though doomed to pedestrianism, were likely to develop high intelligence. Thus it was hoped to raise a specialized group of persons whose work should be biological research untrammelled by the intoxication of flight.

The brilliant cripples that resulted from this policy looked at existence from a new angle. Deprived of the supreme experience for which their fellows lived, envious of a bliss which they knew only by report, yet contemptuous of the naïve mentality which cared for nothing (it seemed) but physical exercise, love-making, the beauty of nature, and the elegances of society, these flightless intelligences sought satisfaction almost wholly in the life of research and scientific control. At the best, however, they were a tortured and resentful race. For their natures were fashioned for the aerial life which they could not lead. Although they received from the winged folk just treatment and a certain compassionate respect, they writhed under this kindness, locked their hearts against all the orthodox values, and sought out new ideals. Within a few centuries they had rehabilitated the life of intellect, and, with the power that knowledge gives, they had made themselves masters of the world. The amiable fliers were surprised, perplexed, even pained; and yet withal amused. Even when it became evident that the pedestrians were determined to create a new world order in which there would be no place for the beauties of natural flight, the fliers were only distressed while they were on the ground.

The islands were becoming crowded with machinery and flightless industrialists. In the air itself the winged folk found themselves outstripped by the base but effective instruments of mechanical flight. Wings became a laughing stock, and the life of natural flight was condemned as a barren luxury. It was ordained that in future every flier must serve the pedestrian world-order, or starve. And as the cultivation of wind-borne plants had been abandoned, and fishing and fowling rights were strictly controlled, this law was no empty form. At first it was impossible for the fliers to work on the ground for long hours, day after day, without incurring serious ill-health and an early death. But the pedestrian physiologists invented a drug which preserved the poor wage-slaves in something like physical health, and actually prolonged their life. No drug, however, could restore their spirit, for their normal aerial habit was reduced to a few tired hours of recreation once a week. Meanwhile, breeding experiments were undertaken to produce a wholly wingless large-brained type. And finally a law was enacted by which all winged infants must be either mutilated or destroyed. At this point the fliers made an heroic but ineffectual bid for power. They attacked the pedestrian population from the air. In reply the enemy rode them down in his great aeroplanes and blew them to pieces with high explosive.

The fighting squadrons of the natural fliers were finally driven to the ground in a remote and barren island. Thither the whole flying population, a mere remnant of its former strength, fled out of every civilized archipelago in search of freedom: the whole population – save the sick, who committed suicide, and all infants that could not yet fly. These were stifled by their mothers or next-of-kin, in obedience to a decree of the leaders. About a million men, women and children, some of whom were scarcely old enough for the prolonged flight, now gathered on the rocks, regardless that there was not food in the neighbourhood for a great company.

Their leaders, conferring together, saw clearly that the day of Flying Man was done, and that it would be more fitting for a high-souled race to die at once than to drag on in subjection to contemptuous masters. They therefore ordered the population to take part in an act of racial suicide that should at least make death a noble gesture of freedom. The people received the message while they were resting on the stony moorland. A wail of sorrow broke from them. It was checked by the speaker, who bade them strive to see, even on the ground, the beauty of the thing that was to be done. They could not see it; but they knew that if they had the strength to take wing again they would see it clearly, almost as soon as their tired muscles bore them aloft. There was no time to waste, for many were already faint with hunger, and anxious lest they should fail to rise. At the appointed signal the whole population rose into the air with a deep roar of wings. Sorrow was left behind. Even the children, when their mothers explained what was to be done, accepted their fate with zest; though, had they learned of it on the ground, they would have been terror-stricken. The company now flew steadily west, forming themselves into a double file many miles long. The cone of a volcano appeared over the horizon, and rose as they approached. The leaders pressed on towards its ruddy smoke plume; and unflinchingly, couple by couple, the whole multitude darted into its fiery breath and vanished. So ended the career of Flying Man.

3. A MINOR ASTRONOMICAL EVENT

The flightless yet still half avian race that now possessed the planet settled down to construct a society based on industry and science. After many vicissitudes of fortune and of aim, they produced a new human species, the Eighth Men. These long-headed and substantial folk were designed to be strictly pedestrian, physically and mentally. Apt for manipulation, calculation and invention, they very soon turned Venus into an engineer's paradise. With power drawn from the planet's central heat, their huge electric ships bored steadily through the perennial monsoons and hurricanes, which also their aircraft treated with contempt. Islands were joined by tunnels and by millipede bridges. Every inch of land served some industrial or agricultural end. So successfully did the generations amass wealth that their rival races and rival castes were able to indulge, every few centuries, in vast revelries of mutual slaughter and material destruction without, as a rule, impoverishing their descendants. And so insensitive had man become that these orgies shamed him not at all. Indeed, only by the ardours of physical violence could this most philistine species wrench itself for a while out of its complacency. Strife, which to nobler beings would have been a grave spiritual disaster, was for these a tonic, almost a religious exercise. These cathartic paroxysms, it should be observed, were but the rare and brief crises which automatically punctuated ages of stolid peace. At no time did they threaten the existence of the species; seldom did they even destroy its civilization.

It was after a lengthy period of peace and scientific advancement that the Eighth Men made a startling astronomical discovery. Ever since the First Men had learned that in the life of every star there comes a critical moment when the great orb collapses, shrinking to a minute, dense grain with feeble radiation, man had periodically suspected that the sun was about to undergo this change, and become a typical 'White Dwarf'. The Eighth Men detected sure signs of the catastrophe, and predicted its date. Twenty thousand years they gave themselves before the change should begin. In another fifty thousand years, they guessed, Venus would probably be frozen and uninhabitable. The only hope was to migrate to Mercury during the great change, when that planet was already ceasing to be intolerably hot. It was necessary then to give Mercury an atmosphere, and to breed a new species which should be capable of adapting itself finally to a world of extreme cold.

This desperate operation was already on foot when a new astronomical discovery rendered it futile. Astronomers detected, some distance from the solar system, a volume of non-luminous gas. Calculation showed that this object and the sun were approaching one another at a tangent, and that they would collide. Further calculation revealed the probable results of this event. The sun would flare up and expand prodigiously. Life would be quite impossible on any of the planets save, just possibly, Uranus, and more probably Neptune. The three planets beyond Neptune would escape roasting, but were unsuitable for other reasons. The two outermost would remain glacial, and, moreover, lay beyond the range of the imperfect etherships of the Eighth Men. The innermost was practically a bald globe of iron, devoid not merely of atmosphere and water, but also of the normal covering of rock. Neptune alone might be able to support life; but how could even Neptune be populated? Not only was its atmosphere very unsuitable, and its gravitational pull such as to make man's body an intolerable burden, but also up to the time of the collision it would remain excessively cold. Not till after the collision could it support any kind of life known to man.

How these difficulties were overcome I have no time to tell, though the story of man's attack upon his final home is well worthy of recording. Nor can I tell in detail of the conflict of policy which now occurred. Some, realizing that the Eighth Men themselves could never live on Neptune, advocated an orgy of pleasure-living till the end. But at length the race excelled itself in an almost unanimous resolve to devote its remaining centuries to the production of a human being capable of carrying the torch of mentality into a new world.

Ether-vessels were able to reach that remote world and set up chemical changes for the improvement of the atmosphere. It was also possible, by means of the lately rediscovered process of automatic annihilation of matter, to produce a constant supply of energy for the warming of an area where life might hope to survive until the sun should be rejuvenated.

When at last the time for migration was approaching, a specially designed vegetation was shipped to Neptune and established in the warm area to fit it for man's use. Animals, it was decided, would be unnecessary. Subsequently a specially designed human species, the Ninth Men, was transported to man's new home. The giant Eighth Men could not themselves inhabit Neptune. The trouble was not merely that they could scarcely support their own weight, let alone walk, but that the atmospheric pressure on Neptune was unendurable. For the great planet bore a gaseous envelope thousands of miles deep. The solid globe was scarcely more than the yolk of a huge egg. The mass of the air itself combined with the mass of the solid to produce a gravitational pressure greater than that upon the Venerian ocean floor. The Eighth Men, therefore, dared not emerge from their ether ships to tread the surface of the planet save for brief spells in steel diving suits. For them there was nothing else to do but to return to the archipelagos of Venus, and make the best of life until the end. They were not spared for long. A few centuries after the settlement of Neptune had been completed by transferring thither all the most precious material relics of humanity, the great planet itself narrowly missed collision with the dark stranger from space. Uranus and Jupiter were at the time well out of its track. Not so Saturn, which, a few years after Neptune's escape, was engulfed with all its rings and satellites. The sudden incandescence which resulted from this minor collision was but a prelude. The huge foreigner rushed on. Like a finger poked into a spider's web, it tangled up the planetary orbits. Having devoured its way through the asteroids, it missed Mars, caught Earth and Venus in its blazing hair, and leapt at the sun. Henceforth the centre of the solar system was a star nearly as wide as the old orbit of Mercury, and the system was transformed.

CHAPTER XIV

NEPTUNE

1. BIRD'S-EYE VIEW

I have told man's story up to a point about half-way from his origin to his annihilation. Behind lies the vast span which includes the whole Terrestrial and Venerian ages, with all their slow fluctuations of darkness and enlightenment. Ahead lies the Neptunian age, equally long, equally tragic perhaps, but more diverse, and in its last phase incomparably more brilliant. It would not be profitable to recount the history of man on Neptune on the scale of the preceding chronicle. Very much of it would be incomprehensible to terrestrials, and much of it repeats again and again, in the many Neptunian modes, themes that we have already observed in the Terrestrial or the Venerian movements of the human symphony. To appreciate fully the range and subtlety of the great living epic, we ought, no doubt, to dwell on its every movement with the same faithful care. But this is impossible to any human mind. We can but attend to significant phrases, here and there, and hope to capture some fragmentary hint of its vast intricate form. And for the readers of this book, who are themselves tremors in the opening bars of the music, it is best that I should dwell chiefly on things near to them, even at the cost of ignoring much that is in fact greater.

Before continuing our long flight let us look around us. Hitherto we have passed over time's fields at a fairly low altitude, making many detailed observations. Now we shall travel at a greater height and with speed of a new order. We must therefore orientate ourselves within the wider horizon that opens around us; we must consider things from the astronomical rather than the human point of view. I said that we were halfway from man's beginning to his end. Looking back to that remote beginning we see that the span of time which includes the whole career of the First Men from Pithecanthropus to the Patagonian disaster is an unanalyzable point. Even the preceding and much longer period between the first mammal and the first man, some twenty-five millions of terrestrial years, seems now inconsiderable. The whole of it, together with the age of the First Men, may be said to lie half-way between the formation of the planets, two thousand million years earlier, and their final destruction, two thousand million years later. Taking a still wider view, we see that this aeon of four thousand million years is itself no more than a moment in comparison with the sun's age. And before the birth of the sun the stuff of this galaxy had already endured for aeons as a nebula. Yet even those aeons look brief in relation to the passage of time before the myriad great nebula themselves, the future galaxies, condensed out of the all-pervading mist in the beginning. Thus the whole duration of humanity, with its many sequent species and its incessant downpour of generations, is but a flash in the lifetime of the cosmos.

Spatially, also, man is inconceivably minute. If in imagination we reduce this galaxy of ours to the size of an ancient terrestrial principality, we must suppose it adrift in the void with millions of other such principalities, very remote from one another. On the same scale the all-embracing cosmos would bulk as a sphere whose diameter was some twenty times greater than that of the lunar orbit in your day; and somewhere within the little wandering asteroid-like principality which is our own universe, the solar system would be an ultramicroscopic point, the greatest planet incomparably smaller.

We have watched the fortunes of eight successive human species for a thousand million years, the first half of that flicker which is the duration of man. Ten more species now succeed one another, or are contemporary, on the plains of Neptune. We, the Last Men, are the Eighteenth Men. Of the eight pre-Neptunian species, some, as we have seen, remained always primitive; many achieved at least a confused and fleeting civilization, and one, the brilliant Fifth, was already wakening into true humanity when misfortune crushed it. The ten Neptunian species show an even greater diversity. They range from the instinctive animal to modes of consciousness never before attained. The definitely sub-human degenerate types are confined mostly to the first six hundred million years of man's sojourn on

Neptune. During the earlier half of this long phase of preparation, man, at first almost crushed out of existence by a hostile environment, gradually peopled the huge north; but with beasts, not men. For man, as man, no longer existed. During the latter half of the preparatory six hundred million years, the human spirit gradually awoke again, to undergo the fluctuating advance and decline characteristic of the pre-Neptunian ages. But subsequently, in the last four hundred million years of his career on Neptune, man has made an almost steady progress toward full spiritual maturity.

Let us now look rather more closely at these three great epochs of man's history.

2. DA CAPO

It was in desperate haste that the last Venerian men had designed and fashioned the new species for the colonization of Neptune. The mere remoteness of the great planet, moreover, had prevented its nature from being explored at all thoroughly, and so the new human organism was but partially adapted to its destined environment. Inevitably it was a dwarf type, limited in size by the necessity of resisting an excessive gravitation. Its brain was so cramped that everything but the bare essentials of humanity had to be omitted from it. Even so, the Ninth Men were too delicately organized to withstand the ferocity of natural forces on Neptune. This ferocity the designers had seriously underestimated; and so they were content merely to produce a miniature copy of their own type. They should have planned a hardy brute, lustily procreative, cunning in the struggle for physical existence, but above all tough, prolific, and so insensitive as to be scarcely worthy of the name man. They should have trusted that if once this crude seed could take root, natural forces themselves would in time conjure from it something more human. Instead, they produced a race cursed with the inevitable fragility of miniatures, and designed for a civilized environment which feeble spirits could not possibly maintain in a tumultuous world. For it so happened that the still youthful giant, Neptune, was slowly entering one of his phases of crustal shrinkage, and therefore of earthquake and eruption. Thus the frail colonists found themselves increasingly in danger of being swallowed in sudden fiery crevasses or buried under volcanic dust. Moreover, their squat buildings, when not actually being trampled by lava streams, or warped and cracked by their shifting foundations, were liable to be demolished by the battering-ram thrust of a turbulent and massive atmosphere. Further, the atmosphere's unwholesome composition killed all possibility of cheerfulness and courage in a race whose nature was doomed to be, even in favourable circumstances, neurotic.

Fortunately this agony could not last indefinitely. Little by little, civilization crumbled into savagery, the torturing vision of better things was lost, man's consciousness was narrowed and coarsened into brute-consciousness. By good luck the brute precariously survived.

Long after the Ninth Men had fallen from man's estate, nature herself, in her own slow and blundering manner, succeeded where man had failed. The brute descendants of this human species became at length well adapted to their world. In time there arose a wealth of sub-human forms in the many kinds of environment afforded by the lands and seas of Neptune. None of them penetrated far toward the Equator, for the swollen sun had rendered the tropics at this time far too hot to support life of any kind. Even at the pole the protracted summer put a great strain on all but the most hardy creatures.

Neptune's year was at this time about one hundred and sixty-five times the length of the old terrestrial year. The slow seasonal change had an important effect on life's own rhythms. All but the most ephemeral organisms tended to live through at least one complete year, and the higher mammals survived longer. At a much later stage this natural longevity was to play a great and beneficial part in the revival of man. But, on the other hand, the increasing sluggishness of individual growth, the length of immaturity in each generation, retarded the natural evolutionary process on Neptune, so that compared with the Terrestrial and Venerian epochs the biological story now moves at a snail's pace.

After the fall of the Ninth Men the sub-human creatures had one and all adopted a quadruped habit, the better to cope with gravity. At first they had indulged merely in occasional support from their knuckles, but in time many species of true quadrupeds had appeared. In several of the running types the fingers, like the toes, had grown together, and a hoof had developed, not on the old fingertips, which were bent back and atrophied, but on the knuckles.

Two hundred million years after the solar collision innumerable species of sub-human grazers with long sheep-like muzzles, ample molars, and almost ruminant digestive systems, were competing with one another on the polar continent. Upon these preyed the sub-human carnivora, of whom some were built for speed in the chase, others for stalking and a sudden spring. But since jumping was no easy matter on Neptune, the cat-like types were all minute. They preyed upon man's more rabbit-like and rat-like descendants, or on the carrion of the larger mammals, or on the lusty worms and beetles. These had sprung originally from vermin which had been transported accidentally from Venus. For of all the ancient Venerian fauna only man himself, a few insects and other invertebrates, and many kinds of micro-organisms, succeeded in colonizing Neptune. Of plants, many types had been artificially bred for the new world, and from these eventually arose a host of grasses, flowering plants, thick-trunked bushes, and novel sea-weeds. On this marine flora fed certain highly developed marine worms; and of these last, some in time became vertebrate, predatory, swift and fish-like. On these in turn man's own marine descendants preyed, whether as sub-human seals, or still more specialized sub-human porpoises. Perhaps most remarkable of these developments of the ancient human stock was that which led, through a small insectivorous bat-like glider, to a great diversity of true flying mammals, scarcely larger than humming birds, but in some cases agile as swallows.

Nowhere did the typical human form survive. There were only beasts, fitted by structure and instinct to some niche or other of their infinitely diverse and roomy world.

Certainly strange vestiges of human mentality did indeed persist here and there even as, in the fore-limbs of most species, there still remained buried the relics of man's once cunning fingers. For instance, there were certain grazers which in times of hardship would meet together and give tongue in cacophonous ululation; or, sitting on their haunches with fore-limbs pressed together, they would listen by the hour to the howls of some leader, responding intermittently with groans and whimpers, and working themselves at last into foaming madness. And there were carnivora which, in the midst of the spring-time fervour, would suddenly cease from love-making, fighting, and the daily routine of hunting, to sit alone in some high place day after day, night after night, watching, waiting; until at last hunger forced them into action.

Now in the fullness of time, about three hundred million terrestrial years after the solar collision, a certain minute, hairless, rabbit-like creature, scampering on the polar grasslands, found itself greatly persecuted by a swift hound from the south. The sub-human rabbit was relatively unspecialized, and had no effective means of defence or flight. It was almost exterminated. A few individuals, however, saved themselves by taking to the dense and thick-trunked scrub, whither the hound could not follow them. Here they had to change their diet and manner of life, deserting grass for roots, berries, and even worms and beetles. Their fore-limbs were now increasingly used for digging and climbing, and eventually for weaving nests of stick and straw. In this species the fingers had never grown together. Internally the fore-paw was like a minute clenched fist from the elongated and exposed knuckles of which separate toes protruded. And now the knuckles elongated themselves still further, becoming in time a new set of fingers. Within the palm of the new little monkey-hand there still remained traces of man's ancient fingers, bent in upon themselves.

As of old, manipulation gave rise to clearer percipience. And this, in conjunction with the necessity of frequent experiments in diet, hunting, and defence, produced at length a real versatility of behaviour and suppleness of mind. The rabbit throve, adopted an almost upright gait, continued to increase in stature and in brain. Yet, just as the new hand was not merely a resurrection of the old hand, so the new regions of the brain were no mere revival of the atrophied human cerebrum, but a new organ, which overlaid and swallowed up that ancient relic. The creature's mind, therefore, was in many respects a new mind, though moulded to the same great basic needs. Like his forerunners, of course, he craved food, love, glory, companionship. In pursuit of these ends he devised weapons and traps, and built wicker villages. He held pow-wows. He became the Tenth Men.

3. SLOW CONQUEST

For a million terrestrial years these long-armed hairless beings were spreading their wicker huts and bone implements over the great northern continents, and for many more millions they remained in possession without making further cultural progress; for evolution, both biological and cultural, was indeed slow on Neptune. At last the Tenth Men were attacked by a micro-organism and demolished. From their ruins several primitive human species developed, and remained isolated in remote territories for millions of decades, until at length chance or enterprise brought them into contact. One of these early species, crouched and tusked, was persistently trapped for its ivory by an abler type, till it was exterminated. Another, long of muzzle and large of base, habitually squatted on its haunches like the kangaroo. Shortly after this industrious and social species had discovered the use of the wheel, a more primitive but more war-like type crashed into it like a tidal wave and overwhelmed it. Erect, but literally almost as broad as they were tall, these chunkish and bloody-minded savages spread over the whole arctic and sub-arctic region and spent some millions of years in monotonous reiteration of progress and decline; until at last a slow decay of their germ-plasm almost ended man's career. But after an aeon of darkness, there appeared another thick-set, but larger brained, species. This, for the first time on Neptune, conceived the religion of love, and all those spiritual cravings and agonies which had flickered in man so often and so vainly upon Earth and Venus. There appeared again feudal empires, militant nations, economic class wars, and, not once but often, a world-state covering the whole northern hemisphere. These men it was that first crossed the equator in artificially cooled electric ships, and explored the huge south. No life of any kind was discovered in the southern hemisphere; for even in that age no living matter could have crossed the roasting tropics without artificial refrigeration. Indeed, it was only because the sun's temporary revival had already passed its zenith that even man, with all his ingenuity, could endure a long tropical voyage.

Like the First Men and so many other natural human types, these Fourteenth Men were imperfectly human. Like the First Men, they conceived ideals of conduct which their imperfectly organized

nervous systems could never attain and seldom approach. Unlike the
First Men, they survived with but minor biological changes for three
hundred million years. But even so long a period did not enable
them to transcend their imperfect spiritual nature. Again and again
and again they passed from savagery to world-civilization and back
to savagery. They were captive within their own nature, as a bird in
a cage. And as a caged bird may fumble with nest-building materials
and periodically destroy the fruit of its aimless toil, so these cramped
beings destroyed their civilizations.

At length, however, this second phase of Neptunian history, this
era of fluctuation, was brought to an end. At the close of the six
hundred million years after the first settlement of the planet, unaided
nature produced, in the fifteenth human species, that highest form
of natural man which she had produced only once before, in the
second species. And this time no Martians interfered. We must not
stay to watch the struggle of this great-headed man to overcome his
one serious handicap, excessive weight of cranium and unwieldy
proportions of body. Suffice it that after a long-drawn-out immaturity,
including one great mechanized war between the northern and
southern hemispheres, the Fifteenth Men outgrew the ailments and
fantasies of youth, and consolidated themselves as a single world-
community. This civilization was based economically on volcanic
power, and spiritually on devotion to the fulfilment of human
capacity. It was this species which, for the first time on Neptune,
conceived, as an enduring racial purpose, the will to remake human
nature upon an ampler scale.

Henceforth in spite of many disasters, such as another period
of earthquake and eruption, sudden climatic changes, innumerable
plagues and biological aberrations, human progress was relatively
steady. It was not by any means swift and sure. There were still to be
ages, often longer than the whole career of the First Men, in which
the human spirit would rest from its pioneering to consolidate its
conquests, or would actually stray into the wilderness. But never
again, seemingly, was it to be routed and crushed into mere animality.

In tracing man's final advance to full humanity we can observe
only the broadest features of a whole astronomical era. But in fact
it is an era crowded with many thousands of long-lived generations.

Myriads of individuals, each one unique, live out their lives in rapt intercourse with one another, contribute their heart's pulses to the universal music, and presently vanish, giving place to others. All this age-long sequence of private living, which is the actual tissue of humanity's flesh, I cannot describe. I can only trace, as it were, the disembodied form of its growth.

The Fifteenth Men first set themselves to abolish five great evils, namely, disease, suffocating toil, senility, misunderstanding, ill-will. The story of their devotion, their many disastrous experiments and ultimate triumph, cannot here be told. Nor can I recount how they learned and used the secret of deriving power from the annihilation of matter, nor how they invented ether ships for the exploration of neighbouring planets, nor how, after ages of experiments, they designed and produced a new species, the Sixteenth, to supersede themselves.

The new type was analogous to the ancient Fifth, which had colonized Venus. Artificial rigid atoms had been introduced into its bone-tissues, so that it might support great stature and an ample brain; in which, moreover, an exceptionally fine-grained cellular structure permitted a new complexity of organization. 'Telepathy', also, was once more achieved, not by means of the Martian units, which had long ago become extinct, but by the synthesis of new molecular groups of a similar type. Partly through the immense increase of mutual understanding, which resulted from 'telepathic' rapport, partly through improved co-ordination of the nervous system, the ancient evil of selfishness was entirely and finally abolished from the normal human being. Egoistic impulses, whenever they refused to be subordinated, were henceforth classed as symptoms of insanity. The sensory powers of the new species were, of course, greatly improved; and it was even given a pair of eyes in the back of the head. Henceforth man was to have a circular instead of a semicircular field of vision. And such was the general intelligence of the new race that many problems formerly deemed insoluble were now solved in a single flash of insight.

Of the great practical uses to which the Sixteenth Men put their powers, one only need be mentioned as an example. They gained control of the movement of their planet. Early in their career they were able, with the unlimited energy at their disposal, to direct it into a wider orbit, so that its average climate became more temperate, and snow occasionally covered the polar regions. But as the ages advanced, and the sun became steadily less ferocious, it became necessary to reverse this process and shift the planet gradually nearer to the sun.

When they had possessed their world for nearly fifty million years, the Sixteenth Men, like the Fifth before them, learned to enter into past minds. For them this was a more exciting adventure than for their forerunners, since they were still ignorant of Terrestrial and Venerian history. Like their forerunners, so dismayed were they at the huge volume of eternal misery in the past, that for a while, in spite of their own great blessings and spontaneous gaiety, existence seemed a mockery. But in time they came to regard the past's misery as a challenge. They told themselves that the past was calling to them for help, and that somehow they must prepare a great 'crusade to liberate the past'. How this was to be done, they could not conceive; but they were determined to bear in mind this quixotic aim in the great enterprise which had by now become the chief concern of the race, namely the creation of a human type of an altogether higher order.

It had become clear that man had by now advanced in understanding and creativeness as far as was possible to the individual human brain acting in physical isolation. Yet the Sixteenth Men were oppressed by their own impotence. Though in philosophy they had delved further than had ever before been possible, yet even at their deepest they found only the shifting sands of mystery. In particular they were haunted by three ancient problems, two of which were purely intellectual, namely the mystery of time and the mystery of mind's relation to the world. Their third problem was the need somehow to reconcile their confirmed loyalty to life, which they conceived as embattled against death, with their ever-strengthening impulse to rise above the battle and admire it dispassionately.

Age after age the races of the Sixteenth Men blossomed with culture after culture. The movement of thought ranged again and again through all the possible modes of the spirit, ever discovering new significance in ancient themes. Yet throughout this epoch the three great problems remained unsolved, perplexing the individual and vitiating the policy of the race.

Forced thus at length to choose between spiritual stagnation and a perilous leap in the dark, the Sixteenth Men determined to set about devising a type of brain which, by means of the mental fusion of many individuals, might waken into an altogether new mode of consciousness. Thus, it was hoped, man might gain insight into the very heart of existence, whether finally to admire or loathe. And thus the racial purpose, which had been so much confused by philosophical ignorance, might at last become clear.

Of the hundred million years which passed before the Sixteenth Men produced the new human type, I must not pause to tell. They thought they had achieved their hearts' desire; but in fact the glorious beings which they had produced were tortured by subtle imperfections beyond their makers' comprehension. Consequently, no sooner had these Seventeenth Men peopled the world and attained full cultural stature, than they also bent all their strength to the production of a new type, essentially like their own, but perfected. Thus after a brief career of a few hundred thousand years, crowded with splendour and agony, the Seventeenth gave place to the Eighteenth, and, as it turns out, the Last, human species. Since all the earlier cultures find their fulfilment in the world of the Last Men, I pass over them to enlarge somewhat upon our modern age.

CHAPTER XV

THE LAST MEN

1. INTRODUCTION TO THE LAST HUMAN SPECIES

If one of the First Men could enter the world of the Last Men, he would find many things familiar and much that would seem strangely distorted and perverse. But nearly everything that is most distinctive of the last human species would escape him. Unless he were to be told that behind all the obvious and imposing features of civilization, behind all the social organization and personal intercourse of a great community, lay a whole other world of spiritual culture, round about him, yet beyond his ken, he would no more suspect its existence than a cat in London suspects the existence of finance or literature.

Among the familiar things that he would encounter would be creatures recognizably human yet in his view grotesque. While he himself laboured under the weight of his own body, these giants would be easily striding. He would consider them very sturdy, often thick-set, folk, but he would be compelled to allow them grace of movement and even beauty of proportion. The longer he stayed with them the more beauty he would see in them, and the less complacently would he regard his own type. Some of these fantastic men and women he would find covered with fur, hirsute, or mole-velvet, revealing the underlying muscles. Others would display brown, yellow or ruddy skin, and yet others a translucent ash-green, warmed by the under-flowing blood. As a species, though we are all human, we are extremely variable in body and mind, so variable that superficially we seem to be not one species but many. Some characters, of course, are common to all of us. The traveller might perhaps be surprised by the large yet sensitive hands which are universal, both in men and women. In all of us the outermost finger bears at its tip three minute organs of manipulation, rather similar to those which were first devised for the Fifth Men. These excrescences would doubtless revolt our visitor. The pair of occipital eyes, too, would shock him; so would the upward-looking astronomical eye on the crown, which is peculiar to the Last Men. This organ was so cunningly designed that, when fully extended, about a hand-breadth from its bony case, it reveals the heavens in as much detail as your smaller astronomical telescopes. Apart from such special features as these, there is nothing definitely novel about us; though every limb, every contour, shows unmistakably that much has happened since the days of the First Men. We are both more human and more animal. The primitive explorer might be more readily impressed by our animality than our humanity, so much of our humanity would lie beyond his grasp. He would perhaps at first regard us as a degraded type. He would call us faun-like, and in particular cases, ape-like, bear-like, ox-like, marsupial, or elephantine. Yet our general proportions are definitely human in the ancient manner. Where gravity is not insurmountable, the erect biped form is bound to be most serviceable to intelligent land animals; and so, after long wanderings, man has returned to his old shape. Moreover, if our observer were himself at all sensitive to facial expression, he would come to recognize in every one of our innumerable physiognomic types an indescribable but distinctively human look, the visible sign of that inward and spiritual grace which is not wholly absent from his own species. He would perhaps say, 'These men that are beasts are surely gods also.' He would be reminded of those old Egyptian deities with animal heads. But in us the animal and the human interpenetrate in every feature, in every curve of the body, and with infinite variety. He would observe us, together with hints of the long-extinct Mongol, Negro, Nordic, and Semetic, many outlandish features and expressions, deriving from the sub-human period on Neptune, or from Venus. He would see in every limb unfamiliar contours of muscle, sinew or bone, which were acquired long after the First Men had vanished. Besides the familiar eye-colours, he would discover orbs of topaz, emerald, amethyst and ruby, and a thousand varieties of these. But in all of us he would see also, if he had discernment, a facial expression and bodily gesture peculiar to our own species, a certain luminous, yet pungent and ironical significance, which we miss almost wholly in the earlier human faces.

The traveller would recognize among us unmistakable sexual features, both of general proportions and special organs. But it would take him long to discover that some of the most striking bodily and facial differences were due to differentiation of the two ancient sexes into many sub-sexes. Full sexual experience involves for us a complicated relationship between individuals of all these types. Of the extremely important sexual groups I shall speak again.

Our visitor would notice, by the way, that though all persons on Neptune go habitually nude, save for a pouch or rucksack, clothing, often brightly coloured, and made of diverse lustrous or homely tissues unknown before our time, is worn for special purposes.

He would notice also, scattered about the green countryside, many buildings, mostly of one story; for there is plenty of room on Neptune even for the million million of the Last Men. Here and there, however, we have great architectural pylons, cruciform or star-shaped in section, cloud-piercing, dignifying the invariable planes of Neptune. These mightiest of all buildings, which are constructed in adamantine materials formed of artificial atoms, would seem to our visitor geometrical mountains, far taller than any natural mountain could be, even on the smallest planet. In many cases the whole fabric is translucent or transparent, so that at night, with internal illumination, it appears as an edifice of light. Springing from a base twenty or more miles across, the star-seeking towers attain a height where even Neptune's atmosphere is somewhat attenuated. In their summits work the hosts of our astronomers, the essential eyes through which our community, on her little raft, peers across the ocean. Thither also all men and women repair at one time or another to contemplate this galaxy of ours and the unnumbered remoter universes. There they perform together those supreme symbolic acts for which I find no adjective in your speech but the debased word 'religious'. There also they seek the refreshment of mountain air in a world where natural mountains are unknown. And on the pinnacles and precipices of these loftiest horns many of us gratify that primeval lust of climbing which was ingrained in man before ever he was man. These buildings thus combine the functions of observatory, temple, sanatorium and gymnasium. Some of them are almost as old as the species, some are not yet completed. They embody, therefore, many styles. The traveller would find modes which he would be tempted to call Gothic, Classical, Egyptian, Peruvian, Chinese, or American, besides a thousand architectural ideas unfamiliar to him. Each of these buildings was the work of the race as a whole at some stage in its career. None of them is a mere local product. Every successive culture has expressed itself in one or more of these supreme monuments. Once in forty thousand years or so some new architectural glory would be conceived and executed. And such is the continuity of our cultures that there has scarcely ever been need to remove the handiwork of the past.

If our visitor happened to be near enough to one of these great pylons, he would see it surrounded by a swarm of midges, which would turn out to be human fliers, wingless, but with outspread arms. The stranger might wonder how a large organism could rise from the ground in Neptune's powerful field of gravity. Yet flight is our ordinary means of locomotion. A man has but to put on a suit of overalls fitted at various points with radiation-generators. Ordinary flight thus becomes a kind of aerial swimming. Only when very high speed is desired do we make use of closed-in air-boats and liners.

At the feet of the great buildings the flat or undulating country is green, brown, golden, and strewn with houses. Our traveller would recognize that much land was under cultivation, and would see many persons at work upon it with tools or machinery. Most of our food, indeed, is produced by artificial photosynthesis on the broiling planet Jupiter, where even now that the sun is becoming normal again, no life can exist without powerful refrigeration. As far as mere nutrition is concerned, we could do without vegetation; but agriculture and its products have played so great a part in human history that today agricultural operations and vegetable foods are very beneficial to the race psychologically. And so it comes about that vegetable matter is in great demand, not only as raw material for innumerable manufactures, but also for table delicacies. Green vegetables, fruit, and various alcoholic fruit drinks have come to have the same kind of ritual significance for us as wine has for you. Meat also, though not a part of ordinary diet, is eaten on very rare and sacred occasions. The cherished wild fauna of the planet contributes its toll to periodic symbolical banquets. And whenever a human being has chosen to die, his body is ceremoniously eaten by his friends.

Communication with the food factories of Jupiter and the agricultural polar regions of the less torrid Uranus, as also with the automatic mining stations on the glacial outer planets, is maintained by ether ships, which, travelling much faster than the planets themselves, make the passage to the neighbour worlds in a small fraction of the Neptunian year. These vessels, of which the smallest are about a mile in length, may be seen descending on our oceans like ducks. Before they touch the water they cause a prodigious tumult with the downward pressure of their radiation; but once upon the surface, they pass quietly into harbour.

The ether ship is in a manner symbolic of our whole community, so highly organized is it, and so minute in relation to the void which engulfs it. The ethereal navigators, because they spend so much of their time in the empty regions, beyond the range of 'telepathic' communication and sometimes even of mechanical radio, form mentally a unique class among us. They are a hardy, simple, and modest folk. And though they embody man's proud mastery of the ether, they are never tired of reminding landlubbers, with dour jocularity, that the most daring voyages are confined within one drop of the boundless ocean of space.

Recently an exploration ship returned from a voyage into the outer tracts. Half her crew had died. The survivors were emaciated, diseased, and mentally unbalanced. To a race that thought itself so well established in sanity that nothing could disturb it, the spectacle of these unfortunates was instructive. Throughout the voyage, which was the longest ever attempted, they had encountered nothing whatever but two comets, and an occasional meteor. Some of the nearer constellations were seen with altered forms. One or two stars increased slightly in brightness; and the sun was reduced to being the most brilliant of stars. The aloof and changeless presence of the constellations seems to have crazed the voyagers. When at last the ship returned and berthed, there was a scene such as is seldom witnessed in our modern world. The crew flung open the ports and staggered blubbering into the arms of the crowd. It would never have been believed that members of our species could be so far reduced from the self-possession that is normal to us. Subsequently these poor human wrecks have shown an irrational phobia of the stars, and of all that is not human. They dare not go out at night. They live in an extravagant passion for the presence of others. And since all others are astronomically minded, they cannot find real companionship. They insanely refuse to participate in the mental life of the race upon the plane where all things are seen in their just proportions. They cling piteously to the sweets of individual life; and so they are led to curse the immensities. They fill their minds with human conceits, and their houses with toys. By night they draw the curtains and drown the quiet voice of the stars in revelry. But it is a joyless and a haunted revelry, desired less for itself than as a defence against reality.

2. CHILDHOOD AND MATURITY

I said that we were all astronomically minded; but we are not without 'human' interests. Our visitor from the earth would soon discover that the low buildings, sprinkled on all sides, were the homes of individuals, families, sexual groups, and bands of companions. Most of these buildings are so constructed that the roof and walls can be removed, completely or partially, for sun-bathing and for the night. Round each house is a wilderness, or a garden, or an orchard of our sturdy fruit trees. Here and there men and women may be seen at work with hoe or spade or secateurs. The buildings themselves affect many styles; and within doors our visitor would find great variety from house to house. Even within a single house he might come on rooms seemingly of different epochs. And while some rooms are crowded with articles, many of which would be incomprehensible to the stranger, others are bare, save for a table, chairs, a cupboard, and perhaps some single object of pure art. We have an immense variety of manufactured goods. But the visitor from a world obsessed with material wealth would probably remark the simplicity, even austerity, which characterizes most private houses.

He would doubtless be surprised to see no books. In every room, however, there is a cupboard filled with minute rolls of tape, microscopically figured. Each of these rolls contains matter which could not be cramped into a score of your volumes. They are used in connexion with a pocket-instrument, the size and shape of the ancient cigarette case. When the roll is inserted, it reels itself off at any desired speed, and interferes systematically with ethereal vibrations produced by the instrument. Thus is generated a very complex flow of 'telepathic' language which permeates the brain of the reader. So delicate and direct is this medium of expression that there is scarcely any possibility of misunderstanding the author's intention. The rolls themselves, it should be said, are produced by another special instrument, which is sensitive to vibrations generated in the author's brain. Not that it produces a mere replica of his stream of consciousness; it records only those images and ideas with which he deliberately 'inscribes' it. I may mention also that, since we can at any moment communicate by direct 'telepathy' with any person on the planet, these 'books' of ours are not used for the publication of merely ephemeral thought. Each one of them preserves only the threshed and chosen grains of some mind's harvest.

Other instruments may be observed in our houses, which I cannot pause to describe, instruments whose office is either to carry out domestic drudgery, or to minister directly in one way or another to cultured life. Near the outer door would be hanging a number of flying-suits, and in a garage attached to the house would be the private air-boats, gaily coloured torpedo-shaped objects of various sizes.

Decoration in our houses, save in those which belong to children, is everywhere simple, even severe. None the less we prize it greatly, and spend much consideration upon it. Children, indeed, often adorn their houses with splendour, which adults themselves can also enjoy through children's eyes, even as they can enter into the frolics of infants with unaffected glee.

The number of children in our world is small in relation to our immense population. Yet, seeing that every one of us is potentially immortal, it may be wondered how we can permit ourselves to have any children at all. The explanation is two-fold. In the first place, our policy is to produce new individuals of higher type than ourselves, for we are very far from biologically perfect. Consequently we need a continuous supply of children. And as these successively reach maturity, they take over the functions of adults whose nature is less perfect; and these, when they are aware that they are no longer of service, elect to retire from life.

But even though every individual, sooner or later, ceases to exist, the average length of life is not much less than a quarter of a million terrestrial years. No wonder, then, that we cannot accommodate many children. But we have more than might be expected, for with us infancy and adolescence are very lengthy. The foetus is carried for twenty years. Ectogenesis was practised by our predecessors, but was abandoned by our own species, because, with greatly improved motherhood, there is no need for it. Our mothers, indeed, are both physically and mentally most vigorous during the all too rare period of pregnancy. After birth, true infancy lasts for about a century. During this period, in which the foundations of body and mind are being laid, very slowly, but so securely that they will never fail, the individual is cared for by his mother. Then follow some centuries of childhood, and a thousand years of adolescence.

Our children, of course, are very different beings from the children of the First Men. Though physically they are in many respects still childlike, they are independent persons in the community. Each has either a house of his own, or rooms in a larger building held in common by himself and his friends. Thousands of these are to be found in the neighbourhood of every educational centre. There are some children who prefer to live with their parents, or with one or other of their parents; but this is rare. Though there is often much friendly intercourse between parents and children, the generations usually fare better under separate roofs. This is inevitable in our species. For the adult's overwhelmingly greater experience reveals the world to him in very different proportions from those which alone are possible even to the most brilliant of children; while on the other hand with us the mind of every child is, in some potentiality or other, definitely superior to every adult mind. Consequently, while the child can never appreciate what is best in his elders, the adult, in spite of his power of direct insight into all minds not superior to himself, is doomed to incomprehension of all that is novel in his own offspring.

Six or seven hundred years after birth a child is in some respects physically equivalent to a ten-year-old of the First Men. But since his brain is destined for much higher development, it is already far more complex than any adult brain of that species. And though temperamentally he is in many ways still a child, intellectually he has already in some respects passed beyond the culture of the best adult minds of the ancient races. The traveller, encountering one of our bright boys, might sometimes be reminded of the wise simplicity of the legendary Child Christ. But also he might equally well discover a vast exuberance, boisterousness, impishness, and a complete inability to stand outside the child's own eager life and regard it dispassionately. In general our children develop intellectually beyond the level of the First Men long before they begin to develop the dispassionate will which is characteristic of our adults. When there is conflict between a child's personal needs and the needs of society, he will as a rule force himself to the social course; but he does so with resentment and dramatic self-pity, thereby rendering himself in the adult view exquisitely ridiculous.

When our children attain physical adolescence, nearly a thousand years after birth, they leave the safe paths of childhood to spend another thousand years in one of the antarctic continents, known as the Land of the Young. Somewhat reminiscent of the Wild Continent of the Fifth Men, this territory is preserved as virgin bush and prairie. Sub-human grazers and carnivora abound. Volcanic eruption, hurricanes and glacial seasons afford further attractions to the adventurous young. There is consequently a high death-rate. In this land our young people live the half primitive, half sophisticated life to which their nature is fitted. They hunt, fish, tend cattle and till the ground. They cultivate all the simple beauties of human individuality. They love and hate. They sing, paint, and carve. They devise heroic myths, and delight in fantasies of direct intercourse with a cosmic person. They organize themselves as tribes and nations. Sometimes they even indulge in warfare of a primitive but bloody type. Formerly when this happened, the adult world interfered; but we have since learned to let the fever run its course. The loss of life is regrettable; but it is a small price to pay for the insight afforded even by this restricted and juvenile warfare, into those primitive agonies and passions which, when they are experienced by the adult mind, are so transformed by philosophy that their import is wholly changed. In the Land of the Young our boys and girls experience all that is precious and all that is abject in the primitive. They live through in their own persons, century by century, all its toilsomeness and cramped meanness, all its blind cruelty and precariousness; but also they taste its glamour, its vernal and lyrical glory. They make in little all the mistakes of thought and action that men have ever made; but at last they emerge ready for the larger and more difficult world of maturity.

It was expected that some day, when we should have perfected the species, there would be no need to build up successive generations, no need of children, no need of all this schooling. It was expected that the community would then consist of adults only; and that they would be immortal not merely potentially but in fact, yet also, of course, perennially in the flower of young maturity. Thus, death should never cut the string of individuality and scatter the hard-won pearls, necessitating new strings, and laborious re-gatherings. The many and very delectable beauties of childhood could still be amply enjoyed in exploration of the past.

We know now that this goal is not to be attained, since man's end is imminent.

3. A RACIAL AWAKENING

It is easy to speak of children; but how can I tell you anything significant of our adult experience, in relation to which not only the world of the First Men but the worlds of the most developed earlier species seem so naïve?

The source of the immense difference between ourselves and all other human races lies in the sexual group, which is in fact much more than a sexual group.

The designers of our species set out to produce a being that might be capable of an order of mentality higher than their own. The only possibility of doing so lay in planning a great increase of brain organization. But they knew that the brain of an individual human being could not safely be allowed to exceed a certain weight. They therefore sought to produce the new order of mentality in a system of distinct and specialized brains held in 'telepathic' unity by means of ethereal radiation. Material brains were to be capable of becoming on some occasions mere nodes in a system of radiation which itself should then constitute the physical basis of a single mind. Hitherto there had been 'telepathic' communication between many individuals, but no super-individual, or group-mind. It was known that such a

unity of individual minds had never been attained before, save on
Mars; and it was known how lamentably the racial mind of Mars
had failed to transcend the minds of the Martians. By a combination
of shrewdness and good luck the designers hit upon a policy which
escaped the Martian failure. They planned as the basis of the super-
individual a small multi-sexual group.

Of course the mental unity of the sexual group is not the direct
outcome of the sexual intercourse of its members. Such intercourse
does occur. Groups differ from one another very greatly in this
respect; but in most groups all the members of the male sexes have
intercourse with all the members of the female sexes. Thus sex is
with us essentially social. It is impossible for me to give any idea
of the great range and intensity of experience afforded by these
diverse types of union. Apart from this emotional enrichment of the
individuals, the importance of sexual activity in the group lies in
its bringing individuals into that extreme intimacy, temperamental
harmony and complementariness, without which no emergence into
higher experience would be possible.

Individuals are not necessarily confined to the same group for
ever. Little by little a group may change every one of its ninety-six
members, and yet it will remain the same super-individual mind,
though enriched with the memories grafted into it by the newcomers.
Very rarely does an individual leave a group before he has been in it
for ten thousand years. In some groups the members live together in
a common home. In others they live apart. Sometimes an individual
will form a sort of monogamous relation with another individual
of his group, homing with the chosen one for many thousands
of years, or even for a lifetime. Indeed some claim that life-long
monogamy is the ideal state, so deep and delicate is the intimacy
which it affords. But of course, even in monogamy, each partner
must be periodically refreshed by intercourse with other members
of the group, not only for the spiritual health of the two partners
themselves, but also that the group-mind may be maintained in full
vigour. Whatever the sexual custom of the group, there is always in
the mind of each member a very special loyalty toward the whole
group, a peculiar sexually toned *esprit de corps*, unparalleled in any
other species.

Occasionally there is a special kind of group intercourse in which, during the actual occurrence of group mentality, all the members of one group will have intercourse with those of another. Casual intercourse outside the group is not common, but not discouraged. When it occurs it comes as a symbolic act crowning a spiritual intimacy.

Unlike the physical sex-relationship, the mental unity of the group involves all the members of the group every time it occurs, and so long as it persists. During times of group experience the individual continues to perform his ordinary routine of work and recreation, save when some particular activity is demanded of him by the group-mind itself. But all that he does as a private individual is carried out in a profound absent-mindedness. In familiar situations he reacts correctly, even to the extent of executing familiar types of intellectual work or entertaining acquaintances with intelligent conversation. Yet all the while he is in fact 'far away', rapt in the process of the group-mind. Nothing short of an urgent and unfamiliar crisis can recall him; and in recalling him it usually puts an end to the group's experience.

Each member of the group is fundamentally just a highly developed human animal. He enjoys his food. He has a quick eye for sexual attraction, within or without the group. He has his personal idiosyncrasies and foibles, and is pleased to ridicule the foibles of others – and of himself. He may be one of those who abhor children, or one of those who enter into children's antics with fervour, if they will tolerate him. He may move heaven and earth to procure permission for a holiday in the Land of the Young. And if he fails, as he almost surely does, he may go walking with a friend, or boating and swimming, or playing violent games. Or he may merely potter in his garden, or refresh his mind though not his body by exploring some favourite region of the past. Recreation occupies a large part of his life. For this reason he is always glad to get back to work in due season, whether his function is to maintain some part of the material organization of our world, or to educate, or to perform scientific research, or to co-operate in the endless artistic venture of the race, or, as is more likely, to help in some of those innumerable enterprises whose nature it is impossible for me to describe.

As a human individual, then, he or she is somewhat of the same type as a member of the Fifth species. Here once more is the perfected glandular outfit and instinctive nature. Here too is the highly developed sense perception and intellection. As in the Fifth species, so in the Eighteenth, each individual has his own private needs, which he heartily craves to fulfil; but also, in both species, he subordinates these private cravings to the good of the race absolutely and without struggle. The only kind of conflict which ever occurs between individuals is, not the irreconcilable conflict of wills, but the conflict due to misunderstanding, to imperfect knowledge of the matter under dispute; and this can always be abolished by patient telepathic explication.

In addition to the brain organization necessary to this perfection of Individual human nature, each member of a sexual group has in his own brain a special organ which, useless by itself, can co-operate 'telepathically' with the special organs of other members of the group to produce a single electro-magnetic system, the physical basis of the group-mind. In each sub-sex this organ has a peculiar form and function; and only by the simultaneous operation of the whole ninety-six does the group attain unified mental life. These organs do not merely enable each member to share the experience of all; for this is already provided in the sensitivity to radiation which is characteristic of all brain-tissue in our species. By means of the harmonious activity of the special organs a true group-mind emerges, with experience far beyond the range of the individuals in isolation.

This would not be possible did not the temperament and capacity of each sub-sex differ appropriately from those of the others. I can only hint at these differences by analogy. Among the First Men there are many temperamental types whose essential natures the psychologists of that species never fully analysed. I may mention, however, as superficial designations of these types, the meditative, the active, the mystical, the intellectual, the artistic, the theoretical, the concrete, the placid, the highly-strung. Now our sub-sexes differ from one another temperamentally in some such manners as these, but with a far greater range and diversity. These differences of temperament are utilized for the enrichment of a group self, such as could never have been attained by the First Men, even if they had been capable of 'telepathic' communication and electro-magnetic unity; for they had not the range of specialized brain form.

For all the daily business of life, then, each of us is mentally a distinct individual, though his ordinary means of communication with others is 'telepathic'. But frequently he wakes up to be a group-mind. Apart from this 'waking of individuals together', if I may so call it, the group-mind has no existence; for its being is solely the being of the individuals comprehended together. When this communal awakening occurs, each individual experiences all the bodies of the group as 'his own multiple body', and perceives the world equally from all those bodies. This awakening happens to all the individuals at the same time. But over and above this simple enlargement of the experienced field, is the awakening into new kinds of experience. Of this obviously, I can tell you nothing, save that it differs from the lowlier state more radically than the infant mind differs from the mind of the individual adult, and that it consists of insight into many unsuspected and previously inconceivable features of the familiar world of men and things. Hence, in our group mode, most, but not all, of the perennial philosophical puzzles, especially those connected with the nature of personality, can be so lucidly restated that they cease to be puzzles.

Upon this higher plane of mentality the sexual groups, and therefore the individuals participating in them, have social intercourse with one another as super-individuals. Thus they form together a community of minded communities. For each group is a person differing from other groups in character and experience somewhat as individuals differ. The groups themselves are not allocated to different works, in such a manner that one group should be wholly engaged in industry, another in astronomy, and so on. Only the individuals are thus allocated. In each group there will be members of many professions. The function of the group itself is purely some special manner of insight and mode of appreciation; in relation to which, of course, the work of the individuals is constantly controlled, not only while they are actually supporting the group self, but also when they have each fallen once more into the limited experience which is ordinary individual selfhood. For though, as individuals, they cannot retain clear insight into the high matters which they so recently experienced, they do remember so much as is not beyond the range of individual mentality; and in particular they remember the bearing of the group experience upon their own conduct as individuals.

Recently another and far more penetrating kind of experience has been attained, partly by good fortune, partly through research directed by the group-minds. For these have specialized themselves for particular functions in the mental life of the race, as previously the individuals were specialized for functions within the mind of a group. Very rarely and precariously has this supreme experience been achieved. In it the individual passes beyond this group experience, and becomes the mind of the race. At all times, of course, he can communicate 'telepathically' with other individuals anywhere upon the planet; and frequently the whole race 'listens in' while one individual addresses the world. But in the true racial experience the situation is different. The system of radiation which embraces the whole planet, and includes the million million brains of the race, becomes the physical basis of a racial self. The individual discovers himself to be embodied in all the bodies of the race. He savours in a single intuition all bodily contacts, including the mutual embraces of all lovers. Through the myriad feet of all men and women he enfolds his world in a single grasp. He sees with all eyes, and comprehends in a single vision all visual fields. Thus he perceives at once and as a continuous, variegated sphere, the whole surface of the planet. But not only so. He now stands above the group-minds as they above the individuals. He regards them as a man may regard his own vital tissues, with mingled contempt, sympathy, reverence, and dispassion. He watches them as one might study the living cells of his own brain; but also with the aloof interest of one observing an ant hill; and yet again as one enthralled by the strange and diverse ways of his fellow men; and further as one who, from above the battle, watches himself and his comrades agonizing in some desperate venture; yet chiefly as the artist who has no thought but for his vision and its embodiment. In the racial mode a man apprehends all things astronomically. Through all eyes and all observatories, he beholds his voyaging world, and peers outward into space. Thus he merges in one view, as it were, the views of deck-hand, captain, stoker, and the man in the crow's-nest. Regarding the solar system simultaneously from both limbs of Neptune, he perceives the planets and the sun stereoscopically, as though in binocular vision. Further, his perceived 'now' embraces not a moment but a vast age. Thus, observing the galaxy from every point in succession along Neptune's wide orbit, and watching the nearer stars shift hither and thither, he actually perceives some of the constellations in three dimensions. Nay, with the aid of our most recent instruments the whole galaxy appears stereoscopically. But the great nebulae and remote universes remain mere marks upon the flat sky; and, in contemplation of their remoteness, man, even as the racial self of the mightiest of all human races, realizes his own minuteness and impotence.

But chiefly the racial mind transcends the minds of groups and individuals in philosophical insight into the true nature of space and time, mind and its objects, cosmical striving and cosmical perfection. Some hints of this great elucidation must presently be given; but in the main it cannot be communicated. Indeed such insight is beyond the reach of ourselves as isolated individuals, and even beyond the group-minds. When we have declined from the racial mentality, we cannot clearly remember what it was that we experienced.

In particular we have one very perplexing recollection about our racial experience, one which involves a seeming impossibility. In the racial mind our experience was enlarged not only spatially but temporally in a very strange manner. In respect of temporal perception, of course, minds may differ in two ways, in the length of the span which they can comprehend as 'now', and the minuteness of the successive events which they can discriminate within the 'now'. As individuals we can hold within one 'now' a duration equal to the old terrestrial day; and within that duration, we can if we will, discriminate rapid pulsations such as commonly we hear together as a high musical tone. As the race-mind we perceived as 'now' the whole period since the birth of the oldest living individuals, and the whole past of the species appeared as personal memory, stretching back into the mists of infancy. Yet we could, if we willed, discriminate within the 'now' one light-vibration from the next. In this mere increased breadth and precision of temporal perception there is no contradiction. But how, we ask ourselves, could the race-mind experience as 'now' a vast period in which it had no existence whatever? Our first experience of racial mentality lasted only as long as Neptune's moon takes to complete one circuit. Before that period, then, the race-mind was not. Yet during the month of its existence it regarded the whole previous career of the race as 'present'.

Indeed, the racial experience has greatly perplexed us as individuals, and we can scarcely be said to remember more of it than that it was of extreme subtlety and extreme beauty. At the same time we often have of it an impression of unspeakable horror. We who, in our familiar individual sphere are able to regard all conceivable tragedy not merely with fortitude but with exultation, are obscurely conscious that as the racial mind we have looked into an abyss of evil such as we cannot now conceive, and could not endure to conceive. Yet even this hell we know to have been acceptable as an organic member in the austere form of the cosmos. We remember obscurely, and yet with a strange conviction, that all the age-long striving of the human spirit, no less than the petty cravings of individuals, was seen as a fair component in something far more admirable than itself; and that man ultimately defeated, no less than man for a while triumphant, contributes to this higher excellence.

How colourless these words! How unworthy of that wholly satisfying beauty of all things, which in our awakened racial mode we see face to face. Every human being, of whatever species, may occasionally glimpse some fragment or aspect of existence transfigured thus with the cold beauty which normally he cannot see. Even the First Men, in their respect for tragic art, had something of this experience. The Second, and still more surely the Fifth, sought it deliberately. The winged Seventh happened upon it while they were in the air. But their minds were cramped; and all that they could appreciate was their own small world and their own tragic story. We, the Last Men, have all their zest in private and in racial life, whether it fares well or ill. We have it at all times, and we have it in respect of matters inconceivable to lesser minds. We have it, moreover, intelligently. Knowing well how strange it is to admire evil along with good, we see clearly the subversiveness of this experience. Even we, as mere individuals, cannot reconcile our loyalty to the striving spirit of man with our own divine aloofness. And so, if we were mere individuals, there would remain conflict in each of us. But in the racial mode each one of us has now experienced the great elucidation of intellect and of feeling. And though, as individuals once more, we can never recapture that far-seeing vision, the obscure memory of it masters us always, and controls all our policies. Among yourselves, the artist, after his phase of creative insight is passed, and he is once more a partisan in the struggle for existence, may carry out in detail the design conceived in his brief period of clarity. He remembers, but no longer sees the vision. He tries to fashion some perceptible embodiment of the vanished splendour. So we, living our individual lives, delighting in the contacts of flesh, the relations of minds, and all the delicate activities of human culture, co-operating and conflicting in a thousand individual undertakings and performing each his office in the material maintenance of our society, see all things as though transfused with light from a source which is itself no longer revealed.

I have tried to tell you something of the most distinctive characteristics of our species. You can imagine that the frequent occasions of group mentality, and even more the rare occasions of race mentality, have a far-reaching effect on every individual mind, and therefore on our whole social order. Ours is in fact a society dominated, as no previous society, by a single racial purpose which is in a sense religious. Not that the individual's private efflorescence is at all thwarted by the racial purpose. Indeed, far otherwise; for that purpose demands as the first condition of its fulfilment a wealth of individual fulfilment, physical and mental. But in each mind of man or woman the racial purpose presides absolutely; and hence it is the unquestioned motive of all social policy.

I must not stay to describe in detail this society of ours, in which a million million citizens, grouped in over a thousand nations, live in perfect accord without the aid of armies or even a police force. I must not tell of our much prized social organization, which assigns a unique function to each citizen, controls the procreation of new citizens of every type in relation to social need, and yet provides an endless supply of originality. We have no government and no laws, if by law is meant a stereotyped convention supported by force, and not to be altered without the aid of cumbersome machinery. Yet, though our society is in this sense an anarchy, it lives by means of a very intricate system of customs, some of which are so ancient as to have become spontaneous taboos, rather than deliberate conventions. It is the business of those among us who correspond to your lawyers and politicians to study these customs and suggest improvements. Those suggestions are submitted to no representative body, but to the whole world-population in 'telepathic' conference. Ours is thus in a sense the most democratic of all societies. Yet in another sense it is extremely bureaucratic, since it is already some millions of terrestrial years since any suggestion put forward by the College of Organizers was rejected or even seriously criticized, so thoroughly do these social engineers study their material. The only serious possibility of conflict lies now between the world population as individuals and the same individuals as group-minds or racial mind. But though in these respects there have formerly occurred serious conflicts, peculiarly distressing to the individuals who experienced them, such conflicts are now extremely rare. For, even as mere individuals, we are learning to trust more and more to the judgment and dictates of our own super-individual experience.

It is time to grapple with the most difficult part of my whole task. Somehow, and very briefly, I must give you an idea of that outlook upon existence which has determined our racial purpose, making it essentially a religious purpose. This outlook has come to us partly through the work of individuals in scientific research and philosophic thought, partly through the influence of our group and racial experiences. You can imagine that it is not easy to describe this modern vision of the nature of things in any manner intelligible to those who have not our advantages. There is much in this vision which will remind you of your mystics; yet between them and us there is far more difference than similarity, in respect both of the matter and the manner of our thought. For while they are confident that the cosmos is perfect, we are sure only that it is very beautiful. While they pass to their conclusion without the aid of intellect, we have used that staff every step of the way. Thus, even when in respect of conclusions we agree with your mystics rather than your plodding intellectuals, in respect of method we applaud most your intellectuals; for they scorned to deceive themselves with comfortable fantasies.

4. COSMOLOGY

We find ourselves living in a vast and boundless, yet finite, order of spatio-temporal events. And each of us, as the racial mind, has learned that there are other such orders, other and incommensurable spheres of events, related to our own neither spatially nor temporally but in another mode of eternal being. Of the contents of those alien spheres we know almost nothing but that they are incomprehensible to us, even in our racial mentality.

Within this spatio-temporal sphere of ours we remark what we call the Beginning and what we call the End. In the Beginning there came into existence, we know not how, that all-pervading and unimaginably tenuous gas which was the parent of all material and spiritual existence within time's known span. It was in fact a very multitudinous yet precisely numbered host. From the crowding together of this great population into many swarms, arose in time the nebulae, each of which in its turn condenses as a galaxy, a universe of stars. The stars have their beginnings and their ends; and for a few moments somewhere in between their beginnings and their ends a few, very few, may support mind. But in due course will come the universal End, when all the wreckage of the galaxies will have drifted together as a single, barren, and seemingly changeless ash, in the midst of a chaos of unavailing energy.

But the cosmic events which we call the Beginning and the End are final only in relation to our ignorance of the events which lie beyond them. We know, and as the racial mind we have apprehended as a clear necessity, that not only space but time also is boundless, though finite. For in a sense time is cyclic. After the End, events unknowable will continue to happen during a period much longer than that which will have passed since the Beginning; but at length there will recur the identical event which was itself also the Beginning.

Yet though time is cyclic, it is not repetitive; there is no other time within which it can repeat itself. For time is but an abstraction from the successiveness of events that pass; and since all events whatsoever form together a cycle of successiveness, there is nothing constant in relation to which there can be repetition. And so the succession of events is cyclic, yet not repetitive. The birth of the all-pervading gas in the so-called Beginning is not merely similar to another such birth to occur long after us and long after the cosmic End, so-called; the past Beginning is the future Beginning.

From the Beginning to the End is but the span from one spoke to the next on time's great wheel. There is a vaster span, stretching beyond the End and round to the Beginning. Of the events therein we know nothing, save that there must be such events.

Everywhere within time's cycle there is endless passage of events. In a continuous flux, they occur and vanish, yielding to their successors. Yet each one of them is eternal. Though passage is of their very nature, and without passage they are nothing, yet they have eternal being. But their passage is no illusion. They have eternal being, yet eternally they exist with passage. In our racial mode we see clearly that this is so; but in our individual mode it remains a mystery. Yet even in our individual mode we must accept both sides of this mysterious antinomy, as a fiction needed for the rationalizing of our experience.

The Beginning precedes the End by some hundred million million terrestrial years, and succeeds it by a period at least nine times longer. In the middle of the smaller span lies the still shorter period within which alone the living worlds can occur. And they are very few. One by one they dawn into mentality and die, successive blooms in life's short summer. Before that season and after it, even to the Beginning and to the End, and even before the Beginning and after the End, sleep, utter oblivion. Not before there are stars, and not after the stars are chilled, can there be life. And then, rarely.

In our own galaxy there have occurred hitherto some twenty thousand worlds that have conceived life. And of these a few score have attained or surpassed the mentality of the First Men. But of those that have reached this development, man has now outstripped the rest, and today man alone survives.

There are the millions of other galaxies, for instance the Andromedan island. We have some reason to surmise that in that favoured universe mind may have attained to insight and power incomparably greater than our own. But all that we know for certain is that it contains four worlds of high order.

Of the host of other universes that lie within range of our mind-detecting instruments, none have produced anything comparable with man. But there are many universes too remote to be estimated.

You may wonder how we have come to detect these remote lives and intelligences. I can say only that the occurrence of mentality produces certain minute astronomical effects, to which our instruments are sensitive even at great distances. These effects increase slightly with the mere mass of living matter on any astronomical body, but far more with its mental and spiritual development. Long ago it was the spiritual development of the world-community of the Fifth Men that dragged the moon from its orbit. And in our own case, so numerous is our society today, and so greatly developed in mental and spiritual activities, that only by continuous expense of physical energy can we preserve the solar system from confusion.

We have another means of detecting minds remote from us in space. We can, of course, enter into past minds wherever they are, so long as they are intelligible to us; and we have tried to use this power for the discovery of remote minded worlds. But in general the experience of such minds is too different in fibre from our own for us to be able even to detect its existence. And so our knowledge of minds in other worlds is almost wholly derived from their physical effects.

We cannot say that nowhere save on those rare bodies called planets does life ever occur. For we have evidence that in a few of the younger stars there is life, and even intelligence. How it persists in an incandescent environment we know not, nor whether it is perhaps the life of the star as a whole, as a single organism, or the life of many flame-like inhabitants of the star. All that we know is that no star in its prime has life, and therefore that the lives of the younger ones are probably doomed.

Again, we know that mind occurs, though very seldom, on a few extremely old stars, no longer incandescent. What the future of these minds will be, we cannot tell. Perhaps it is with them, and not with man, that the hope of the cosmos lies. But at present they are all primitive.

Today nothing anywhere in this galaxy of ours can compare with man in respect of vision and mental creativeness.

We have, therefore, come to regard our community as of some importance, especially so in the light of our metaphysics; but I can only hint at our metaphysical vision of things by means of metaphors which will convey at best a caricature of that vision.

In the Beginning there was great potency, but little form. And the spirit slept as the multitude of discrete primordial existents. Thenceforth there has been a long and fluctuating adventure toward harmonious complexity of form, and toward the awakening of the spirit into unity, knowledge, delight and self-expression. And this is the goal of all living, that the cosmos may be known, and admired, and that it may be crowned with further beauties. Nowhere and at no time, so far as we can tell, at least within our own galaxy, has the adventure reached further than in ourselves. And in us, what has been achieved is but a minute beginning. But it is a real beginning. Man in our day has gained some depth of insight, some breadth of knowledge, some power of creation, some faculty of worship. We have looked far afield. We have probed not altogether superficially into the nature of existence, and have found it very beautiful, though also terrible. We have created a not inconsiderable community; and we have wakened together to be the unique spirit of that community. We had proposed to ourselves a very long and arduous future, which should culminate, at some time before the End, in the complete achievement of the spirit's ideal. But now we know that disaster is already near at hand.

When we are in full possession of our faculties, we are not distressed by this fate. For we know that though our fair community must cease, it has also indestructible being. We have at least carved into one region of the eternal real a form which has beauty of no mean order. The great company of diverse and most lovely men and women in all their subtle relationships, striving with a single purpose toward the goal which is mind's final goal; the community and super-individuality of that great host; the beginnings of further insight and creativeness upon the higher plane – these surely are real achievements – even though, in the larger view, they are minute achievements.

Yet though we are not at all dismayed by our own extinction, we cannot but wonder whether or not in the far future some other spirit will fulfil the cosmic ideal, or whether we ourselves are the modest crown of existence. Unfortunately, though we can explore the past wherever there are intelligible minds, we cannot enter into the future. And so in vain we ask, will ever any spirit awake to gather all spirits into itself, to elicit from the stars their full flower of beauty, to know all things together, and admire all things justly?

If in the far future this end will be achieved, it is really achieved even now; for whenever it occurs, its being is eternal. But on the other hand if it is indeed achieved eternally, this achievement must be the work of spirits or a spirit not wholly unlike ourselves, though infinitely greater. And the physical location of that spirit must lie in the far future.

But if no future spirit will achieve this end before it dies, then, though the cosmos is indeed very beautiful, it is not perfect.

I said that we regard the cosmos as very beautiful. Yet it is also very terrible. For ourselves, it is easy to look forward with equanimity to our end, and even to the end of our admired community; for what we prize most is the excellent beauty of the cosmos. But there are the myriads of spirits who have never entered into that vision. They have suffered, and they were not permitted that consolation. There are, first, the incalculable hosts of lowly creatures scattered over all the ages in all the minded worlds. Theirs was only a dream life, and their misery not often poignant; but none the less they are to be pitied for having missed the more poignant experience in which alone spirit can find fulfilment. Then there are the intelligent beings, human and otherwise; the many minded worlds throughout the galaxies, that have struggled into cognizance, striven for they knew not what, tasted brief delights and lived in the shadow of pain and death, until at last their life has been crushed out by careless fate. In our solar system there are the Martians, insanely and miserably obsessed; the native Venerians, imprisoned in their ocean and murdered for man's sake; and all the hosts of the forerunning human species. A few individuals no doubt in every period, and many in certain favoured races, have lived on the whole happily. And a few have even known something of the supreme beatitude. But for most, until our modern epoch, thwarting has outweighed fulfilment; and if actual grief has not preponderated over joy, it is because, mercifully, the fulfilment that is wholly missed cannot be conceived.

Our predecessors of the Sixteenth species, oppressed by this vast horror, undertook a forlorn and seemingly irrational crusade for the rescue of the tragic past. We see now clearly that their enterprise, though desperate, was not quite fantastic. For, if ever the cosmic ideal should be realized, even though for a moment only, then in that time the awakened Soul of All will embrace within itself all spirits whatever throughout the whole of time's wide circuit. And so to each one of them, even to the least, it will seem that he has awakened and discovered himself to be the Soul of All, knowing all things and rejoicing in all things. And though afterwards, through the inevitable decay of the stars, this most glorious vision must be lost, suddenly or in the long-drawn-out defeat of life, yet would the awakened Soul of All have eternal being, and in it each martyred spirit would have beatitude eternally, though unknown to itself in its own temporal mode.

It may be that this is the case. If not, then eternally the martyred spirits are martyred only, and not blest.

We cannot tell which of these possibilities is fact. As individuals we earnestly desire that the eternal being of things may include this supreme awakening. This, nothing less than this, has been the remote but ever-present goal of our practical religious life and of our social policy.

In our racial mode also we have greatly desired this end, but differently.

Even as individuals, all our desires are tempered by that relentless admiration of fate which we recognize as the spirit's highest achievement. Even as individuals, we exult in the issue whether our enterprises succeed or fail. The pioneer defeated, the lover bereaved and overwhelmed, can find in his disaster the supreme experience, the dispassionate ecstasy which salutes the Real as it is and would not change one jot of it. Even as individuals, we can regard the impending extinction of mankind as a thing superb though tragic. Strong in the knowledge that the human spirit has already inscribed the cosmos with indestructible beauty, and that inevitably, whether sooner or later, man's career must end, we face this too sudden end with laughter in our hearts, and peace.

But there is the one thought by which, in our individual state, we are still dismayed, namely that the cosmos enterprise itself may fail;

that the full potentiality of the Real may never find expression; that never, in any stage of time, the multitudinous and conflicting existents should be organized as the universal harmonious living body; that the spirit's eternal nature, therefore, should be discordant, miserably tranced; that the indestructible beauties of this our sphere of space and time should remain imperfect, and remain, too, not adequately worshipped.

But in the racial mind this ultimate dread has no place. On those few occasions when we have awakened racially, we have come to regard with piety even the possibility of cosmical defeat. For as the racial mind, though in a manner we earnestly desired the fulfilment of the cosmical ideal, yet we were no more enslaved to this desire than, as individuals, we are enslaved to our private desires. For though the racial mind wills this supreme achievement, yet in the same act it holds itself aloof from it, and from all desire, and all emotion, save the ecstasy which admires the Real as it is, and accepts its dark-bright form with joy.

As individuals, therefore, we try to regard the whole cosmic adventure as a symphony now in progress, which may or may not some day achieve its just conclusion. Like music, however, the vast biography of the stars is to be judged not in respect of its final moment merely, but in respect of the perfection of its whole form; and whether its form as a whole is perfect or not, we cannot know. Actual music is a pattern of intertwining themes which evolve and die; and these again are woven of simpler members, which again are spun of chords and unitary tones. But the music of the spheres is of a complexity almost infinitely more subtle, and its themes rank above and below one another in hierarchy beyond hierarchy. None but a God, none but a mind subtle as the music itself, could hear the whole in all its detail, and grasp in one act its close-knit individuality, if such it has. Not for any human mind to say authoritatively, 'This is music, wholly,' or to say, 'This is mere noise, flecked now and then by shreds of significance.'

The music of the spheres is unlike other music not only in respect of its richness, but also in the nature of its medium. It is a music not merely of sounds but of souls. Each of its minor themes, each of its chords, each single tone of it, each tremor of each tone, is in its own degree more than a mere passive factor in the music; it is a listener, and also a creator. Wherever there is individuality of form, there is also an individual appreciator and originator. And the more complex the form, the more percipient and active the spirit. Thus in every individual factor within the music, the musical environment of that factor is experienced, vaguely or precisely, erroneously, or with greater approximation to truth; and, being experienced, it is admired or loathed, rightly or falsely. And it is influenced. Just as in actual music each theme is in a manner a determination of its forerunners and followers and present accompaniment, so in this vaster music each individual factor is itself a determination of its environment. Also it is a determinant, both of that which precedes and that which follows.

But whether these manifold interdeterminations are after all haphazard, or, as in music, controlled in relation to the beauty of the whole, we know not; nor whether, if this is the case, the beautiful whole of things is the work of some mind; nor yet whether some mind admires it adequately as a whole of beauty.

But this we know: that we ourselves, when the spirit is most awake in us, admire the Real as it is revealed to us, and salute its dark-bright form with joy.

CHAPTER XVI

THE LAST OF MAN

1. SENTENCE OF DEATH

Ours has been essentially a philosophical age, in fact the supreme age of philosophy. But a great practical problem has also concerned us. We have had to prepare for the task of preserving humanity during a most difficult period which was calculated to being about one hundred million years hence, but might, in certain circumstances, be sprung upon us at very short notice. Long ago the human inhabitants of Venus believed that already in their day the sun was about to enter the 'white dwarf' phase, and that the time would therefore soon come when their world would be frost-bound. This calculation was unduly pessimistic; but we know now that, even allowing for the slight delay caused by the great collision, the solar collapse must begin at some date astronomically not very distant. We had planned that during the comparatively brief period of the actual shrinkage, we would move our planet steadily nearer to the sun, until finally it should settle in the narrowest possible orbit.

Man would then be comfortably placed for a very long period. But in the fullness of time there would come a far more serious crisis. The sun would continue to cool, and at last man would no longer be able to live by means of solar radiation. It would become necessary to annihilate matter to supply the deficiency. The other planets might be used for this purpose, and possibly the sun itself. Or, given the sustenance for so long a voyage, man might boldly project his planet into the neighbourhood of some younger star. Thenceforth, perhaps, he might operate upon a far grander scale. He might explore and colonize all suitable worlds in every corner of the galaxy, and organize himself as a vast community of minded worlds. Even (so we dreamed) he might achieve intercourse with other galaxies. It did not seem impossible that man himself was the germ of the world-soul, which, we still hope, is destined to awake for a while before the universal decline, and to crown the eternal cosmos with its due of knowledge and admiration, fleeting yet eternal. We dared to think that in some far distant epoch the human spirit, clad in all wisdom, power, and delight, might look back upon our primitive age with a certain respect; no doubt with pity also and amusement, but none the less with admiration for the spirit in us, still only half awake, and struggling against great disabilities. In such a mood, half pity, half admiration, we ourselves look back upon the primitive mankinds.

Our prospect has now suddenly and completely changed, for astronomers have made a startling discovery, which assigns to man a speedy end. His existence has ever been precarious. At any stage of his career he might easily have been exterminated by some slight alteration of his chemical environment, by a more than usually malignant microbe, by a radical change of climate, or by the manifold effects of his own folly. Twice already he has been almost destroyed by astronomical events. How easily might it happen that the solar system, now rushing through a somewhat more crowded region of the galaxy, should become entangled with, or actually strike, a major astronomical body, and be destroyed. But fate, as it turns out, has a more surprising end in store for man.

Not long ago an unexpected alteration was observed to be taking place in a near star. Through no discoverable cause, it began to change from white to violet, and increase in brightness. Already it has attained such extravagant brilliance that, though its actual disk remains a mere point in our sky, its dazzling purple radiance illuminates our nocturnal landscapes with hideous beauty. Our astronomers have ascertained that this is no ordinary 'nova', that it is not one of those stars addicted to paroxysms of brilliance. It is something unprecedented, a normal star suffering from a unique disease, a fantastic acceleration of its vital process, a riotous squandering of the energy which should have remained locked within its substance for aeons. At the present rate it will be reduced either to an inert cinder or to actual annihilation in a few thousand years. This extraordinary event may possibly have been produced by unwise tamperings on the part of intelligent beings in the star's neighbourhood. But, indeed, since all matter at very high temperature is in a state of unstable equilibrium, the cause may have been merely some conjunction of natural circumstances.

The event was first regarded simply as an intriguing spectacle. But further study roused a more serious interest. Our own planet, and therefore the sun also, was suffering a continuous and increasing bombardment of ethereal vibrations, most of which were of incredibly high frequency, and of unknown potentiality. What would be their effect upon the sun? After some centuries, certain astronomical bodies in the neighbourhood of the deranged star were seen to be infected with its disorder. Their fever increased the splendour of our night sky, but it also confirmed our fears. We still hoped that the sun might prove too distant to be seriously influenced, but careful analysis now showed that this hope must be abandoned. The sun's remoteness might cause a delay of some thousands of years before the cumulative effects of the bombardment could start the disintegration; but sooner or later the sun itself must be infected. Probably within thirty thousand years life will be impossible anywhere within a vast radius of the sun, so vast a radius that it is quite impossible to propel our planet away fast enough to escape before the storm can catch us.

2. BEHAVIOUR OF THE CONDEMNED

The discovery of this doom kindled in us unfamiliar emotions. Hitherto humanity had seemed to be destined for a very long future, and the individual himself had been accustomed to look forward to very many thousands of years of personal life, ending in voluntary sleep. We had of course often conceived, and even savoured in imagination, the sudden destruction of our world. But now we faced it as a fact. Outwardly every one behaved with perfect serenity, but inwardly every mind was in turmoil. Not that there was any question of our falling into panic or despair, for in this crisis our native detachment stood us in good stead. But inevitably some time passed before our minds became properly adjusted to the new prospect, before we could see our fate outlined clearly and beautifully against the cosmic background.

Presently, however, we learned to contemplate the whole great saga of man as a completed work of art, and to admire it no less for its sudden and tragic end than for the promise in it which was

not to be fulfilled. Grief was now transfigured wholly into ecstasy.
Defeat, which had oppressed us with a sense of man's impotence
and littleness among the stars, brought us into a new sympathy and
reverence for all those myriads of beings in the past out of whose
obscure strivings we had been born. We saw the most brilliant of our
own race and the lowliest of our prehuman forerunners as essentially
spirits of equal excellence, though cast in diverse circumstances.
When we looked round on the heavens, and at the violet splendour
which was to destroy us, we were filled with awe and pity, awe for
the inconceivable potentiality of this bright host, pity for its self-
thwarting effort to fulfil itself as the universal spirit.

At this stage it seemed that there was nothing left for us to do but
to crowd as much excellence as possible into our remaining life, and
meet our end in the noblest manner. But now there came upon us once
more the rare experience of racial mentality. For a whole Neptunian
year every individual lived in an enraptured trance, in which, as the
racial mind, he or she resolved many ancient mysteries and saluted
many unexpected beauties. This ineffable experience, lived through
under the shadow of death, was the flower of man's whole being. But
I can tell nothing of it, save that when it was over we possessed, even
as individuals, a new peace, in which, strangely but harmoniously,
were blended grief, exaltation, and god-like laughter.

In consequence of this racial experience we found ourselves faced
with two tasks which had not before been contemplated. The one
referred to the future, the other to the past.

In respect of the future, we are now setting about the forlorn task
of disseminating among the stars the seeds of a new humanity. For
this purpose we shall make use of the pressure of radiation from
the sun, and chiefly the extravagantly potent radiation that will later
be available. We are hoping to devise extremely minute electro-
magnetic 'wave-systems', akin to normal protons and electrons,
which will be individually capable of sailing forward upon the
hurricane of solar radiation at a speed not wholly incomparable
with the speed of light itself. This is a difficult task. But, further,
these units must be so cunningly inter-related that, in favourable
conditions, they may tend to combine to form spores of life, and to
develop, not indeed into human beings, but into lowly organisms

with a definite evolutionary bias toward the essentials of human nature. These objects we shall project from beyond our atmosphere in immense quantities at certain points of our planet's orbit, so that solar radiation may carry them toward the most promising regions of the galaxy. The chance that any of them will survive to reach their destination is small, and still smaller the chance that any of them will find a suitable environment. But if any of this human seed should fall upon good ground, it will embark, we hope, upon a somewhat rapid biological evolution, and produce in due season whatever complex organic forms are possible in its environment. It will have a very real physiological bias toward the evolution of intelligence. Indeed it will have a much greater bias in that direction than occurred on the Earth in those subvital atomic groupings from which terrestrial life eventually sprang.

It is just conceivable, then, that by extremely good fortune man may still influence the future of this galaxy, not directly but through his creature. But in the vast music of existence the actual theme of mankind now ceases for ever. Finished, the long reiterations of man's history; defeated, the whole proud enterprise of his maturity. The stored experience of many mankinds must sink into oblivion, and today's wisdom must vanish.

The other task which occupies us, that which relates to the past, is one which may very well seem to you nonsensical.

We have long been able to enter into past minds and participate in their experience. Hitherto we have been passive spectators merely, but recently we have acquired the power of influencing past minds. This seems an impossibility; for a past event is what it is, and how can it conceivably be altered at a subsequent date, even in the minutest respect?

Now it is true that past events are what they are, irrevocably; but in certain cases some feature of a past event may depend on an event in the far future. The past event would never have been as it actually was (and is, eternally), if there had not been going to be a certain future event, which, though not contemporaneous with the past event, influences it directly in the sphere of eternal being. The passage of events is real, and time is the successiveness of passing events; but though events have passage, they have also eternal being. And in certain rare cases mental events far separated in time determine one another directly by way of eternity.

Our own minds have often been profoundly influenced by direct inspection of past minds; and now we find that certain events of certain past minds are determined by present events in our own present minds. No doubt there are some past mental events which are what they are by virtue of mental processes which we shall perform but have not yet performed.

Our historians and psychologists, engaged on direct inspection of past minds, had often complained of certain 'singular' points in past minds, where the ordinary laws of psychology fail to give a full explanation of the course of mental events; where, in fact, some wholly unknown influence seemed to be at work. Later it was found that, in some cases at least, this disturbance of the ordinary principles of psychology corresponded with certain thoughts or desires in the mind of the observer, living in our own age. Of course, only such matters as could have significance to the past mind could influence it at all. Thoughts and desires of ours which have no meaning to the particular past individual fail to enter into his experience. New ideas and new values are only to be introduced by arranging familiar matter so that it may gain a new significance. Nevertheless we now found ourselves in possession of an amazing power of communicating with the past, and contributing to its thought and action, though of course we could not *alter* it.

But, it may he asked, what if, in respect of a particular 'singularity' in some past mind, we do not, after all, choose to provide the necessary influence to account for it? The question is meaningless. There is no possibility that we should not choose to influence those past minds which are, as a matter of fact, dependent on our influence. For it is in the sphere of eternity (wherein alone we meet past minds), that we really make this free choice. And in the sphere of time, though the choosing has relations with our modern age, and may be said to occur in that age, it also has relations with the past mind, and may be said to have occurred also long ago.

There are in some past minds singularities which are not the product of any influence that we have exerted today. Some of these singularities, no doubt, we shall ourselves produce on some occasion before our destruction. But it may be that some are due to an influence other than ours, perhaps to beings which, by good fortune, may spring long hence from our forlorn seminal enterprise; or they may be due perhaps to the cosmic mind, whose future occurrence and eternal existence we earnestly desire. However that may be, there are a few remarkable minds, scattered up and down past ages and even in the most primitive human races, which suggest an influence other than our own. They are so 'singular' in one respect or another, that we cannot give a perfectly clear psychological account of them in terms of the past only; and yet we ourselves are not the instigators of their singularity. Your Jesus, your Socrates, your Gautama, show traces of this uniqueness. But the most original of all were too eccentric to have any influence on their contemporaries. It is possible that in ourselves also there are 'singularities' which cannot be accounted for wholly in terms of ordinary biological and psychological laws. If we could prove that this is the case, we should have very definite evidence of the occurrence of a high order of mentality somewhere in the future, and therefore of its eternal existence. But hitherto this problem has proved too subtle for us, even in the racial mode. It may be that the mere fact that we have succeeded in attaining racial mentality involves some remote future influence. It is even conceivable that every creative advance that any mind has ever made involves unwitting co-operation with the cosmic mind which, perhaps, will awake at some date before the End.

We have two methods of influencing the past through past individuals; for we can operate either upon minds of great originality and power, or upon any average individual whose circumstances happen to suit our purpose. In original minds we can only suggest some very vague intuition, which is then 'worked up' by the individual himself into some form very different from that which we intended, but very potent as a factor in the culture of his age. Average minds, on the other hand, we can use as passive instruments for the conveyance of detailed ideas. But in such cases the individual is incapable of working up the material into a great and potent form, suited to his age.

But what is it, you may ask, that we seek to contribute to the past? We seek to afford intuitions of truth and of value, which, though easy to us from our point of vantage, would be impossible to the unaided past. We seek to help the past to make the best of itself, just as one man may help another. We seek to direct the attention of past individuals and past races to truths and beauties which, though implicit in their experience, would otherwise be overlooked.

We seek to do this for two reasons. Entering into past minds, we become perfectly acquainted with them, and cannot but love them; and so we desire to help them. By influencing selected individuals, we seek to influence indirectly great multitudes. But our second motive is very different. We see the career of Man in his successive planetary homes as a process of very great beauty. It is far indeed from the perfect; but it is very beautiful, with the beauty of tragic art. Now it turns out that this beautiful thing entails our operation at various points in the past. Therefore we will to operate.

Unfortunately our first inexperienced efforts were disastrous. Many of the fatuities which primitive minds in all ages have been prone to attribute to the influence of disembodied spirits, whether deities, fiends, or the dead, are but the gibberish which resulted from our earliest experiments. And this book, so admirable in our conception, has issued from the brain of the writer, your contemporary, in such disorder as to be mostly rubbish.

We are concerned with the past not only in so far as we make very rare contributions to it, but chiefly in two other manners.

First, we are engaged upon the great enterprise of becoming lovingly acquainted with the past, the human past, in every detail. This is, so to speak, our supreme act of filial piety. When one being comes to know and love another, a new and beautiful thing is created, namely the love. The cosmos is thus far and at that date enhanced. We seek then to know and love every past mind that we can enter. In most cases we can know them with far more understanding than they can know themselves. Not the least of them, not the worst of them, shall be left out of this great work of understanding and admiration.

There is another manner in which we are concerned with the human past. We need its help. For we, who are triumphantly reconciled to our fate, are under obligation to devote our last energies not to ecstatic contemplation but to a forlorn and most uncongenial task, the dissemination. This task is almost intolerably repugnant to us. Gladly would we spend our last days in embellishing our community and our culture, and in pious exploration of the past. But it is incumbent on us, who are by nature artists and philosophers, to direct the whole attention of our world upon the arid labour of designing an artificial human seed, producing it in immense quantities, and projecting it among the stars. If there is to be any possibility of success, we must undertake a very lengthy programme of physical research, and finally organize a world-wide system of manufacture. The work will not be completed until our physical constitution is already being undermined, and the disintegration of our community has already begun. Now we could never fulfil this policy without a zealous conviction of its importance. Here it is that the past can help us. We, who have now learnt so thoroughly the supreme art of ecstatic fatalism, go humbly to the past to learn over again that other supreme achievement of the spirit, loyalty to the forces of life embattled against the forces of death. Wandering among the heroic and often forlorn ventures of the past, we are fired once more with primitive zeal. Thus, when we return to our own world, we are able, even while we preserve in our hearts the peace that passeth understanding, to struggle as though we cared only for victory.

3. EPILOGUE

I am speaking to you now from a period about twenty thousand terrestrial years after the date at which the whole preceding part of this book was communicated. It has become very difficult to reach you, and still more difficult to speak to you; for already the Last Men are not the men they were.

Our two great undertakings are still unfinished. Much of the human past remains imperfectly explored, and the projection of the seed is scarcely begun. That enterprise has proved far more difficult than was expected. Only within the last few years have we succeeded in designing an artificial human dust capable of being carried forward on the sun's radiation, hardy enough to endure the conditions of a trans-galactic voyage of many millions of years, and yet intricate enough to bear the potentiality of life and of spiritual development. We are now preparing to manufacture this seminal matter in great quantities, and to cast it into space at suitable points on the planet's orbit.

Some centuries have now passed since the sun began to show the first symptoms of disintegration, namely a slight change of colour toward the blue, followed by a definite increase of brightness and heat. Today, when he pierces the ever-thickening cloud, he smites us with an intolerable steely brilliance which destroys the sight of anyone foolish enough to face it. Even in the cloudy weather which is now normal, the eye is wounded by the fierce violet glare. Eye-troubles afflict us all, in spite of the special glasses which have been designed to protect us. The mere heat, too, is already destructive. We are forcing our planet outward from its old orbit in an ever-widening spiral; but, do what we will, we cannot prevent the climate from becoming more and more deadly, even at the poles. The intervening regions have already been deserted. Evaporation of the equatorial oceans has thrown the whole atmosphere into tumult, so that even at the poles we are tormented by hot wet hurricanes and incredible electric storms. These have already shattered most of our great buildings, sometimes burying a whole teeming province under an avalanche of tumbled vitreous crags.

Our two polar communities at first managed to maintain radio communication; but it is now some time since we of the south received news of the more distressed north. Even with us the situation is already desperate. We had recently established some hundreds of stations for the dissemination, but less than a score have been able to operate. This failure is due mainly to an increasing lack of personnel. The deluge of fantastic solar radiation has had a disastrous effect on the human organism. Epidemics of a malignant tumour, which medical science has failed to conquer, have reduced the southern people to a mere remnant, and this in spite of the migration of the tropical races into the Antarctic. Each of us, moreover, is but the wreckage of his former self. The higher mental functions, attained only in the most developed human species, are already lost or disordered, through the breakdown of their special tissues. Not only has the racial mind vanished, but the sexual groups have lost their mental unity. Three of the sub-sexes have already been exterminated by derangement of their chemical nature. Glandular troubles, indeed, have unhinged many of us with anxieties and loathings which we cannot conquer, though we know them to be unreasonable. Even the normal power of 'telepathic' communication has become so unreliable that we have been compelled to fall back upon the archaic practice of vocal symbolism. Exploration of the past is now confined to specialists, and is a dangerous profession, which may lead to disorders of temporal experience.

Degeneration of the higher neural centres has also brought about in us a far more serious and deep-seated trouble, namely a general spiritual degradation which would formerly have seemed impossible, so confident were we of our integrity. The perfectly dispassionate will had been for many millions of years universal among us, and the corner stone of our whole society and culture. We had almost forgotten that it has a physiological basis, and that if that basis were undermined, we might no longer be capable of rational conduct. But, drenched for some thousands of years by the unique stellar radiation, we have gradually lost not only the ecstasy of dispassionate worship, but even the capacity for normal disinterested behaviour. Every one is now liable to an irrational bias in favour of himself as a private person, as against his fellows. Personal envy, uncharitableness, even murder and gratuitous cruelty, formerly unknown amongst us, are now becoming common. At first when men began to notice in themselves these archaic impulses, they crushed them with amused contempt. But as the highest nerve centres fell further into decay, the brute in us began to be ever more unruly, and the human more uncertain. Rational conduct was henceforth to be achieved only after an exhausting and degrading 'moral struggle', instead of spontaneously and fluently. Nay, worse, increasingly often the struggle ended not in victory but defeat. Imagine then, the terror and disgust that gripped us when we found ourselves one and all condemned to a desperate struggle against impulses which we had been accustomed to regard as insane. It is distressing enough to know that each one of us might at any moment, merely to help some dear individual or other, betray his supreme duty toward the dissemination; but it is harrowing to discover ourselves sometimes so far sunk as to be incapable even of common loving-kindness toward our neighbours. For a man to favour himself against his friend or beloved, even in the slightest respect, was formerly unknown. But today many of us are haunted by the look of amazed horror and pity in the eyes of an injured friend.

In the early stages of our trouble lunatic asylums were founded, but they soon became over-crowded and a burden on a stricken community. The insane were then killed. But it became clear that by former standards we were all insane. No man now can trust himself to behave reasonably.

And, of course, we cannot trust each other. Partly through the prevalent irrationality of desire, and partly through the misunderstandings which have come with the loss of 'telepathic' communication, we have been plunged into all manner of discords. A political constitution and system of laws had to be devised, but they seem to have increased our troubles. Order of a kind is maintained by an over-worked police force. But this is in the hands of the professional organizers, who have now all the vices of bureaucracy. It was largely through their folly that two of the antarctic nations broke into social revolution, and are now preparing to meet the armament which an insane world-government is devising for their destruction. Meanwhile, through the breakdown of the economic order, and the impossibility of reaching the food-factories on Jupiter, starvation is added to our troubles, and has afforded to certain ingenious lunatics the opportunity of trading at the expense of others.

All this folly in a doomed world, and in a community that was yesterday the very flower of a galaxy! Those of us who still care for the life of the spirit are tempted to regret that mankind did not choose decent suicide before ever the putrescence began. But indeed this could not be. The task that was undertaken had to be completed. For the Scattering of the Seed has come to be for every one of us the supreme religious duty. Even those who continually sin against it recognize this as the last office of man. It was for this that we outstayed our time, and must watch ourselves decline from spiritual estate into that brutishness from which man has so seldom freed himself.

Yet why do we persist in the forlorn effort? Even if by good luck the seed should take root somewhere and thrive, there will surely come an end to its adventure, if not swiftly in fire, then in the ultimate battle of life against encroaching frost. Our labour will at best sow for death an ampler harvest. There seems no rational defence of it, unless it be rational to carry out blindly a purpose conceived in a former and more enlightened state.

But we cannot feel sure that we really were more enlightened. We look back now at our former selves, with wonder, but also with incomprehension and misgiving. We try to recall the glory that seemed to be revealed to each of us in the racial mind, but we remember almost nothing of it. We cannot rise even to that more homely beatitude which was once within the reach of the unaided individual, that serenity which, it seemed, should be the spirit's answer to every tragic event. It is gone from us. It is not only impossible but inconceivable. We now see our private distresses and the public calamity as merely hideous. That after so long a struggle into maturity man should be roasted alive like a trapped mouse, for the entertainment of a lunatic! How can any beauty lie in that?

But this is not our last word to you. For though we have fallen, there is still something in us left over from the time that is passed. We have become blind and weak; but the knowledge that we are so has forced us to a great effort. Those of us who have not already sunk too far have formed themselves into a brotherhood for mutual strengthening, so that the true human spirit may be maintained a little longer, until the seed has been well sown, and death be permissible. We call ourselves the Brotherhood of the Condemned. We seek to be faithful to one another, and to our common undertaking, and to the vision which is no longer revealed. We are vowed to the comforting of all distressed persons who are not yet permitted death. We are vowed also to the dissemination. And we are vowed to keep the spirit bright until the end.

Now and again we meet together in little groups or great companies to hearten ourselves with one another's presence. Sometimes on these occasions we can but sit in silence, groping for consolation and for strength. Sometimes the spoken word flickers hither and thither amongst us, shedding a brief light but little warmth to the soul that lies freezing in a torrid world.

But there is among us one, moving from place to place and company to company, whose voice all long to hear. He is young, the last born of the Last Men; for he was the latest to be conceived before we learned man's doom, and put an end to all conceiving. Being the latest, he is also the noblest. Not him alone, but all his generation, we salute, and look to for strength; but he, the youngest, is different from the rest. In him the spirit, which is but the flesh awakened into spirituality, has power to withstand the tempest of solar energy longer than the rest of us. It is as though the sun itself were eclipsed by this spirit's brightness. It is as though in him at last, and for a day only, man's promise were fulfilled. For though, like others, he suffers in the flesh, he is above his suffering. And though more than the rest of us he feels the suffering of others, he is above his pity. In his comforting there is a strange sweet raillery which can persuade the sufferer to smile at his own pain. When this youngest brother of ours contemplates with us our dying world and the frustration of all man's striving, he is not, like us, dismayed, but quiet. In the presence of such quietness despair wakens into peace. By his reasonable speech, almost by the mere sound of his voice, our eyes are opened, and our hearts mysteriously filled with exultation. Yet often his words are grave.

Let his words, not mine, close this story:

Great are the stars, and man is of no account to them. But man is a fair spirit, whom a star conceived and a star kills. He is greater than those bright blind companies. For though in them there is incalculable potentiality, in him there is achievement, small, but actual. Too soon, seemingly, he comes to his end. But when he is done he will not be nothing, not as though he had never been; for he is eternally a beauty in the eternal form of things.

Man was winged hopefully. He had in him to go further than this short flight, now ending. He proposed even that he should become the Flower of All Things, and that he should learn to be the All-Knowing, the All-Admiring. Instead, he is to be destroyed. He is only a fledgling caught in a bush-fire. He is very small, very simple, very little capable of insight. His knowledge of the great orb of things is but a fledgling's knowledge. His admiration is a nestling's admiration for the things kindly to his own small nature. He delights only in food and the food-announcing call. The music of the spheres passes over him, through him, and is not heard.

Yet it has used him. And now it uses his destruction. Great, and terrible, and very beautiful is the Whole; and for man the best is that the Whole should use him.

But does it really use him? Is the beauty of the Whole really enhanced by our agony? And is the Whole really beautiful? And what is beauty? Throughout all his existence man has been striving to hear the music of the spheres, and has seemed to himself once and again to catch some phrase of it, or even a hint of the whole form of it. Yet he can never be sure that he has truly heard it, nor even that there is any such perfect music at all to be heard. Inevitably so, for if it exists, it is not for him in his littleness.

But one thing is certain. Man himself, at the very least, is music, a brave theme that makes music also of its vast accompaniment, its matrix of storms and stars. Man himself in his degree is eternally a beauty in the eternal form of things. It is very good to have been man. And so we may go forward together with laughter in our hearts, and peace, thankful for the past, and for our own courage. For we shall make after all a fair conclusion to this brief music that is man.

Time Scale 1

2,000 — years ago	JESUS CHRIST
1,500 —	A.D. 500
	Charlemagne
1,000 —	A.D. 1000 Norman Conquest, 1066
	America Discovered, 1492
500 —	A.D. 1500 Newton
'Today' 2000 A.D.	EUROPEAN WAR, 1914 Anglo-French War Russo-German War Euro-American War
	Sino-American War *First World State* founded
500 —	A.D. 2,500
1,000 —	A.D. 3000
1,500 —	A.D. 3500
2,000 — years hence	A.D. 4000

Americanized World ↓

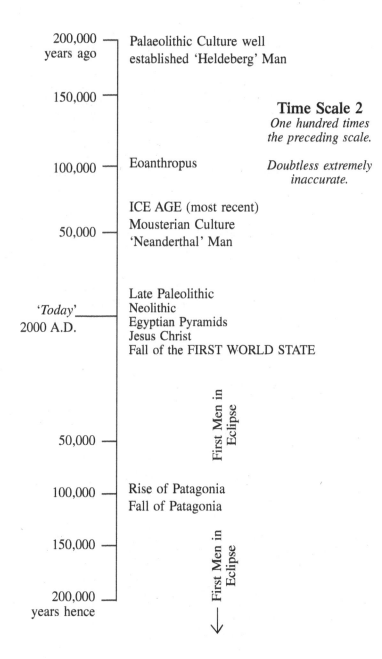

200,000 years ago — Palaeolithic Culture well established 'Heldeberg' Man

150,000 —

Time Scale 2
One hundred times the preceding scale.

100,000 — Eoanthropus

Doubtless extremely inaccurate.

ICE AGE (most recent)
Mousterian Culture
'Neanderthal' Man

50,000 —

Late Paleolithic
Neolithic
Egyptian Pyramids
Jesus Christ
Fall of the FIRST WORLD STATE

'Today'
2000 A.D. —

First Men in Eclipse

50,000 —

100,000 — Rise of Patagonia
Fall of Patagonia

First Men in Eclipse

150,000 —

200,000 years hence —

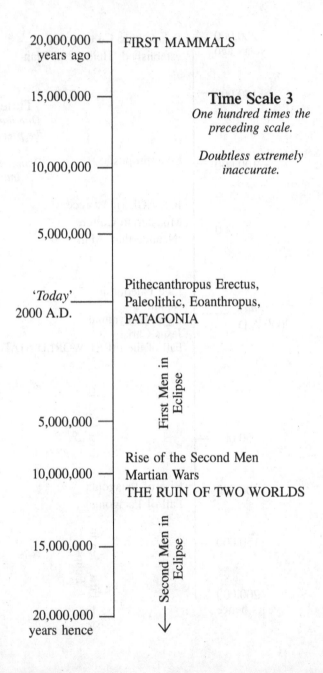

2,000,000,000 years ago	PLANETS FORMED
1,500,000,000	**Time Scale 4** *One hundred times the preceding scale.* *Doubtless extremely inaccurate.*
1,000,000,000	
	'Life' appears on Earth
500,000,000	
	First Reptiles
'Today' 2000 A.D.	FIRST MAMMALS Second Men
	The Great Brains Fifth Men Migration to Venus Period of Eclipse
500,000,000	
	Flying Men
1,000,000,000	Migration to Neptune
	} Period of Eclipse
	} Period of Fluctuation
1,500,000,000	
	Fifteenth Men
	Last Men appear
2,000,000,000 years hence	END OF MAN

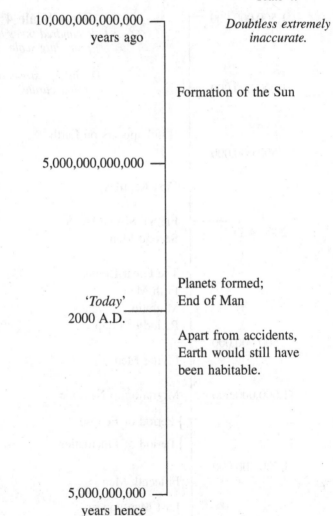

Time Scale 5
*Ten thousand times
scale 4.*

10,000,000,000,000
years ago

*Doubtless extremely
inaccurate.*

Formation of the Sun

5,000,000,000,000

Planets formed;
End of Man

'Today'
2000 A.D.

Apart from accidents,
Earth would still have
been habitable.

5,000,000,000
years hence